The Emperor of Khalindain
into the hands of the fanat
declare all forms of vice illeg
wenching or fun in the king
Akbar, city of sin, and all
of death by *auto-da-fé*.

Streetpoet, a wandering
and has no desire to be burnt at the stake. He must use all
charm, nerve and luck to save his skin, and to track down the
beautiful Lara – the only woman who can bring the Emperor
back to his senses.

TROUBADOUR

RICHARD BURNS

UNWIN
PAPERBACKS

LONDON SYDNEY WELLINGTON

First published in paperback by Unwin ® Paperbacks, an imprint of
Unwin Hyman Limited in 1988

UNWIN HYMAN LIMITED
15/17 Broadwick Street
London W1V 1FP

Allen & Unwin Australia Pty Ltd
8 Napier Street, North Sydney, NSW 2060, Australia

Allen & Unwin New Zealand Pty Ltd with the Port Nicholson Press
60 Cambridge Terrace, Wellington, New Zealand

British Library Cataloguing in Publication Data

Burns, Richard, 1958–
    Troubadour.
I. Title
823'.914[F]
ISBN 0-04-440225-2

Printed in Great Britain by Cox & Wyman Ltd, Reading

Contents

Chapter 1

Auto-da-fé

The dark day was made darker by gathering crowds, but despite the rain a large crowd had formed in the square. Everyone enjoys an execution. And of the various methods of execution – lynching, drowning, impaling, decapitation, mutilation, strangulation, and all the rest – none provides a more delightful spectacle than a burning.

There were ten prisoners in all: three Kapatan jugglers, one minstrel, a group of five strolling players, and the landlord of the tavern in which this miscellaneous bunch had staged their last fatal performance. Five sturdy stakes had been erected in the centre of the square and the centre of the crowd; two prisoners were tied back-to-back to each. At the prisoners' feet were bundles of firewood, ready to be lit, and not one of these entertainers had ever drawn a keener audience.

The regional Master of the Brotherhood read the charges. He had a deep, ponderous voice, but was loud enough for all to hear. 'By Order of the Emperor Consatiné,' he read, speaking through the sinister grey silk mask the officers of the Brotherhood affected on official occasions. 'All Travelling Players, Actors, Whores, Mimics, Mummers, Dancers, Tragedians, Comedians, Minstrels, Jugglers, Tumblers and other Perverts will be denied, on Pain of Death, their much-abused Right to Perform in any City, Town, Village, Hamlet, or in any Field pertaining to the Same, in the Empire of Khalindaine. This Proclamation Signed and Sealed by the Hand of Kamrot Hedchkeeper, First Lord of the Council and Grand-Master of the Brotherhood of the Faithful, in the Fifty-Eighth Day of the Second Quartering of the Fourth Year of the Most Glorious Reign of the Emperor Consatiné.' He stopped reading, which pleased the crowd, and addressed the prisoners directly. 'All of you have been found guilty under this order, and it is my duty therefore to execute the sentence.'

'Execute the execution?' asked the minstrel from his place at the stake. 'Sounds daft put like that.' The spectators smiled their appreciation: an execution is even better when there is a joker among the victims.

'Silence!' the Master demanded. 'It is my duty,' he repeated, 'to execute the sentence.' He paused, futilely hoping to recapture the drama that had been lost. 'The sentence is death!'

'You mean you're going to kill us?' asked the minstrel innocently. 'I thought you'd just tied us here to show us off because we're all of us so good looking. After all, if you didn't have such a high regard for good looks, you wouldn't be wearing that mask.'

'Silence!' bawled the Master again.

It was no good. The minstrel was determined to talk on, and had the crowd behind him now. 'What about woods?' he asked.

'What?' the Master responded, incautiously.

'Woods. What about them?'

'What about them?' echoed the Master. 'What have woods to do with anything?'

'You've said we can't perform in cities and towns and fields, and all the rest of the places on your list, but I didn't hear you mention woods.'

'You were caught in a tavern!' the Master said, exasperated. 'Woods are irrelevant.'

'I'll grant that it won't make any difference to us; I'm thinking about you. You're going to look such a chump when the next lot of travelling players you get round here performs in a wood though.'

'But *no one* performs in a wood!'

'No one used to,' agreed the minstrel. 'But they will be doing it in future, you just bet.'

The rain was getting heavier, the day later. Visibility decreased all the time. 'Let's get on with the execution!' called the Master. The crowd was no longer amused by the minstrel's interruptions. They agreed with the Master, and their heads lifted in anticipation.

'Just hold on a minute.' It was the minstrel again. The raised heads dropped with a sigh. 'Hadn't we better get this sorted out once and for all. Reread that bit of paper you're holding.'

'No!'

'It's for your peace of mind as well as mine,' reminded the minstrel. 'It won't take long. Just reread it.'

The mask hid the Master's face. He unrolled the proclamation and began to read. 'By Order of the...' The rain suddenly became a deluge. Fat splashes fell on the page, smearing it. 'This is ridiculous. I can't read this. The ink's running all over the place.'

'So is everyone else,' the minstrel pointed out. It was true. The crowd had decided enough was enough and fled, leaving just a few old women and fewer youths to brave the weather. The Master and his guards stood in a moist and miserable ring around the prisoners, and around the guards the buildings faded to silhouettes against a barely lighter sky.

'Quickly!' urged the Master. 'Fire the pyres!'

'Pyre the fires!' mocked the minstrel. 'Sire the liars! Wire the briars! Oh, and by the way, before I die, I'd just like to say a big thank you for finding such a pretty girl for me to get incinerated with.'

'Just shut up!' called the Master from the gloom. 'And get on with it!' he shouted to his men.

The minstrel misunderstood. 'I'd love to get on with it,' he called, 'but you've tied us back-to-back and stuck this stake in the way.'

The wood was sodden, the flames reluctant to hold.' Hurry up,' called the minstrel. 'I'm getting cold.'

The guard shoved his burning brand at the pile of wood again. There was a crackle, extinguished almost at once.

'Magnificent' observed the minstrel. 'They fetch us out here in this weather and then can't even light a fire. There's hospitality for you.'

'I'm doing my best,' complained the guard.

'Haven't you any fire-spell?'

'No. Any more suggestions?'

'Well, as you mention it, yes. You're doing it all wrong.'

'Me!' The guard was affronted. 'Listen, mate. I've lit more auto-da-fés than you've had hot dinners.'

'I'd never have had a hot dinner if you'd been lighting the stove. You're just dabbling round the edges. Ram the torch right in. That'll get it started.'

'Put the torch out altogether, more like. I'll stick to doing it my way, if you don't mind.'

'If you're sure that's what you want. But I thought the idea was to burn us to death, not drown us.'

'You should be grateful,' muttered the guard, making another ineffectual attempt at the pyre. 'If it wasn't for this rain you'd be dead already.'

'Look,' said the minstrel. 'I've lived rough. I've lit fires in weather ten times worse than this.'

'Oh yeah. If you're so clever you do it.'

'Right. I will. Probably.'

'Probably?' mocked the guard. 'You backing down already?'

'No. Of course not. It's just that it is, well, rather wet.'

'Rather wet!' The guard was sneering openly. 'I thought you'd lit fires in weather ten times worse than this'.

'I have. I'll do it then. Get me down.'

The guard clambered up the piled wood. 'Careful now,' warned the minstrel. 'You'll snag yourself on the branches.'

'Don't you mind about me, sunshine. You just worry about lighting this pyre. *If* you can.'

Balancing awkwardly the guard cut the minstrel's bonds with a knife. 'Go on then mate. Get this thing lit then.'

'Well...'

'Excuses, excuses. Get on with it.'

Reluctantly the minstrel climbed down, took the torch, and smashed it as hard as he could over the guard's head. 'Come on love,' he told the actress he had been tied to. 'Time to go.'

'What about the others?' she asked as he helped her from the pyre.

'We won't even be able to find them in this weather, never mind help them. They'll just have to take care of themselves.'

'Please,' she pleaded. 'I can't leave them. My father, my mother, my sister, her husband!'

'Father, mother, sister, husband?'

'We're a family troupe.'

'All things are relative,' said the minstrel.

'Is that a joke?'

'No, not a joke. A justification. A reason for helping you when reason tells me to run away, when the real reason I'm going to help is I'll do anything for a pretty face. You wait here. I'll probably not be back because I'll probably get myself killed, but if I do survive I'll at least want to be able to find you.' He vanished into the rain, shaking his head. 'I must be mad,' she heard him mutter.

The rain-filled darkness was sinister now she was alone. Malevolent water found its way into her clothes, pulling them to her, stifling her. Then there was a brief cry of pain, and another.

'What's going on?' She recognised the Master's deep voice. He sounded perilously close.

'Tripped, didn't I,' growled a voice that might have been the minstrel's.

'What's going on?' persisted the Master. He sounded nervous. 'Tell you what, lads. Let's forget it. Let's burn 'em tomorrow when we can see what we're doing.'

Another cry penetrated the Master's words, cut off by the ugly sound of a death rattle.

'For Hedch's sake,' called the Master. 'We'll leave the prisoners and get inside. I've had enough of this.'

'I wish you'd told me earlier,' said the minstrel's voice close by. There was a morbid, mortal grunt and the sound of something heavy falling onto the flagstones. 'I needn't have killed anyone then.'

The actress peered through the rain as the minstrel approached. He held a sleek and vicious dagger. 'Stolen,' he explained, tossing it aside.

'Are the others safe?' asked the girl.

'They're all free,' replied the minstrel. 'What they do next is up to them.'

He led her from the pyre. After a few paces she stumbled over something that lay in her path. Bending, she saw the body of the Master. His grey mask had twisted sideways untidily, and the eye-holes sprouted tufts of grey hair. 'I'm going to be sick,' said the actress, and was. The body dammed her vomit.

'Just hurry up!'

They reached the edge of the square and found an alley where they took shelter of a sort between the eaves of mean houses. 'Thank you,' said the actress.

'For what?'

'For saving my life, silly. And for saving my family.'

He was a shape in the darkness next to her. 'Just remember: in future you only perform in woods.'

'I'll remember.' She smiled. Her teeth were white in the gloom, and then their brightness was extinguished as he placed his mouth over hers. The kiss was long and tender.

'By the way,' he said when they had separated. 'You must tell me your name. I'll want to whisper it in my dreams.'

'You're daft,' she said.

'Probably. Who are you anyway?'

'My name is Amila, daughter of Aulcun the Player. And who are you?'

'They call me Streetpoet,' said the minstrel, and then he was gone, and the girl was alone in the streaming night rain.

Further north the rain was falling as snow. In the palace of Verdre, several thousand strides up-river from the capital city, Cythroné, the Emperor Consatiné was being prepared for sleep. Despite the snow the room was hot, for not only was there a good fire burning but also – an innovation designed by the emperor's adoptive father, the Gros of Ra – hot air was pumped between the floors from a large furnace in the basement. The Gros of Ra was a man whose ingenuity was matched only by his intolerance, a man who found others offensive and therefore made it his affair to be offensive back; fortunately, thought Consatiné as his courtiers undressed him, the Ra-Lord was at Mornet, at the other end of the empire, and was likely to remain there for many years to come. The one compensation Consatiné had found, on learning he was the adopted bastard of the previous empress rather than the heir of the Gros of Ra as he had always supposed, was that he knew he did not have that man's awkward blood in his veins.

This ritual of going to bed was a complicated and puzzling one. A small battalion of courtiers seemed to be required to remove the emperor's clothes. Then there was the strict protocol about the business, and the equally strict hierarchy. Each courtier was assigned a separate article, and should for instance the Lord of the Third Waistcoat Button join his illustrious ancestors in the family vault, his place would be filled by the Lord of the Fourth Waistcoat Button; the Fifth Waistcoat Button would then become the Fourth Waistcoat Button, and so on down the imperial body, concluding with the elevation of the Lord of the Left Shoe to Lord of the Right Shoe; a new Lord of the Left Shoe would then be required and the post, though it carried no remuneration, was always eagerly contested.

The ritual had the advantage of keeping a large number of otherwise quite useless noblemen occupied, but the disadvantage of taking half the night. When he considered that the whole process would have to be repeated, in reverse, in the morning, Consatiné sometimes marvelled he got any sleep at all.

When at last the Lord of the Inner Vest was done, and Consatiné stood naked, ready, and uncharacteristically grateful to the Gros of Ra who had heated the chamber so effectively, a new group of courtiers came in to wash, powder and dress their emperor for bed; when at last the Lord of the Nightcap had finished and Consatiné, alone and glad of it, climbed into the gigantic bed, to dream his regular dreams about the pretty girl from Northreach he had known once and loved, he wished – as he had so often wished – he had never become emperor at all.

The moon waxed and waned, and the midwinter solstice dawned, unenthusiastically, on a lone rider crossing the Trema Hills. He reined in his horse at the brow of the last of the hills and surveyed the view ahead. Below him stretched the towns and vineyards of the county of Marq. The rider held the reins loosely in one hand; in the other was a spiced sausage. He took steady bites of the sausage as he watched the morning begin. Grey clouds formed dark kingdoms against the lightening sky, and the kingdoms came and went just as they do in history. The wind gusted strongly, though the day was mild, and the rider's travelling cloak was sometimes a blanket and sometimes a flag, while the winter trees rattled and snapped and the occasional stalk of smoke from an outlying house was bent and made to disappear.

He finished the sausage and tossed away the skin: it joined the sweep of dead leaves and animal droppings at the side of the track. He jabbed his horse rather inexpertly with his spurs and the animal continued on its way. An orange sun had appeared, coming through the trees and clouds like a bronze coin beneath water, as he reached the first of the towns.

Ordagyn, like most of the towns in the peaceful county of Marq, requires neither walls nor towers to defend it: history has never interfered much here, and even the terrible events that had marked the first days of Consatiné's reign, when the inhuman Agaskan had risen in force to threaten the empire, had caused no more than a flurry of gossip and an increase in the price of wheat. The rider travelled the length of the wide main street, noting with contempt the elegant houses, the well-tended gardens, and the frequent taverns he passed; with equal contempt the occasional burger he passed noted the rider's black and white outfit and his long black cloak, and recognised the newcomer as an officer of the Brotherhood.

The rider reached the basilica, stopped, and dismounted. He strapped his horse to a ringbolt set in the walls and drew a single sheet of paper from a roll in his saddlebag. Walking to the basilica door he took a hammer from his belt and two nails from his purse. The wind was awkward but the man was practised; he had nailed up many similar documents since joining the Brotherhood. He hammered the top of the paper to the door and only then unrolled the rest of the proclamation, fixing it with a further two nails.

> By Order of the Emperor Consatiné, the Manufacture, Retail and Consumption of Intoxicating Beverages be they Wines, Beers or Spirits is Forbidden throughout Khalindaine. This Law shall be Enforced with utmost Vigour and any Transgressions shall be Punished by Execution. Signed and Sealed by the hand of Kamrot Hedchkeeper, First Lord of the Council, Grand-Master of the Brotherhood of the Faithful, on the Ninetieth Day of the Second Quartering of the Fifth Year of the most Glorious Reign of the Emperor Consatiné.

The officer of the Brotherhood did not bother to read it; he already knew what it said. Tired after his long journey over the Trema Hills, he stretched his aching back and entered the basilica, intending to rest. But before he rested he prayed, as he regularly did, to the gods the Brotherhood had made. He knelt before the altar and took off his leather helm. The head beneath was quite bald. Around him the stained glass, old but of the highest quality, depicted the legendary exploits of the heroes of the past. The messenger despised them – if the decision had been his he would have had them torn down, these symbols of decadence, and replaced with decent respectable plain glass. 'Akhran the Golden, Akhran the Avenger,' he began, 'Strengthen Me Your Servant. Hedch the

First Martyr, Hedch the Proclaimer of the Coming of Ormaas, Lend Me Your Determination. Ormaas the Second Martyr, Rightful Heir to the Throne of Khalindaine, Give Power to my Cause.' And so it went on, a quaint misinterpretation of recent history retold in the bigoted terms of the Brotherhood. 'For in the Beginning there was Akhran, and all was Good, and only the Strong and Faithful filled the Land. And then came the Time of Darkness, and of Softness, and of Unbelief, and the People of Khalindaine grew Weak. And then came the Time of Crisis, when the Agaskan rose in *Ingsvaal* against the People of Khalindaine. And only Hedch the First Martyr knew of their coming' – this was almost true: Hedch, who had been employed by the scheming Gros of Weir to find the bastard son of the Empress Elsban, had been the first to bring news of the Ingsvaal to Cythroné – 'and He was Heeded Not. And only Hedch the First Martyr knew the True Identity of the Rightful Heir to the Throne of Khalindaine' – this was not true at all, proving that even martyrs can make mistakes – 'and Again He was Heeded Not. And just as Hedch was Martyred for Proclaiming the Truth, thus Ormaas the True Heir was martyred for *Being* the Truth and the Light and the Salvation of...'

'Oh, do shut up!'

The bald man turned round. There was no one to be seen; the basilica was deserted. 'Who spoke?' he demanded, drawing his sword.

'I did.' A thin, rather handsome young man with a slight beard and a mocking smile climbed from beneath a pile of stacked prayer mats. 'You're keeping me awake with your drivel.'

'Drivel! How dare you!' The bald man's face writhed as bafflement and fury contended. 'Who are you to speak of the Mysteries this way?'

'Allow me to introduce myself. Men call me Streetpoet.' He leapt to his feet and made an insolent bow towards the other before leaping back to avoid the blow. 'And you are?'

'Od the Hedchenlightened,' said the older man with dignity. 'An Officer of the Brotherhood of the Faithful. And that alone should ensure your respect.'

'Bollocks,' said Streetpoet, who rather prided himself on his ability to find the appropriate word for any situation. 'Your precious Brotherhood is a collection of misguided busybodies whose only pleasure is depriving other people of pleasure.'

'Misguided!' Od smashed his sword to the floor. The clang echoed as Streetpoet took another prudent step back.

'Yes, misguided. I'm tired of all this fuss about Ormaas. I knew him: he was a very pleasant, very ordinary bloke. And he was no more the rightful heir to the throne of Khalindaine than I am.'

'You knew him?'

'We travelled together from Northreach, heading for Cythroné, but got separated in Khalinrift. He was in love with his cousin Lara. So was Consatiné.'

'You mean you knew the Emperor as well!'

'I know it sounds unlikely.' The minstrel looked down at his threadbare clothes and worn boots. 'But I assure you it's true, just as it is true that Consatiné, despite the rumours, really was the son of Elsban. Your friend Hedch was sent to find the bastard, discovered that Ormaas was the right age and had been adopted, and made the obvious mistake. Anyone would, but that doesn't stop it being a mistake.'

'I don't believe a word of this,' said Od the Hedch-enlightened. 'You do not look like an intimate of princes. And anyway, if Consatiné really is the rightful emperor, how come he never performs the Rite of Endyear?'

This was a good question, and one that had been asked many times before. The Rite of Endyear demands the emperor should stab himself in public: the rightful emperor will be saved by the atavar of his ancestor Akhran the Golden; an imposter, as the Gyr Orland had discovered just before Consatiné ascended to the throne, dies. 'I can't say for certain,' said Streetpoet, rather lamely, and before he could finish what he was going to say, Od had butted in.

'I thought as much. Consatiné is not the rightful emperor; Ormaas should have been and was murdered. That's all there is to it.'

Streetpoet shook his head sadly. 'I wish I'd time to explain the whole story to you, though I'm not sure you'd listen, but unfortunately I've got a rather pressing engagement with a sweet young thing in Haal tonight, so I must be off. Wine beckons, a woman beckons: I can't be late.'

'Wine, eh? You'll be lucky.'

'I generally am.'

'Haven't you read the proclamation?'

'What proclamation?'

'The one I've just nailed to the door of the basilica.' Streetpoet turned to the door, which was as blank as the look he gave Od. 'On the outside,' Od explained.

'Oh. *That* proclamation. How silly of me to miss it. You wouldn't mind reading it for me, I hope, only I can't quite make out the letters through two finger-breadths of wood.'

'It says drinking is banned throughout Khalindaine.'

'It says what!'

'Drinking is banned. It'll do the empire good.'

'You're barmy. Did I hear you say you've just hammered that thing to the door? Did anyone see you?'

'I don't think so. Why should it matter if they did?'

'Because, my hairless friend, the people of Marq are going to want your blood. Tell me, what do people do in Marq?'

'Grow vines.'

'And what happens to all those grapes?'

'They're made into wine.'

'And what happens when drinking is banned?' This time Od did not need to reply. 'That's right. They starve. But before they do they are going to make absolutely sure that you don't survive. They'll tear you limb from limb.'

'Limb from limb?' asked Od the Hedchenlightened.

'Limb from limb,' confirmed Streetpoet.

'What do I do?'

'Hope no one's read your proclamation and then get out of here fast.' Od looked suddenly pathetic, and as his self-righteous certainty evaporated Streetpoet felt sympathy for him. 'I'll see if the coast is clear,' he said. He went towards the door but stopped before he reached it, driven back by a hum of angry voices from outside.

'What's the matter?' asked Od.

'Either there's an unseasonable hive of hornets out there or the townsfolk have found your proclamation. Listen!'

The sounds were getting louder. The low dangerous buzz that had first greeted the news was being replaced by a fresh sound, full of incomprehension and anguish. It was the sound of animals in pain, and like any wounded animal, the wine-growers were dangerous. 'What do I do?'

asked Od again, his voice so low Streetpoet had to strain to hear him.

'I'd go back to what you were doing before I butted in,' whispered Streetpoet: 'I'd pray.'

Suddenly there was a yell outside, and the repeated cry of 'The horse, the horse'. 'They've found your horse,' observed Streetpoet.

'What do I do?' asked Od the Hedchenlightened for the third time.

'There's only one thing for it.' Briefly Streetpoet outlined his plan. They were only just in time. The door was flung open and, stark against the winter sun, an armed and angry mob burst in, screaming for the messenger's blood.

Had he known of the events in Orgagyn, the Emperor Consatiné might have felt sympathy for the persecuted messenger. He was feeling persecuted himself. Ever since that morning, when the Vaine of Hethopas, in his rôle as Lord of the Ruff, had told him that legislation banning alcohol had been announced in the imperial name, Consatiné had been besieged by protesting petitioners. The usual restraint of the court was forgotten; incredulous and offended aristocrats had been demanding to see their emperor all day.

Consatiné sent at once for Kamrot, the First Lord of the Council and the initiator of the new laws, and the two of them shut themselves into a spacious chamber in Verdre while beyond the door a noisy crowd demanded to be heard. 'I wish you'd told me what you'd intended,' said the emperor regretfully. 'How in Khalindaine did you think you'd get away with it.'

'It is not a question of "getting away with it", returned Kamrot. 'Alcohol has sapped the spirit of the people. It is the will of the Masters of the Brotherhood of the Faithful that it should be prohibited.'

There was a pun in that 'spirit of the people' line but Consatiné was not in the mood. 'It's lunatic,' he insisted. 'You can't stop people drinking.'

'We already have,' Kamrot pointed out. 'It has been proclaimed thus.'

'Proclamation or not, will people obey?'

'It is the law,' replied the First Lord.

His complacency infuriated Consatiné. 'That doesn't mean a thing. Have you thought about what is involved when alcohol is banned.'

'Certainly,' said Kamrot. 'The empire will be purified; a pollution will be driven out.'

'And what about the people who'll lose their jobs?'

'Those who live by the bottle do not deserve jobs.'

Consatiné refused to accept this. 'What about the people who make the barrels then? The ones who transport it? Do they "live by the bottle"? They'll still lose their jobs. What are they supposed to do?'

'They are supposed to do what they are told.' Kamrot's mouth was as narrow as his mind, and as full of bad ideas as bad teeth. 'That is the point of government.'

'But you can't govern if the people won't let you!'

'Why not?'

'Why not! Because…' There were so many reasons Consatiné had to pause before he could list them. 'Because who is going to enforce this ridiculous law? The Brotherhood? They're strong, but hardly strong enough to patrol the entire empire from Northreach to Nerith. The army? I've served with the army: they'll not like being told they can't drink; they won't be on your side. The nobility? Hardly! Can you see the Gros of Ghaof giving up his wine? And though I'm always the last person to hear anything, even I know that Karim-vaine-Hethopas has invested four hundred million rubecks and bought up the entire barrel production of Ilynés province for the next twelve years. What's he going to do with the barrels? Carry water? And I can only thank Menketh that the Gros of Weir is on his voyage of exploration. Most of his fortune comes from the wine trade from Nerith and Ilynés.'

'Corrupt and decadent nobles,' said Kamrot primly, 'cannot oppose the will of the Faithful.'

Consatiné looked at his First Lord glumly. 'I expect they can,' he said.

Kamrot thumped the table, suddenly animated. 'Then they *shall* not!' he said. His water jug rattled. 'I rule Khalindaine and I have issued my command.'

'I'm still the emperor,' mentioned Consatiné.

'You are a figurehead and a weak fool.' Consatiné said nothing for he knew that this was true; Kamrot continued.

'Remember the Convention of Weir. The Brotherhood of the Faithful was brought into government to prevent civil war: if we weren't standing beside you half Khalindaine would oppose you. Everyone knows you are not the true heir.'

'Perhaps, perhaps...'

'There is no question! You said yourself it was the ghost of Ormaas who led the troops at the battle of Klau, when the Agaskan were defeated, and since then there has been no doubt that the Brotherhood of the Faithful, ruling in Ormaas's sacred name, is the legitimate government of Khalindaine.'

'Do you think banning drinking is what Ormaas would have wanted? I knew him, remember: you didn't.'

'I know that he was the Avatar of Akhran the Golden and the true heir to the throne of Khalindaine,' said Kamrot stubbornly. 'That is all I need to know.'

Consatiné smiled sadly. 'But what if that wasn't true. What if I really was the avatar? What if I really was the heir?'

'You are not. You admitted as much when you told the world how Ormaas's ghost had inspired the troops at Klau. And if you are the avatar, why have you never performed the Rite of Endyear?'

'You answered that yourself: it is because I am a weak fool. I told the world Ormaas had led the troops at Klau because I was in love with Ormaas's cousin Lara and I wanted to do something for her, to preserve his memory and make his silly death a little more worthwhile. And I have never performed the Rite of Endyear because I was – because I am – terrified of the avatar. Kamrot, you've never had another being take possession of you. Akhran is a monster, not a man. When he was inside me I was a monster too. It happened at Klau; it must never happen again. I would go mad. Other emperors were brought up to be the avatar of Akhran; I wasn't. He simply took possession of me, unexpectedly, terrifyingly. And I never, ever want it to happen again.'

Kamrot was not really listening. 'You cannot squirm and lie your way out of this,' he said.

Suddenly Kamrot's face changed. The fanatical certainty drained away, leaving a grey and frightened old man with hollow cheeks and eyes. But it was not the change in Kamrot's face that was so remarkable: Consatiné was transforming before his First Lord's eyes.

Strange and harsh expressions tore at Consatiné's soft flesh.
The eyes turned black in concentrated fury. The mouth
stretched to show hungry teeth. The cheekbones swelled above
sunken, sucking cheeks. The Avatar of Akhran the Golden,
first Emperor of all Khalindaine, inspiration of a thousand
sagas, taker of ten thousand lives, had taken possession of his
pale young descendant. The creature that had been Consatiné
flung back the table. The water jug smashed against the wall.
A second blow caught Kamrot in the throat. The First Lord's
neck snapped in the instant; shocked blood squeezed from his
mouth and eyes; he slumped to the floor at the foot of the
wall, and his blood messed with the spilt water in a spreading
scarlet pool.

Outside the chamber the petitioners heard the loud crash.
Their noise was silenced for the first time that day as they
wondered what had happened or what to do and looked to one
another for inspiration. Meanwhile, the creature sat upright on
the delicately crafted chair for another tense and dangerous
moment, and then his gasps became sobs as Consatiné, restored
and shocked, discovered what his body had done.

It was the Vaine of Ghry who took the initiative. He
knocked on the door, and then again, louder. Then he opened
the door. The emperor, elbows pressed against knees, fists
pressed against eyes, sat rigidly in his chair, while Kamrot, First
Lord of the Inner Council, Grand-Master of the Brotherhood
of the Faithful, stretched discarded and broken at the foot
of a far wall.

'Hi!' said Streetpoet cheerfully. 'What can I do for you?'

Fortunately for Streetpoet the door was narrow and the
mob disorganised. The first impetus of their rush broke like
a wave against the arched frame. 'Who you be?' asked a man
at the front of the crowd.

'You know me, you dope. I'm Streetpoet. I was drinking
at your tavern last night.'

'Oo-ar,' said a woman's voice. 'You remember him, Kliung:
he be the one sang them songs. And you've been here before,
bain't you?'

'I get about,' said Streetpoet modestly. 'I'm sorry by the way:
I didn't have the money to enjoy a bed at your tavern last night
so I slept here. Very nice basilica it is too. I like the windows.'

There were various cries of 'What be happening?' and 'It bain't be the man we's looking for,' from behind the leaders.

'Well, I reckons it bain't you stuck this thing' – the man waved a scrap of paper, all that survived of the offending pamphlet – 'onto the door of the basilica, because we knows as him as did it come by horse this morn. But what we want to know is, where be he now? You seen him?'

'I don't think he's been here. Not that I've been awake long. I was woken by someone banging on the door.'

'Banging on door?' asked one voice.

'That'd be he sticking his proclamation up,' replied another.

'I knows where I'd be sticking his proclamation up if I be given the chance,' said a third.

'It doesn't sound as if he came in here,' said Streetpoet. 'Where do you want to try next? I'll help you look.'

'We bain't be needing no help,' said the leader, the man called Kliung. 'This be our fight.'

'But I'd like to help,' said Streetpoet. 'Until a moon's turn ago I was a travelling minstrel. I had a job I enjoyed, good hours, income unreliable but sufficient for my needs, nice working conditions and congenial company in any tavern the length of Khalindaine. Now I'm reduced to sleeping in basilicas. If this carries on I'll soon need to look for a proper job. So let me help you look for the sod.'

It all sounded perfectly reasonable to the crowd, and when they left the basilica, Streetpoet was in their midst, improvising a song as he went. *'No damn good, no damn good, ever came of the Brotherhood,'* he chanted, and those around him joined in this primitive chorus while he sang the verses solo.

> In Ordagyn in the Country of Marq
> They make the best wine ever drunk.
> They've made enough wine to float an ark
> But they're never ever ever drunk.
> So no wonder they're cross when a man on a horse
> Tells them that drink is forbidden.
> But we'll get the bloke and settle up the scores
> No matter where the bugger is hidden!

Od the Hedchenlightened, hanging desperately from a rafter, was not greatly reassured by this song.

The Vaine of Ghry walked slowly into the room. His polished shoes tapped the wooden floor; the noise seemed to him to be the crash of masonry as it fell from an impossibly high tower, but the emperor made no movement. Firstly, the Vaine went up to the corpse of Kamrot. Only a look was needed to prove the First Lord was dead. The eyes had seeped tears of blood and the head was at an inhuman angle. Then he turned to his emperor. 'Your majesty?'

Consatiné raised his head. His eyes were vacant and his tongue lolled loosely in his mouth.

'Your majesty!' insisted the Vaine of Ghry. 'Are you all right?'

The emperor did not reply. A snail trail of saliva dribbled down his chin, making a dark stain on his velvet doublet.

'Your majesty,' repeated the Vaine, but this time his words were a howl.

The Ordagyn mob searched diligently until the early solstice nightfall made their hunt impractical; then, despite the claims Streetpoet had made for their abstinence, they got thoroughly drunk. 'Bain't no point wasting it,' they told one another, dragging out vast glass demijohns that had been stored since the summer harvest. Streetpoet stayed with the party until midnight, leading the carousing through the streets and squares, then made his excuses and left. Few were capable of even noticing he was gone; no one thought to follow him. He went straight to the basilica and cautiously opened the door. *'No damn good, no damn good, ever came of the Brotherhood,'* he sang softly into the darkness. 'Od, it's me.'

The only response was a sort of groan from high in the roof.

'Od? Are you all right?'

Again came the groan, though this time it might have been a desperate 'No'.

'You can come down now. There's no one much about. There's no one much standing except me.'

'Oh? I can come down now, can I? That's easier said than done, I can tell you.'

'You got up, didn't you.'

'When I climbed up it was different. For one thing, if I hadn't I'd have been torn limb from limb. Secondly, I was fresh then: I'd only been riding all night long: I hadn't been hanging from a rafter all day too. And thirdly, I could see what I was doing.'

'Tough,' agreed Streetpoet. 'But never mind. You haven't got a lot of choice: you either come down now or you stay till you drop, because I'm not looking after you any more.'

'I might like it up here,' said Od.

'Then you stay there. I'm off.'

'All right. I'm coming. Only it really was much easier when I could see what I...'

There was a thump in the dark, a crash, a squeal. 'Hello?' said Streetpoet. Only silence replied, and silence, as is its habit, was not saying very much.

'Od?' tried Streetpoet again, advancing into the darkness. Still there was no sound from the fallen officer of the Brotherhood.

Worried now, Streetpoet felt his way through the blackness, groping his way from chair to chair as he advanced down the aisle. In the bell tower above him a lone owl hooted. He was half way down the basilica when a noise behind him made him turn. 'Od?'

The noise, as of manhandled bedding, was repeated. 'Od?' Streetpoet retraced his steps to the door, where the prayer mats were piled for the faithful to collect. He knelt down and shuffled his way through them. 'Od? Are you there?'

There was a long drawn out sigh, and then the whole pile of mats started thrashing about in the darkness. Streetpoet had found Od. 'Hello, bald friend,' said the troubadour. 'Are you all right.'

Od did not answer the question, exactly. Nor did he avoid it. He swore, however, repeatedly, viciously, variedly and fluently. His curses, in quick succession, struck Streetpoet, Ordagyn, the wine trade, the basilica, the rafters, the prayer mats and the floor, before turning to wider subjects. Od swore at his father and mother for bringing him into the world, at his late wife for dying on him, at the Brotherhood for engaging him, at Hedch for inspiring the Brotherhood, and at the god Menketh for creating Hedch. Streetpoet listened impatiently. He had heard better swearing, though charitably he acknowledged that, as an officer of the Brotherhood, Od was probably out of practice. At last the stream of imprecations was exhausted. 'Finished?' asked Streetpoet.

'Did I curse you?'

'Right at the beginning.'

'Then I've finished.'

'Good.' Streetpoet led the way to the door and, opening it, peered out. 'I want us well clear of Ordagyn by daybreak. The whole town is sozzled, thank Menketh, but you know what they'd do to you if they got the chance.'

'Tear me limb from limb.'

'Exactly. So let's get away.'

They set off rapidly through the dark streets, and as they left the town Streetpoet and Od encountered many bodies sprawled in the gutters. 'Disgusting,' said Od the Hedchenlightened.

'Do shut up,' said his companion. 'You sound like one of the Brotherhood.'

'I am one of the Brotherhood.'

'That's still no excuse for sounding like one. I'd give the Brotherhood a miss if I was you. It really is all tosh, you know.'

Od scratched his bald head in the dark. 'I'll think about it,' he said.

They left the town and clambered through the vineyards. The vines were pruned low for the winter, but still offered enough cover for two men running at the crouch. 'We'd better keep off the roads,' said Streetpoet.

'Where are we going?' asked Od.

'Somewhere else.'

It began to rain, which was not unusual for the time of year. The rain made the vineyards muddy and treacherous. They both tumbled over several times, and dawn found them still within sight of Ordagyn, though several thousand strides further up the hillside.

'What's going to happen next?' asked Od.

'We're going to have something to eat.' Streetpoet pulled a loaf and a small joint of beef from under his jerkin. 'I borrowed these last night. The man they used to belong to won't be eating for a fortnight after what he drank.'

'I wasn't talking about having something to eat. I was talking about the fate of the empire.'

'Oh?'

'Do you think there really will be trouble because of that proclamation?'

'Yes,' said Streetpoet. 'I think there will be. I can feel trouble in my bones.'

'If feelings in the bones are any indication,' said Od, rubbing as many parts of his anatomy as he could whilst scoffing his bread and beef, 'then my bones say we're in for catastrophe.'

Streetpoet smiled. 'We'll wait here until afternoon, I think, and sleep. At this time of year there'll be no one in the fields.'

There was a long pause. Both men thought the other asleep. And then Streetpoet looked up to find Od staring at him. 'What's the matter?' asked the minstrel.

'Why did you save me?' asked Od. 'I heard what you told that mob. You should have turned me over.'

Streetpoet shrugged. 'Actually, I can think of three possible reasons why I helped.'

'Well?'

'Because I'm daft, or because I'm daft, or because I'm daft. Now, can we get some sleep?'

The court physician was helpless and aghast. So was everyone else. Consternation spread rapidly round the palace and then leaked to the outside world. The palace of Verdre lies several thousand strides to the east of Cythroné, the capital: news of the disaster in the palace travelled to the city faster than a horseman would. The rumours were confused. Cythroné was already seething as a result of the proclamation about drink; the news that some awful event had occurred at the palace, which had resulted in the death of the Grand-Master of the Brotherhood and the imbecility of the emperor, fetched people onto the streets in their thousands. The thoroughfares were paralysed; the only commodity exchanged in the markets was gossip.

'Kamrot tried to kill the emperor with poison and was killed by the palace guards,' said a young carpenter to his wife as they entered the inn for a meal, 'but now who's to say the emperor will live?'

'It was a great beast, I've heard,' said a serving-woman, routinely slapping her customers' hands from her buttocks as she spoke, 'that killed Kamrot and so terrified the emperor it scared his wits right out of him.'

'It's a judgement on them for banning booze, that's what it is,' replied one of the customers. The ban did not seem to have had much effect, judging from this man's breath.

A lunching scribe wiped his nose on his sleeve before speaking. 'I've heard that Consatiné killed Kamrot, but was so struck with remorse it addled his brain,' he said with authority.

And finally a theory emerged that was to achieve almost general currency in the confusion of the next few days. 'No,' said an unshaven soldier as he stabbed a pickle with his knife. 'You've all got it wrong. Consatiné killed Kamrot, and then the ghost of Ormaas appeared and scared the emperor right off his head.'

The people in the streets and taverns became mobs as the daylight faded. Many chanted for the emperor, many more against him. Rioting spilled even into the lovely grounds of the palace itself, and several palace guards as well as several hundred rioters were injured in the gardens. Arson and looting damaged many shops and houses in Cythroné and the surrounding area, and the city militia, as divided as any group in that divided town, did nothing to prevent it.

Meanwhile, Consatiné, unconscious and oblivious after a sleeping draft, was lain carefully on his great bed. The usual formalities were dispensed with. On his side, curled protectively around his own belly, the emperor looked foetal, and as exposed as an embryo without a womb.

Morning revealed the extent of the devastation. Palls of smoke hung over the city. In the slums of the Quarter to the south of the river Khalin, several noted supporters of the Brotherhood had been burnt in an impromptu auto-da-fé which engulfed not only them but their houses and families. Several of the great trading houses along the river Carpaccio had been ransacked, and all had been damaged by the rioters. Public anger had exposed many private grievances. Cuckolded husbands had slain their wives' lovers. Profiteering landlords lay dead in dark alleys. Moneylenders found their loans repaid by a knife in the gut or a rope. Brutal bosses' brutality was returned. Unpopular magistrates were sentenced to death.

Nor did the morning bring real peace. The mobs were not satisfied. In Fragma Square a demonstration against the emperor turned into a spree of looting which again the militia did nothing to prevent. A ship-of-war on the Khalin mutinied for a short while against the drink law until its officers promised the rum ration would be retained, and then

hanged the ringleaders. And an aristocratic member of the
Council, the Gros of Querostan-Cully, died when his carriage
was overturned by protesters.

In the end it was the weather that saved Cythroné. A blizzard
swept down from the north, over the exposed Plains of Myr,
and by noon the snows were scouring the streets, burying the
dead and forcing the living to seek shelter. At the same time,
a panicky meeting of the Council – minus the late Gros of
Querostan-Cully – found itself unable to cope with the crisis
and sent a message to the highly respected Gros of Peltyn. The
Gros commanded the imperial armies on the Khalinwatch; the
Council asked him to accept the Regency of Khalindaine until
the emperor was recovered.

The day ended in enforced truce. The weather persisted: the
ships moored on the Khalin found themselves iced in; chestnut
vendors did well in the indoor markets of Hythrapos and Giran;
the half-hearted militia patrols were driven from the streets,
and the taverns took advantage of it all. Still gossip persisted,
and perhaps the greatest curiosity of all was that, despite the
plethora of rumours, no one stumbled on the truth.

This time the snow did reach as far south as the county of
Marq, falling on Streetpoet and Od as they slept. Streetpoet
was woken first: 'Come on,' he said, 'we've got to get
a move on.'

'Why?'

'Because if we don't we'll freeze to death.'

'Is that the only reason you woke me?'

'Isn't it enough?'

'No. Can I go back to sleep now?' And Od closed his eyes.

Amused as well as exasperated, Streetpoet raised his own
eyes to the snow, which fell in dark shapes that seemed to
come out of nowhere. 'Well,' he told himself, 'this won't do.'
And he woke his companion again.

'Now what?' asked the sleeper.

'It's still snowing.'

'Good.' Od rolled over and settled again.

This time Streetpoet shook him, hard. 'How you can sleep
when we're in danger of our lives is beyond me.'

'How you can expect me to wake after all I went through
yesterday is just as obscure to me, I'm telling you!'

'We must move though.'

'I suppose so. Botheration!' Od the Hedchenlightened struggled out of comfortable sleep, sat up, and rubbed his face and hands. 'I'm not enthusiastic,' he warned. 'I've nowhere to go.'

'No wife, no family, no friends?'

'My wife and children were killed in the plague; my friends were in the Brotherhood, and now you've taken even that from me.'

'You must have had a trade before you joined the Brotherhood.'

'I was a pilot on the Hasfaine river.'

'That's a *good* job,' said Streetpoet, impressed. 'Why can't you go back to that?'

Od shook his head. 'I haven't worked the river for three years. It changes every three days because of the silt. No one would employ me any more.'

'Looks like you're stuck with me then. Or I'm stuck with you.'

'Looks like it,' agreed Od, smiling. 'Are you going anywhere in particular.'

'I'm not sure.' Streetpoet stood and led on, Od following. 'I've a good mind to go to Northreach. That's where Lara, the cousin of Ormaas that I mentioned, lives. I want to find her, bring her down to Cythroné, and see if Consatiné will meet us. I've a feeling that with Lara's help I might be able to knock some sense into Consatiné and make him accept that he really *is* emperor, whether he likes it or not.'

Od the Hedchenlightened puckered his hairless face into a wistful smile. 'I've often wanted to travel,' he said.

Life is a strange place to inhabit. Almost anything can be explained except the things that matter. What life *is*, for instance, or death. Or why, at the very moment Streetpoet mentioned her name, the Emperor Consatiné on his immense state bed suddenly opened his mouth and cried, quietly but distinctly, 'Lara!' four times before relapsing into his customary inertia.

The snow was deeper in the hills, and the companions, although catching only the edge of the blizzard that raged in Cythroné, were unable to make much headway. Od's battered limbs still caused him particular discomfort, but Streetpoet was falling down as often as his friend and both of them were feeling the cold more intensely with every step. 'I came south this winter to get away from this sort of weather,' complained Streetpoet.

'It is bad for the time of year, I suppose.'

'It's exactly right for the time of year,' Streetpoet corrected. 'It's bad for *us*.'

They carried on. They were no longer climbing: they seemed to be walking along a kind of ridge, though the steady snow made it hard to see exactly where they were. Each step required them to sweep aside a gout of snow, for they were too tired and the snow was too deep for them to raise their legs over it now.

'Can you still feel your toes?' asked Streetpoet.

'I can't even feel my knees,' admitted his companion.

'Oh well, maybe we'll find somewhere soon.'

'What's this "maybe"?' demanded Od. 'I've lost my faith in the Brotherhood; I was pinning it all on you. You've saved me once, don't say you're going to let me down this time?'

'I'll try not. I'm glad you've given up on the Brotherhood, by the way.'

'Just call me Od the Disenchanted from now on.'

'All right.' They were chattering to keep out the cold, Streetpoet realised. 'And I suppose my luck will hold. I've been pretty lucky in the past. I was even saved from the House of the Condemned once, and I'll bet there aren't many people in Khalindaine who...'

'Shhh.'

'It's an interesting story, honestly. And I'll make up something exciting to gloss over the boring bits.'

'Shhhhhh. Look over there.' Od pointed to the right, at nothing at all so far as his companion could see. None the less, Od was insistent, through tugging and dumb-show, that their path lay in that direction. All directions were the same to Streetpoet by then: he followed.

He soon saw what had attracted Od's attention. A light showed briefly through the snow flurries, was hidden, and then revealed again. 'Better be careful,' they warned one another as they approached, though both desired nothing so much as to run up to the light and throw themselves at the mercy of its owner.

'How do we find out if they're friendly?' wondered Od.

'We ask them.'

'Oh.'

Still moving as cautiously as they could, the two figures approached the stranded wagon, then waited outside. Od coughed politely; Streetpoet waved an impatient arm to tell him to shut up and sang a brief snatch of song.

> *The Night is cold and so are we,*
> *The snow is very deep.*
> *We've got no gold but we're friendly*
> *– Please, let us in to sleep.*

The edge of the awning was pushed back and a handsome, elderly and very tired face looked out. 'Come on in if you're going to,' he said.

This welcome was not exactly enthusiastic, perhaps, but to Od and Streetpoet it was the most delightful invitation they could recall. Inside the crowded but comfortable quarters they saw, by the light of a suspended brazier, three figures on three beds. The first was the man who had let them in; the second belonged to a woman of equal age and attractiveness; the third was a pretty girl's, and this girl stared so hard at Streetpoet that even he felt something approaching embarrassment.

'Have we met?' he felt compelled to ask her. 'I usually remember so pretty a face.'

She smiled, certain from this that she had identified him correctly. 'Well,' she said. 'It was dark. And we were back to back most of the time.'

'How novel,' he remarked. And then he remembered. 'Amila! The actress at the auto-da-fé!'

'There's no acting at an auto-da-fé,' put in Od. 'The Brotherhood wouldn't allow it.'

'She was being burnt, twit,' said Streetpoet. He addressed Amila again. 'And this must be your family.'

'This is half of them. My sister and her husband are stranded further down the hill. We were trying to make it over the brow before the snow got deep, but we failed.'

'Aulcun,' said the man, suddenly introducing himself. 'And this is the light of my life, my wife Ryhtal. We are honoured to have you as a guest, young man, and I'm only sorry I didn't recognise you at once.'

'I'm Streetpoet,' said Streetpoet.

'We know all about you,' said the man called Aulcun.

'And it's lovely to meet you again,' said Ryhtal. 'We've heard so much about you from Amila.'

'It's good to meet you again,' replied Streetpoet.

Aulcun had fetched out a bottle. 'I've heard it's been banned,' he said, waving it, 'but never mind that. A curse on the Brotherhood: this deserves a drink! By the way, who is your friend?'

'Ah,' said Streetpoet. 'This is Od.' Od gave him a searching look. 'Od the Disenchanted.'

'I'm very pleased to meet you,' said Od.

Chapter 2

A Question of Values

The blizzard blew for thirteen nights, and was the worst for thirteen years. Cythroné huddled beneath the onslaught, politics forgotten in the need to keep warm. The victims of the solstice violence remained preserved and unburied beneath the drifts, or provided food for enterprising dogs; the streets were abandoned to the raging wind and the snow. In wooden shanties whole rooms were pulled down for firewood; in merchants' cold houses sick children coughed and gasped against the chill; even the palaces of the nobles offered little comfort, and their elegant courtyards were filled daily with frostbitten and half-dead mendicants flushed from the alleys by the cold. Commerce and rioting were equally impossible. When solitary wanderers met in the street their greetings were always the same: 'Four days now', 'Five days', 'Eleven days'; it was a solemn scoreboard which demonstrated the extent of the winter's victory; it was as though the paralysis which gripped the emperor had enveloped his capital city.

On the fourteenth day, though Consatiné's condition remained unchanged, the blizzards stopped, and a summons was issued from the palace, calling the Council for a meeting.

Wriknek the Faithfollower was in his house at the end of the Street of Lawyers when the call came. It was an unpretentious house, for Wriknek was an unpretentious man. Like many of the Brotherhood's more enthusiastic members Wriknek had been born and brought up in the Plains of Myr; even now, as a respected member of the Council, he chose to live as quietly as possible. Yet despite his modest upbringing and his modest house, Wriknek had far from modest ambitions. For within him was a worm, buried so deep that even Wriknek knew nothing of its existence, and the worm's name was syphilis.

Wriknek lived alone, except for his servants. His wife had died some years before and, although the Brotherhood did not demand celibacy, like most of its senior officers, Wriknek lived a life of chastity. It was as well for the female population of Cythroné that he did so: his syphilis was no fault of his own – he had inherited it from his father, a small-town and small-minded solicitor like his son who had nevertheless indulged in prostitutes – but was contagious and growing daily.

Syphilis was known in Khalindaine long ago. Ancient disinterred skeletons had been found which bore the disease's distinctive mark. But it was in that memorable year, in which the trade route with distant Ehapot was opened, that a new and fatal chapter in the disease's history began. As though fortified by contact with the exotic tropics, the terrifying effects of syphilis were noted from the time of the explorer Kelgratan's triumphant return to Nerith onwards, and its success could be measured on a map of the cities it visited: Cythroné, Myr, Ilynés, Comtas, Mornet. Always the disease travelled under an assumed name, a euphemism which laid blame for the disease on somewhere else. In Cythroné it was called 'the Southern plague'; in Ilynés it was 'the Nerith disease'; in Myr it was 'the Curse of Akbar'; and in Comtas it was the Cythron disease. Wriknek's father had met the disease on a business trip to Morn, and had passed it on to his wife and unborn son: poor Wriknek, had he but known it, had no choice but to suffer its ravages; he would suffer and would die, and would never know the cause. All he knew was that within his mind something special had been born, and he thought this a mark of divinity.

The Council Chamber was a high, gilded room, its walls and ceilings decorated with ornate stylised vegetation. In addition to the Gros of Ra's underfloor heating, four great fires, one set in each wall, warmed the room. None the less, Wriknek noted a certain reluctance on the part of the Brotherhood Councillors to remove their coats: their coats marked them off from the corrupt court.

There was a long table in the centre of the Council Chamber. The Brotherhood sat on the right, the nobility on the left. Two chairs in the centre were conspicuously vacant, that of the First Lord and that of the emperor. Another space was left by the Gros of Querostan-Cully. Wriknek sat down determinedly, but the meeting refused to begin. The Gros of Yrksa discussed the work of the musician Bhanre with the Vaine of Thren; Corval Hedchbeloved and Prajik Ormaaslover discussed, in rather less respectful tones, the hollow comforts of the Council Chamber; the Vaine of Ferênq told the Vaine of Loutaxi a risqué story involving two virgins and a candle; Januslav the Believer demanded to know why Konuskat the Disciple was wearing a dark blue cloak contrary to the rules of the Brotherhood. This last discussion was getting as heated as anything was likely to get in that climate.

'My cloak was ripped,' explained the Disciple. 'I could hardly come out in this temperature without a cloak to my back, could I?'

'It will not do,' warned Januslav the Believer. 'Senior officers of the Brotherhood are in no way above the rules; on the contrary, we have a particular duty and responsibility to uphold the rules, for it is our perseverance and diligence which preserves the purity of the Faith. Your attire will have to be raised at the next meeting of the General Congress, Brother.'

'Kinky,' said the Vaine of Thren, overhearing.

Konuskat, meanwhile, was smiling at the younger man, looking at him with a mixture of pity and respect. 'I admire your dedication, Januslav, just as I envy your youth. A man of my age, however, would not last long without a cloak in these conditions.'

'Better to be without a cloak than in defiance of the Rules,' replied the Believer.

'And better dead?'

'Aye. If that is what it takes. Decadence cannot be defeated without sacrifice, Brother.'

In the midst of all this a new voice sounded, loudly and clearly, addressing the whole assembly. Wriknek the Faithfollower stood at his place, his pinched face and small eyes illuminated by the light of the several fires, and demanded to be heard.

'Councillors, councillors!' he shouted, moderating his voice only when he was sure he had their attention. 'We are here to discuss the fate of the empire, yet all I have heard so far has been idle chit-chat and trivial bickering. Cythroné is in crisis, and Menketh knows what is happening elsewhere in Khalindaine: *we've* certainly had no news. The whole of Khalindaine could be up in arms, or buried beneath the snow, for all you know or care. Now, discussing nothing and delighting in the noise we make might suit our noble colleagues at the other end of the table – they're used to indolence – but it isn't the way of the Brotherhood and it isn't the way to get things done. We must organise. To my mind we have already made a mistake. In our panic after Kamrot's death we sent for this Gros of Peltyn, but we were irresponsible that day – we ignored our own responsibility, and I for one am ashamed I was party to inviting him to Cythroné; I've no desire to replace the legitimate government of Khalindaine with the dictatorship of this Gros of Peltyn and his troops.'

He waved a parchment scroll at the Council. 'Do you recognise this?' he asked them. 'This is the Convention of Weir, the constitution of Khalindaine as laid down by the Gros of Weir and the Grand-Master of the Brotherhood when Consatiné took the throne.'

'We know, only too well,' said the Gros of Llire-Brenzoq wearily.

'But do you!' demanded Wriknek the Faithfollower, turning triumphantly on his fellow councillor. 'Do you! Then why do you seek to ignore it? The Convention clearly states that Khalindaine be governed by a council, made up equally of members of the Brotherhood and the nobility. It says that the emperor shall be chairman and that the Grand-Master of the Brotherhood in his rôle as First Lord, shall be vice-chairman. What it most certainly does not say is that, in the event of the death or incapacity of either of those two – and I will not speculate as to what happened on that dreadful day: we all have our own theories on that – the Council should hand over power to some jumped-up, trumped-up nobleman with his own private army. We of the Brotherhood are representatives of the people...'

'Some of the people,' interjected the Llire-Brenzoq-Lord accurately.

'And who do you represent?' asked Wriknek. 'No one but yourselves.' This was equally accurate: the Gros of Llire-Brenzoq was silenced and Wriknek able to proceed. 'We are the representatives of the people and of the True Faith. I therefore move, on behalf of the Brotherhood, the people and the Faith, that our unconstitutional invitation to the Gros of Peltyn be withdrawn immediately, and that the running of the empire should continue to be the prerogative of the Council. I further propose that in the absence of the emperor we should, constitutionally, see that the vice-chairman should take the chair.'

'He's dead, you blithering idiot,' called the Vaine of Ferenq.

'And therefore should be replaced forthwith. The Convention of Weir states that the First Lord should be chosen from the Brotherhood: therefore, it should be a member of the Brotherhood, and not some fumbling aristocrat, who should rule Khalindaine at this time of crisis.'

'And who do you have in mind for the job?' enquired the Vaine of Thren. 'You perchance?'

'That is for the Brotherhood to decide,' replied Wriknek primly. 'And is beside the question. The point, the vital point, is one of principle, and I for one am not going to stand back and let some *noble* lord trample on my rights as his forebearers trampled on mine.'

'A moment, please.' The new speaker was the Gros of Hyopenrah, elderly and astute. 'As I understand it, Wriknek wants the invitation to the Gros of Peltyn to be withdrawn, on the grounds that, with the Gyr in charge, Khalindaine would be ruled by a member of the nobility.'

'And because such an appointment would be in gross contravention of the Convention of Weir,' Wriknek answered.

'And because he wants the job of First Lord,' said the Vaine of Thren.

'Let's not enquire into Wriknek's motives, let's just establish exactly what he wants,' said the Hyopenrah-Lord. 'The second point, as my noble friend has just intimated, is that Wriknek wants power to pass instead to a new First Lord, chosen from the ranks of the Brotherhood.'

'Exactly!' said Wriknek. His sallow face wore an unhealthy flush. 'In accordance with the Convention of Weir!'

'It seems to me,' continued the Gros smoothly, 'that this would cause exactly the same problem in reverse. Too much power in the Brotherhood's hands has already caused chaos in Khalindaine. Look at the fiasco over alcohol. Kamrot went over the head of the Council, sent out the proclamation without full consultation, and by doing so caused turmoil. It is not a question of who is *appointed* to govern; what we must ask is who is *fit* to govern, and in my belief, on the evidence of the appalling mishandling of the alcohol legislation, the Brotherhood has proved itself *un*fit!'

Like many of his colleagues the Faithfollower was on his feet and shouting: 'The Convention of Weir!' he yelled. 'What about the Convention of Weir?'

'Ah yes, the Convention of Weir,' said the Hyopenrah-Lord. 'I was coming to that. Not only are Wriknek's proposals unacceptable' – there was a chorus of approval from his peers – 'they are entirely misplaced, for the Convention of Weir demands the balancing presence of the emperor at the head of government.. Without the emperor the Convention is in suspension: the conditions required for it to operate do not pertain until the Emperor Consatiné, may Menketh preserve him, is restored to us.'

'Rubbish,' retorted Wriknek. 'The emperor lives. That he is moonstruck is neither here nor there.'

'That the emperor *lives* is neither here nor there,' corrected the Hyopenrah-Lord. 'The conditions required for the Convention no longer apply, and therefore the Convention no longer applies, and I believe that this ill-mannered attempt to revoke our previous decision should be disregarded absolutely.'

'The Brotherhood will oppose any interference with the convention,' affirmed Wriknek.

'Just as the nobility will oppose any power-grabbing opportunism by the so-called Brotherhood,' returned the Gros of Hyopenrah.

It looked as if argument was inevitable, but then a messenger arrived with the news that the Gros of Peltyn had arrived. Order was restored to the chamber, though it was of a seething, precarious kind.

The Gros's entry was dramatic and forceful, as he had intended. With the snow still clinging to his boots he flung open the double doors and marched straight to the First Lord's vacant chair: the nobility all stood for him, as did one or two of the more impressionable members of the Brotherhood.

'Sit down, sit down,' he told them. 'We've no time for ceremony. My information is sparse but I hope accurate: Kamrot is dead, the emperor ill, and Cythroné riots. Is that the case?'

There were murmurs of agreement from around the table. 'What about the Convention of Weir?' cried Wriknek, predictably, but for the time being the Convention was forgotten as the Peltyn-Lord's personality swamped the opposition.

'Our first priority must be to restore order,' continued the Gros, 'and make it clear that the good government of Khalindaine will not be interrupted by these unfortunate events. I have three proposals. Firstly, immediately, my troops will march into the city. I believe a show of strength at this time will convince the rioters to return to their homes; any who disregard this reassurance will be dealt with harshly. Secondly, the ridiculous proclamation forbidding drinking will have to be modified. We can't do away with it entirely, for that would be to admit we were wrong. Instead I suggest we amend it, to prohibit public drunkenness, which is a reasonable prohibition and one the people will accept. And thirdly, we must arrive at some sort of explanation for the curious events surrounding Kamrot's death and the emperor's illness, which will satisfy the population and put an end to the rumours which circulate even amongst my own troops. That explanation I leave to you: you are politicians, and I am sure you are far more experienced at concocting lies than I, a mere soldier. And now, gentlemen, I must leave you. My presence is required in the city.'

With a flourish of his cloak the Gros of Peltyn left. There was a silence, followed by a babble. The nobles were unequivocal in their support, and even some of the Brotherhood had been impressed by the decisive speed with which the Peltyn-Lord had acted. To others, however, the Gyr's autocratic assumption that the Council would fall in with his plans was a confirmation of their worst fears, and they lost no time in announcing this.

'You see,' said Wriknek. 'He is acting the tyrant already. He has no right to meddle with existing legislation. The law against alcohol is a just and proper one.'

'Yet I have heard that it is unpopular,' pointed out Konuskat the Disciple, considerably understating what he had actually heard.

'The Truth is always unpopular,' said Korval the Hedchite.

'But is now the right time to enforce such legislation?' asked Prajik Ormaaslover. 'The Gros of Peltyn might be right about that at least. Such a law was bound to cause trouble.'

'Trouble!' mocked Wriknek. 'Unpopularity!' He looked scornfully at the Brothers. 'You talk as if we act by the will of the people; we act by the will of the gods!'

'He was happy enough citing the people earlier,' muttered Prajik, but only to himself. More loudly he said: 'Yet, by accepting the Gros of Peltyn's recommendation temporarily we might be able to kill two birds with one sling-shot. Those misguided but plentiful people who enjoy a drink now and again will be satisfied, whilst the enlightened ones who support our attempts to purify Khalindaine will know we are not responsible for this change in the law.'

'Fool!' cried Wriknek. A vein on his forehead bulged. 'Temporiser! Now is not the time for subtlety! Now is the time for action! We will strike a blow that will alter the history of Khalindaine! The time is ours. Are we going to sit back and be browbeaten by the Gros of Peltyn and his aristocratic cronies, or are we going to claim our natural and legal rights? You may be deceived by the Peltyn-Lord's aristocratic arrogance, but I am not, and the people will be with me...'

'Oh. Them again,' muttered Prajik.

'...when the struggle begins. You are either for me or against me, Brothers; there is no middle way. I speak with the voice of the Faithful and only the Faithful shall hear! Stand with me, you who share the faith, or stay seated, and show yourselves to be time-servers, hypocrites, power-seekers or cowards! Stand up and join me, I say, and show yourselves true men, true believers, true Brothers!'

One by one the Brothers stood. Some were eager, others reluctant. Eventually only Konuskat and Prajik remained seated. They looked at one another, shrugged, and stood at last with the rest. Meanwhile, Wriknek, full of the certainty that this was his moment, strode up to the Gros of Hyopenrah. 'We leave you to your deliberations. We leave you to your lies. We shall not be cheated of our rightful place in government, nor shall we fail to let the men of Khalindaine know how you have attempted to thwart us. Goodbye. You shall not see us at this table again whilst the Peltyn-Lord rules.'

Steadily the brothers filed out after their new leader. 'Good riddance!' called the Vaine of Ferênq cheerfully, but several of his peers were less sanguine about this turn of events.

'This could mean civil war,' warned the Vaine of Thren.

'I hope not,' replied the Vaine of Loutaxi. 'Surely a compromise can be reached.'

'Why worry?' asked the Gros of Llire-Brenzoq calmly. 'What are a handful of lawyers and tailors going to do?'

'Should it come to war,' said the Vaine of Loutaxi, 'they're going to try to do for you.'

'Let them!' said the Llire-Brenzoq-Lord, who apparently viewed the prospect with relish. 'It's time we put them in their place.'

On the snowbound hill above Marq the family of Aulcun and their new companions were eating. Lunch was a rabbit Streetpoet had snared. It was solid when he brought it back from the trap and needed to be defrosted before he could skin it. Still, with the addition of a few rather yellow sprouts and a handful of dried herbs, it made a reasonable stew, though hardly a feast for five.

'Is there any more?' Amila asked.

'Plenty,' replied Streetpoet. 'Only they need catching first.'

'You knew what I meant!' she complained.

'Sorry, my lovely. No more stew.'

She smiled back at him and, though she would have liked some more to eat, she was content.

The Cythron riots had resumed, and once again Fragma Square was their focus. A large mob of republican apprentices, Hedchite artisans, and several thousand junior members of the Brotherhood assembled there, almost as if their meeting was prearranged, but were attacked at once by other groups loyal to Consatiné. Fragma Square lies at the point where the Namamorn, running from west to east, meets the Mercantile Way, which runs north and south, and the roads exit through the square's four corners; in the centre stands the statue that the Empress Elsban had erected of her forbidden lover Ravenspur. The mobs were armed with improvised weapons: billhooks that were kitchen knives tied to broom handles, staves that, demobbed, were fence-poles, knobkerries that were once knob-handled canes. Perhaps for this reason the violence, though intense, was rarely fatal: many were hurt but few were killed.

The total absence of uniforms among the contending sides led to much confusion. Only the members of the Brotherhood of the Faithful, dressed in their distinctive black cloaks and tall hats, could be identified clearly, and because of this they became rallying points for their own side and targets for their opponents. Round them the fighting raged.

The captains of the city militia, and the aldermen and leading burghers of Cythroné, knew full well that there was trouble in Fragma Square, which is why they kept away, but the Gros of Peltyn, at the head of his troops, felt no such inhibitions. He marched straight down the Namamorn, passed the icebound hovels on the outskirts of Cythroné, beneath city gates which had once marked the boundaries of the town, and which were now swamped by buildings, and through towards the square. The noise of the fighting could be heard clearly in the snow-filled and still largely deserted streets: loud wails, the crash of wood on wood, the heaving sounds of the crowding throng. The next evidence of the events in the square was dragged figures, wounded in the fighting, who were being escorted home by their friends. It was noticeable, and a tribute to the appearance of the Gros's veterans, that the friends tended to scuttle up alleys at the troops' approach, leaving the wounded in the gutter.

Finally, the troops reached the edge of the square. The Gros of Peltyn called for his officers. They rode round him rapidly, their blue cloaks swirling. His instructions were terse: the officers rejoined their men, and the operation to clear the square began.

The arrival of so many troops did not go unnoticed, and the combatants nearest their regimented ranks broke off their skirmishing in a mutually agreed desire to get away. Smashing the head of a chandler or a carter was one thing; trying to fight a seasoned veteran of the Khalinwatch campaign was another. Unfortunately for the refugees, dispersing through the mob was by no means easy. Those further from the entrance to the Namamorn were unaware of the troops, and resented the pushing, shoving intruders. Meanwhile, in accordance with the Gros's commands, companies of pikemen under his lieutenant, the Vaine of Talen, were filing through the side-streets around the square, preparing to muster at the other exits.

The Gros now led his cavalry forward. Sabre-flourishing, breastplate-sparkling, and mounted on great chargers, the horsemen advanced through the square at the trot. Prudently, the mob parted to let them through, and almost all the injuries at this stage were inflicted on those who could not escape the horses' hoofs in time. At the same time the pikemen were beginning to form up at the other exit: it was not a perfectly co-ordinated operation, there having been no time for advanced planning; on the other hand, as a rough and ready way of controlling the mob it seemed to be working quite well. But even the admirable Gros of Peltyn had overlooked one thing – the sheer numbers in the square.

On the north-west side of the square was a row of ancient shops; exposed timbers were black against the plaster; coloured banners proclaimed what each shop sold; everything was dingy in the snow-drenched day. The shops were all closed and boarded against looters, but this made no difference. With a sound like an eruption first one and then another of these ancient buildings tumbled down as the pressure of the mob increased. What had been a relatively harmless pitched battle, certainly by the standards of the fighting that was to follow, became a massacre. Men were broken beneath great beams, and then further mashed as their companions' feet were driven over the ruins. Families who had barricaded themselves in the upper storey were thrown fatally into the mob. The entire north-west side of the square became a scene of devastation. Corpses were mingled in the ruins like rice in a sauce. The wailing injured became a threnody to mourn the many dead.

That evening, while Cythroné counted the casualties, a discussion took place in a snowbound wagon on a hill above the county of Marq.

'I have no reputation in the east,' Aulcun was protesting, whilst his son-in-law, Bazadore, lit his pipe. 'How could we find work? Menketh knows, it's hard enough finding work here.'

'Exactly,' said Bazadore. 'It's too hard here. We've been harried from village to village ever since your theatre in Nerith was closed. We've had no time to rehearse nor learn new material; we've had no rest to speak of; we were nearly burnt to death in Téres, and would have been had this bloke not saved us.' Streetpoet smiled modestly; Bazadore continued. 'If we went east, to Comtas, we'd be safe.'

'You're half-Kapatan,' said Aulcun. 'Your father's race is used to leading a wandering life. But I'm just an actor, as my father was before me and his before that. My family managed that theatre in Nerith for three generations, building it up and building up its reputation. Well, since the Brotherhood closed down the theatre, all that's left is the reputation. But who has heard of Aulcun on the east coast? We may only be a shadow of what the company was once, but at least here we get an audience.'

'An audience for our execution? Is that what you want? It's what we're likely to get. Even if you don't want to leave, what about your wife and daughters? Do you want to see them killed?'

'Of course not. But I don't want to see them starve either. There are too many good companies in the east.'

'Name them if they're so famous.'

'I can't,' returned the older man. 'I don't know their names any more than they would know mine. But Feodh Linesinger was from Comtas, and he twice took the Actor's Spoils in Cythroné!'

'That was years ago. Feodh's probably dead by now.'

'He'll have trained others.'

'Then why haven't we heard of them?'

'The same reason they won't have heard of me. It's too far away. It's too alien. Menketh alive! They barely speak the same language over there!'

'You exaggerate the difficulties there, ignore the dangers here,' said Bazadore.

'And you overestimate the difficulties here while ignoring the impossibility of working there.'

'You are a stubborn man, Aulcun,' said his son-in-law, not without a certain amount of respect. 'You are also misled. We know that the Brotherhood has much less influence in Comtas. We know that the theatres have not even been closed. Here, between Ilynés and Nerith, where the Brotherhood is strong, we are in perpetual danger. There we should be safe.'

'He is right,' said Ryhtal. 'We're too old to be on the run like this.'

'We're too old to move to another part of the country,' argued her husband.

'No. Not for that.' Ryhtal smiled at Aulcun. 'We could start a theatre there. We still have some money. Imagine it, a real theatre again, with scenery and seats for the wealthy. And we could hire more actors, do more ambitious performances.

You are old enough now to play Emperor Tylarq just as you always wanted. In Comtas you could do it. How does the great speech from that play go?'

Reluctantly at first, but with increasing vigour as the lines of the poet worked on his actor's soul, Aulcun recited.

> Old as I am, and blind, there's mischief yet
> Behind these sightless eyes and year-etched lines
> Puzzled across my face. For don't forget
> That as the years improve the finest wines
> So man can be improved. Once I was young,
> A livid lover, vivid in bright clothes.
> Then was I a fool. I too have sung
> Ditties for my mistress, praised her toes,
> And damned her eyes an instant on that she
> Spake three words to another; swore
> She loved me not though she loved me,
> And drove her to the streets, forced her to whore
> And be the things she had not been till I
> Suspected them of her. Oh! What a fool!
> And I have fought in wars, and praised the sword
> That killed the fine young man, fresh out of school,
> Who faced me full of fears upon the sward.
> Then was I the fool! And I have ruled
> An empire made of dust and men who die
> Though I knew that not, for I was fooled
> And did not recognise that life goes by
> For then I was the fool! And then! And then!
> And only now, purblind, I feel I gaze
> Evenly on life and love and men,
> And recognise the jests, the wayward ways,
> We find to hide the fact we die, and know
> That mischief is the way of gods, the tool
> By which they sway us, and indeed I know
> That still I am the fool, the happy fool!

Ryhtal smiled indulgently at her husband. 'We're going east then,' she stated.

'We'll see,' said Aulcun, smiling back, and Ryhtal knew that, like every sympathetic person who says 'We'll see', her husband meant 'Yes'.

'Are you coming with us?' Amila asked Streetpoet.

'Sadly, no,' the minstrel replied. 'Od and I are journeying to Northreach in search of a certain young lady called Lara.'

'Oh,' said the actress.

In the winter evening dark, lit only by the fire suspended in its bracket, it was easy for Amila to hide her tears. But for Consatiné, waking again in response to that distant mention of Lara's name, the tears could not be hidden. Surrounded by courtiers, advisers, doctors and quacks, he had no privacy at all in which to weep.

Amila went to Streetpoet that night, climbing beneath the blanket with him as he slept and waking him with gentle kisses. Her body was warm and naked beside him, her mouth and limbs inviting.

Od, sleeping well wrapped on the floor, was woken by a slight but rhythmic shudder that ran through the wagon. He yawned his eyes open but could see nothing. Bazadore and his wife had returned to their own caravan; the fire had been extinguished. But though his eyes were useless, his ears were alert: he heard the groaning of Streetpoet's bed and the different groans Amila made. The tempo grew faster; Amila gasped; Streetpoet grunted, and Od, who had been a married man, knew for certain what was happening. Then the groans reached a suppressed climax, the shaking stopped, and Od went back to sleep. When he next awoke it was morning. A winter dawn lit the peaceful caravan. Amila had returned to her own bed, and Streetpoet, with a look of blissful innocence, slept as though all the rage of an Agaska could not disturb him.

'No!' screamed the Emperor Consatiné suddenly, though the Lord of the Left Sleeve was dressing him just as if this were an ordinary morning. 'I shall not be buried in the sword shop!'

'Sire?' enquired the Lord of the Left Sleeve politely.

Consatiné seemed to have forgotten his first statement already. 'Bring me sweetmeats!' he ordered.

Servants were dispatched at once. Consatiné sat on his bed, stopping the dressing ceremony in its tracks. 'Have you ever seen a swan drink cider?' he asked. 'I haven't.'

The tray of sweetmeats arrived. Consatiné looked at them closely, picking over them carefully but never tasting them. 'All dead,' he pronounced sadly. 'It must have been an awfully long wait for the boat.' He started to cry, sobbing and sniffing gently to himself. 'I suppose they caught cold and could never get warm.'

'What boat?' asked a courtier, in the hope of humouring his emperor.

'I expect it sank in the bath,' explained Consatiné. 'They do, you know.'

The courtiers looked around rather helplessly. Previously, at least, the addled wits of their emperor had kept him quiet; now it seemed he could not stop talking.

'Do you know how to drink the health of the Brotherhood?' Consatiné asked.

A reply seemed expected. 'No, sire,' said one or two dutiful voices.

'With an empty glass.'

There was a pause and then, spontaneously, the Lord of the Left Leg of the Under Nether Garment started to laugh. Others began to laugh too, and Consatiné seemed cheered by this.

'What,' he asked, 'is a dog that goes backwards wagging its head?'

The courtiers did not know.

'Why, a backwards dog is a god!' said Consatiné. 'And what colour is a bald man's hair?'

'We don't know sire.'

'Neither does he,' said Consatiné cheerfully. The emperor had become court fool.

The Gros of Peltyn was called for. As always he was businesslike, intelligent and sensible, but there was precious little sense to be had from Consatiné.

'There has been rioting in Cythroné,' he informed his emperor.

'Then the wind must have blown from the east,' replied Consatiné sagely.

'I don't understand the relevance, sire,' admitted the Gros.

'Nor I,' admitted Consatiné cheerfully.

'The riots have largely been contained,' continued the Peltyn-Lord, pressing on with his report.

'In a large container?' asked Consatiné.

'In Fragma Square.'

'How curious,' said Consatiné. 'Have you ever seen what a blind man sees?'

'No sire.'

'You're fooling yourself if you believe that. Fetch me Lara.'

'Who, your majesty?' asked the Gros of Peltyn.

'Lara. I want her to be my wife.'

'Sire?'

'What colour is rain?' asked the emperor.

'Why, no colour, sire.'

'Wrong again. My reign shall be green, bright green, and we shall have flowers in the city. But first I must marry my Lara.'

Hurried consultations took place. 'He appears much recovered,' said the Gros. 'At least he is talking now, though he's not making much sense. That must be a good sign.'

The doctors did not like to commit themselves. It was safer to commit a patient. 'Strong possibility of change,' said one.

'Despite the likelihood of continuation,' added another.

'Given all factors,' said a third.

'And taking them into consideration,' said a fourth.

'With a suitable margin of error,' said the fifth.

'Stop!' demanded the Peltyn-Lord. 'I got more sense out of Consatiné! What exactly are you trying to tell me? That you don't know any more about the emperor's condition than I do?'

'I wouldn't say that,' said the first doctor.

'Not in so many words,' said the second.

'More a question of weighing things up...'

'...balancing the evidence...'

'...forming a hypothesis...'

'...checking the metabolism...'

'...the pulse...'

'...the arteries...'

'...the melancholic humours...'

'...the phrenological significances...'

As the doctors' discussion degenerated into increasingly obscure jargon, the Gros wondered about this 'Lara' the emperor had spoken of so forcefully. At least the name had a concrete ring to it; finding 'Lara' was something a man could try; anything was better than listening to the doctors' waffle.

'Send for the Vaine of Talen!' he instructed, cutting through the physicians' discourse.

The Vaine of Talen arrived almost at once, a handsome active young man whose courage had already been proven on the battlefield. 'Your Grosarch,' said the Vaine, taking off his velvet hat and bowing his dark curls at the Gros of Peltyn.

'Have you ever heard of anyone called Lara?' he asked.

'No, sir. Should I have?'

'I can't think why you should,' agreed the Gros of Peltyn. 'But that name is going to become second nature to you from now on. I want you to scour Khalindaine to find her.'

'What does she look like?'

'I don't know.'

'Where does she live?'

'I don't know that either. But the name has a Northreach ring to it, and the emperor was originally from Northreach. I suggest you travel to Mornet at once, with a company of troops. We'll choose them for their brains rather than their bravery; you're hunting for a woman, not a wild bear. Our emperor has become rather voluble today, and demands this woman as his wife; for want of anything better at this stage, we ought to at least look for her. It might help him.'

'Certainly sir. Is there nothing else to go on?'

'Only speculation. If he wants to marry her she's presumably of marrying age, though that doesn't necessarily follow. In his present condition she could be the nurse he had when he was two. Still, we'll worry about that when we find her. Start at the Ranbrunsvag, the home of the Ra-Lord and his wife in Mornet. The Lady Ra might be helpful, though I doubt her husband will be.'

'Is this mission to be secret, sir?'

'The reason for it is. Otherwise, no. You may ask as many people as many questions as you like.'

'Thank you, your Grosarch.'

'I tell you, Talen, I envy you. I'd rather be going to Northreach than hanging around here all the time. I'd rather be going anywhere. But a duty is a duty, I suppose: you've got yours and I've got mine, and the best thing we can do is our best. Set off as soon as possible, and get back soon too.'

'Yes sir,' said the Vaine of Talen smartly as he turned to leave.

That night the snow turned to rain. The rivers rose, the drifts
subsided into obstinate heaps, and grass began to show through
the whiteness;. Consatiné's reign was indeed becoming green.

Streetpoet and Od left the troupe that morning. Streetpoet
felt an inexplicable sense of urgency about finding Lara
now, though he had not seen her for five years, and barely
thought of her for four. He needed to speak to someone who
shared the truth.

They trudged through the receding snow. Streetpoet sang
as they walked, a marching song he composed in time to
their footsteps.

> I'm with a bod
> Whose name is Od…
> You think that's odd?
> Well so's his god.
> I want a lass
> Who knew Ormaas
> To prove Od wrong
> Tum-deedle-bong.

Od did not rise to this teasing, however; he did not speak to
his companion at all. Streetpoet tried again.

> I saved Od's skin
> And stayed with him
> Through thick and thin
> But he's so dim
> He doesn't talk
> While we walk.
> That's rather rude.
> Tum-doodle-dood.

'Come on,' added the minstrel. 'What's up with you? You
haven't said a word, civil or uncivil, all morning.'

Still Od remained silent. Streetpoet tried his excruciating
song again.

> Od is bald.
> I've heard him called
> Many names.

And yet he claims
It's just 'receded',
'Hair's not needed',
'My hair's just thin',
Tum-doodle-BALLS!

'Just shut up,' said Od, who had indeed claimed the things Streetpoet had listed.

'Ah! What was that I heard? It can't have been Od because he doesn't speak. Or perhaps he does? I'll try talking to him again.'

'I said shut up!'

'That's better,' said Streetpoet. 'You look a lot less like an egg with your mouth open. You ought to speak more often: keep your mouth closed too long and someone will hard-boil your head.'

'Haven't you got a conscience?' Od demanded.

'I suppose I have. What a strange question for a bright day.'

'It doesn't show,' said Od.

'What are you talking about?'

But Od had relapsed into silence.

'Look,' said Streetpoet. 'I'm in a good mood. The sun is shining, the snow is melting, there's a sparkle to the day. And you just walk beside me with a face like an undertaker's mother-in-law. What's got into you?'

'Amila is a lovely girl.'

'Agreed. So what? You haven't fallen for her, have you? Is that why you're moping?'

'Of course not,' said Od firmly. 'I'm far too old for that sort of thing.'

'Do you mean you can get too old for it?' asked Streetpoet incredulously. 'I'd better make sure I get my quota before my time is up.'

'It looks to me as if you're already knocking up quite a score.'

'What are you talking about?'

'About you and Amila!' said Od. 'I heard the two of you last night! I know what was going on!'

'You're jealous,' said Streetpoet.

He was wrong. 'I was thinking about that poor girl. One minute you're making love to her; the next minute you've gone without a backward glance. Is that fair? Is that honourable?'

'She came into my bed,' protested Streetpoet. 'What was I meant to do? Throw her out? Would that have been fair and honourable?'

'She's in love with you. You saved her life, and then you took advantage of her.'

'I'm always doing things like that,' said Streetpoet.

'That,' said Od, 'is hardly an excuse.'

They walked on in silence for a while. At last Streetpoet spoke. 'I'm sorry,' he said. 'I hadn't realised you'd be upset.'

'There's no point apologising to me. I'm not the one you ruined.'

'I hardly "ruined" her!'

'I suppose it's just a question of values,' said Od. 'But personally I think you've behaved like a swine. Still, at least you know what was bothering me now. We've a long journey in front of us. Let's not talk about it any more.'

'You still want to come with me?' asked Streetpoet contritely.

Od had no doubts. 'Her's wasn't the only life you saved, remember.'

Chapter 3

The Namacythron

Two days later the companions reached Ilynés, the western sea-board's second port and the one-time capital of Khalindaine's most prosperous kingdom. They walked together through crowded streets. Though the city had grown since the days of its predominance, its status had shrunk: now commerce, rather than politics, counted for most there, and the old palace had become the wine exchange, complete with an ugly new porch of vast size beneath which the merchants haggled, and the ancient military fort now housed the fish market, where the sharp salty smells and the circling flies were confined by high thick walls and patrolled – almost quarantined – by tall half-ruined towers.

Streetpoet watched his companion's antics with some amusement. 'Why are you walking with your hand up against your face?' he asked.

'Shhhh. I don't want anyone to see me. I'm well known here: I'm a member of the Ilynés Chapter of the Brotherhood, remember.'

'All right, but for Menketh's sake stop looking so furtive. You might as well be carrying a banner saying "Look at me, I'm suspicious".'

'Really?' asked Od, his hand falling to his side.

'Really. I wouldn't worry about it if I were you. I'm sure the Brotherhood won't miss you.'

'Thanks,' muttered Od.

'You know what I mean. There's been a lot going on in Khalindaine since you were last here: they probably assume you were killed in the riots in Marq.'

'Torn limb from limb,' agreed Od mournfully.

'Cheer up,' said Streetpoet. 'You'll feel better when you've some food inside you.'

'I certainly will,' said Od with more enthusiasm. 'How much money have we got?'

'Two rubecks.'

'Two rubecks!' Od's face relapsed into misery. 'We couldn't buy a stale loaf for that.'

'Who said anything about buying? I'm going to sing for my supper.'

'Singing's banned,' reminded Od.

'So's drinking. So let's find a tavern and do both.'

It did not take them long. They left the main thoroughfares and went down the narrow, confused streets of the old town. The Brotherhood's prohibitions had caused the taverns to close their doors; they had not caused the taverns to lock them. There was always the risk of a Brotherhood raid, of course, but the ban on drinks had pushed up the prices and the love of profit outweighed the fear of prosecution. Besides, what else was there for the innkeepers to do but keep serving: the alternative was starvation.

'This looks a likely place,' said Streetpoet. The inn sign had been taken down from above the door but its frame was still there, distinguishing the place's function. Streetpoet walked in, and Od followed.

In the gloom within Od saw a middle-aged woman, rather scrawny for a landlady, who was standing behind her bar and exchanging cheerful insults with a rat catcher. Four or five loungers stood by a table discussing a game of cards, and a drunk sat in a far corner.

Streetpoet went up to the bar. For a second he pretended not to notice the landlady and then, when she asked him what he wanted, he let his eyes fall full on her. It was a long, admiring stare. 'Why, hello,' he said, in apparent confusion. Od, who found all this vaguely embarrassing, remained near the door.

'Hello,' agreed the landlady, returning Streetpoet's admiration. The rat catcher, who knew when to cut his losses, left them and joined the loungers. 'What do you want?' asked the landlady.

Streetpoet gave her a conspiratorial, almost reproving smile. 'You know what I want,' the smile seemed to say, though his voice said something quite different. 'A tankard of ale, if you please.'

She turned to pour his drink from her long handled jug; Streetpoet climbed onto the bar itself and sat there quite relaxed. 'A song for a lovely lady,' he announced.

When love is love and life is life,
A man needs nothing more
Than cheery dreams, an absent wife,
A lady to adore.
In Ilynés, that lovely city
A woman I have seen,
She keeps an inn, she's very pretty,
She is the perfect queen.
What more could any man require
Than a lady sweet.
What more could any man desire
Save something good to eat.

The landlady laughed appreciatively. 'You're hungry,' she deduced. 'Been travelling long?'

'The turn of twenty years,' said Streetpoet. 'All my life I've been on the road, singing for my supper.'

'What about your bald mate? What's he do?'

'Aha!' said the minstrel. 'Allow me to introduce Od, my walking talking conscience. You see,' he continued, giving the landlady a knowing stare, 'although in many ways a well put-together sort of chap, nature in her infinite diversity forgot to endow me with a conscience. To remedy this omission I have been supplied instead with Od.'

'And he's hungry too, I suppose,' said the landlady.

'Ravenous,' agreed Streetpoet before Od could speak.

'All right. Boiled beef do you?'

'Washed down with a tankard of ale?' asked Streetpoet.

'You're pushing your luck,' she decided, but relented when he smiled. 'All right, a tankard of ale as well.'

'Not for me,' said Od firmly.

'All the more for me,' said Streetpoet.

Luncheon was served. 'You'll stay this evening?' asked the landlady with a leer.

'For myself nothing could please me more. However, my conscience' – he indicated Od – 'would never allow such an abuse of your hospitality.'

She weighed this up, smiled wryly to herself, and shrugged. 'A convenient thing, this conscience of yours.'

Streetpoet smiled back. 'Something I have to bear. And now, with copious thanks for your kindness, we must away!'

'Up yours,' said the landlady succinctly. 'I've been done, good and proper.'

Streetpoet and Od opened the door and stepped out into the street. 'Your very good health!' called the minstrel.

The landlady laughed, picked a tankard of ale from the nearest table, and launched its contents at the closing door. Foaming amber splashed across the wood and was soaked up by the rush-matted floor.

Talen-vaine-Talen led a troop of two hundred horsemen from the gates of Verdre and north along the Namamorn towards Morn and Rhalman. As his superior had suggested, these troops, though hand-picked, were not the most effective fighting force to have ever left Cythroné; they were, however, an intelligent bunch. Because of this method of selection they wore the uniforms of several regiments. Some seventy came from the Vaine of Talen's own company, and an equal number from the Verdre guard. The rest were drawn from a miscellany of companies: the scarlet plumes of the Hrondian militia mixed with the yellow crests of Gyfroth; their blue cloaks of the Vaine of Heront's company swirled between the greens of the Taraqota regiment; cuirassiers from Myr rode alongside lancers from Jaskar. At the head of the column the Vaine rode, helmetless, enjoying the crisp winter air and the speed of his stallion; behind him was his standard bearer, carrying the pale blue flag embroidered with a golden lion that was the mark of Talen. They crossed the Freyth Bridge, looked their last on the towers and spires of Cythroné, and galloped colourfully across a plain of retreating snows.

The marshes north of Ilynés are strange and inhospitable. Drainage ditches, often overgrown and hidden like mantraps, cross flat banks of gathered silt. The occasional houses are raised on wooden stilts, ugly overseers of the reeds. The winding paths are often ill defined, and only the Namacythron, pushing through the bleakness, makes an indelible impression on the landscape. Even this can be deceptive: the continuing process of erosion and deposition changes the route from year to year, and the inexperienced traveller can easily miss his way, which was exactly what Streetpoet and Od had achieved.

'I told you we shouldn't have turned right there,' said Od.

'It wasn't turning right there that did for us. It was your insistence we should carry on past those trees.'

'It was like that the last time I came this way,' said Od.

'Maybe. It wasn't the last time *I* came this way,' replied the minstrel. 'I thought you used to be a pilot on the river. We can't even find the Menketh-cursed thing!'

The mid-afternoon dusk of a winter's day was making a grey world greyer, and though in the distance they could still see Ilynés smudging the horizon, they found themselves increasingly uncertain of their direction.

'Now where?' asked Od.

As it grew darker it grew colder, and the cold fetched a spectral mist out of the dykes. Twice they waded ankle deep in water they had not seen.

'This is no good,' said Streetpoet. 'I don't know where we are or how we can find out. And I don't like all this water. To be truthful, I don't like *any* water.'

Od walked ahead a few strides. 'I think this directionnnnn...' There was a loud splash. Streetpoet hurried to where the bald man had been.

'Od!' he called.

For a reply there was nothing but a string of gurgled oaths.

'Are you all right? Can you swim?'

'Of course I can swim! I used to be a riverman, remember! But this water is freezing.'

Od's shiny head appeared at Streetpoet's feet; the minstrel gave his friend a hand and heaved him from the water. Od stood shivering. 'You need a fire,' Streetpoet said. 'We'd best search out some wood.'

They walked round the edge of the water slowly, looking for wood for a fire, and found nothing. Their journey seemed to take them in a full circle, an impression confirmed when Od spotted the marks he had left climbing from the water.

'That's peculiar,' said Streetpoet. 'How come we're on an island?'

'O Menketh!' replied Od. 'I know what must be happening. The snows are melting; the river's rising.'

'How high will it get?'

'I don't know. Ormaas alive, I'm cold.'

'Here,' said Streetpoet, taking off a layer of jerkins. 'Wrap this round you.'

'Thanks'.

They squatted by the water's edge and watched the level suspiciously. The darkness intensified; the water turned from grey to black. As it became darker it seemed also to become more noisy. 'I wish we'd found some firewood,' said Streetpoet.

Od made no reply. Despite the cold that penetrated his bones, he was fast asleep.

Streetpoet too began to nod off. His head felt heavy, heavier, insupportable. Then his body jerked and he was awake. Slowly the same process was repeated, with the same jerk as its conclusion. He rubbed his eyes, yawned, and lay down at his companion's side, sharing his meagre warmth.

It was Od who woke first, with a powerful urge to relieve himself. But this urge didn't seem to be coming from the usual place; it was his hand that seemed to feel the pressure most. Without reaching full consciousness, Od put that hand to his face. It was sopping wet.

'Streetpoet!'

The minstrel rubbed his own eyes. 'What's the matter?'

'Look at the water!'

'Where?' asked Streetpoet sleepily.

'Everywhere!'

This was no exaggeration. As far as the eye could see may not have been very far; it was far enough. East and west, north and south, the world was water entirely. Only their tiny island, a few strides across, seemed to be above the black surface, and the companions, precarious on the edge of this haven, shivered with something that was not only the cold.

'What do we do?' they asked, but neither had a reply.

It was Od who had the first intelligent suggestion to make. 'Look,' he said. 'This water can't be all that deep. I mean, in the light I didn't even notice that this bit was higher than all the rest. We could probably wade all the way to Ilynés if we knew which way to go.'

'You're right! It's probably only knee deep at the most. Which way do you reckon we should go? Or would it be better to stay here?'

'I think we ought to move. The level is probably still rising.' Od pointed, choosing a direction at random as far as Streetpoet could see. 'That way.'

'What makes you say that?'

'The old riverman's sense of direction, though I'd be happier if I could see the stars.'

'I'd be happier if I could see a hog roasted whole on a spit. Still, can't have everything, I suppose.'

They set off in the direction Od had indicated. Od's supposition had been correct: the water was no deeper than their calves, and they waded through it with increasing confidence.

'You're sure we're headed in the right direction?' asked Streetpoet.

'No.'

That was the end of the conversation.

The cold water deadened sensation in their feet. Their boots became an encumbrance and they stopped, removed them, and strung them round their necks. The night became a long journey of pushing, slushing strides, until suddenly they hit a deeper channel and found themselves swimming and sinking.

For a second neither of them knew what had happened. Immersion had been instant and absolute: they were not wading but drowning now, and then spluttering up to the surface, both pairs of boots lost, and calling out the other's name.

Od was a good swimmer, Streetpoet a poor but determined one. They struck off in the direction they thought they had been heading, and almost at once Od's feet touched firm land. 'This way!' he called, but when he stepped forward for Streetpoet to join him on the landfall he found he had stepped straight off.

Streetpoet tried a step in another direction, and he too found nothing but deep water, and flailed his arms in his panic. Their landfall had obviously been illusory, perhaps a rock jutting above the rest, or the stump of a tree. Again they were forced to swim.

The water was cold, the companions colder. Exhaustion was rapidly draining through them, washing the strength from their limbs. To begin with they encouraged one another, asked questions, made hopeful remarks; soon they swam in silence, and the water stretched on forever.

Had it not been for the debris they would certainly have drowned, for a slight but significant current was pushing them through the marshlands and into the Hasfaine itself. But the flood had released many stranded things from the river's margin, and one of these, an abandoned stilt-house with rotted legs that had failed to withstand the strain, drifted by to the swimmers' right.

'Od!' cried Streetpoet. 'Look!'

They turned towards the floating house, still upright on the waters. It reminded Streetpoet of a boat; at first he had thought it was a boat, until it came close enough to make it out.

Od reached the drifting house first. There was a door, but the waters reached half way up this, so instead he climbed in through the window. Wearily, Streetpoet followed.

The interior was darker than the night. To begin with neither could see a thing, though they bumped into many items that floated in the waist-high water. One of the things Streetpoet found in this way seemed to be anchored in the middle of the room. He explored it with his hands and found a ladder.

'Let's climb out of this water,' said the minstrel, relieved at the opportunity.

Od traced his voice through the dark. 'All right. Wait for me.'

Streetpoet climbed up first, into a density of black. Od followed closely, not wishing to lose his companion. At the top, Streetpoet tentatively stretched out a toe and felt for flooring, and as he did so the entire house turned turtle.

Spluttering once again, immersed once again, and now trapped in the inverted upper storey of a floating or sinking house, Streetpoet found he had lost the will to fight. Had Od, who had been in the trap between floors when the house capsized, not grabbed his companion's wrist as they went, Streetpoet could not have survived. As it was they surfaced together, Streetpoet bruised by painful contact with the trap, the ladder, and a dozen floating chairs, and surfaced in a pocket of air that was barely the size of their heads.

'What next?' asked Streetpoet.

'We'll have to get out onto the roof...sorry, the floor.'

Od dived into the water and disappeared; Streetpoet did not have the strength to follow but waited, treading water, for his friend.

It was a long wait. The first thing Streetpoet was aware of was a scrabbling sound near his head and then footsteps above him. 'Od!' he called through the floor.

'Hello!'

'What's happening out there?'

'Not a lot so far as I can see.'

'Oh.'

'Mind, I think it's getting lighter.'

'Fine.'

'Though I might be wrong.'

'Sure.'

Streetpoet's exhaustion, which had subsided briefly at the sight of the floating house, was returning. His legs were numb. Treading water was becoming too much for him. Twice he sank; going down the third time he knew would lead to death.

'Streetpoet!' Od called.

'Here,' said the other weakly.

'It's getting lighter.'

'Good.'

'I can see land.'

'Where?'

'Everywhere. All around, though a fair way off.'

'How far?'

'A few thousand strides. At most.' Od sat cross-legged on the upturned floor of the house, between broken sticks that had once been stilts. Streetpoet did not reply. 'Streetpoet!' Od insisted.

'What?' Though tired, Streetpoet forced himself to answer.

'Are you all right?'

'No,' Streetpoet replied. 'My muscles are jelly, my bones turned to ice, and now you tell me I'm a thousand unswimmable strides from shore. Do you expect me to be all right?'

'Don't worry,' said Od, scanning the horizon. 'We're floating nearer all the time. Just hang on.'

Just hang on! thought Streetpoet. I would, if there was something to hang on to. But Od's encouragement gave brief new strength, and though as exhausted as ever, he no longer felt resigned.

The shore grew. Od, who had sailed the river often, scanned the skyline for landmarks. He was no longer worried. Not only was he back in a world he knew well, but a few brief days spent with Streetpoet, brief days which admittedly seemed a lifetime, had taught him to be phlegmatic if nothing else. Fate, he had decided, is what happens to a man, and Od did not feel fate wanted him to drown. Since his meeting with Streetpoet he had turned from a respected and respectable officer of the Brotherhood of the Faithful to a vagrant, a fugitive, and now apparently a stowaway on a stolen house! That's life, he mused, then the house struck the river-bed and Od fell off.

He swam beneath the water around the house, feeling for the door. It was already open. For a moment he thought Streetpoet had found it and escaped, then realised that the latch had been released when the house had capsized. He swam in and upwards; he banged his head without surfacing and set about trying to find the minstrel.

He found him, grasped him, and got kneed in the chest for his pains. 'Oi!' he complained, surfacing.

'Oh, it's you,' said Streetpoet.

'Who did you think it was?' asked Od. 'The Gros of Yrksa?'

'What's up?'

'Nothing. We're aground.'

'On shore!' asked Streetpoet, swallowing water in his excitement.

'Almost,' said Od, which was almost true.

'Thank Menketh for that,' said Streetpoet.

Od led Streetpoet out through the door and they came to the surface together. The shore was further away than Streetpoet had hoped but nearer than he had feared. 'Where are we?' he asked.

'Not sure,' gasped Od, swimming away. 'River's flowing that away; must be the north bank.'

'Well,' said Streetpoet, swallowing more water. 'That's where we want to be.' He gargled and followed Od. 'I know one thing, old chum. Next time you want to prohibit drinking, start with river water will you.'

Consatiné played with the cat. The doctors observed him gravely. 'Aha!' cried the emperor, waving a hand above the animal's claws. 'So! you would scratch me with your swords, your spears.'

'No grasp of reality,' the doctors decided. 'No knowledge of what's what.' Consatiné overheard this, which was not hard: the doctors followed him wherever he went yet treated him as if he were not there. 'Silly men,' he told the cat. 'Can't tell a metaphor from a bucket.'

The doctors nodded wisely and noted down this confirmation of their diagnosis.

Exhausted entirely by now, Streetpoet and Od pulled themselves onto the river-bank. The sun was out, and though it was not warm at least the bitterness of the previous days had gone. They did not notice the sun. They did not notice the grass on which they sprawled. They did not even notice the inquisitive cows that ambled up to them, nuzzled them, and went on their chewing way. They slept.

It was midday when Od awoke, and it was hunger that woke him. They had not eaten for a turn of the sun, and his belly demanded food. He woke Streetpoet; the latter, more used to the vagrant's way by far, woke at once and was ready to move.

'Where did you say we are?' he asked Od.

'I didn't. There are one or two spots like this along the river, though that looks like the Tower of Trahorn. I'd recognise it from a boat, but we're too low down here.'

'Oh well. We'll soon find out.'

They walked through the pasture, disturbing the cows. A strip of snow still clung to the hedgerows' shade but otherwise there was little trace of winter. It was a balmy day. Ahead of them, on a mound above the river's flood plain, was a tower of wood, a watch-tower from times gone by, and for want of another destination the companions, by mutual and silent agreement, headed for it.

A line of trees ahead of them disguised a tall and stately wall, so that they did not realise until they were committed that the way ahead was blocked. 'That's a blow', said Od. 'I wonder where we are now.'

'Well, I'm bothered if I'm going to walk round it,' said Streetpoet. 'Give me a leg up.' Od hesitated. He was not a natural law-breaker. 'Ah, who gives a Kapatan's curse,' he decided. 'Up you go.'

Streetpoet reached the top, reached down, and hauled Od up. The two of them perched awhile at the top of the wall and then jumped. The grass absorbed their fall.

They looked round again, expecting discovery, and then ran through the cover of the trees. Some five hundred strides away they could see the elegant facade of a modern country house, obviously the property of some local dignatory: white marble, tall spires, steeply pitched roofs, broad windows. They ran swiftly past it; Od puffed but kept up with his friend. Behind it the ancient watch-tower glowered from its rise, irrelevant to the companions now.

From a window of the mansion house the elderly Vaine of Trahorn looked out. It was a fine day for looking out: the grass was green after the snowfall, the bare trees opened out his view; beyond his walls the river was a band of gold stretching from horizon to horizon. He was a little surprised to see two figures running across this scene, however, and sent for his manservant, Hyvek.

Hyvek arrived immediately and confirmed what his master had seen.

'Send someone to fetch them back,' said the Vaine. 'I want to know who they are and why they're in my garden.'

It seemed a reasonable, moderate request, and Hyvek at once put it into action. A rider was sent to the gate, which was closed, and the woods were combed straightaway.

Before long two bedraggled, damp, and pathetic figures were escorted to the Vaine of Trahorn's presence. 'Who are you?' asked the Vaine.

'He's Od,' said Streetpoet.

'I'm Od,' agreed Od.

'I didn't ask what he is, I asked who.'

They sorted the confusion out. 'I'm Streetpoet,' added Streetpoet.

'And what,' asked the nobleman portentously, coming to the point of his questions, 'were you doing in my garden?'

'We're looking for a woman,' began Od.

The Vaine interrupted. 'In my garden!'

'No, no,' said Od.

'I'll explain,' said Streetpoet suavely. 'In a sense Od's words are correct although, being somewhat soft in the head, he has not grasped the whole story. We are indeed looking for a woman, in Northreach...'

'You're lost?' asked the Vaine. 'Northreach is the other side of Khalindaine.'

'We are on our way to Northreach. We were following the Namacythron when the river rose and swept us away. We came to shore outside your palace and, exhausted and without boots, decided to risk a short cut through your beautiful grounds.'

'I knew we shouldn't have,' muttered Od, but Streetpoet cut him off.

'We had heard, of course, of your charity, and knew we had nothing to fear from so noble and generous a man if we did no harm. And I assure you we neither meant nor did harm.'

'You'd heard of me then,' said the Vaine of Trahorn.

'Indeed sir,' said Streetpoet, who had not the faintest idea who he was addressing but could spot a soft touch from five thousand strides. 'Your magnanimity is quite famous.'

The old man was obviously delighted, and chuckled to himself. 'Well, well.' He rang a bell and Hyvek returned. 'Fetch some food for these gentlemen.'

'Certainly sir.'

Hyvek went away. 'I see your reputation barely does you justice, sir,' said Streetpoet.

'Why, thank you,' returned the Vaine. 'One does one's bit, one does one's bit. But tell me, under what circumstances does a man like yourself and your manservant travel all the way to Northreach to look for a woman. I've never been the marrying kind myself, but it seems to me there's no shortage round here.'

'A matter of honour,' said Streetpoet while Hyvek returned with a tray of food. 'And I hope you will hold it no disrespect if I fail to divulge my mission in all its detail. Sadly, sir, I am sworn to secrecy, and whilst I have no doubt that you, of all people, would never pass on any secret entrusted to you I also know that you, of all people, would be the last to ask me to betray my word. The word of a gentleman must always be his bond.'

'Of course,' agreed the old man sincerely, though he was intrigued by his young guest. 'Do tell me though why you are dressed like beggars. You are obviously a man of some background.'

'We are travelling incognito.'

'Ah. I thought maybe you'd been robbed.'

Streetpoet cursed inwardly: being robbed would attract more sympathy. 'No, sir, though we lost our boots and my purse in the flood.'

The Vaine of Trahorn rang his bell again. 'See if you can find this gentleman and his servant some boots.'

'Old ones,' specified Streetpoet. 'We wouldn't want anyone to penetrate our disguise.'

It was mid-afternoon by the time Streetpoet and Od were on their way again. Well fed, well shod, and with a purse of money presented to them by the Vaine, Streetpoet was fully content; despite sharing the same comfort in his belly and his toes, Od looked rather less pleased.

'Now what's the matter?' asked Streetpoet, as they left the Vaine's pleasant gardens and walked along the road from his estate to the nearest town. 'You're not going to get pious on me again? That charming man enjoyed our company; he could easily spare what he gave us; our mission may well be very important.'

'It isn't that.'

'What is it then?'

'It's that Hedchblasted "Manservant" business. That's what really got to me.'

Many miles further north, on the road between Morn and Rhalman, a different nobleman was also being misled. Talen-vaine-Talen was a handsome and able young man; even his best friends, however, would not deny his impetuosity. At the moment that trait in his nature was being engaged by a tale he heard at the wayside. A pretty young girl of some fourteen summers lay weeping in the gutter; a young man of perhaps two summers more stood over her, bleeding from a cut in his forehead, and explaining how, in the woods south of the road, were the robbers that had caused their anguish.

'Our mother was taken from us,' said the boy, and the girl confirmed this with a wail.

'Robbers?' Talen-vaine-Talen listened with great sympathy as the boy and girl between them pieced together their tale: how they had been travelling to Mourn for the fair; how their mother had sent them on ahead; how robbers had burst from the south and dragged their mother and their possessions, cattle for the market and gold for the auctions, into the trees; how they had heard their mother scream.

There was not a word of truth in all this, except that there were robbers in the wood. The robber leader had seen the Vaine of Talen's troops approaching and assumed, egotistically, that it was he they were after. He had thus arranged this diversion: his son and daughter were to decoy the cavalrymen south while he and his brigands hid in the woods to the north.

The robber chief's children were entirely convincing. They led the gallant Vaine and his men deep into the wood where the track was narrow and confined. The cavalrymen had to dismount. Suddenly the children were gone, of course, and the troops were lost.

'Excuse me saying so,' said one of the cavalrymen. 'But I think we've been had.'

The soldier's hypothesis matched the facts. 'You seem a bright man,' said Talen-vaine-Talen. 'What's your name?'

'Ossius, sir. From the Verdre guard.' Ossius looked sadly at the Vaine. 'But you overestimate me. If I was bright I'd have caught on sooner and would not be in this pickle.'

'We can get out easily enough by retracing our steps. What annoys me is the waste of time.'

'Well, there's nothing much we can do about that.'

'The philosopher Herx,' said a soldier in the crimson cloak of the Talen's own company, 'suggests that the concept "time" has no validity except in the context of human awareness'.

'Araton,' added a cavalryman in a green cloak, possibly one of the Taraqota regiment, 'tends to agree with that notion, I believe, regarding the moment "Now" as a convenient fiction between the certainty of "Past" and the unknown but sure to occur "Future".'

'I've often seen it that way myself,' chipped in Ossius. 'Though that being the case all our perceptions are based on a fallacy, because surely it is only by reference to the notional "Now" that we can understand the diversity of the world.'

'Can we get on our way?' asked the Vaine of Talen.

'If that *is* the case,' said a trooper from the Vaine of Heront's company, 'it is presumably another proof of Gythé's famous dictum "I think therefore I think I am", proving also...'

'Back to the road men!' ordered the Vaine.

'...that though I think I am, I am not necessarily what I think.'

'I think therefore I think I am what I think,' suggested the man from the Taraqota regiment.

'We've more important things to worry about,' shouted the Vaine, 'than whether we are what we think!'

'That's true,' the soldiers agreed.

'For instance,' said a new voice, 'does Araton's notion deny free will, or is the fact that *a priori* there will be a future not determine exactly what that future shall be?'

The Vaine of Talen, leading his men slowly back to the road, was beginning to regret the Peltyn-Lord's decision to give him only intelligent soldiers.

Streetpoet and Od rejoined the Namcythron at Orlong, eight thousand strides north of the river Hasfaine. The flood waters had delayed many travellers: the friends joined a large group who had crossed on the first ferry of the day and who, like them, were making for Cythroné.

For the first time they learnt of the curious events at the palace, the death of Kamrot, the incapacity of the emperor, and the subsequent violence. They also learnt that the differences of opinion continued.

'Emperor indeed! Bain't be nothing but an imposter!'

'Ooh aye? And I suppose you think Brotherhood be right? Them as stopped us having a drink when us felt like it!'

'Least they know who right emperor be.'

'If they get it wrong 'bout drink they could be got it wrong about that and all.'

'Maybe it's like new decree says. Maybe it be a mistake. Maybe it should've read "no public drunkenness" after all.'

'No public drunkenness!' exclaimed Od to Streetpoet. 'I risked my life to send out that decree, and now the council's changed it.'

'Nothing is worth risking your life for,' said Streetpoet, who had frequently risked his life for nothing. 'But it sounds like there's all the turmoil I feared and more. Your aching bones were right.'

The road to Cythroné was always busy, but it seemed to Streetpoet, who had several times passed this way before, that there was a new urgency to the travellers: something more than the usual pressures of commerce seemed to drive these people on.

The Namacythron then was as much as it is today. Few parts were paved. In many places the outline is barely visible, and the route, especially in dry weather, can only be worked out by following the constant traffic; in wet weather the pot holes fill with water, horses are up to their hocks in the mud, and peasant women on their way to the country fairs forget their modesty and hoist their skirts to their knees. This was such a day. The snow survived in mucky ruts, its coarse crystals stained with dung and dirt. Muleteers cursed and their phlegmatic mules ignored them. The rough clothes of the peasants, already the colours of mud, took on the consistency of mud too as the carriages passed.

The bulk of the day's traffic seemed to be travelling north. Streetpoet and Od, hurrying, passed through various groups, and each group seemed to have a different verdict on the recent affairs of state. At one stage they were with a group of journeymen. The money for the market hall they had been constructing in Ilynés had run out, and they were moving to Cythroné in the hope of similar work in the capital. Unusually, this group seemed to have royalist sympathies: most artisans tended to support the Brotherhood.

'Never thought much of the Brotherhood any road,' announced a mason, his heavy callipers swinging from his pack.

'Nay,' replied another. 'No fun, that lot.'

'Miserable swine,' concurred a carpenter. The last led a mule loaded with tools of his trade: hand planes, saws, chisels and hammers hung from neat pouches tied to the animal's back.

'I would have thought you'd support the Brotherhood,' mentioned Od. 'I mean, they usually recruit from people like you, don't they?' Od knew full well that they did; he had been a tradesman himself until the call of the Faithful had taken him away from that.

'Us?' The second mason was incredulous. 'Support them? Fat chance!' said the carpenter. 'Till they came along we were building basilicas. Good detailed work it was. Plenty of satisfaction, regular earnings, good rate of pay. And people used to appreciate what we was doing. Now we're lucky if we can get a job building anything. Look at last job we were on: a market hall! We're skilled craftsmen, not bloody labourers. But all they wanted us for in Ilynés was a bit of fancy work in the ceilings. There's no challenge to that, no pleasure. It's like asking Vlatri tan Bul' – Khalinadaine's leading artist throughout the period – 'to paint a barn door.'

'So where're you heading?' asked Od.

'Cythroné. And if we can't find work I reckon we'll find something to do with our hands, right lads?'

There was general agreement.

The journeying journeymen stopped for a meal at a wayside inn; Streetpoet and Od continued. 'A lot of people seem to be on the road today,' said the minstrel, 'and a lot of them are spoiling for a fight.'

They passed a short caravan laden with fruit: eight two-wheeled waggons, each pulled by a pair of heavy horses. The carters had been drinking, probably at the inn now filled with journeymen, and sang a republican ballad.

> In days long gone when there was none
> To take the tax and leave the debt,
>   We used to be both true and free,
>   We shared the fruit of every tree
> But we'll all be equal yet
>
> Those days are gone but from now on
> We've had enough of toil and sweat:
>   Streets will flood with noble blood!
>   All blood's equal equal mixed with mud!
> We'll all be equal yet.

'Your friend Consatiné doesn't seem to be popular everywhere,' observed Od.

'Frankly,' said Streetpoet, 'I don't think he's popular anywhere, really. He hasn't worked hard enough to be a good emperor. But he's still the rightful ruler, despite everything.'

'Do you think it'll come to a fight?'

'If enough people want a fight,' said Streetpoet, 'there is a fight.'

They continued on their way. They passed herdsmen leading their cattle to the slaughterhouses, and solitary merchants riding filth-dappled ponies. Sometimes a dashing horseman passed them on an errand, and sometimes a carriage containing a bourgeois family. They saw live animals transported in stinking wicker cages, and fat barrels bound with ropes strapped to the backs of bored mules. The colours around them were muted by the low winter sun and splashed by the omnipresent mud. Beyond the road the fields, dotted with sprawling windmills and lumpy hamlets, showed green and brown to their snow-white edges. Fat fractious crows croaked beneath the pale blue sky. The frequent trees were stark shadows, a blue-green that edged to grey where the light failed; a purer green that hinted yellow in direct sunlight. Evergreens' dark green mourned the winter weather. Branches scratched the clouds. The distance hazed to grey hills and the hills hazed into the sky.

For a while they were on their own between two bends. They talked of the situation. 'Do you think it will come to war?' Od asked.

'I hope not. There's a difference between fighting and warfare. And I don't see how the Brotherhood could raise an army.'

'I don't know. There were a lot of soldiers sympathetic to the Brotherhood. They used to come to our meetings.'

'Perhaps things aren't as bad as they seem. After all, we haven't seen any actual fighting yet.'

But then they rounded a corner, and Streetpoet's words were instantly belied.

Ahead of them was a small but determined battle. Some sixty or so travellers seemed to be involved: two were members of the Brotherhood and, as had happened earlier, in Fragma Square, the Brothers' distinctive dark clothes proved a focus for the fighting. The fight spread across the road, blocking it and smearing the edges of the tracks, so that the road dissolved into a width of churned earth for a few score strides before returning to its usual muddy but linear form.

Streetpoet and Od looked on aghast. There was no doubting the seriousness of the combatants: two lifeless bodies by the wayside proved as much. But far more worrying were the screams and cries: 'Kill the Consatiné-lovers'; 'Brotherhood for ever'; 'Death to the Faithful'; 'Up the Revolution'.

There did not seem to be much point trying to get along the road. Already other travellers were appearing from round the bend, and one or two had rushed immediately into the fray. 'Remember the Diehards!' cried an intoxicated carter, before being felled by a royalist fist. Od and Streetpoet, their faces dark, watched with mounting horror.

The Vaine of Talen endured a discussion about the duality of existence, with particular reference to the internal world described by Thero tan Thet, in which the philosopher proves the impossibility of a construct of reality that ignores the subjective point of view, and the views of Yruthon the Juprethe about the inability of the individual to perceive anything beyond his own perceptions. He was bored by an analysis of the mathematical problems involved in squaring the circle, despite a learned discourse from one of the Cythron cuirassiers, and survived, just, an interminable argument about the perfectibility of man. But when it came to a discussion of the issues involved in the categoric imperative he was forced to admit defeat. As the argument continued around him he rode steadily, quietly, and entirely listlessly at the head of his troops.

As Streetpoet and Od continued on their way, skirting the frequent skirmishes, listening to the various arguments, they were forced to acknowledge just how deep the division was between the two sides. There were many factors involved in the division between the Royalists and the Opposition. One was religion: the Brotherhood of the Faithful, for many, represented a truer, purer and more fundamental faith than did the antiquated, discredited pro-royalist religious orders; equally, the doubt held by many that Consatiné was not the true heir had been virtually confirmed by his refusal to perform the Rite of Endyear. The second factor was a social one: the expansion of trade in recent years, particularly after the destruction of the Agaskan nation, had enriched many without giving them political clout, and the Brotherhood's position in the Council made it the only voice of the unfranchised. And thirdly, a factor unacknowledged at the time, the population was rising. Streetpoet and Od were by no means the only people on the road: for many, as land grew scarcer, the vagrant's life was the only life possible. Trade had benefited the few at the expense, it seemed, of many, and a large body of people was available to espouse any cause, royalist or republican, out of sheer dissatisfaction with their current lot. Families were split. Younger sons sided with the Brotherhood, fathers and inheriting elder brothers supported Consatiné; the stable peasantry on large aristocratic estates followed their masters happily enough, but the expanding smallholders of the Plains of Myr and the landless, craftless workers who found only seasonal employment tended towards the Opposition; the richest merchants in the cities, whose wealth came from royal monopolies and was preserved by the status quo, were for the emperor, but the lesser merchants and those artisans not directly threatened by the activities of the Brotherhood would have happily seen him overthrown.

If the troubles on the Namacythron seemed worrying, much worse was to be found in Cythroné itself. The city was divided utterly, and at the time Streetpoet and Od arrived there was home for the staunchest supporters of both sides. The companions entered through the ugly southern suburbs, where ancient hamlets were incorporated haphazardly into ugly rows of cheap timber houses, and sought somewhere to spend the night. They were stopped twice on their way. The first time two men in an unfamiliar uniform of black and orange held them and interrogated them as they entered the commercial district of Carpaccio. 'What do you want coming to Cythroné?'

Streetpoet answered. 'Please sir, my old dad here, he's deaf and dumb. We didn't mean no harm sir. We didn't honest.'

'Dumb is he. He seemed to understand well enough when I told him to halt.'

'That's because he saw you waving a sword at him, sire.'

'And what is your business in Cythroné? Answer me that?'

'We've come for the gold, your highness.'

'Gold?'

'Yes, your majesty. We've heard that the streets of Cythroné are paved with gold so we've come for our share.'

'You're barmy. You know that?'

'Yes your holiness.'

'Can you hold a sword?'

'I don't know.'

The soldiers, laughing at the simpletons who had landed in their midst, handed Streetpoet a sword of blackiron. The minstrel held it diffidently, tried waving it in emulation of one of the soldiers' air-swiping thrusts, and tossed it half across the street in his clumsiness.

'Try again,' instructed the soldiers, and Streetpoet did.

This time one of the soldiers confronted the minstrel. Streetpoet's incompetent attempts to defend himself provoked great laughter from the troops, while the soldier danced facetiously and jabbed at the minstrel's clothes. Visibly annoyed, Streetpoet made a sudden rush at the soldier, fell flat on his face, and again sent the sword sprawling.

'Get on your way,' said the soldier who had challenged them. 'We'll not be enlisting you. You'd be more use to the enemy than us if it came to a fight, I reckon.'

Streetpoet hurried off.

'And take your old man with you!' the soldier called.

Streetpoet returned, dragging Od away behind them. As soon as they were out of sight of the soldiers, Od shoved Streetpoet off him. 'Father!' he said, in disgust. 'It's worse than being your manservant!'

'All right,' said Streetpoet. 'We'll try you as my brother, but fathers and sons attract more sympathy and less suspicion.'

The second challenge came at the Bridge of Towers, which crosses the river Khalin and links the old town of Cythroné to the more recent expansion to the south. This time the soldiers were wearing the familiar uniform of the city militia.

'State your business!' demanded a sergeant.

'Our old mam's dying,' said Streetpoet. 'I've just travelled down to Ilynés to fetch my big brother here to her bedside. Pray Menketh we're not too late.'

'Big brother!' asked the sergeant. 'He ain't got no hair. Looks more like your dad to me. You can pass. But did you see any other troops on your way?'

'Wearing orange and black?' asked Streetpoet.

'Them's the ones.'

'Yes.'

'Opposition troops,' nodded the sergeant. 'Whereabouts?'

'They blocked the Mikas Road just after where the Namacythron ends.'

'Aye. That's what we heard.' He turned to a soldier. 'Best let the Captain know. Sounds certain there's a band of rebels to the south of the city, and well equipped they must be too. Where'd the likes of them get uniforms?'

'The rebels've got some wealthy supporters, sergeant,' replied the soldier. 'Not all the rich folk are behind Consatiné.'

'Aye. That's as maybe. Now you get that message to headquarters.'

The soldier left; Od and Streetpoet, no longer of interest to the worried Royalist troops, walked with him a while.

'Where are you two bound?' the soldier asked Od.

'Fragma Square,' he replied. It was the first place in Cythroné that came into his head.

'I'll walk that way with you.'

They arrived with the dusk in Fragma Square. The square was full of people, and the people were being herded into queues. A young man, in the uniform of a cavalry trooper, seeing Streetpoet, Od, and their companion, intercepted them. 'I'll relieve you of these two,' he told the soldier. 'Thanks.'

The young man prodded Streetpoet and Od to one side. 'What's he doing?' asked Od.

The soldier they'd been with shrugged. 'Don't know. But I haven't time to argue. You'll be all right. I've got to deliver this message.'

'Come on you!' said the young trooper, and Od found himself shoved into a queue, with Streetpoet just behind.

'Now what?' wondered the troubadour.

'Silence in the queue,' said the trooper, watching them suspiciously.

Night came. The queues moved slowly, inefficiently. Gradually the sullen line which contained Od and Streetpoet was whittled down, and at last Od found himself in front of a trestle table, behind which a tired clerk wrote a report by candle light.

'Name?'

'Od. But what's this about?'

The man yawned and ignored the question. 'Let's have your story then. What did you see on the day?'

'What day?' asked Od.

'What do you mean, what day? *The* day. The day all them people got killed.'

'I don't know what you mean. I've only arrived in Cythroné today.'

'Where were you before?' The clerk had stopped writing Od's answers down.

'Coming here.'

'You messing me about?'

'No.'

'You'd better not be.'

'I'm not.'

'Then why are you answering these questions?'

'Because you're asking them.'

'Right. That does it. Get this bloke out of the line. Have him for wasting official time.'

'I'm sorry,' said Streetpoet in the nick of time. 'My grandfather here is a little strange in the head. His hair has all fallen out and I reckon the cold has got to his brain. I'll take him home.'

Streetpoet led Od back through the streets, helping the older man carefully over the cobbles. In this way they left the square.

'Grandfather!' exclaimed Od. 'I've barely ten years on you.'

'It saved you a beating, didn't it?'

'It'll cost you one.'

'Threats, threats, threa...'

Streetpoet was suddenly silenced: Od hurled himself at the minstrel's waist. They fell to the floor in a heap, Od holding tight. Streetpoet raised a leg and tried to knee Od in the groin, but Od had anticipated this and, still clinging to his opponent, twisted himself out of range. Streetpoet flailed his arms about wildly and then realised that the pressure was relaxing.

'Are you all right?' Streetpoet asked, concerned.

Od looked up. 'I'm laughing, you idiot.'

'What at?'

'At us.'

Streetpoet laughed too. 'Come on, son,' said Od.

'Grandson,' corrected Streetpoet, and they laughed again as they picked themselves up. 'Has anyone ever told you you're lovely when you're angry?'

'No,' said Od, emphatically, as they walked companionably together through the darkened streets.

Chapter 4

Uncivil War

Wriknek sat in the guttering light of a candle and stared at a sea of shadowed papers. Maps showed approximate degrees of Brotherhood influence across Khalindaine; tables listed sympathisers who would be able to contribute funds; columns of figures gave the cost of equipping an armed man; schematic diagrams explained potential chains of command. And then there were the reports, covering everything from discussions of the quality of Myrian pork to the likelihood of infiltration into the imperial staff. Wriknek picked one up, almost at random, almost in despair. He was a methodical man but there was no method in this mess. He looked blankly at the paper in front of him: it suggested one Gryfag as a potential senior officer in the Brotherhood's forces. Very helpful, thought Wriknek sourly, if we had any forces to speak of. He knew of maybe a thousand Cythrons, dressed in yellow and black, who had been sponsored by the Brotherhood in the city, which might make the beginning of an army; he also knew that there was much too much confusion in Cythroné for him ever to marshal that army there. He put down the paper. Everything stopped at him, he felt: he was expected to do it all, from issuing edicts on harlotry to providing nails for horseshoes. In sudden malice, tinged with despair, he picked up another random report and, without reading it, held it in the candle's flame. It lit at once, a burning brand in his hand, and he moved it to the edge of the table where it ignited further overhanging reports.

Compulsively he encouraged the fire, pushing more and more pieces of paper within its hungry range until his desk top and his floor were illuminated by a hundred orange flames that danced and writhed and destroyed. He watched the destruction with satisfaction. Now the table itself was alight, blackening, burning. Casually he walked to the door of his room and called for his servants. 'Fetch me my carriage!' he cried. 'We're leaving Cythroné. We're moving north, to Ghell, my home town.' Behind him the growing fire cast an eerie light:

he was a man in the mouth of hell. 'I want messages to all
our supporters, everywhere. We are raising our standard in
the Plains of Myr.' Behind him the fire, fanned by the draught
from the open door, was well beyond control, but Wriknek
ignored it as he gave his instructions. 'The war has begun,' he
announced, and the disease that was within him laughed with
sheer delight.

All night long the messengers of the Brotherhood were busy
and by the following morning the tension in the city appeared
to have lessened. There had been a fire in the northern part
of the city, where the lawyers lodged, but apart from that
the Royalists were pleased to note that there had been
little trouble.

Dawn brought fresh intelligence reports. An inevitable
factor in a civil war is that both sides have spies in the other
camp. Some spy for the best of motives, others for the worst,
and it is the latter group that survives the longest. It did not
take long before the Peltyn-Lord had learnt that Wriknek had
left Cythroné, nor that the Brotherhood were raising an army
in the Plains of Myr. And even had there been no spies, no
informers, no double agents, the news would have reached
him soon enough, for Cythroné was awash with rumour.

For Streetpoet and Od, however, a more immediate problem
was how they should leave their accommodation without
paying, a problem Streetpoet solved by the simple expedient
of climbing through a window. Outside the day was cold but
bright: good travelling weather. They wrapped their cloaks
around them and blew their breath in visible plumes, but they
were not unhappy. Their journey was well under way.

The euphoria lasted only as far as the Anxious Gate, that
gate in the city walls which leads out to the Namamorn and
which earnt its curious name because it was from these towers
that threats were to be first seen. Normally the gate is simply
an inconvenience, narrowing the roadway and causing queues;
today it was an obstacle because, for the first time in memory,
the portcullis was down and the gates were locked.

Streetpoet did not need to be told that some crisis had
happened. Even during the Ingsvall, the terrible Agaskan
rising five years previously, the gates had never been closed.
Without even attempting to get through the gates he pulled

Od down a side-street. 'There's no chance of getting out that way,' he told his friend. 'But never mind. Three-quarters of the city walls have been pulled down. We'll have no problem getting round.'

But Streetpoet's confidence was misplaced. Where there were no walls there were troops, and where there were no troops there were bands of loyal civilians. Streetpoet led Od up to one of this last. 'What's going on?'

'The Gyr Peltyn's orders. Apparently the Brotherhood are raising their standard in a place called Ghell, wherever that is.'

'It's in the middle of the Plains of Myr,' said Streetpoet, who had been there. 'But what do you mean, raising their standard. Raising their standard of what?'

'Raising the flag of war, stupid. They're gathering an army.'

'But what in Hrakar for!'

'What do you think they want an army for? We're at war, civil war. That's why no one's allowed north: we don't want anyone else joining them.'

Streetpoet looked his most innocent. 'Do we look like we're on our way to fight? We're heading for Northreach. Do we look like rebels?'

'What do rebels look like?' replied the citizen. 'My own brother has joined them. And your bald mate looks just the sort of bloke who'd be on the Brotherhood's side: he's got that tight-lipped Brotherhood look written all over him. So there's no chance we'll let you through.'

'You carry on,' said Od. 'I'd better stay here.'

'No,' said Streetpoet and the citizen together.

'Just a thought,' said Od, and the friends turned back towards the centre of the city.

'What next?' asked Od.

'We'll just have to go south and go right round Cythroné.'

'That'll take days.'

'We're in no hurry.'

'No?' said Od. 'I'd have thought we were. The country's at war or soon will be. Communications can only get worse. If we don't get to Northreach soon we'll never get there. And anyway, I thought you said this Lara of yours could maybe help sort things out in Khalindaine. The sooner the better, I should say, from the way things are going now.'

'I suppose you're right,' said Streetpoet. 'But I don't see what choice we have.'

'Why don't we steal a boat?'

'A boat?' Streetpoet stopped walking. 'And sail to Akbar that way?'

'Why not?'

Streetpoet thought, though not for long. 'Because I don't know the first thing about boats, that's why: the only boat I've ever been in apart from the odd ferry was one that took me up the Khalin through Khalinrift to Northreach, and I was sick all the way then. And because I've drunk enough water out of the Hasfaine, thank you, to last me the rest of my days.'

'Look, I can handle a boat. We'll pinch something small, I'll sail it, you can just sit in the stern with your eyes shut.'

'I'll be sick,' Streetpoet warned.

'You can do what you like,' said Od, 'as long as you do it over the side.'

Wriknek's manic energy did not subside as he rode through the morning. The rhythm of the horses' hoofs, the uncomfortable bucketing of the carriage, and the frequent cries of the drivers would have made sleep difficult even had he desired it, but Wriknek was not interested in sleep. He drew up new plans in his head – writing was out of the question as the carriage lurched – for the requisition of bundles of black and orange cloth from the merchants of the Plains, and of further cloth for tents; the thought of cloth led him to think of flags, and he wondered what his regimental standards should look like.

His own banner, he decided, would be black. He wondered if it needed a symbol: a bear, perhaps, to signify Ormaas's Northreach origins, or a death's head, which more suited his tastes? What about a death's head supported by two rearing bears? Yes, that's it! he decided: that shall be my mark!

He started to envisage a special force, chosen from the élite of the Brotherhood. The Brothers Militant, he would call them, and they would wear black tabards bearing his design: he would not risk them in fighting, but would use them to enforce his rule and to purge the enemy within. For already the paranoia which is a symptom of syphilis was worming its way through his skull, warning him to trust no one. In fact, the more he thought about it, the more his worries about the future focused on those who were meant to be on his side: his megalomania predicted victory over the Royalists, but his paranoia foresaw treachery from his colleagues. Still, he thought, smiling to himself, I shall be ready for their betrayal when it comes, and shall deal with it most severely.

His thoughts turned away from this towards strategy. Wriknek was no soldier. He had never seen a battle, never even seen a parade ground, and no matter how hard he concentrated, he could not imagine his troops except as ranks of men, marching, matching, dressed in orange and black, with him and his Brothers Militant at their head. Warfare, death, decimation did not fit his picture: he saw banners that flew in the wind, with his own sinister flag flying highest; he heard drums in his head and heard bugles, and never heard the wounded as they screamed.

Another consideration struck him. What title should he use? Grand-Master declared his control of the Brotherhood, but did not do justice to his wider ambitions. Supreme Master maybe? Or his predecessor's title of First Lord? But he did not want to be a lord; he wanted no lords in the land. Perhaps Prophet would suit him? Grand Prophet? Supreme Prophet? But these titles smacked too much of self-importance. Monomania does not always demand grandiloquence: many dictators have called themselves 'colonel', for instance, secure that their reputation transcends their rank, whilst the self-effacement suggested by such modesty enhances their reputation and disarms criticism. Wriknek shared this characteristic. He had never been interested in display. He would be known simply as the Commander, he decided. He liked it: it was suitably ambiguous, neither proclaiming nor limiting the extent of his power. Wriknek smiled. This proved what a special moment this was for it was his second smile of the day. Wriknek smiled, and felt that in choosing his title he had made the most important decision yet.

The days passed. Streetpoet and Od reconnoitred the waterfront carefully. Streetpoet was an accomplished thief, though he would have denied that title, preferring to think of himself as a man who could improvise; Od had never stolen anything in his life, yet it was he who was initiating this enterprise and the minstrel who followed like a novice.

They soon realised that stealing a boat was going to be relatively easy. The emergency had caused the waterfront to be more confused than usual, whilst those of Wriknek's supporters who had followed him north had left several boats disused and available in the harbour. The difficulty was the journey up-river. The bridges were manned with soldiers and the galley fleet was patrolling. The companions had seen many boats stopped before they could leave Cythroné, and Od reluctantly decided that they would have to abandon the plan.

'Oh well,' said Streetpoet. 'Never mind.'

Their alternative plan was no more successful, however. Going south was equally impossible. The soldiers on the bridge were not only preventing river traffic, but also stopping people crossing the Khalin. Once more it was apparent that argument would be futile.

'Now what?' asked Od, as they walked impotently up and down the quay once more.

'I don't know.'

'Why do you think the soldiers are so keen on everyone staying in Cythroné anyway?'

'I'm not honestly sure,' said Streetpoet. 'I suppose they don't want people leaving and joining the Opposition in the north, or roaming the countryside taking advantage of the panic. But it seems a dangerous policy to me. Consatiné is quite likely to have a rebellion in his own capital if he contains all the rebels like this.'

Od shook his head. 'Hardly *all* the rebels,' he said. 'The real heart of the Brotherhood is the Plains of Myr. That's where Consatiné's main opposition is going to come from.'

They walked back along the waterfront. 'Look at that boat too,' said Od in disgust. 'Perfect.'

He was looking at a small vessel, little more than a dinghy with a mast. 'There's no point,' said Streetpoet. 'We'd never get up-river. We'd never even get to the south bank.'

'It's a pity. It looks a nice little craft.'

A thought occurred to Streetpoet. 'Where does the river go in the other direction?'

'What do you mean? It goes the same place all rivers go.'

'But where's that?' demanded Streetpoet.

'The sea, of course.'

'Oh!' Streetpoet mused a while. 'Do *all* rivers go to the sea then? I didn't know that.'

'Where did you think they went? Climbing mountains?' Od was frankly incredulous, but Streetpoet had no experience of the sea at all, as his next remark proved.

'Comtas is by the sea.'

'So?' asked Od.

'Well, why don't we take the boat and go to Comtas?'

'Because Comtas is the other side of Khalindaine. We'd have to sail half way round the empire to get there.'

'But it's all the same sea, isn't it?'

'It's wet and salty,' agreed Od. 'But it's also, as you appear to have overlooked, huge. It's much further to Comtas by sea than it would be by land.'

'Oh.' Streetpoet was deflated.

'Mind you. At least going towards the sea would get us out of Cythroné, and that'd be a start.'

Temporarily, Streetpoet let his anxiety to be on his way override his anxiety about the sea. 'All right,' he said, but his change of heart was not to last long.

They climbed down to the boat, using a ladder of blackiron hoops, and Od stepped aboard. The boat rocked beneath his weight.

'It isn't safe,' said Streetpoet. 'It's rocking now. It'll sink when I get on.'

'Just get aboard and stop being daft.'

'How?'

'The same way I did. Take a step.'

'No!'

'Why not?'

Streetpoet thought, came up with no reason except sheer fear, and reluctantly stretched his leg to the gunwale. 'Come on,' encouraged Od. 'If anyone sees you they'll know you're not a sailor.'

Tentatively Streetpoet tried to transfer his weight to his outstretched leg without letting go of the iron rings. The boat refused to co-operate, however, and moved away, leaving Streetpoet dangling from the ladder with his feet in the river. Quickly he pulled his legs up. 'See,' he said, 'It can't be done.'

Od had not been paying much attention to his companion's efforts, busying himself instead with an inspection of the boat. 'Aren't you on board yet?' he asked.

'Does it look like it?'

'Menketh alive,' muttered Od; he walked to where Streetpoet still hung and reached out for the ladder, bringing the boat skilfully in. 'Just step aboard for goodness sake!'

Streetpoet did.

'Is that better?' asked Od sarcastically. 'Can we go now?'

Streetpoet took the question at face value. 'I feel sick already,' he announced.

'Just shut up,' Od said good humouredly, 'and watch out for sea snakes.'

'*Sea snakes!*'

'It was a joke.'

'Ha ha ha. Very funny.'

Od climbed back up the ladder swiftly, unfastened the painter, and climbed down again, still holding the rope. He stepped easily from the ladder into the stern of the already drifting boat, and gave it an extra push as he parted from the shore. 'We're going downstream anyway,' he explained to Streetpoet as he wound the painter into a skilful coil. 'So we could just drift. But I'll raise the sail as soon as we're clear of the lee of this wharf.'

Streetpoet, his hands clinging to the gunwale, said nothing.

Talen-vaine-Talen and his colourful armed philosophers travelled north through the Plains of Myr towards Akbar. They heard nothing of the imminent war except wild rumours, and these they dismissed as incredible. When they saw a large company of men approaching, in an unfamiliar uniform, they were curious but not concerned. In a land where every second aristocrat and every second town has a band of troops, some in uniform, others not, it takes an experienced man indeed to recognise every soldier he sees.

It does not take much experience, however, to recognise an attack when it comes. The charge was swift and unexpected, and then the newcomers were amongst them, slashing and hacking, killing four in their initial violence. Then the mêlée began, and Talen-vaine-Talen, though outmanoeuvred by his troops when it came to speculative ontology, proved why he was their leader. With reckless gallantry he led a counter-charge, swinging at the nearest enemy soldier and smashing the cheek guard of the other's helm before finishing him with a jabbed chop to the neck. There was a small hill, barely more than a mound, by the side of the road, and Talen made for it, almost dragging his horse up the muddy cutting at the edge of the track.

Another of the attackers, in his orange and black uniform, rode to intercept the Vaine. Talen did not pause: he spurred his horse forward; his scything blade caught the trooper across the chest. The trooper sat bolt upright on his horse before slumping dead to the dusty earth.

Talen reached his objective and waved his blooded sword above his head. 'For the Empire!' he cried, as he looked for the place in the fighting where his intervention would achieve most. One or two of his men heard his cry and repeated it in ragged fashion.

Once the element of surprise was spent the two sides were evenly matched. Talen's force was actually a little larger than the Opposition's, and though the Vaine of Talen's philosophers might not have been the most effective fighting force in Khalindaine, they were well trained and outraged at this unprovoked attack. The Vaine, on his hillock, noted all this with a professional eye, taking in the situation at once and deciding on his priorities. His instincts all told him to fight, to teach his unexpected enemy the folly of attacking the Vaine of Talen; his sense spoke otherwise, however, and told him that his mission was more important, at this stage, than a moment of military glory. He would have to disengage his troops, lead them off in good order, and prevent the enemy pursuing them; he was not sure quite how this was to be managed but, being a man of action rather than introspection, joining the fight seemed a good way to start. He urged his horse into the fray. What he needed to do, he decided, as he parried a half-hearted blow, was to capture the enemy standard or kill the enemy leader. And then he let his instincts take over entirely, for he was fighting for his life.

The mêlée was confused. There was no order to the wheeling soldiers, no line they could have called their own. Not far from him was the enemy standard. It looked not unfamiliar, despite the legend 'Remember the Diehards' emblazoned across it, and he recognised it as that of a small town in Myr he had served in only a few years before. This meant, almost certainly, he had once fought alongside these men who were now his enemy. It no longer mattered. Sentiment was for when the fighting was done. All that mattered at this moment was to capture that flag and get away before he lost too many men.

He fought steadily through. He was a fine soldier and a fine horseman, trained from birth in the arts of war. Despite the confusion around him, the bucking, rearing horses and the wildly swinging swords, he felt under no threat. With well-timed feints and new attacks he succeeded in isolating the standard bearer and went in for the kill.

A standard bearer is always at a disadvantage in a mêlée. The flag, though impressive, is unwieldy; it rests in a leather cup by its bearer's left foot and, though his right arm is free for defence, because the reins have to be held in the outstretched left hand, the hand that supports the standard, the horse often feels itself pulled round. This was exactly what was happening in front of Talen-vaine-Talen. The standard bearer, though trying to engage the vaine, found his horse was having none of this: Talen had no difficulty in riding round the poor man and killing him with a single, well-aimed thrust. Sentiment, he recalled, was for when the fighting was done. He did not need to capture the enemy standard after all, he decided: it fell to the ground and was trampled, and that was enough.

Anyway there was no time to think: it was time to act only. The mêlée was utter confusion. Talen could feel himself tiring as he swung, struck, parried and thrust, and he could see all around him others were feeling the same. Suddenly the retreat sounded, a short low note followed by a longer higher one, and the figure thrice repeated.

This was civil war. Both sides were trained in the same conventions, and both sides gravitated to the same bugle call.

It was the opposition that had in fact called the retreat, though both sides were grateful for the opportunity to rest. Talen sought out Dagon and together they rode back to the hummock. The end of the battle was as confused as the beginning. The cavalrymen broke off fighting but did not know which way to turn. In the end, by mysterious mutual agreement, the Royalists gathered round their standard whilst the Opposition returned the way they had come. Even then, six of Talen's men got it wrong and became the first prisoners of the war.

Around the hummock the Vaine of Talen restored order to his men. Injured horses had to be killed, dead comrades and opponents cremated. The cavalrymen wiped their swords clean on the grass and, dismounting, watered their horses at a nearby stream.

'We saw them off,' said Dagon with pleasure.

'I suppose so,' said Talen. 'But who were they.'

'Bandits?'

'In uniform?' It seemed unlikely. 'They must have been Brotherhood supporters.'

'But why should *they* wear uniform, come to that?'

There was only one conclusion. 'Civil war!'

Talen-vaine-Talen may have lacked the intellectual accomplishments of many of those he led, but he was no fool. He recognised two things immediately: that there were likely to be those amongst his troops who would wish to desert, and that there were unlikely to be any friendly villages until they reached Akbar. He ordered his troops to remount and then addressed them.

'Well men, as we've agreed, it looks like Khalindaine is at war with itself. I can think of nothing that disgusts me more than the thought of civil war, but the situation has happened now and there is nothing any of us can do to prevent it. For myself, I have sworn my allegiance to my emperor, and that is where my own loyalty will lie, but some of you may wish to fight for the Brotherhood. These are strange times and the normal rules of discipline do not obtain. I am prepared to let any man who so chooses desert the flag of Talen, on condition that the deserter promises not to inform our enemy of our position or destination. So, anyone who wants to leave, leave now. I do not want traitors in my ranks.'

There was muttering. One or two soldiers seemed on the point of taking up Talen's offer, only to change their minds, and one group in particular seemed undecided what to do for the best. It was from this group that a young trooper called Baruny rode forward.

'Talen-vaine-Talen,' he said formally. 'Like many of my companions I am from the Plains of Myr. I suspect that come a fight my family will be with the Brotherhood and I do not

want to oppose them. But when I joined the army I too took
a vow of allegiance to Consatiné and the Empire, and I do not
wish to betray that vow now. I am certain I speak for all your
soldiers when I say I would rather follow you and the emperor
than desert.'

The speech did the trick: not a single man left Talen's side.
And though there was muttering from time to time, Talen's
brave offer had disarmed mutiny, because anyone who felt like
stirring trouble would be quickly reminded that he had had his
chance to go and not taken it. And besides, as one of them
put it, 'In what other army do you get such a high standard
of conversation?'

'I am grateful for your loyalty,' said Talen, 'and humbled
by it. Thank you all very much. And now, business. For we
cannot afford to hang around here. We are on what I am sure
must be Brotherhood territory: the Plains of Myr have always
been dominated by the Hedchites. If we are to reach Akbar
safely and swiftly we must be careful how we travel.'

It was a trooper called Hjek who came up with the suggestion. 'There'll be quite a few deserters around, I reckon. Why
don't we pretend to be amongst 'em? Coming from so many
different regiments, we can get away with that I'd say. All of
us, that is, and with respect, excepting you, sir.'

'Why can't I get away with that?' demanded Talen-vaine-
Talen.

'You're obviously an aristocrat, if you know what I mean,
sir.'

'You mean I should borrow a trooper's uniform?'

Hjek looked doubtful still. 'Well, that *might* make a difference.'

Without much relish, Talen-vaine-Talen stripped off his
exquisite armour and donned a dead man's clothes. He ordered
the soldiers to divide the expensive suit of armour between
them: he hoped he would have the chance to reclaim it at
Akbar. And then he mounted a horse.

'How do I look?' he asked.

'Like a nobleman in a trooper's uniform,' said Ossian.

'It's too rough,' said Streetpoet. 'We'll have to turn back.'

'Eh?' was Od's distracted reply. 'What's too rough?'

'The sea. it's awful. We'll drown.'

'Streetpoet,' said Od, speaking carefully. 'First, this isn't rough, this is calm. And second, it isn't even the sea. We're in the Khalin estuary.'

'O Menketh!' said Streetpoet, and was promptly sick.

Wriknek had established his headquarters in an inn, this being the largest single building in the small town of Ghell. He sat, dressed in black, amid a web of charts and tables, working his way through them steadily, with that uninspired doggedness which had been his only outstanding characteristic until the pox ate through his brain. As often before, when the demon madness he thought was divinity had left him, he found himself wondering how in Hedch's name he had found himself in this situation. His army was growing steadily. The towns of the Plains of Myr had each sent their garrisons to his flag; the general muster had attracted many; even several of the noblemen of the Plains were raising troops on his behalf, and the sea of tents around Ghell had quadrupled the town's population. But as the army multiplied, so did Wriknek's problems. Already his trusted Brotherhood was at full stretch, collecting information, distributing uniforms as fast as they could be manufactured, and trying, with limited success, to cut lasciviousness and irreligion from the ranks; the Brotherhood, however, was showing itself incapable of actually leading an army, and his great need was for experienced and loyal soldiers. But there lay the heart of Wriknek's dilemma: the more he promoted someone, the more he suspected him.

Wriknek suddenly threw down his quill. He wanted to see the army, he decided: he needed to check his troops. He wanted to inspire them and inspect them, and most of all he wanted to reassure himself of their loyalty.

The orders were given for a general turn-out on the fields beyond Ghell. The troops were bustled from their city of tents and told to assemble before their Commander. It was a long slow job. Clerks who had been hard at work issuing new uniforms in exchange for civilian clothes – an exchange, probably practised by all armies, which made desertion harder – took advantage of the respite by stretching and gossiping. Gamblers, their card games disturbed by the call to muster, concealed their winning hands inside their cloaks. Sergeants who felt their men had almost got their drill right worried

that suddenly, in front of the Commander, one of them would
get it wrong.

Despite the large number of men there was not much noise.
The day was grey, listless, oppressive. A storm threatened.
Heavy clouds hung damply over the plains. Wriknek, an
unimpressive figure who had to be helped onto his large
horse, rode between the companies. The wind strengthened.
Tent flaps buffeted, cavalry horses whinnied, and sergeants
barked hasty commands. Perhaps a third of the troops were
fully equipped, a third partially so, and the final third still in
civilian dress. It is a measure of the progress of his disease that
Wriknek had trouble distinguishing between the half-equipped
troops of reality and the perfect soldiers who marched through
his mind. Meanwhile, the wind brought the first of the rain.

The tiny boat left the shelter of the Khalin's bank and
headed for the open sea. The blustery day sometimes scattered
the clouds, allowing the sun to break through. They sailed
along the wide bleak estuary. The land was an ochre ribbon
round their horizon, broken only where the river finally
met the sea.

To Streetpoet's surprise he found himself getting used to the
boat: he would not have claimed that he felt happy or secure,
but at least he had learnt to tolerate the movement, which was
a start. Od, however, was undeniably enjoying himself. He had
not realised how much he had missed the movement of a boat
beneath him, nor how much he relished the clean sea-filtered
air. He tacked the boat skilfully into the rising wind, and as
the sail swung from side to side it passed dangerously over
Streetpoet's ducked head.

They travelled slowly. Streetpoet kept half an eye on the
swinging boom and watched the shore go by. A cormorant
perched on an abandoned jetty. They passed a hamlet of
reed-roofed fishermen's cottages, draped with drying nets, and
an old watch-tower, derelict and overgrown. A tall ship passed
in the other direction, sailing down the middle of the channel
with the wind behind it and its sails bulging.

The headland that led them into the sea was marked by a
tumble of grey rocks. Od steered the little boat carefully round,
and Streetpoet watched with something between interest and
fear as the water suddenly grew rougher on the far side of

this shelter, and saw the coarse waves reach for the rocks like desperate hands that grasped yet could not grip.

The wind was getting stronger all the time, and the sea was flecked with white as gusts caught the top of the waves. 'We'll have to make our way further out!' shouted Od, and Streetpoet had to snatch at the words before they were blown to the shore.

'Why?' Streetpoet wanted to know, but Od did not hear or was not listening. All he was aware of was the worsening weather.

The clouds on the western horizon were threatening now, darker and more troubled than the grey sky above. Od continued to sail away from the coast, knowing he would need sea-room if the storm broke. Tacking was becoming harder though, and their zigzag course seemed to be making no impression.

'Have you seen those clouds?' asked Streetpoet through the wind.

Again Od did not seem to have heard, but Streetpoet saw from the tension and concentration in his friend's face that he had.

Od held on until the last minute before making his decision. 'We can't get any further in this weather,' he shouted. 'We'll have to run for the shore!'

'What?'

'Run for the shore!'

'Thank Menketh,' exclaimed Streetpoet, not understanding Od's reluctance.

The little boat responded alertly to Od's command, as though it too wanted to race ahead of the storm. To the west the first lashings of rain were beginning to obscure the horizon. The coastline stretched away to the north and east of them, familiar yet inhospitable, and the boat tossed alarmingly. Streetpoet, already wet from the flying spray and the vanguard of the rain, was soaked now as a succession of waves broke over their stern. He shut his eyes, and when he looked up was surprised to find neither the boat sinking nor Od washed away. The shoreline jumped crazily ahead. Sometimes it vanished entirely; at others it swung above them, ready it seemed to fall on their heads. The sea, it appeared, was given new purpose by the nearby land, and instead of the earlier chaos of waves the companions had now to cope with rollers that smashed into the shore, white horses that charged the grey beach. Od knew his only chance of getting them ashore was to ride the breakers and hope to be flung high enough up the beach to survive: should the boat deviate at all from its course in this venture, it would be turned and capsized at once.

The full force of the storm was still to come, as Od knew. This gave resolution to his desire to get ashore. He wished he knew this shoreline better, for there was no way of telling what lay at the foot of the cliffs. Was it sand? Or more rocks?

Od let out a little sail. He would need speed for steerage. Streetpoet's eyes, he noticed, were tight shut, and his hands just as tight on the gunwales. They were less than a hundred strides from the shore. The waves raced them in. And disaster struck, suddenly. A receding wave revealed a rock, low and smooth, ahead of them. There was only one way to avoid hitting it, which was to hope the waves would carry them over. It was a forlorn hope. The bows scraped the stone. The stern came round and smashed like a broadside. The boat tumbled over the low rock and tumbled the companions out. Streetpoet, eyes wide open now, saw a confused swirl of green-grey spume and felt an angry pain in his left shoulder as he was hurled against the rock. He reached out instinctively and grabbed the still-intact hull of the boat. The waves pulled him and his salvation sullenly back and then hurled him at the rocks again, maliciously. The hull cracked and splintered. Then the sucking respite was repeated, until Streetpoet was driven forward once again.

He was still on the seaboard side of the rock but Od had been thrown to the other side. He was bruised in many places where he had rolled over the stone, but knew he was alive. When the boat had capsized the mast had snapped off, and the jutting stump had been pushed into his leg the moment he sprawled on top of the low rock, in the instant between the collision and the next damaging wave. Now he was clear, his leg smarting and probably bleeding.

There was no point searching for Streetpoet. Od knew only too well that in these flailing seas two men could be but a stride apart and yet unable to see or save one another. The only thing for it was to swim to the shore and, perhaps, to raise the alarm. And even that modest ambition was not going to be easy to achieve: where he was, behind the low rock that had sunk them, the sea was relatively calm, but as if in compensation the waters to either side of him, disturbed by the rock's obstruction, were confused and fierce. Od knew the only certainty about broken waves is no one can be certain which way they will break, and knew too he would just have to hope to stay afloat and alive long enough for the waves to ground him. And he had been washed ashore often enough to know that being close to the beach was not enough: the undertow, the shingle, and the danger of striking his head on a rock made the last few strides the most dangerous of all. Taking a lungful of air, he pushed himself into the torrents.

For the third time the broken hull, with Streetpoet still clinging on desperately, was forced into the rock. Streetpoet saw, as through a kaleidoscope, water, stone and wood meet, part, turn and fragment. His mouth filled with sea-water. His lungs coughed through the waves. Still holding to what was left of the hull, he felt his arms, legs and chest scraped through his clothes by the rough and barnacled rock. There were no thoughts in his head. Survival was a matter of hanging on, and instinct was the only thing that kept his hands tight round the wood.

Od was bobbed and tossed. Forced under water he held his breath, struck upwards, and was rewarded by a gasp of air. Then he was under the water again, swimming blindly but strongly, and surfacing gratefully, unexpectedly. His bald head streamed water. Ahead was the shore, closer than he had dared hope, and as he made a stroke through the water another wave picked him up and carried him closer still. Now was the most dangerous stage of the landing. He put his feet down, trying to find the bed, but was immediately swept up, turned over, and forced to flail again for another desperate mouthful of air. The water was too powerful: he could not hope to wade through it but must ride the surface waves, avoid the fatal undertow and hope he would be washed ashore somewhere safe and sandy, and not pummelled against some rock. It was asking too much, but what choice had he? He could hardly turn back. So he kicked his legs up to the surface of the surf and let a wave shove him ashore like a piece of jetsam.

The world for Streetpoet was a sucking smash of salt water that stung and numbed the cuts on his sides. Somehow clear

of the rock, he was in fact moving not towards the shore but
parallel to it, caught between conflicting waves and driven
north in the conflux. A large wave struck him, knocking him
towards the dangerous headland nearby, and then relenting
and driving him on past.

Od braced himself for the grinding collision with the shore.
At least it was a beach he was headed for, he saw. His wave did
not throw him far enough though. He was swept back and it was
left to a second breaker to shove him onto the pebbled beach,
where a third wave struck him, bruising him against the shingle
and lifting him back into the water. He struggled desperately.
To drown after having been ashore! Another wave bore down
on him and hurled him forward, headlong, and when at last
this wave had receded Od found himself high and dry.

Streetpoet could not have told how he survived the storm;
the only witness was an ancient albatross that lived in the cliffs
and saw the minstrel swept into the smooth water beneath the
sheer cliffs of the headland. The boat had been well made
and even now, despite the shipwreck, the gunwale held, a flat
boat-shape on the water as though the rest of the vessel was
submerged rather than destroyed. The wreckage was twisted by
the waves, washed over by the breakers, and finally deposited
some six hundred strides north of where Od had gone ashore.
The albatross stretched her elegant wings, flew low over the
fallen minstrel, and let the wind carry her home.

The soldiers found Od first. They kicked him in the chest
to find if he was dead; learning he was not they kicked him
again. Od woke to a clear and cloudless day, and stared up
at the waspish uniforms of the Opposition.

'What you doing here?' asked the sergeant.

'I was washed ashore.'

'We can see that. What from?'

'A small boat. I was sailing from Cythroné...'

'Cythroné! What are you, a spy?'

'I've escaped... I'm of the Brotherhood.'

The soldiers stepped back and had a sort of consultation,
which meant in practice that the sergeant wanted the others to
back him up before returning to the prone figure on the sand.
'All right,' said the sergeant. 'That's as may be. Prove it.'

'Are you of the Brotherhood?' asked Od in his turn.

'Me? No! I'm just a soldier, like.'

'Then how will you recognise the secret signs? Take me to the local Master of the Brotherhood and I'll prove myself to him.' Od sat up. Even his bruises wore bruises by now, and the night had left him cold. 'Help me to my feet, will you. Have you found my manservant?'

'Who'll he be when he's at home?'

'He was with me when we sank. Youngish chap, scruffy, hasn't shaved. Good talker.'

'He'll have drowned,' said the sergeant with confidence.

It made sense. Od himself had been lucky to survive, and he had a far greater understanding of the sea than the minstrel. Yet somehow he could not imagine Streetpoet dead. 'Go and look for him,' Od demanded.

The troops had not expected orders from their prisoner. 'You're kidding!'

'I have vital information about the disposition of Royalist troops,' lied Od easily, proving that his time with Streetpoet had not been wasted. 'But I am going nowhere and telling no one until a thorough search has been carried out for my manservant. You have the power to force me to come with you, of course, but I assure you that such disrespect to an officer of the Brotherhood will not be overlooked.'

Again the soldiers consulted, and again the sergeant told them what to agree. 'Look, fellow,' he told Od. 'We've only just met you. You might be Wriknek's brother-in-law for all we know, or the Gyr Peltyn himself in disguise. You might be telling the truth but you could just as well be lying. How should we know? We're just a shore patrol, sent by headquarters to keep our eyes on this bit of coast and make sure the locals don't get up to anything silly. But I'll tell you what: you've an honest face, despite your bald head; we'll take you up to the village and then I'll leave you with a couple of guards while we hunt for this bloke of yours. But we're not wasting the whole day looking: if we haven't found him by lunchtime then that's it, we're going to visit Oprech, the Master of the Brotherhood round here, willy-nilly, and it'll be up to him what happens to you next. All right?'

'Fine by me,' said Od, who was tired of arguing anyway.

There was a narrow path from the cove to the headland. The soldiers escorted Od up it, supporting him where necessary and twice having to wait for him. 'I'm doing my best,' protested Od when they complained. 'Just a bit battered, that's all. A bit battered, a bit out of breath.'

The village was close, which was as well, because the pain in his leg where the mast had pierced his thigh was growing more intense with every step. The houses nestled just behind the headland, in the lea of a rocky outcrop. Od noticed how the village children, who had been playing in the streets, fled as the soldiers approached. The garrison had housed itself in a long white barn fitted with rough beds and subdivided by rougher curtains. Od was allowed to lie down while the troops searched for Streetpoet. 'I don't hold out much hope though,' cautioned the sergeant as he left. 'It was a bad night last night.'

Through the open door Od could see the bright day. Spring seemed to be arriving at last. Flowers grew in the fresh grass, and in the distance he could hear the bleating of lambs. He suddenly realised he was hungry. 'Any chance of a meal?' he asked one of his captors.

'Sure. Bacon and eggs do you?'

'Lovely.'

'Boy!' This was to an aged man who hurried from the far recesses of the barn. 'Boy. We want anything you've got. No, make that everything. Bacon, eggs, good bread if you've got any, whatever.'

'We've no eggs left, begging your pardon sir,' said the old man, his head bent so low he seemed to be trying to address his own chest.

'Bugger that!' The soldier grasped the old man by the shoulders and shook him. 'I said I wanted eggs.'

'Where from, please sir?' The man's voice was pathetically low.

'Where the Menketh do I care where from! If you want to walk again, just get us some eggs.'

The old man hurried off.

'Only way to deal with these beggars,' confided the soldier.

Od nodded, thoughtfully.

After a good meal, however acquired, everyone feels better. Od put down his plate, stood, and limped around the cliff top. The day was beautiful. The cold sunlight on the sea, the yellow flowers on the cliffs, the seabirds circling overhead, conspired to make Od feel almost at peace with the world, until he saw the soldiers coming along the cliff path, with Streetpoet's body between them.

Od hurried lamely back to the billet. The soldiers dropped Streetpoet onto a bed.

'Is he?' asked Od.

'No. He isn't. You say he's a manservant? Scruffy looking so-and-so, though but!'

'I suppose he is,' agreed Od. 'But I'd miss him. Been in the family for years.'

'Best wake him up, I suppose,' said the sergeant. There was a pail of water at the foot of the bed which he tossed over the minstrel; Streetpoet blinked towards consciousness, wiping his eyes. 'Ouch. It must have been a heavy night.' He looked round. 'Where am I?'

'We've reached the edge of the Plains of Myr,' put in Od, in case Streetpoet came out with anything indiscreet. 'We're among friends at last.'

'Fine friends,' said the minstrel, ringing water from his jerkin. 'Still, I should've got used to it by now. I've never been anything but wet since I met you.'

'Met you?' asked the sergeant. 'I thought he was some old retainer or something.'

'Ever since we rendezvoused in Ilynés,' amended Od. 'We split up to escape from the south. The Brotherhood's none too popular in the wine regions, you know.'

The soldier laughed. His generous jaws wobbled. 'I'll believe that!'

The companions were loaded onto a mule waggon and driven inland. A pair of magpies crossed the sky above them, landing in a neighbouring tree and jeering. Shaggy grey sheep, losing their winter coats, looked up with bored black eyes. A gibbet swung in the breeze making the dead man moan.

They came to a deserted village. Many of the buildings were burnt to the ground. 'What's been going on here?' asked Od.

The soldier who drove the waggon answered over his shoulder. 'This place? Oh, we had fun there, I can tell you. The villagers decided they'd prefer to be on the Royalist side, so we were sent along to change their minds.' He gestured towards a roughly heaped mound of soil that was circled by carrion crows. 'They're mostly buried there.' Od looked and then looked away.

'Has there been much of that?' asked Streetpoet, his voice sounding unconcerned.

'Well, you know how it is. Some noisy bigwig says their village is staying loyal to the emperor and we have to make an example of the place. But it doesn't happen so much any more. I guess they're getting the message.'

'Fancy,' said Streetpoet.

'Pity, really,' continued the soldier. 'Easiest job in Khalindaine: move in, slaughter a few villagers, take what you can and get off.'

'Positively straightforward,' Streetpoet agreed. 'So how many villages suffered – sorry, were made loyal – in that way?'

'Couldn't tell you, mate. I only know this section. But there's nineteen villages and we've only had to deal with two, so I guess the rest were with us.'

'I'm sure they will be by now at any rate.'

'Oh yes,' said the soldier. 'Yes, they're right with us now.'

They reached their destination, Tehkan, the local market town. Tehkan was typical of the towns of the southern Plains. It retained its gates, built into steeply roofed towers, but the walls had long ago been pulled down to allow for the spreading houses. The streets seemed unusually quiet to Od. Instead of the bustle of traders and craftsmen there was silence; instead of the throng of servants buying for their masters there was just the occasional shuffling passer-by. Many of the shops were closed, though not all. They passed a print shop, where diligent wood carvers bent over their blocks to score their designs, and a blacksmith's smithy where pungent clouds of black smoke told of business as usual.

'Where is everyone?' asked Od.

'How do you mean?'

'The town seems deserted.'

'Oh aye,' said the soldier. 'Well, we don't encourage too much gossip, and so we've cut down the market to one day a week and kept folks inside the rest of the time.'

'I see.'

They reached a fortified mansion near the edge of the town. 'Who've you got there?' asked a guard at the mansion's gate.

'Couple of refugees. Bald bloke reckons he's one of the Brotherhood; other one's his servant.'

'You'd best take 'em in yourself. Oprech Fatefollower is trying a few cases at the moment: I've orders to stay at the gate.'

'No problem.'

Streetpoet had somehow thought of cases of wine when he had heard the soldier's words; Od was not deceived. They were taken into a room which had been converted to serve as a court. At one end sat an elderly man in black, flanked by half a dozen soldiers in the by now familiar black and orange uniform of the opposition. 'Who've you got there?' demanded the old man.

'Refugees, Oprech Fatefollower, sir.'

'What's the charge?'

'Bald chap reckons to be Brotherhood, your worship.'

'Does he now?'

Od walked forward confidently and raised his right hand. The first and third fingers were crossed beneath the second. The old man nodded. 'What's your name?'

'Od Hedchenlightened. Of the Ilynés chapter.'

'Ilynés, eh? Most of your lot have already reached the Plains.'

'I have not seen my Brothers for some time. I was charged with the glorious mission of carrying the message prohibiting alcohol to the towns of Marq; the degenerate citizens of the region chased me and I was forced to flee for my life. I have been on the run since then, trying to get north and join my fellows.'

'Well, you'll be welcomed, Od Hedchenlightened, no doubt of that. The Brotherhood's at full stretch and we're short of good men. But are you fit to travel? You look a bit damaged, and you've a nasty limp.'

'We were shipwrecked, Brother. But we are recovering.'

'Good. Well, you'd better get off for Ghell. I got a message only this morning saying any Brothers without specific duties were to head there at once: I guess that'll apply to you. There's too much work and not enough time. Even in the Plains of Myr there are those who'd oppose us. I'll be seeing a few cases when you've gone. I was just signing the death warrants when you came in.'

'You sign before you try the cases?'

'Saves time, Brother. And now, if you'll forgive me, I must get on.' He waved the first case in, and Od and Streetpoet left the courtroom. Alone outside, they looked grimly at one another, and then Streetpoet gave a faint smile. 'Well,' he said, 'I know one thing. You're getting good at this businesss of lying.'

'What do you mean, lying? I told Oprech the truth, pure and simple.'

'Yes,' agreed Streetpoet, but Od was not through.

'Yes, *sir*,' Od corrected.

Streetpoet shrugged. 'Yes, *sir*,' he repeated, and if Od heard the irony, he ignored it.

Chapter 5

A Small Town Called Ghell

Konuskat the Disciple, in his cramped quarters in Ghell, sat on his camp bed and looked at the floor. The knotted wooden boards made patterns as he watched, made sinister faces and eyes that stared him out. Sometimes, when Konuskat wondered about life in general, and his own life in particular, he felt that somehow something had gone wrong. Until – what was it now? – five years ago he had been a minor part of the family firm. He had enjoyed his life, enjoyed having an office to go to and nothing much to do when he arrived, enjoyed looking out of the window at the prostitutes and the dark skinned southern immigrants who quartered in the commercial districts. Perhaps, he now wondered, that was where I went wrong? For if I hadn't been looking out of the window I wouldn't have seen the crowd round Hedch, Hedch the Messenger, Hedch the First Martyr, nor heard him say, in tones of the deepest conviction, that Ormaas was the rightful heir to Khalindaine.

Life's vagaries did not stop there. Konuskat, the mildest of men, had, by virtue of his respected family and his early conversion, found himself unwillingly promoted: local Master, senior Brother of Western Cythroné, member of the Council of Khalindaine; his Hedch-inspired faith had kept him going, sustaining him through the weariest of meetings and the most tedious of official reports. Why is it that now, he asked himself, just when I need strength most, I have lost it? He felt a panic in his throat. Have I lost my faith?

A knock interrupted his thoughts, but before he had a chance to open the door it was thrown open and a group of burly young men had forced their way in.

'Konuskat? Formerly known as the Disciple?' demanded their leader.

Why formerly? But Konuskat nodded despite this worry.

'You have been charged with entertaining disloyal thoughts. You have been tried in your absence by the Commander in person. I have a warrant here for your execution.'

'Oh!' said Konuskat, formerly the Disciple. 'Oh! I say!'

He was led bewildered to the door and down the stairs, then taken to a quiet square near Wriknek's commandeered inn where the dust was matted with blood.

They prayed for him before they killed him.

The cavalry squadron which had engaged the Talen-vaine-Talen's force rode fiercely, triumphantly, across the Plains, and, as the rest of his troops looked after their horses and their prisoners in the city of tents, the commander carried on to Wriknek's headquarters.

'Captain Kelvaz reporting,' he announced at the door of the inn.

Wriknek was informed and the cavalry officer, carrying his horned helmet under his arm, was led to the Commander's presence.

'Yes, Captain Kelvaz?' asked Wriknek, barely troubling to look up from the papers he was signing.

'Commander. Patrolling the road between Rhalman and Akbar, my squadron encountered a large force of enemy cavalrymen. I have returned with six prisoners.'

'Excellent. But did you lose any men?'

'Sixteen fell on the field of battle, and as many or more of the enemy.'

'But none of our men was captured? That is the important thing.'

'No, sir. And if I tell you that no two men amongst these prisoners wear the same uniform, perhaps that will indicate the size of the force we were up against?'

'It does indeed, Congratulations are doubly in order. We shall have to consider some sort of battle honour for your flag. After all, this was the first fighting of the war. That it was our victory surprises me not at all, but I do feel we should note the precedent. You must report with your standard tomorrow at dawn.'

'Sir.' Kelvaz drew his lower lip into his mouth and played with it before continuing. 'The fighting was very fierce...'

'So!' exclaimed Wriknek impatiently.

'And the standard...' The captain faltered guiltily.

'I see.' it seemed to Kelvaz that it was suddenly very quiet. The Commander was talking to him in a voice so low, and so malicious, that the words were barely audible. 'My congratulations were misplaced. The standard is the heart and soul of the regiment.' The fuse burnt down. Then came the explosion. 'Get out of my sight! You are a disgrace to the uniform you wear! Get away from me! You'll not see active service again. I'm going to send you to the meanest outpost on the furthest coast, where you can dig latrines until you drop. We could break your hands for this, pull your member from you, smash your legs for less. Get away from me! Get out! Get out!'

Kelvaz almost ran. The man's mad, he thought: he's barmy. But Wriknek's insanity had already passed, it seemed. He settled back and continued with his work.

Od and Streetpoet arrived in Ghell. Their journey from Tehkan had taken seven uneventful days; they had grown first familiar then bored with the monotonous scenery of the Plains of Myr. Wheatfields and dykes divided the land; villages and windmills cut into the sky. Ghell came as a welcome change of scenery.

Ghell's city of tents had already taken on a more or less permanent appearance, with smokestacks and wooden porches. Wriknek and his staff had encouraged the soldiers to chop down all the trees in the surrounding area: firewood would soon be scarce, maybe, but they now had an uninterrupted view over many thousand strides. To take full advantage of this a party of soldiers were erecting a tall wooden watch-tower along the southern perimeter.

The outer ring of the camp, almost a fortification, was a noisome trench the soldiers used as their latrine. A party of soldiers was filling in a section of this; another party was strengthening the bridge which would take Od and Streetpoet into Wriknek's domain. The companions had to wait for a while until the bridge was fixed.

'What are we going to do when we get in?' Streetpoet asked, not for the first time.

'Just wait and see,' replied Od.

'That's what you keep saying.'

'I know,' said Od.

Streetpoet had to accept that. It was strange, he reflected, how the initiative seemed to have passed to his friend: the result of their situation in the heart of Brotherhood country, he guessed, where Streetpoet's talent for a song might be fatal but Od's assumed piety was a certain winner.

Od too found it strange to be in charge, but rather enjoyed the novelty. He had never been a leader before. He had never been a liar either. Now he was both, and despite the obvious dangers he found himself rather relishing events. 'Don't worry,' he told the minstrel. 'All we've got to do is get a posting to Akbar and we're laughing.'

'That's encouraging,' said Streetpoet, but he did not sound much encouraged.

'What was your name again?'

'Od the Hedchenlightened.'

'Well, Od Hedchenlightened. You are welcome indeed, Ilynés Chapter, you say you were in? Fine Chapter that. Knew old Hjei well: pity he was killed.'

'Killed?'

'You didn't know? You have been out of touch! Yes, all the senior officers from Ilynés were killed: there was rioting after the proclamation banning alcohol, as I suppose you'd know, and the wine merchants of Ilynés strung them all up. Not a thing anyone could do. Very sad. Of course, quite a lot of junior Brothers from there are here, but you'll not find many with more seniority than you. You'll probably find you're the master of the Chapter.'

'I should rather have a more active role in the war,' said Od. He was moved by pity for his erstwhile companions; he was grateful that there was unlikely to be anyone in Ghell to question his movements between the riots and the present.

Suddenly a messenger had burst into the room and Od's thoughts. 'Begging your pardon, sir, but can you spare anyone? Wriknek wants an interrogation doing. Some captured Royalists.'

'Everyone's engaged at present,' said the senior Brother. 'It'll have to wait.'

'I don't think it can wait, sir.' The man was obviously afraid, noted Od. 'The army's leaning on Wriknek and Wriknek's leaning on me, sir. The officers are talking about doing the interrogation themselves; Wriknek won't hear of it; and all

Ingsvaal's going to break loose unless something happens soon. Can't you do it, sir?'

The senior Brother shook his head. 'Out of the question. I just haven't time. There's new information coming in all the time and I'm the only one manning this desk.'

'Perhaps I could take over here?' suggested Od helpfully.

'I'm afraid not. You just wouldn't know what to refer where. But you could do the interrogation I suppose.'

'Me? But I've only just arrived. I wouldn't know what to ask, what to do with the information, anything.'

'Neither would anyone else,' said the senior Brother sadly. 'Just ask where they've come from, what they're doing, that sort of thing. I'm sure you'll manage.'

'Hurry, sir. I've Wriknek breathing down my neck,' said the messenger.

'Yes, you'd better get on with it. Don't want Wriknek annoyed with us,' said the senior Brother.

Od found himself virtually manhandled out of the room by the grateful messenger. Streetpoet was waiting outside the door and followed Od without asking questions as Od was bustled into the street.

'I'm very grateful, sir,' the messenger was saying. 'You know what Wriknek's like.' Od didn't, nor did he want to learn. He followed the messenger to the ironic inn that served now as Wriknek's headquarters. The streets were full of soldiers and dark dressed members of the Brotherhood. The soldiers lounged; the Brothers dashed frantically around. There were no women or children in the town, Od noted, and the soldiers seemed bored and bad tempered. There seemed no love lost between them and the Brotherhood.

Od was surprised at the variations on the theme of black and yellow that the soldiers had managed to get into their uniforms. The men of Myr, the large city at the north of the Plains, wore blackiron breastplates over a black jerkin, and the only lighter colour was an almost orange plume in their helms. The men of Cythroné who had beaten the Peltyn-Lord's blockade wore, in contrast, jerkins with orange and black hooped sleeves under their breastplates. Quite why black and yellow, or black and orange as it frequently was, had become the Opposition colours no one knew: some said, reasonably, it was because there were no Royalist regiments who wore those colours; others, more cynically, pointed out that the family of Corval Hedchbeloved was the major importer of yellow dyes. What could not be denied was the effectiveness of these uniforms: attractive yet oppressive, they made their wearers look invincible.

The messenger led Od, and Streetpoet, round the inn to the stables. The bright colours of the well-guarded Royalist prisoners were almost a relief after the Opposition troops' sombre shades. Od announced himself and his authority, and a room was found in the stable block where the interrogation could be held. Od sat on the only chair in a distempered, straw-floored room and Streetpoet stood respectfully behind him. The soldiers were shown in one by one. Od asked the questions, Streetpoet made a clumsy note of the answers. 'Name? Regiment?' He was told. 'And the nature of your mission?'

It was with this question that the confusion started. The first man said his regiment was on its way to reinforce the garrison at Akbar, the second that they were on their way to Mornet. The third claimed they were scouting the Rhalman road, and the fourth said they were hunting bandits. It was the fifth who most interested Streetpoet. 'We were looking for a girl believed to be in Northreach,' he said.

Streetpoet leant curiously over Od's bald head. 'What girl?' he demanded. 'Why?'

'How should I know. You'd have to ask Talen about that.'

'Who?'

'Talen-vaine-Talen. Our commander.'

Od looked up at Streetpoet, who shrugged, and then dismissed the man. 'They couldn't be looking for the same person we are,' he said, but he sounded as though he was seeking reassurance.

'Menketh knows. Anything's possible. Consatiné could have sent them himself. I've often wondered why he hadn't searched for her before. I guess he was too busy or too proud.'

'We'd better find out what the last prisoner has to say.'

He too was ushered in, but like the first he said they were reinforcing Akbar.

'We'd better have them all in again,' said Od. 'Goodness knows what my report is going to look like.'

'Make something up,' said Streetpoet. 'It's what most of this lot must have done.'

The soldiers were shown in again. The first two denied all knowledge of the girl, but the third was surprised by the name Lara and his surprise showed.

'Exactly,' pressed Streetpoet. 'And now perhaps you'll tell us *all* you know.'

'And we want the truth this time,' added Od, who did not know the peculiar nature of the Vaine of Talen's force. He was soon to learn.

'Ah, but what is truth?' asked the trooper rhetorically. 'Surely the notion of truth requires an objectivity which is beyond any individual's powers. Indeed, the differences in our situations, as the fact you perceive me as an enemy testifies, are sufficient to create insurmountable ontological barriers between any mutual notion of externally realised truth.'

'What's he talking about?' asked Od.

'Beats me,' admitted Streetpoet.

The soldier had not finished. 'These ontological differences, especially when taken in conjunction with differences of personality, background, and even possibly the formation of our sentient parts, will surely confirm this.'

'I don't want to know about the deformities of your private parts,' misunderstood Streetpoet. 'I want to know about Lara.'

'Why?'

'Because if you don't we'll have your belly slit open and your entrails burnt under your nose.'

'That's a pretty good reason,' admitted the trooper. 'What do you want to know?'

'All you can tell me.'

'All right, though it isn't much. The Gyr Peltyn chose us to find this Lara, arrest her, and return her to Cythroné. There wasn't a war on then, of course; I don't suppose he'd spare the Vaine of Talen today.'

'Who is this Vaine of Talen anyway?'

'Who's he! He's the Peltyn-Lord's second in command. I must say, for intelligence officers you two certainly don't seem too intelligent. Anyway, have you finished? I was involved in a discussion about the correct formula of pi.'

'Don't you mean the correct recipe for pie?'

'Your really are idiots, aren't you. Now, can I go?'

'You still haven't said why you were looking for Lara.'

'I still don't *know* why I was looking for Lara.'

They dismissed him.

'Well, now what?' asked Od.

'I don't know, but I don't like it. Have you written your report?'

'Give me a chance.'

'Well, hurry up with it, take it to Wriknek, and get that posting. We can't afford to waste any more time than we have to here; we must find Lara soon.'

The initiative, Od realised, had passed back to his friend. 'All right. Give me a hand. Which of the stories will help us most?'

'The one about reinforcing Akbar, I reckon. With any luck it'll give us an excuse to go that way. You know, checking up the veracity of what we've learnt, that sort of thing.'

'Fine by me.' And, tongue between his teeth, Od compiled his report in his laborious longhand.

Talen-vaine-Talen and his philosophers reached Akbar and rode in through the houses and warehouses of the west bank, the area known as Baoz. Despite the devastating plague only five years earlier, Akbar seemed as thriving, as boisterous and as licentious as ever. Its peculiar economy was based entirely on providing what others required, however esoteric those requirements might be. Little girls and big girls, little boys and big boys, goats, drugs, whips, bladders, broom handles, all were available for a price in Akbar.

There are philosophies to match almost every practice. Araton practised and preached celibacy; Alapochon advocated free love and freedom. Although, as several of those who tended towards Araton's point of view were arguing as the troop rode into Akbar, 'Free love is the last thing you'll get here. You'll pay through the nose.'

One thing that could be guaranteed, apart from high prices, was that Akbar would remain loyal to Consatiné, or at least, would remain steadfast against the Opposition party. The Brotherhood, and all it stood for, were anathema in Akbar's bazaars and brothels, for obvious reasons; equally, Akbar symbolised for the Brotherhood all that was decadent and corrupt in Khalindaine.

The Vaine of Talen crossed the Bridge of Traders to the Isle of Meaak, in the middle of the river, and approached a large and elaborate modern palace on the square to the south of the castle known as the Stronghold. This palace was the recently completed home of the Vaine of Akbar, a relative of the emperor who, by advertising his non-existent influence to the gullible, had made himself a small fortune. Once his estates had been mortgaged to the hilt, and he had been forced to live many thousand strides from Akbar in a derelict castle where the sanitation was even suspected by the rats. Now, thanks to promises he had never intended to keep and offers he should never have made, he was doing very nicely, and back in his hereditary and spiritual home, Akbar.

Luetah-vaine-Akbar sat in a purple robe at the head of a long and loaded table. In front of him, in chaotic procession, were goblets and platters of silver and gold which held the exquisite delicacies of the empire. The Vaine of Akbar was not eating, however. He slumped morosely forward, his hands cupped beneath his chin, and his dark eyes seemed focused beyond the splendour of his table into some distant future, a future, it appeared from the Vaine's expression, which was far from bright.

Sitting near him, chewing a hunk of meat from the bone, was Krunf, the captain of the Akbar guard. 'I knew it couldn't last,' said the Vaine of Akbar. 'We've been too lucky. I knew it wouldn't last.'

The captain of the guard chased the meat down his throat with a deep draught of wine. A red trickle of wine ran down his chin, where it mingled with the stubble and greasy smears of animal fat. 'Don't say that. It's not over yet.'

'Don't be more stupid than you need, Krunf. It's the end, I'm telling you. I knew things were going too well.'

'You're always looking on the black side,' said Krunf. 'All right. So the Brotherhood have got control of the Plains. Big surprise: they were always strong there anyway. But south of the Khalin is still Royalist, and so is Cythroné.'

'But we're not south of Khalin,' pointed out Luetah. 'And we're not Cythroné.'

'We're not north of the Khalin either though, are we?' asked Krunf with impeccable logic. 'We're on it.'

'Exactly. Strategically we're a perfect target for a Brotherhood attack. And, of all the places in Khalindaine, we're the one they'd enjoy attacking most.'

'Don't worry.'

'Don't worry! Why ever not! Have you any idea what the Brotherhood would do to us if they captured us?'

Krunf furrowed his brow. 'I see what you mean. Yes,' he continued, 'I certainly wouldn't want to be in your shoes.'

'*My* shoes! What about yours?'

'Me, I'm just a common soldier...'

'Common, yes. Soldier, no.'

'...so why should they harm me?'

'Because I'll tell them it was you who first arrested the Ormaas bloke, that's why.'

'You wouldn't.'

The Vaine of Akbar smiled, for the first time since the war had become inevitable. 'Oh yes I would.'

This friendly discussion was brought to an end by the announcement of a visitor. 'A soldier to see you,' said a man servant unceremoniously.

The Vaine and his captain of guard blanched simultaneously. Leutah-vaine-Akbar was first to speak. 'Menketh!' he cried aloud. 'They're here already.'

'They can't be,' complained Krunf. 'I haven't even put a guard on the town gates yet.'

'You haven't what!' The Vaine was livid. His blood pressure, always high, reached danger point, and the veins on his forehead bulged beneath his skin.

Talen-vaine-Talen strolled in. 'Are you the Vaine of Akbar?' he asked.

'He is,' said the Vaine and his captain, speaking together and pointing at one another.

'You can't both be,' said the Talen good humouredly. He identified the rightful Vaine correctly by the splendour of Leutah's robes and saluted him; the magnate made no response.

'It wasn't me who did it,' put in Krunf. 'Ask anyone... anyone except *him*,' he added, pointing at Leutah.

'Did what?' asked Talen politely.

'Oh, don't you know?' said Leutah, seizing his moment. 'This is my captain of guard. He's the man who arrested Ormaas, years ago.'

'No, it wasn't me,' protested Krunf. 'It was someone else who looked like me.' He tried to be ingratiating. 'Honestly, Brother.'

'Brother?' Talen-vaine-Talen looked perplexed, and then laughed. 'I'm not one of the Brotherhood. I'm the Vaine of Talen; I'm on your side.'

'You're not dressed like the Vaine of Anywhere,' pointed out Leutah.

'That was in case we met more Opposition patrols,' said the Vaine of Talen. 'But this isn't an Opposition uniform anyway.'

'Of course it isn't,' said Leutah. He turned indignantly on his captain. 'You should have spotted that straight away, you fool. You're meant to be a soldier.'

'You know I haven't left the palace for five circuits of the moon,' protested Krunf. 'Not since my wife found out about Minski. How should I know what an Opposition uniform looks like?'

'You'll find out soon enough,' said the Vaine of Talen. 'We've seen off one of their patrols but I don't doubt there will be more.'

Leutah had recovered himself. 'And what can we do for you, noble Vaine?'

'My men and I are on an urgent mission to Northreach. We need a boat, probably more than one, to take us there.'

'You mean you're not staying?'

'No.'

'But who's going to defend Akbar?'

'You are, I suppose. You've got a garrison, haven't you?'

'After a fashion. But it's commanded by this idiot.' Leutah indicated Krunf. 'He can't even recognise an Opposition uniform, for Menketh's sake!'

'My wife'd kill me if I went out again,' said Krunf in apology. 'You know what she's like.'

'You see what I mean,' said Leutah. 'Terrified of his wife; what earthly use will he be against the army of the Brotherhood?'

'Be fair,' said Krunf. 'I'd rather face an army than my wife any day.'

Leutah ignored this. 'So you see, you'll have to stay, or
else Akbar will fall to the Opposition and the only bridgehead
north of Toas will be in enemy hands.'

'Why can't you take command?' asked the Talen-vaine-
Talen.

'Me?'

'You're the obvious choice.'

'But I'm a coward!'

'Baoz will almost certainly fall: all the walls seem to have
been pulled down. But Akbar has excellent walls, strong gates,
fine towers, and the Isle of Meaak is in an excellent defensive
position. All you have to do is keep the enemy out.'

'I don't think you appreciate the seriousness of the situation,'
said the Vaine of Akbar. 'People *die* in wars.'

Od presented himself at the office of the Commander. He was
by no means the only one who wanted to see Wriknek. The
corridors of the inn were full of people with urgent reports
to make. Some walked back and forth impatiently; others sat
still and silent, and waited half asleep at the foot of the rough
walls. There seemed no logic about who would be shown into
Wriknek's presence first: an orderly would step out, be assailed
by a hundred protests, and select in an apparently arbitrary way
who the Commander would next see. The system was breaking
down already, many realised; Wriknek would have to delegate
some of the decision-making to others.

Od's wait was not a particularly long one. Wriknek seemed
to be giving precedence to members of the Brotherhood rather
than soldiers, a sensible policy as it was to the Brotherhood
that most important tasks were entrusted; theirs was the only
effective system operating at that time in the Opposition camp.

'Od the Hedchenlightened,' said Od as he entered. He
was getting used to the clipped brusque style of Wriknek's
headquarters. 'Report from troops captured on road between
Rhalman and Akbar.'

'Proceed,' said the Commander.

'Report indicates considerable reinforcements on way to
Akbar. Each trooper captured of a different regiment, but all
cavalry: seem to have been vanguard of larger unit destined
for Akbar.'

'Recommendations?'

'Further information required. Suggest self and limited number of men check report.'

Wriknek dropped out of this curious style of discourse before Od; Od had more to lose. 'We've already got lots of patrols down there. We're going to besiege the place as soon as the army is ready.'

'Oh.'

'Still,' the ex-lawyer confided to the ex-river-pilot, 'it would be nice to have someone down there who really understood the military situation.' Wriknek turned to one of his harassed aides. 'Give this man a travel warrant.' He turned back to Od. 'How many men do you want to take?'

'As few as possible. I have a manservant I can trust with my life.'

'Is he one of the Faithful?'

'Alas, he is soft in the head and could not remember the initiation ceremony, but though he has never actually joined his loyalty to the cause is beyond doubt.'

'Troops?'

'I know how few you can spare. My man and I shall travel alone.'

'Then depart at once. Good day.'

Od, feeling very pleased with his handling of the interview, left the Commander and headed back to his friend.

Streetpoet was not alone. This was no surprise given the cramped conditions of Wriknek's headquarters; the corner of the stables they had used for the interrogation of the prisoners was now being used as the headquarters of Wriknek's nascent private army, his Brothers Militant. Half a dozen of these fanatics were instructing a group of co-opted soldiers about the way they wanted their room. 'Get this straw out of here and find us some that's fresh. We'll want the desk against the window, there, and the big map against the wall.'

Streetpoet stood in the middle of this, neither helping nor heeding. Meanwhile, the Brothers Militant, their black tabards marked with Wriknek's design, were talking all around him.

'The whole problem is spying,' said one. 'It just isn't possible to check the credentials of everyone around here.'

'The solution is stiffer penalties.'

'We're already killing anyone we suspect,' pointed out another.

'We'll just have to kill more of them,' said the first speaker.

'How do we trap them?'

'I don't know. There has to be a way. The Spirit of Hedch is with us.'

Od entered the room. 'Who are you?' demanded one of the Brothers Militant.

'Od the Hedchenlightened, of Ilynés chapter. About to depart by special instruction of Commander Wriknek Faithfollower to investigate the situation in the Akbar region.'

A shudder seemed to run through the Brothers Militant at the very mention of Akbar: a shudder of disgust, a shudder of anticipation.

'You are a brave man to risk the home of the Anti-Ormaas,' said one, whilst another demanded to see Od's travel document.

Od handed it over whilst he replied. 'For the Faith, Brother, no sacrifice is too great.'

'It is a pleasure to hear a man talking like that.'

'Yes indeed,' said a different voice. 'There are too many time-servers even in the ranks of the Brotherhood.'

'True, Brother true. Too many of our number joined for political favour and not out of the fervour of their own hearts.'

'Have you heard of our organisation?' asked the first Brother Militant.

'I don't know,' said Od. 'What's it called?'

'We are the Brothers Militant,' said the man, with pride.

'That's nice,' said Od. 'Come on Streetpoet, we'd better get off.'

'Streetpoet?' asked one of the Brothers. 'The name has a decadent ring.'

One of the Brothers Militant grabbed Streetpoet by the front of his jerkin. 'Are you a spy?'

'Yes,' said Streetpoet.

'Deny it would …' The man had never had so straightforward a response before. 'What did you say?' he asked suspiciously.

'I said I was a spy. But I'm spying for you, not on you. Isn't that right Od?'

'Yes,' said Od, feeling this was safest, although in honesty his nerve had almost failed him when Streetpoet had given the simple affirmative.

'There you are then,' said the minstrel. 'Can we get on our way. Wriknek's orders and all that.'

'Oh yes,' said Streetpoet's inquisitor. 'Of course.'

'But before you go,' said another of the Brothers Militant, 'why don't you two enroll in our organisation? You are obviously men of the right calibre: well, Od Hedchenlightened is anyway. Why don't you join us in our righteous fight to eradicate wickedness from the Opposition forces?'

'I say, that's ever so good of you,' said Streetpoet. 'What do we have to do?'

'Just a simple initiation.'

'Sorry,' said Od. 'We haven't time.'

'I'm sure we have,' said Streetpoet. 'It won't take long, will it lads?'

'No time at all.' The six Brothers Militant bustled their co-opted servants from the mean room and put on their masks. 'Right. First of all we'll say together the prayer of the Faithful. You start, Streetpoet.'

Od heard this with horror. He had known they should leave. Now they would be exposed, discovered, revealed, laid bare, unveiled, disclosed, unmasked and detected. There was a pause, and then Streetpoet's voice rang out, clear and honest. 'Akhran the Golden, Akhran the Avenger, Strengthen Me Your Servant,' and the others had joined in. They went through the long prayer. As far as Od could tell Streetpoet recited it all, although amid seven other voices it was not always easy to be sure. Then the Brothers Militant demanded, in the flat ritualistic voices their organisation adopted at such times, that the friends reveal their stomachs. They did so, and a sharp knife was produced. Od braced himself. He looked with distaste at his own belly, where a stylised initial letter was being drawn in dots of blood.

Whilst the knife-wielder was moving to do the same to Streetpoet's more streamlined stomach, another Brother was rubbing a purple powder into Od's wounds. A black candle was lit within a skull. 'Repeat after us,' said one of the Brothers Militant. 'Death to the Unfaithful.'

'Death to the Unfaithful.'

'May the flesh of the Wicked perish.'

'May the flesh of the Wicked perish.'

'May their Giblets be boiled in Oil.'

'May their Giblets be boiled in Oil.'

'May their Arms and Legs be seized in Spasms.'

'May their Arms and Legs be seized in Spasms.'

'And their Tongues suffused with Boils.'

'And their Tongues suffused with Boils.'

'For this is the Will of our Master.'

'For this is the Will of our Master.'

'Wriknek on Hrakar's Skull.'

'Wriknek on Hrakar's Skull.'

'And Ormaas in the World Beyond.'

'And Ormaas in the World Beyond.'

'I Now Pronounce You.'

'I Now Pronounce...'

'No! You don't say that bit. I Now Pronounce You Brothers of the Militant, Companions of the Commander and part of the Secret Infiltration of Mankind which shall lead to the Supremacy of the Faithful.'

Thank Menketh for that, thought Streetpoet. I thought he was going to marry us.

'Is that it?' asked Od. 'Can we go now?'

'Wait. You need your identity cards.'

The wounds were blown on, which removed the purple powder except where the blood had dissolved it. Printed sheets of paper, barely larger than the wounds, were pressed against them, and marked with the purple and red stain. 'There you are,' said the Brothers Militant to their new colleagues. 'You can go now.'

'Fine. Bye bye.'

Streetpoet and Od left the Brothers. 'Well,' said Streetpoet. 'That might be useful.'

'I don't see how,' grumbled Od. 'You took an awful risk. If they'd discovered you weren't even a Brother they'd have boiled your Tongue in Oil, I can tell you.'

'No,' said Streetpoet, 'you've got it wrong. It's the *Giblets* that are boiled in Oil; the Tongue is suffused with Boils, remember?'

'The principle is much the same,' observed Od dryly. 'How you got away with it I don't know.'

'I've a good memory,' said Streetpoet. 'I'd heard the prayer once or twice, and parodied it sometimes in taverns. A very popular act it was too, I can tell you. But it was hard work not to begin as my parody begins, 'Akbar the Golden, Akbar the Avenger, Harden me your servant...'

'Is that what you used to chant?'

'I'm afraid so. Went down very well: all about Gonorrhoea.'

'You know,' said Od. 'Sometimes you disgust me.'

'You know,' said Leutah-vaine-Akbar. 'Sometimes you disgust me.'

Krunf smiled knowingly. 'But you couldn't do without me, could you?'

'I suppose not.' The Vaine of Akbar looked with distaste at the prone figure at his feet. 'Quite a handsome young man, this Vaine of Talen. I'm sure he'll make a very good defender of Akbar.'

Quickly the two conspirators gathered what they could from the wealth around them and wrapped it into the table cloth. Leutah went over to a heavy strong-box and tried carrying it but he could not lift it. 'Give me a hand,' he ordered.

'I'm already carrying this lot.' Krunf indicated the cloth full of gold candlesticks and silver platters.

'Stick them on top of the box then. Come on. We've got to get away.'

'All right. One, two, three, lift!'

They took the strong-box, topped with the untidily bundled tablecloth, and staggered over Talen's body. As they passed a heavily carved dresser the Vaine of Akbar stopped. 'A moment,' he instructed, and poured himself a swift drink. 'All right,' he said after he had taken a draught. 'On our way.' He put down the cup; Krunf picked it up, drained it, and lifted the strong-box again. They left by a door to the river. 'Good bye,' the Vaine of Akbar called to his unconscious peer. 'Sorry to leave you like this, but you know how it is. When the going gets tough, the tough get going, as I believe the saying of the commoners has it. And therefore we're going. Bye now.' The door shut behind them and Talen was alone.

'How far is it to Akbar?' wondered Od as they walked through the overcrowded town.

'I'm not sure,' said Streetpoet. 'Three days travel, maybe.'

'I thought you knew. You seem to have been everywhere.'

'I have been everywhere,' said Streetpoet. 'But until recently Ghell was *nowhere*.'

'But you have been to Akbar?'

'Yes.'

'So, what's it like? Is it as bad as people say?'

'It is a source of constant wonder to me the way you Brotherhood types express this prurient interest in Akbar. Well, I'll describe it. On this side of the river is Baoz, in the middle is the island of Meaak, and on the east bank is Akbar proper. Akbar has a lot of brothels, it's true, but a lot of merchants too. It's not as diabolical as some people seem to expect, nor as much fun, but I've always done well there.'

They continued through Ghell's streets. 'What we need is transport,' mused Streetpoet. 'I'm getting tired of walking.'

'What do you mean. We haven't been walking long. We haven't even left Ghell.'

'Haven't been walking long! I've been walking all my life!'

They passed a livery stables. 'Let's see what Wriknek's orders are worth,' said Streetpoet, and called out to a groom. 'Excuse me! Can we requisition a couple of horses?'

'These mounts is spoken for. Get lost.'

'We have orders from Wriknek in person.'

'Nothing to do with me.'

'Well, look at them at least.'

'I can't read.'

'Then find someone who can.'

Grumbling, the groom went in search of the stable-master, whose pleasant face was troubled by too much work. 'Just show these orders of yours to me then. But I warn you, these horses are for the cavalry. You'll not get one here.'

Od handed over the paper bearing Wriknek's signature.

'This is just a travel warrant,' said the stable-master. 'It doesn't say anything about requisitioning horses. Sorry lads, you're out of luck.' Then his face changed. 'Oh.' He turned on the groom. 'You didn't tell me about this!'

'About what?'

The stable-master waved the paper under the groom's nose. With it, disregarded by Od, was the membership certificate of the Brothers Militant, overprinted with a rough and bloody initial. The groom blanched. 'They didn't say.'

'You didn't ask, you mean.'

'I'm sorry, sir.'

'Don't apologise to me,' said the stable-master. 'Apologise to these gentlemen.' He turned to Streetpoet and Od. 'I'm sorry about this. The man's a fool. We'll get you a couple of horses at once.'

Streetpoet and Od exchanged a puzzled look and followed the groom. Behind them came the stable-master, still apologising. Two fine horses were found.

'Well, well, well,' said Od as they rode away. 'There's more to this Brothers Militant bit than I'd supposed.'

They crossed the latrine trench that marked the edge of the camp, passed the still unfinished watch-tower, the trampled fields that served as a training ground and the bare stumps of trees turned now to firewood, and set out across the fertile Plains. The day was cold but neutral, as though the weather were too lazy to commit itself. The horses were strong and fast. 'We'll find somewhere to spend the night,' said Streetpoet. 'With mounts like this we could be in Akbar tomorrow.'

The Vaine of Talen was having trouble with his head. When he shook it the top came off. When he lay still his brain still revolved. With his eyes shut he saw patterns of coloured light. They were there when his eyes were open too.

He struggled to a sitting position. The last thing he could remember was talking to the Vaine of Akbar: after that, nothing. What had happened? Had he been taken ill? He felt his head, found a lump, and knew he had been coshed. He tried to stand, but for some reason had been fitted with someone else's legs while he was unconscious: his own legs, he recalled, had been strong and firm, but these were rubbery and useless. Never mind. He struggled to the door, opened it, and called out as loudly as he could. The cry was not loud, as it happened, but this did not matter. It served his purpose. First one of his troopers and then, the alarm raised, several came running to his assistance.

The Vaine of Akbar sat in the stern of his small boat and his captain of the guard rowed. There are, of course, two ways of pronouncing the word r-o-w-e-d, and both would be appropriate, for as he pulled the boat through the water he argued furiously about their destination.

'We can't row all the way to Cythroné.'

'Where do *you* suggest we go? Up the river to Mornet?' replied the Vaine. 'That's fine by me if you're prepared to do the rowing.'

'I don't mean going to Mornet.'

'Then where else is there?'

'We could pull into a nearby village and lie low till the war ends.'

'A nearby village!' Leutah was incredulous. 'This is where the war is going to be fought, you fool.' Despite the urgency with which he spoke the Vaine of Akbar's bulk reclined comfortably enough in the back of the boat. 'We don't want to get caught up in that We've got money, but that can't buy off soldiers: they take lives, not bribes. At least in Cythroné the civilised standards of bribery and corruption still prevail, Menketh be praised.'

'I still think we could find somewhere safe that's nearer.'

'And I don't, so get rowing.'

Scowling, facing his master, the captain of the guard heaved another clumsy stroke through the water. Behind him, yet looking him in the eye, the Vaine of Akbar smiled pleasantly. 'Just think of all the good it's doing you.'

Krunf thought about this, and caught a crab with his oars, splashing water over Leutah. Got you, you swine, thought the captain of the guard, though his mouth was apologising profusely.

The Vaine of Talen was instructed to rest, an instruction which chafed his nature. While he fretted on the bed which had once been Leutah's, a gigantic affair with an unaccountable mirror hanging over it – 'Who wants to see himself sleep?' he asked himself – a report told him that his erstwhile host had been seen in a small boat heading downstream, leaving the city and leaving Talen a quandary. Should he stay to defend Akbar or continue with his mission? He dictated a message to the Gros of Peltyn, advising his commander of the situation, and had it dispatched in the next boat downstream, then reviewed the options, only to discover he had none. Already the word had got about that a party of troops had arrived to defend the town, and he was besieged by grateful petitioners, for the people of Akbar were under no illusions about what would happen to their livelihoods, and perhaps even their lives, should the Opposition capture them.

Wriknek and the Vaine of Talen had little in common. One was a megalomaniac lawyer, the other a gallant knight. One was elderly, hunched and dour, the other handsome and young. But that night as they slept, both were aware of a pressure in their heads, a pressure intensified by worries that, in that late-at-night way worries have, seemed insurmountable.

Chapter 6

The Siege of Akbar

The following day began brightly. The clouds were broken, and a warm breeze came off the Rift. The trooper, Ossius, was stationed in the Tower of Asbik, at the northernmost point both of the Stronghold and the Isle of Meaak. With him was a contingent of what was left of Krunf's soldiers, supplemented by a number of private guards, virtually gangsters, who had been supplied by the bosses of the various brothels and drinking clubs for which the town was famous. Of the two groups, Ossius had no doubts that the more responsible and disciplined was the latter.

He looked down at the river, in spate now as the winter snows of Northreach melted. The water was brown and turbulent, and as Ossius watched it part round the out-thrust base of the tower he got the curious sensation that he was moving upstream. So potent was this feeling that he had to look away, look at the static towns on the shore, Baoz to the west and Akbar to the east, to remind himself that he was stationary.

The tower was tall, though not as tall as the neighbouring keep at the centre of the Stronghold, and from it he could see over the towns to the contrasting landscapes beyond. East was the Plain of Myr, dotted with small villages, cut through with canals and gently curving roads that led, uninterrupted, into the streets of Baoz. West, Akbar was divided and protected from the drifting sands of the Khalinrift by high walls, and beyond the walls was the desert. Ossius had never seen the Rift before, and watched with fascination the wind-raised wraithes of sand that danced there in the face of the sun, until his attention was diverted by the sound of trumpets in the courtyard below. He turned round and looked down, to see his commander, Talen-vaine-Talen, arriving. 'That your boss?' asked one of the gangster-guards.

'Yes,' said Ossius, not without pride, for Talen had recovered his armour from his men's baggage and was looking his most splendid.

'That's mighty peculiar,' continued the other. 'It looks like he's moving his headquarters into the Stronghold. I thought he'd be staying in Leutah's palace, him being a nobleman.'

'He's got more sense,' said Ossius. 'He may be a nobleman, but he's a soldier first.'

The man changed the subject. 'You reckon the Brotherhood army will attack then?'

'I don't know. I wouldn't be surprised if they did. Akbar Bridge is worth capturing for them: they could attack Cythroné from two sides if they could cross the Khalin, and I guess that if they could capture Cythroné that would be the end of the war.'

'We'll just have to keep the miserable swine out then, won't we,' said the gangster. The prospect of fighting did not worry him: he fought daily on his master's behalf in the feuds that characterised Akbar's twilight world. 'My boss, old Prothal One-Eye, ain't one to surrender.'

'I would have thought the decision rested more with *my* boss,' observed Ossius.

'Don't you believe it. It's the gangs that run Akbar, and it'll be up to the gang leaders to decide what happens. They had a meeting last night and agreed to help your Talen bloke, which is why I'm here and my mates. But we'd keep on fighting even if you lot left. Each gang boss's house is a fortress: you can see the towers in Akbar over there. They'll not give in to no Brotherhood in a hurry.'

The towers were indeed prominent, sharply shadowed by the low sun. 'It'll be a long war,' mused Ossius sadly.

'Doesn't have to be,' said his companion. 'If your emperor could get himself sorted out, it'd all be over soon. Why doesn't he perform the Rite of Endyear? That'd take the wind from the Brotherhood's sails.'

But to that Ossius had no answer.

That night Streetpoet and Od had stayed at Hasarl, which is nearer to Ghell than Akbar. The inn had been full, but by proclaiming their membership of the Brothers Militant they had managed to persuade the innkeeper to find them a couple of beds: the innkeeper had been so persuaded, in fact, that he had given them his own rooms. The friends had an early night: there is little to do in a tavern which serves no drink.

'It's very useful, this Brothers Militant lark,' said Streetpoet as they got up the following morning. 'It's amazing what you can get with a bit of cheek. It was easy enough to get into, at any rate.'

Od dressing, looked at the scar on his belly. 'Easier to get into than out of, I shouldn't wonder. I'd never even heard of them, but they've been making an unpleasant name for themselves round hereabouts, judging from the way we're treated. We'll be in trouble if the Royalists capture us, I shouldn't wonder.'

'We'll just have to make sure they don't.'

'I thought the idea was to rejoin them as soon as possible.'

'That doesn't mean we have to flash our tummies at all and sundry,' Streetpoet pointed out.

'They'll be suspicious of anyone trying to get into Akbar from the Plains,' said Od.

'Well, we'll just have to find a way of disarming their suspicion,' said Streetpoet. 'Come on. I want to get there by nightfall.'

They paid for their lodgings and left. The bright morning made travelling a pleasure and, though they were of the wrong social class to be particularly accomplished horsemen, they both knew enough to stay on their mounts and enjoy it. Od's experience as a messenger had taught him that a steady pace was better than bursts of speed; Streetpoet's bottom, softened by a long absence from the saddle, agreed wholeheartedly.

They continued south-east, riding almost directly into a rising sun haloed behind light clouds. The road they followed was an important one, linking Akbar and Myr, but traffic in those troubled early days of the war, before the armies had been fully mobilised, was slight. They passed few travellers.

Talen, feeling much recovered, was making a tour of the defences. He realised early that they could not keep the Opposition from Baoz: there were no walls there, and innumerable roads leading in. He wondered how much time he had before the expected attack came. His best plan, he was sure, was to evacuate Baoz entirely and burn the two bridges connecting the township to the island, but he was reluctant to destroy the bridges until necessary in case they were needed for a Royalist counter-attack. Nor was he sure whether Akbar would accommodate the citizens of Baoz: he had already experienced something of the clannishness of the crime-barons of Akbar when late the previous night they had called, offering their equivocal support; despite his virtuous proclamations of loyalty, their spokesman, a weathered old man with a bejewelled eye-patch, had made it quite clear that such support was to be on their terms, not Talen's. Talen found them rather unsavoury allies.

Wriknek, in his own headquarters, also had reservations about his allies. Like Talen, he was forced to rely on those he considered unreliable, which in Wriknek's case meant pretty well everyone apart from himself. The war council he was holding only confirmed that view.

The officers of the Opposition army had apparently met in caucus before the main council, and, rationally but forcefully, were demanding the appointment of a general to lead the army. At the same time, and from Wriknek's point of view even more worrying, was the attitude of many of the senior Brotherhood who, having realised that their opinions were actually of less value in Wriknek's dictatorship than they had been on the old Council of Khalindaine, seemed determined to question the Commander's every decision. For this the senior Brothers could hardly be blamed: after the death of Konuskat the Disciple none of them felt safe.

'It is imperative,' said a young Captain of the Horse, Celeman of Baalbrecht, 'that a general is appointed. The army must be mobilised without delay: despite desertions to our ranks, the Royalist armies are in better shape; their command structures are organised, their officers appointed. We must not lose the initiative.' His fellow soldiers nodded in agreement.

'Gentlemen,' replied Wriknek. 'Gentlemen.' He paused. His face was drained of colour by long hours of work, and his eyes felt full of grit. He rubbed them. 'I have been studying the situation with great care, and with the help of many intelligence reports from sympathetic sources within that Royalist command structure my young friend Celeman so commends, I believe I have a true picture of the situation.' There was a map behind him, reasonably accurate for the time, showing the Plains of Myr and the region of Cythroné. With a quill Wriknek pointed to places as he listed them. 'The bulk of the decadent Royalist army is assembling at Verdre, the Royal palace east of Cythroné, under the personal command of the Gros of Peltyn, but will not, I suspect, stray far from there. The Peltyn-Lord dares not trust the mood of the citizens of Cythroné, for which, given the untenable and unconstitutional nature of his régime, he cannot be blamed. This has two effects for us. On one hand, it gives us a far greater opportunity to manoeuvre than his; on the other, it means that, for the time being, an all-out attack on Cythroné, with the intention of finishing both the so-called emperor and the war, would be a mistake. We must consolidate our position first, and obviously our first target should be the tainted town of the anti-Ormaas known as Akbar.' The quill stabbed at the place on the map. 'This would give us control of the Khalin between Cythroné and Mornet, and cut Northreach off from the capital. It would also give us a bridgehead to the south, and I am sure there are many of the Faithful living there who would flock to our banners were they given the opportunity.'

It all made sense. Whilst a frontal attack on Cythroné might prove fatal, marching into Royalist territory via Akbar could well attract support from discontented southerners. There were many displaced people on either side of the Khalin who would prefer to be on the other side, but who as things stood kept quiet.

'Excuse me, Commander,' said a distinguished and ambitious officer, Kalomn of Grav. 'The plan seems to me sensible in all respects, but I wonder how large a force you are considering sending to Akbar?'

'As many as it takes,' said Wriknek. His grasp of strategy was better than his understanding of tactics, and he really had no idea.

'My own feeling,' said Kalomn, who was nobody's fool, 'is that three divisions of infantry, a brigade of cavalry, and a regiment of engineers would be the minimum required, though the Commander of course may have other ideas.'

'No, no,' said Wriknek. 'That accords well with my own judgement. How many brigades of cavalry did you suggest?'

'One, Commander.'

'I see. That's fine. And how many engineer regiments?'

'Again one, Commander.'

'Only one? Personally I feel two would be better.'

'I defer to your opinion, Commander.'

'Good. Then that is settled. This army which we shall call the Army of the East, shall set out at once to crush the infernal enemy in Akbar.'

'Commander?'

This time it was Prajik Ormaaslover who was speaking. Wriknek looked at him with distaste. 'Yes?'

'Commander, your plans seem well devised to secure gains to the south, but what of the north? Since the end of the Ingsvall, brought about by the ghost of Ormaas on the field of Klau, the Agaskan pose less of a threat on the northernmost frontiers of Khalindaine. Northreach is Royalist. Some defence is needed in the north, based at Myr.'

'I am glad you raised this,' said Wriknek, lying. 'And I believe that some time ago you suggested a man who could command in the north.'

'Gryfag, Commander. My cousin.'

'Exactly.' Wriknek thought on his feet. Prajik Ormaaslover was no Konuskat, to be disposed of at will, but a fanatical ally and a member of the powerful Taramos family which included Corval the Hedchbeloved. Wriknek had no desire to advance the fortunes of that already powerful family further, but neither did he want to alienate them. 'Gryfag,' he repeated. 'Your cousin. An ideal choice.' After all, Wriknek concluded to himself, Myr is a long way from events of importance; this Gryfag will have little influence there.

'We understand, of course, that supreme command will rest with you, Commander,' interrupted Celeman, 'but obviously the nature of your responsibility will prevent you travelling with the Army of the East. Whilst appointments are being made, perhaps the Commander would care to tell us whom he has chosen to lead the attack on Akbar?'

'Certainly, certainly. I have given this matter much thought,' he said, which was true, 'and am confident in my decision,' he added, which wasn't. 'The attack on Akbar will be led by Kalomn of Grav. Later I shall also be appointing the General of the Army of the West, who will have the task of taking Cythroné itself.'

The appointment was greeted with general satisfaction, and though one or two of the soldiers believed they could have done the job themselves and were less than delighted, there was still the tempting prize of the Generalship of the West to be won. 'And now,' finished the Commander, 'I am sure you have work to do. If the new General of the East will remain here, please, the rest may go.'

The pains in Streetpoet's buttocks seemed to have eased; now it was his back that was aching. As the second day of their journey ended they wondered whether to press on into the night and reach Baoz, or to rest at the first inn they came to, but by the time they finally found an inn, they had decided they would have to rest. They dismounted, tied up their horses, and entered the inn. This time the papers that showed them to be members of the Brothers Militant were greeted with blank stares, because the influence of that notorious body had not yet reached as far from Ghell as this, but it did not matter; they were early in the evening and rooms were still vacant. Indeed, they were soon to consider themselves fortunate that their membership of Wriknek's élite force had gone unrecognised, for this village was still loyal to Consatiné.

Kalomn of Grav, the General of the East, wasted no time. Before nightfall he had mustered the officers who were to be under his command, introduced himself to those who did not know him, and given orders for the march to Akbar to begin as soon as possible. He had already decided, in consultation with Wriknek, that the troops would take no provisions but would forage along the way, so one worry was gone. The only question now was one of time: how soon could they be under way. Two cavalry regiments were available for immediate use, and he gave these orders to set out at first light, to scout the countryside, and to check there was to be no opposition before the gates of Akbar itself. The rest of his army, however, would take at least two days to assemble. The officers, grateful to have something to do, and proud to be involved in the first campaign of the war, went back to their tents and began to organise their men. Kalomn, left alone, took a single draught from the smuggled hip flask he and so many of the Opposition officers sported, and toasted the Opposition's health.

The inn was quiet. 'No drink served, I suppose?' said Streetpoet to the landlord, and his question was greeted with a wink.

'You're a likely looking lad,' a barmaid told him. 'What'll you be drinking?'

'You mean I *can* have a drink? I thought the Plains were all dry. That's one of the reasons me and my friend have been trying to get to Akbar.'

'Well, you're close enough to Akbar for it to make no odds,' said the barmaid. 'So what's your tipple?'

'Porter, please,' Streetpoet looked at Od. 'For *two*,' he added significantly.

'Right you are.'

'You know I don't drink alcohol,' said Od quietly after the girl had gone.

'You do tonight. This place is obviously Royalist, or at least, it isn't on the side of the Brotherhood. If everyone and their great-aunt is right, and the Opposition is going to attack Akbar, I'll lay odds that the people from round here are going to flee into the town. What better way of getting into Akbar than to arrive with a lot of loyal refugees from a loyal village, fleeing the curse of the Brotherhood?'

'I suppose you're right. But I don't like heavy drink, never have.'

'You just sit here and sip it. I'm going to ingratiate myself with the natives.'

'Sleep with the barmaid, you mean,' said Od cynically.

'Sing her a song,' corrected Streetpoet. 'To establish my credentials as a right-thinking man and not some boring member of the killjoy Brotherhood.'

Other people were slipping into the tavern checking everything was all right as they entered and then relaxing as they saw no cause for concern. Soon the place was quite busy. Streetpoet stood with a group of drinkers by the fire; Od supped his porter unhappily in a corner, and wondered how anyone could ever enjoy this foul stuff.

Suddenly his thoughts were broken by Streetpoet's strong voice rising in song.

> Have you heard the tale of Tinfantoe
> Who lived in Akbar long ago?

> Have you heard of Tinfan and his wife?
> How he cut her throat with a carving knife?

His audence had indeed heard the tale of Tinfantoe. Od might not have recognised the song but many others in the room did, and by the time Streetpoet had finished the first verse many had joined in; by the time the second verse was over Od's seemed the only voice in the room that was silent.

Despite its cheerful tune the song seemed pretty macabre to Od. This Tinfantoe, he learnt, had been cuckolded by his wife who, if Od had heard aright, had slept with fourteen bakers, three tailors, seven scribes, a physician, a musician, a mortician, and a regiment of light infantry, before being murdered by her outraged husband. The only moral of this depressing tale seemed to be in the final verse.

> If you want your wife to stay with you
> This is what you ought to do:
> Nail her ankles to the floor
> And find yourself a willing whore.

There were times when Od felt a distinct nostalgia for his innocent Brotherhood days.

Still, he could hardly concern himself with ethics, he decided. The song had produced the desired effect and Streetpoet was the toast of the inn.

Streetpoet capitalised on his success by telling a couple of tall, rude stories. The first was about an impotent carpenter who fashioned himself something obscene out of wood, and whose wife kept complaining of splinters. The second – and hearing it Od winced, for despite appearances to the contrary this was meant to be Opposition territory – was about two members of the Brotherhood in a brothel. But the stories went down famously and Streetpoet's success was assured.

If the drinkers wondered about their new friend's quiet, bald companion they did not probe. Od sat silent in his chair, sipping his porter as slowly as he could, while Streetpoet's songs, fitting the mood of his audience, grew increasingly scurrilous and lewd. He finished the tankard with relief, only to find it refilled before he could protest, and after his second porter Od found he was listening to the songs with something like interest: and why not, he asked himself; this is an education. He was even wondering about joining in the choruses by the time he had finished the third tankard, but he must have fallen asleep instead, for the next thing he knew he was being helped upstairs by Streetpoet and the barmaid. 'Goodnight, old pal,' said the minstrel, leaving Od alone. Od wondered briefly where he was and why, then went to sleep.

The following morning Od awoke to find Streetpoet at the foot of his bed making bugle fanfares through pursed lips.

'What is it?' Od asked irritably.

'Morning.'

'Tell it to go away.'

'It isn't just any morning,' said Streetpoet. 'It's the morning we go to Akbar.'

'Why?' Od was suddenly alert. 'What's happened?'

'So far, nothing. But the rumour has it that the Opposition army will be here tomorrow, and the villagers are all for fleeing today.'

'That's reasonable. But will they take us with them?'

'Oh yes. And I've found someone to buy the horses. He didn't pay what they were worth, but every little counts and they didn't cost us anything. And I've discovered something strange. You remember that bloke Talen-vaine-Talen, the commander of the soldiers we interviewed? It seems he's taken over the garrison at Akbar, which suggests maybe they *weren't* looking for Lara after all and that your report about them reinforcing the defence might have been right.'

'That is peculiar,' agreed Od. 'You seem to have done well last night. I'm sorry I accused you of just wanting to sleep with the barmaid.'

'Oh, I did that as well,' said Streetpoet. He spoke lightly, but refused to meet Od's eye.

Od dressed and they walked outside. It was another bright day, warmed by the wind of Khalinrift. The village street was full of people and their possessions: the villagers obviously took the Opposition threat seriously. Carts and packhorses were laden, and when the beasts of burden were fully loaded it was the turn of the wives and children. In comic procession the village moved, and in the middle of the procession, helping out, were Streetpoet and Od.

Two full regiments of cavalry, each four hundred men strong, rode from Ghell's tent-city and traced the steps of Streetpoet and Od along the road to Akbar. The men were dressed for campaigning. They carried little food, of course, but plenty of clothes and other possessions, strapped in canvas bags and slung over their saddle-cloths. The first regiment was of demi-lancers, wearing leather jerkins piped with orange and carrying long-pennoned lances. The second regiment was of light cavalry, from Cxuma, a town at the foot of the Rhav mountains. These men were less uniform in appearance: though the Opposition colours still predominated they wore a great variety of loose fitting outfits, with cloaks and turbans of muslin and saddle-cloths decorated in many exotic ways. They also rode in a different style, eschewing the conventional upright stance of Khalindaine in favour of the high-stirruped fashion of the Rhav, with their bodies bent low over the reins. They were ideal troops for skirmishing against infantry: their style of riding was exactly suited to cutting swathing blows through men on foot, and their ferocity was legendary; so was the missionary activity of one Ghalvré Believer, who had converted these fiercely independent tribesmen to Hedchism only two years previously, and whose fanaticism seemed to have infected them. Between them, these two regiments were to scout the area west of Akbar, harry any opposition they encountered, and prepare the way for the infantry and siege weapons which were following. Leading them was a small group: Archen of Semdheln, the cavalry commander, and his aides; the standards of the two regiments, the demi-lancers' flag, emblazoned with the familiar injunction to Remember the Diehards across an orange-gold cross on a background of scarlet and white, and the traditional flag of Cxuma, showing a stylised mountain range on a white background; the musicians, sixteen trumpeters of the demi-lancer regiment, their sleeves rich with orange chevrons, and twelve from the Cxuma regiment, wearing gorgeous crimsons and yellows; and the farriers, bearded, with their axes hooded in leather cases.

Much faster than Streetpoet and Od, they hurried towards Akbar. They were full of the desire for glory, and full of the strength of their faith.

'We're here,' said Od. 'Now what?'

'We'll have to get a boat upstream,' replied the minstrel.

'Will they still be sailing?'

'I should think so. It takes more than a piddling little war to stop the Rivermasters earning their keep. They're a proud lot, you know. And anyway, I'd have thought the Gros of Peltyn would want to keep contact with Mornet.'

It became academic. Two of Talen's soldiers and two of the gangster-guards were sorting through the newcomers and picking out any who were remotely able-bodied. Streetpoet was bustled in one direction, Od in another. 'Congratulations, fellow,' said the leader of the press-gang. 'You're in the army.'

'Oh, good,' said Streetpoet. 'What fun.'

He was led across the Bridge of Traders, which joins the wharfs of Baoz to the southern part of Meaak. The bridge was packed with more refugees, evacuated from vulnerable Baoz with their possessions, and compounded by the new immigrants from the outlying villages. Talen's makeshift army tried to organise the influx, but with little success. Twice Streetpoet heard the truncated scream as someone was pushed into the swollen waters of the Khalin.

At the far side the able-bodied ones, who had been mixed with the crowd in the crush, were again identified, and led along the quay to Zantoroch Square, the open area between the Stronghold and Leutah's palace. Here they were given swords and spears, many of which had been confiscated from a cargo of weapons ordered from Perain by Wriknek's commissariat. Across the crowded square Streetpoet saw a bald head which might have been Od's, but before he could be sure he was being led away again, with a party of fellow conscripts, back to Baoz. This time they crossed by the Akbar Bridge, which led straight into the middle of Baoz, and which Talen was sensibly keeping free of refugees. Streetpoet's improvised company was headed by one of Talen's professional soldiers, a trooper in the pale blue of the Vaine of Talen's own regiment. They were taken south through the township to a deserted house on the Rhalman Road and rapidly given their instructions.

'Right lads,' said the trooper. 'You know why you're here. We've all heard the rumours about the Brotherhood heading this way with an army, and you lot have been specially selected to stop them. You haven't been given any choice because there wasn't any choice to give, but if you value your freedom you'll fight with a will, and if you value your life you'll not desert because we're putting to death anyone who tries. You – and me – are part of the force that's going to try to defend this road, to stop the enemy advancing straight up to the Bridge of Traders which is where the road leads. It'll be a hard fight, there's no doubt of it, and we can't be expected to win, so what we've got to do is slow the Opposition down and then get back across the bridge, where we should be safe.'

A tremulous hand was raised amongst the assembled men. 'We haven't any armour. We'll be killed.'

'From what we've all heard about the Brotherhood we'll be killed anyway if we're captured,' said the trooper, falling back on a piece of unjustified gossip brought out in every war. 'How'd you rather die, with a sword in your hand or a rope round your neck?'

'How soon are the Brotherhood expected?' asked another.

'I can't tell you. Any more questions? Right, I'll be off.'

There were many more questions, but it was too late.

Od had been stationed further north, again at the edge of the township, and found himself billeted in a rather charming merchant's house on the Myrian Road. The instructions he received were similar, though delivered in the harsher accent of one of the Akbar soldiery. At midday a woman came round with a wheelbarrow laden with cheap food, which was distributed among the conscripts. Od and his new companions gnawed at the bones of a particularly athletic chicken, and compared regrets. After lunch he wanted to go for a walk, to see if he could find Streetpoet, but was refused permission to leave the house, so he went into the courtyard, along with many others, and sat there until the shadows came and it was too cold. In the evening the whores came round, smuggled across the Khalin from Akbar to service the new army. Od was disgusted, but secretly rather pleased. Even in wartime Akbar was living up to its reputation.

A day passed, and another. For a while the defenders hoped it was all a false alarm, some kind of silly mistake, and then the two Opposition cavalry regiments arrived, riding round the township just beyond bowshot and planting their tents with complete unconcern almost on the edge of the buildings.

Talen was insulted by this, and wanted to gather his cavalrymen together and attack these invaders, but knew in his heart that the enemy was too strong and that he needed his men alive to police the conscripted militia. So the waiting continued, more tense than ever.

Not that Talen wasted his time. He found engineers in the town, and used them to replace the stone central arches of both bridges with wood. These wooden bridges could be more easily destroyed if necessary, and the engineers were posted, with bottles of that curious Northreach speciality know as fire spell, ready to bring the bridges down.

On the fourth day the Opposition's infantry arrived, and leading them was Kalomn of Grav, dressed not in uniform but in the clothes of a fashionable civilian: the Brotherhood's sombre tastes did not always apply to the soldiers who fought alongside them, and Kalomn was in fact something of a dandy. But he was also a good soldier, who had fought in the Agaskan campaign in the north before resigning his commission over a matter of honour and retiring to the life of a country gentleman, and the Brotherhood had been pleased when, like many of the gentry of the Plains, Kalomn had rallied to their flag. His first task was to arrange the disposition of his troops, which he did with a parade-ground precision that infuriated the watching defenders, and then, when at last he was satisfied, he rode slowly, almost sedately, round Baoz, inspecting it, before ordering his trumpeters to blow a fanfare at the mouth of the Myrian Road. Kalomn of Grav wanted to parley.

Talen had been watching his enemy from the upper windows of a house on the edge of the township. 'I suppose I'd better see what he wants,' he remarked and, with a small retinue of his troops, he rode out beneath the flag of truce.

The two men had never met, though each had heard of the other. They exchanged the usual pleasantries men use to disguise the horrors of war, and as they did so each weighed the other up. Kalomn saw a handsome well-built man, the sort who would make an excellent second-in-command but was surely too young for the position he now held; Talen saw a dignified, proud soldier, a man it would be a privilege to follow. Kalomn offered Talen the predictable terms – put down your arms, surrender the town and the bridges intact, and you will be allowed to return to Cythroné –

and Talen, just as predictably, said no. But though they parted
with a sense of mutual respect, and almost regret, as soon as
each was safe behind his lines, battle began.

Suddenly the drums beat out a tattoo. Od found himself pushed
out onto the Myrian Road along with his new companions, and
shoved into a sort of line behind a small phalanx of pikes. He
had barely drawn his sword before the first of the enemy were
upon them. The Rhav cavalry, small targets hunched over their
horses, charged down the road and engaged the pikes, ducking
the fierce points and laying into the untrained and ineffectual
defenders. With mayhem all around him Od tried to fend off a
swinging blade. Shields had been out of fashion, except in
Northreach, for many years now: as he parried the blow with his
sword, Od had time to wonder just why. Then the cavalryman
had passed beyond him, and another was approaching. To his
left Od saw one of his comrades fall, slashed through the skull,
and then heard the instruction to retreat though whether an
officer or a panicking conscript had given it was uncertain.
What was certain, however, was that the conscripts needed no
second bidding. Almost as a man those who could turned and
ran, many dropping their weapons as they fled, and raced for
the bridge. Akbar's first line of defence had barely troubled
the enemy at all.

The second line of defence was at the bridgehead. Talen
himself had ridden there, to supervise the placing of the
fire-charges if they were to prove necessary and to help
the defence of the bridge, and with him was a formidable
body of Akbar gangsters. Suddenly the conscripts were on
them, running in panic as the horsemen picked them off, and
without mercy the gangster-guards closed ranks. Some of
the conscripts were impaled on the swords of their own side,
others made for side-streets. The majority were simply cut
down. Four hundred men died on the rout along the Myrian
Road. The Akbar irregulars, the gangland militia, watched
without emotion; Talen, on his horse behind the lines, also
watched, but he was consumed with guilt. He had ordered the
conscription and stationed the conscripts: he had condemned
them to death.

The Rhav cavalry re-formed. This was no place for complicated manoeuvres, but that was not the Rhav style anyway.

They simply gathered, then charged, and the white flag which portrayed their native mountains was flecked and splashed with blood.

Od was amongst the conscripts who had diverted down side-streets. There was no time to wonder whether he was guilty of cowardice, nor any point in asking the question. The whole troop had broken and individual endeavour counts for nothing in that situation. Against infantry they might have stood their ground, but not against the Rhav tribesmen. Talen had made an error of judgement and his troops had paid for it dearly.

There was a pause, a hiatus, and a sense of curious security down that side-street. Od was not alone. Perhaps ten others had accompanied him, and all of them were citizens of Akbar or Baoz. 'We'll not make it to Akbar Bridge,' they told one another. 'Our only chance is to get down to the Bridge of Traders.'

Stealthily they crept through the deserted streets, panicking at every sound they heard, but they need not have worried. The Rhav cavalrymen were fighting the gangster-guards, and the Opposition infantry, who were mopping up after the carnage, had not even cleared the outskirts. 'This way,' said one of Od's comrades, and they went through narrow alleys and beneath high arches, twisting left and then right as though in a maze.

The Rhalman Road came as a surprise to Od, not least because they did not arrive onto it but above it, on a bridge. Beneath were lines of their fellow conscripts and behind were the wharfs, the heavily guarded Bridge of Traders and the Khalin, but it was the scene ahead which held their attention. Lacking cavalry – and cursing himself for not bringing more; he had not anticipated this sort of fighting – Kalomn had been forced to commit his infantry here, and the conscripts were doing much better. Line after line of them blocked the streets; these men actually seemed to be enjoying the fighting. They were being pushed slowly back, as was inevitable when faced with fully equipped soldiers, but they did not give ground easily and some had even organised themselves into guerilla groups, slipping up side-streets and harrying their enemy's flanks. Some of those with Od wanted to join the fighting in the street below, others to get to the bridge which, despite the

guards, seemed to offer the best chance of escape. Od was
with those who wanted to stay and fight. He felt he had run
far enough for one day and so made his way to street level
down a twisting stair.

At this time, on the Myrian Road, things were taking
a different twist. The very success of the Rhav horsemen
had caused them problems for they were isolated from their
companions, and though Talen did not have the strength to
inflict heavy damage on them, their isolation offered him an
opportunity he was quick to grasp. 'Sound the retreat,' he
told his trumpeters, and the mournful thrice-repeated notes
were sounded. At the same time, mindful of the fact that few
of his troops were professionals, Talen rode among his men.
'Fall back in good order!' he yelled. 'Fall back in good order!'
Slowly the troops pulled back, crossing the bridge, and behind
them came the Rhav.

Secure on the other side, Talen gave the order his engineers
had been expecting, 'Bring down the bridge.' The fire-spell
bottles, suspended by an arrangement of lines from poles
above the wooden part of the bridge, were dropped, and
where they smashed flames quickly spread. Now it was the
Rhavs' turn to worry. Their retreat had been cut off, and
though as many as two hundred of them had reached the
Isle of Meaak, none was to return alive. The men of Akbar
showed no mercy and each in time was hacked down. The quay,
where most of the fighting had taken place, was smeared and
puddled with blood.

Talen wheeled his horse from the bloodshed and, with
his trumpeter and his faithful standard bearer, crossed the
Bridge of Traders. The fighting had reached the wharfs now
and two of the elaborately painted barges moored there were
already alight. But such is the way of war that here, where
his conscripted army was performing wonderfully, there was a
bigger problem. Talen could not fire the bridge without cutting
off his men's retreat, and this he would not do; nor could he
wait for the enemy to drive his men back across the bridge,
for such was the confusion that pockets of men were already
fighting there and soon the two armies, terribly enmeshed,
would both be on it. Already he was cursing his own folly.
If only I had abandoned Baoz. If only I had fired the bridges
before the attack began. If only. If only.

Careless of his own safety, the Vaine of Talen charged the nearest group of Opposition troops. Before he had tried to stay clear of the fighting, believing – though it went against his nature – that he should not risk himself, but now he did not care. Any damned fool could do better than me, he felt: why should I preserve myself longer. He slashed and wheeled and slashed again, making desolate that area of the bridge, and tried to get through to the front of the fighting where the two armies clashed head on. But it was impossible and all he could do was to try to pick off those of the Opposition who broke through.

The narrow streets, and the equally narrow bridge, made conventional warfare impossible, as Streetpoet, in the midst of the battle, realised. Instead of outflanking movements and carefully timed charges, this was simply a matter of weight, of one army shoving another. And slowly but surely his own side was being forced back. He was no longer confined between the walls of buildings, he found, but on the wharfs, and in grave danger of being cut off from the bridge. He looked around but there was no one about to give orders, so he gave them himself. 'Make for the bridge, lads!' he shouted to those around him. 'We don't want to find ourselves this side when the enemy gets control of it!'

Those with him appreciated the sense in what he said. Together they fought their way back to the bridgehead and there, emerging from nowhere or so it seemed, was Od, standing next to him. 'Are you all right?' asked Streetpoet. It was not a very helpful question: I'm alive but I won't be for long was the answer Od might have given, had he had time. Instead he merely grunted, and engaged a soldier in orange and black who was nearby.

The confusion continued as the friends were driven across the bridge and onto the quay at the other side. Both sides were exhausted by now but neither dared break off, and the rearguard action continued as night began to fall. The front line, including Od and Streetpoet, had reached the Isle of Meaak now; the Bridge of Traders was intact and in Opposition hands. Talen, unable to get himself killed in the fighting, or even involved in it properly, now found he faced an entirely new dilemma, for the Opposition, more by accident than design, were infiltrating the island and reaching the single bridge that led to Akbar itself. If that fell to the enemy the Stronghold would be isolated.

Streetpoet swung his sword. His shoulder ached terribly now and he was aware, without being able to do anything about it, that he was being pushed up a side-street away from the quay. He looked around for the bald head of his friend but Od had disappeared again. There was no time to worry or mourn. The Opposition's demi-lancers were crossing the Bridge of Traders now whilst their infantry were falling back.

Talen watched what was happening with growing concern. He wished he had a cavalry, but the only horsemen he had were those he had brought with him and they were being used to command the conscripts. Yet cavalry was the most effective force, without doubt, in these street battles. The Opposition infantry had virtually left the quay now, moving into the side-streets, and the demi-lancers were able to charge along the waterfront, smashing the remaining defenders.

Talen fell back further, to Zantoroch Square. It was crowded with civilians; unlike Baoz, Meaak had not been evacuated, and though the gates of the Stronghold were open its courtyard could not accommodate all who sought shelter there. The fighting was becoming a massacre here. Whole families were being put to the sword by the advancing Opposition. Od, wondering what had become of Streetpoet, was amongst the many in the square, at the foot of the towers that mark the gate of the Stronghold. For some reason he could not fathom, to do with the dynamics of battle and the fortunes of war, he seemed to be away from the fighting for a while, and able to take stock of the situation. He saw Talen-vaine-Talen, dirty and bleeding, ride through, dismount and hurry towards the stairs of the gate towers; the other way, over the heads of those pressed around him, he saw in the other direction a demi-lancer raise his lance in triumph. Speared on the point was a naked baby.

Streetpoet emerged from the side-streets onto the straight road that runs through Meaak, connecting the two sides of the Akbar Bridge. He wondered about trying to get across the bridge and into Akbar where the walls were strong, but saw that the gates at the end of the bridge were firmly closed and that he was unlikely to be allowed in. Instead he crossed the main road and, still pursued, headed for the walls of the Stronghold which he could see over the houses ahead.

As Streetpoet looked up, Talen looked down and saw, in the increasing darkness, that although it was to condemn those outside to death, he would have to close the Stronghold's gates before the Opposition got in. Reluctantly, he gave the order and the great gates began to close.

At their foot was Od. He saw them swinging, moving towards him, and knew to be on the outside when they closed was to give up life. Many others felt the same. For a moment the mechanics of the doors almost foundered as bodies blocked them, and then the bodies were through. There was a sickening crack as the doors closed on a desperate trailing leg, and they were fast shut. Od, dazed but inside, stood in the packed courtyard and breathed in the noisome stenches of fear and despair: it smelt like the pure breath of life to him for at least at that moment he was safe.

Because he carried a sword he was soon singled out and given a job. He was sent to the Tower of Dratorik at the south-east corner of the Stronghold. He was told to keep watch, but it was dark by now. There was nothing to watch except the flames as the Opposition zealously burnt any luxuries that fell into their hands. In Akbar, that meant a lot of fires. Leutah's palace alone was a treasure house, an abomination in the eyes of the Brotherhood.

Streetpoet, hiding in a corner of that palace, was inclined to disagree. He had always had a taste for the gaudy. He was not bothering to hide; he sat in the middle of the great chamber, where an abandoned meal still mouldered, and waited for capture. He was not too upset at the prospect, in so far as he expected the mark of the Brothers Militant would save him from imprisonment, but he was annoyed that his mission to Northreach must surely be over and worried, now he had time, at the fate of Od. Still, he reasoned, as he examined a silver cruet by the light of the fires outside, at least while there's life there's hope.

The battle was over now though the fighting continued. A group of prostitutes at the southern end of Meaak had boarded themselves in and were putting up a spirited defence. Several householders along the quay fought to keep what they owned. And despite Wriknek's sternest injunctions, there was much evidence of rape and pillage, which soldiers the length of Khalindaine and beyond accept as their natural reward.

The following day was quiet. Kalomn rested his men, leaving sufficient outside the Stronghold to pen the defenders in, but billeting the rest in Baoz, where they enjoyed luxuries unexpected by campaigning troops and praised their commander heartily. Streetpoet woke to find himself eye to eye with a mouse: they scared one another mightily. The minstrel blinked and looked around. He was still in Leutah's chamber, head down on the abandoned meal, and uncaptured. He went over to a window and cautiously looked out. It was raining, he noticed, but the pale blue standard of the Vaine of Talen was still flying over the Stronghold which meant it still held out. Streetpoet was pleased to see it. He was no more superstitious than any man in that superstitious age, but felt that the fact he had escaped capture meant capture was not his fate and that freedom would be found in the Stronghold.

It was not a feeling the Vaine of Talen shared. Cooped up in one tiny room in the overcrowded fortress, free was the last word he would have used to describe his situation. Wretched would have come closer. He blamed himself for the defeat of the previous day, and more than that, for the loss of life; he was being unfair on himself because he had not asked for the commission, nor had the chance to train the troops who served under him, but remembering this did not help him. All he could think of was his mistakes.

He looked round. The Stronghold was the oldest building in Akbar and one of the oldest in Khalindaine. It had originally been a pirate fortress, intercepting the ancient trade between Mornet and Cythroné. Later, after Akhran the Golden had tamed Khalindaine and united it, piracy had proved less profitable than commerce, and on the island and the surrounding banks new buildings had sprung up. But the fortress had survived and for that at least Talen could be grateful. He walked out onto the roof of the keep. A large detachment of Opposition troops could be seen in Zantoroch Square, looking bored and careless. 'I'll wake them up,' he thought to himself as he sent for archers.

The arrows stung through the air. Streetpoet watched with interest as the troops in the square in front of him suddenly dispersed and made for cover, leaving several of their comrades behind. Had he been able to see through the stride-thick battlements of the Stronghold, the minstrel would even have recognised one of the less competent of the archers, for once more Od had been conscripted.

Kalomn of Grav, from his headquarters in Baoz, cursed his men for bunglers when he saw the arrow shower added to the rain. 'I told them not to stray within bow shot,' he told his aides. 'Still, they'll have learnt their lesson. Who is in command of that regiment?'

'Galkrefton Hedchworshipper, sir.'

'A member of the Brotherhood, eh? Well, well. Let's have him cashiered and sent back to Wriknek for incompetence: see how the Commander likes that.'

Kalomn continued to stand by the window. 'What's that?' he demanded, as suddenly a sail was raised just beyond the southern tip of Meaak.

'A ship, sir.'

'I can see that. Where's it from?'

'It must have set sail from Akbar, unless it came all the way down river from Mornet.'

'It's too small to have gone through the Rift. It must be an Akbar boat. Ormaas alive! Just when everything seemed to be going so well. How long does it take to sail to Cythroné?'

No one knew, but estimates varied from four to ten days, both of which were in fact reasonable. 'All right, at the worst it'll be four days there, four days back...' Kalomn began.

'No General,' corrected one of his aides. 'It will take longer to return because it'll be going against the stream.'

'True,' said the General, who did not mind being interrupted if the interruption were useful. 'What, six or seven days, minimum, coming back?' Again no one knew. 'That gives us ten days to capture Akbar, before reinforcements arrive. Can it be done?' This time Kalomn corrected himself. 'It'll *have* to be done.'

It was Talen, however, who drew first blood. Sending the besieging Opposition soldiers scurrying had done wonders for morale in the fortress – even Talen felt cheered – and he considered it essential that this should be kept up. So when Ossius and a number of other soldiers suggested a sortie to the Akbar Bridge, and with luck to Akbar itself, Talen was sympathetic. 'But you'll not find it easy,' he warned.

'I don't know. The Opposition might be a bit more wary than they were but they're still being complacent. Most of them are stationed in Baoz, after all. I think if we're swift we might manage it.'

'If you're prepared to risk it. How many men will you take?'

'No more than thirty: we've only got thirty serviceable horses. And we'll want the archers to cover us.'

'All right. When?'

'Late today. We want to catch the last of the light if possible. And I've got another plan if this one is successful.

Talen-vaine-Talen listened. 'Did you think of this on your own?' he asked when Ossius had finished.

'I talked it over with some of my friends,' Ossius admitted.

'You know,' said Talen. 'I'm beginning to think that there might have been wisdom in the Peltyn-Lord's selection of troops after all.'

It was agreed. Ossius and his cavalry, drawn largely from those Talen had brought, but including one or two from Akbar, who would know their way through Meaak and also, with luck, be recognised by the men on the gates of Akbar, were drawn up behind the gates with the archers, including Od, behind them. The gates were opened quickly. The cavalry galloped out. The Opposition troops at the far end of Zantoroch Square heard the great gates open, but even so were taken by surprise by the swiftness of the onslaught; they were even more surprised when the charge, instead of striking them, suddenly veered off to their right down a side turning, onto the main bridge road, and onto the bridge. Immediately after the cavalry came the infantry armed with bows; as soon as the cavalry had cleared the square the bowmen started to fire and soon the Opposition had cleared the square too.

Streetpoet heard the commotion: he could hardly have failed to do so. At once he was on his feet and running down the stairs to the palace's main entrance. He checked that the bald head he had seen, barely thirty strides away, really did belong to Od and then sang clearly from the doorway.

> No damn good, no damn good,
> Ever came of the Brotherhood.

Od looked up as he heard these words and saw Streetpoet sauntering across the square towards the archers. The minstrel nearly overdid it. The archers had been instructed to fire a single volley and then retreat back into the Stronghold, and Streetpoet was forced to break into a run to join them. Od waited at the gates as his friend slipped in. 'Any more casual,' said the bald man critically, 'and you'd have been a casualty. What kept you?'

'Sorry I'm late,' said Streetpoet. 'But I've never lived in a palace before. I was getting to quite like it.'

'Thirty cavalrymen leave, one bedraggled minstrel comes in,' mused Od. 'Hardly a fair exchange.'

'I don't know', said Streetpoet. 'I'd say I'd brought a gift beyond price. I've brought you the Luck of the Troubadours.'

It was dark by now inside the high-walled castle. 'The Luck of the Troubadours!' said Od. 'So that's how he does it!'

Beyond the fortress walls, over the ever-present sound of the river, they heard a high trumpet note repeated four times. Talen-vaine-Talen, on the battlements of the keep, listened with satisfaction. Ossius and his men had arrived safely and the first part of the plan was complete. Talen spoke to the trumpeter who had accompanied him to the battlements, and a different series of notes, loud and silvery, sounded above the Khalin's roar. 'Let's see what the morrow brings,' said Talen-vaine-Talen to his musician. 'Let us see what the morrow brings.'

The trumpeter was not the only musician employed in the Stronghold that night. One of the denizens of the tavern where they had spent their last night before Akbar recognised Streetpoet and Od: by popular demand, to the former's delight and the latter's embarrassment, the minstrel sang 'Tinfantoe'.

Meanwhile, Kalomn planned his attack.

Chapter 7

Going Against the Stream

Kalomn of Grav had chosen to wear full armour that morning, as if to emphasise his determination. He stood at the Baoz end of the Bridge of Traders planning his strategy and watching the heavy waters of the river. He was sure the river was rising, reaching further up the stone piers, but he dismissed this. It was unimportant. His real problem, as he recognised clearly, was that while the Bridge of Traders took him and his troops as far as the Isle of Meaak, it went no further: from Meaak to Akbar was only the intact eastern part of the Akbar Bridge, which Ossius had travelled the night before. Kalomn might control Baoz, and all Meaak except the Stronghold, but that in itself was worthless; as Talen had already discovered, defending Baoz was virtually impossible, and Kalomn was rightly concerned that Royalist reinforcements would drive him out as easily as he had disposed of Talen's conscripts. And meanwhile, most infuriating of all, the town of Akbar was as invulnerable as ever.

'Captain Teleq?'

'Sir,'

'We have a problem,' said the General of the East, with careful understatement. 'Akbar is still secure. We control the bridges but command no defensible positions. There is the strong possibility that enemy reinforcements will soon arrive.' Kalomn demonstrated the same ability to ask leading questions that he had used in his discussion with Wriknek: 'What would you do?'

'I should try to capture the Stronghold, sir. Whilst it is in enemy hands it remains a thorn in our side. We cannot attack Akbar without exposing our flanks to the Stronghold; at the same time, were it in our hands, we would have somewhere to defend.'

'Exactly, captain. And there is another reason for taking it.'

'Sir?'

'The Royalist commander of Akbar is in there. Without him, I wonder if it would be possible to persuade the soft citizens of Akbar to surrender?' Kalomn stopped meditating and made his decision. 'Captain Jargoz?'

'Here, general.'

'Captain Jargoz, take your engineers and raze the buildings of Meaak to the ground. I want a clear area in front of the Stronghold.'

'Yes, sir.'

'Captain Moristal? Will that wooden section of the Bridge of Traders take the weight of our siege engines?'

'I doubt it, sir.'

'Very well. Then the engines must be dismantled and taken across or, if you can do it more quickly, strengthen the bridge. I'll leave that up to you.'

'Yes sir.'

'Colonel Bératon?'

'General?'

'I want your men trained in the use of battering rams. Select the brawniest and have them practise on the basilica here in Baoz. Bringing their basilica down will not improve our enemy's morale.'

'Yes sir.'

'And colonel.'

'Sir.'

'You have until tomorrow.'

'Yes sir.'

Streetpoet and Od stayed together on the battlements, impelled by curiosity rather than discipline. In any case discipline in the castle was slack. Talen lacked officers, although he had made several from the troops he had brought, and many of the conscripts walked from place to place at whim.

'Look,' said Od suddenly, pointing at the Bridge of Traders, just visible beyond the customs post. A column of troops was crossing, taking with them a number of pack horses.

'I wonder what they want?'

'I expect we'll find out,' said Od, morosely.

Meanwhile, Colonel Bératon's men were busy with their battering ram, crashing first against the doors and walls of the basilica before turning their attention to the tall handsome bell tower. The colonel had borrowed one of Captain Jargoz's engineers to supervise this demolition – he did not want the basilica falling on his men – and stood across Baoz Square from the tower, watching as the tall building rocked.

'Back, two, three, four, rest two, three, four, charge!' shouted the sergeant as the men, all well built, sweated in the spring sunlight. As the ram struck the wall, the bells in the tower high above began to ring, tunelessly, in panic. 'Again,' grunted the sergeant, and again the tower vibrated; on the island Streetpoet and Od heard the bells, and wondered what was signified.

'All right! All right!' called the engineer. 'That's enough.' The dust settled a little. 'You've weakened it. Now let's have a bit of science.'

Wooden piles were put into the holes the ram had made in the walls, and the holes were enlarged so that the wood took the weight of the tower. Behind the props was a heap of wood chips soaked in fire-spell. 'Do you want to light it, sir?' the engineer asked Colonel Bératon, but the colonel declined.

'You started it,' he said. 'You go ahead and have the fun.'

The engineer took hold of a burning brand and poked it at the hole in the wall. At once the flames burst out, grabbing at the props as the engineer ran away. From their safe vantage points the watchers could not see the fire, but they could smell and hear it, and they could hear the building too as it cracked and shifted. Small bells rang once again. The whole tower seemed to slip forward half a stride, and turn slightly. Larger bells rang now. And then, with the exaggerated dignity of a drunk, the tower toppled forward through the roof of the basilica. The soldiers gave three cheers.

Streetpoet and Od, though further away, had an equally clear view of the bell tower's end. 'What did they do that for?' they asked one another when the noise of the demolition had cleared, but it was a question that neither could answer.

Od turned away from Baoz and looked at the island. 'Menketh alive!' he exclaimed. 'They're at it again.'

Leutah's palace was already aflame; the customs post likewise. 'What are they doing?' wondered Streetpoet.

'I've no idea. If they were just pulling down buildings on the island I'd say they were clearing the way for an attack, but this lot seem to be pulling down everything they can get their hands on. I can't understand it.'

'Perhaps they just like spoiling things,' suggested Streetpoet.

This view seemed to be confirmed by events on Meaak. Leutah's palace crackled and spat as Captain Jargoz's men set it alight. The fashionable tall windows burst in the heat. A roofing beam fell, taking heavy lead tiles with it, and a column of smoke nosed its way out. Black marks spread above each broken window, and inside the floors were giving way with angry slumping sounds. But Jargoz's men had not finished: before the fire could finish the palace they did, roping pack horses to the columns of the portico and heaving them down. The pediment, the architrave and the columns all tumbled into thick smoke-competing dust, and what was left of the roof fell in, scattering brilliant sparks and bulging the front wall – now unsupported by the portico – out into Zantoroch Square. The wall swelled, sagged and gave way, tossing bricks and burning wood clean across the square and into the river, and chasing Jargoz's men away too. Then, in an earthquake of collapsing masonry, the rest of the palace fell in on itself.

'Spectacular,' commented Od.

In Northreach it was raining. In Northreach it was always raining, or so it seemed that year. The Gros of Ra sat in his study, fingering his grey moustache and working out his money. The Lady Ra was in her parlour, no more bored than usual. The eye of a casual visitor, however, would have taken most pleasure in looking at the maid in the garden who was bringing in the clothes she had only moments earlier hung out, thinking there was a lull in the rain. The heavy raindrops darkened the maid's plain grey dress and pinned it to her shoulders and breasts. They made her fair hair darker too and plastered it flat against her head. None of this mattered nor detracted from her beauty. She had a straight nose, slightly freckled. She had clear grey eyes, intelligent and amused, with long lashes that had to blink as the rain rolled down her face. And she had a liveliness, a brilliance about her mouth, which made every man who saw her want to kiss her.

Fortunately, she was also fairly tough. The manservants of Mornet had learnt not to mess with her. 'Gorgeous looker,' they would remark evasively, 'but a bit too much spirit to her.

Knocked old Fyartar clean out once, and all he'd done was
made to pinch her bum.'

'Aye,' agreed their companions. 'And she's got a tongue in
her head. Remember how she made Typo Gordanbel look half
a stride tall when he was making up to her last Darkfeast?'

Even visiting nobles had learnt, to their infinite disappointment, that this lovely maid was most certainly not available.
'If I was the Ra-Lord,' they muttered to one another as they
nursed their injured pride, 'I'd bed her or sack her. She's no
right to look so warm and act so cold.'

No right perhaps, but also no choice, and the Ra-Lord,
who was never as obtuse as others believed, recognised this
and did neither.

An older, fatter maid called from the open door. 'Lara!
Lara! Her ladyship wants you.'

The maid struggled with the clothes and dumped them into
the arms of the older woman before hurrying off. 'Lara,' said
her ladyship when the maid reached the parlour. 'Is it time for
something to eat?'

'Yes, m'lady, if you wish.'

'Thank Menketh for that.' The Lady Ra, uncharacteristically
observant, characteristically random in her thought processes,
suddenly noted her maid servant was wet. 'Have you fallen
into something?' she asked. 'You are all wet.'

'It is raining, your ladyship.'

'Oh,' said the Lady Ra. 'Is that all. How tedious. I'd like
bread and honey. I thought something exciting might have
happened. And a glass of something mulled. Nothing exciting
ever happens.'

'Yes, m'lady,' replied Lara, in a general sort of way.
She walked back down the sumptuous corridors of the
Ranbrunsvag, looking through the windows as she went.
The rain made everything faint and grey, as though a
long and steady net were being constantly unfurled between
herself and the world. Even from where she was inside the
house she could hear, in the distance, the perpetual thunder
of the Mornet Falls as the swollen Khalin plunged from the
fastnesses of Northreach to the great pool beneath.

'What's the old dear want now?' asked the undercook when
Lara reached the kitchens.

'Nothing much. Bread and honey.'

'Nothing much! You're joking! There's no honey in the castle: I know because I was looking for some yesterday to put on the master's ham – you know what a sweet tooth he's got. I'm afraid you'll just have to send someone down the hill to Mornet if you want honey. I'll ask Maraka. She'll not be doing the laundry in this weather!'

'It's all right,' said Lara. 'I'll go myself.'

'In this rain? You must be crackers.'

'I've been inside all day. All day today, all day yesterday, all day the day before. And the day before that and the day before that. And even, I dare say, the day before that and the day before that. I *will* go crackers if I don't get outside soon.'

'If that's what you want,' said the undercook. 'But you'd better tell her ladyship first. She'll wonder why you're taking so long.'

'Her? Wonder?' The girl known as Lara was scornful. 'The last thing she ever wondered about in her whole life was whether she looked better with her hair in a plait. She hasn't the brains to wonder.'

'Don't be hard on the dear. You'll not find an easier mistress.'

'Nor a harder master than the Gros. But you're right,' admitted Lara. 'The Lady Ra is a sweetheart, even if she does drive me batty with her vagueness.'

'I don't know what you're doing working as a servant anyway,' said the undercook. 'You're too bright and too pretty for this line of work.'

'It's something to do,' said Lara. 'My mother died last year and my uncle, who should be looking after me, has never really recovered from the death of his adopted son in the Ingsvaal. Besides, I couldn't stand living with him: he drinks too much. At least here I earn my keep and pay my way.'

'Well, never mind dear,' said the undercook, who had been dreaming romantic dreams for Lara and not really listening at all. 'Maybe some handsome nobleman will visit the castle, fall madly in love with you, and sweep you off your feet.'

'Maybe,' said Lara. 'And maybe one day the sun will wear bright green breeches.'

Captain Moristal and his men worked assiduously. The siege weapons had to be stripped down, carried across the new wooden section in the middle of the Bridge of Traders, and reassembled. The work was not made any easier by the thick smoke that poured from the burning buildings of Meaak.

'Couldn't you lot have waited before firing the buildings?' Moristal asked Jargoz.

'I'd have thought we had priority,' said Captain Jargoz, his voice hoarse because of the smoke and the dust. 'It's you lot should have waited before crossing the river with these contraptions of yours.'

'They're not contraptions, they're siege engines. And besides, we're acting on the orders of General Kalomn in person.'

'Well, so are we.' Jargoz paused, partly for thought, partly to allow a fat gout of smoke to pass them. 'I guess the general's in a hurry,' he decided.

'It seems he is,' agreed Captain Moristal. 'Come on!' he called to his men. 'Let's get this lot assembled. The general wants us firing as soon as possible.'

Quickly and expertly the soldiers started work on the siege engines, beginning with the trebuchets, great counterweighted catapulets which could hurl rocks or fire-spell at the Stronghold's curtain walls. They had just completed the second of these when, clear over the crackling of burning buildings, though obscured by the sound of a wall collapsing, they heard the call of a trumpet blowing across the river from Akbar. It was answered almost at once by a trumpet from the Stronghold. 'What's that mean?' asked Moristal.

'Not much. They've been playing tunes to one another all morning. It keeps the blokes in the Stronghold from feeling lonely, I guess. Ignore it.'

Moristal accepted Jargoz's advice. The mules which carried the fire-spell were tethered on the Bridge of Traders, beyond the reach of sparks from the burning buildings of Meaak. Moristal sent for them, telling his men to be careful: he had no desire to be accidentally incinerated, and supervised the loading of the first volley onto the great metal spoons of the trebuchets. Cloth, weighted with lead, was soaked in fire-spell. 'Ready?' asked Captain Moristal.

'Ready,' his sergeants assured him.

'Aim.'

Jargoz had been wrong, however, in thinking that the trumpet calls were meaningless. Their messages were simple but carefully worked out. 'Are you ready?', 'Not yet'; 'Are you ready?', 'Not yet'; 'Are you ready?', 'Yes we are.' A final message was relayed across from the Stronghold to Akbar at the very moment when Moristal gave the order to fire: the gates of fortress and city were opened, the trebuchets fired, and as the Royalist troops poured out, infantry from the Stronghold, cavalry from the gates of Akbar, a volley of fire-spell was launched. The Royalists charging towards the Opposition; a shower of fire, temporarily filling the sky, passed over their heads to burst in the courtyard or on the walls of the Stronghold. For a moment all was chaos, and then the Vaine of Talen, who led the attack from the Stronghold in person, rallied his troops to his flag. The Opposition barely had time to defend themselves, and no time to defend their still juddering siege engines. Galloping through the smoke, running through the raised dust, the Royalists fought their way to the very edge of the bare quay between the two bridges to Baoz and pushed the trebuchets and the rest of the siege engines, mostly still incomplete, into the river. The Khalin's hungry waters dragged the wooden structures away in moments.

Then the attack was over: Talen-vaine-Talen gave the order to withdraw, and his troops returned to their bases. The royalists lost four men in the attack, and a further four when the fire-spell burst in the courtyard; the Opposition lost forty, and more significantly, lost their siege engines. Kalomn's attack would have to be postponed.

Lara hurried down the wooded slopes from the Ranbrunsvag to the town of Mornet which spread beneath. The incessant rain, which under other circumstances might have annoyed her, refreshed her after days confined to the castle. She let it run down her hair and her dress. From the fertile volcanic plug on which the Ranbrunsvag stood she could look directly across at the Mornet Falls. She had been in Mornet a year, and had grown accustomed to their dramatic power, but felt she had never seen them look more swollen. An irresistible weight of water seemed to push to the edge of the falls in a fat brown rush that was so constant it appeared to be static, and then it broke into a myriad plummeting bubbles, a column of crushing white. The noise of the water, a constant accompaniment to Mornet life, seemed louder than ever; the pool beneath, though as still and sinister as ever, was undeniably higher, and lapped over the causeway that led down from the Northreach towns to Mornet.

Lara looked at the view a while and then went on her way.

Talen stood in front of a mirror, washing himself in the inefficient soapless way of a serving soldier. For the first time for days he was not displeased by the sight of his own features; for the first time for days he felt satisfied with himself and with life. He had not forgotten the disaster of the first day of battle, when so many troops had been lost, but his was not a naturally introspective nature. The day's action had soothed his fretting mind. He dried himself quickly on the edge of his blanket and walked out to check his guards.

Lara was half way back to the Ranbrunsvag when the noise came. It began as a pressure, a shudder in the air, and then the world cracked, burst, exploded. Lara winced and ducked involuntarily before her natural curiosity got the upper hand and she looked for the source of the sound. It was not difficult to trace. The pool at the foot of the Mornet Falls had been suddenly split asunder, and a wave of black water was rushing headlong, filling the hollows in the riverbank, rising high over the quays of Mornet, and being funnelled again as the Khalin dropped into the crack of Khalinrift. The devastation was instant and awful. Anyone standing at the riverside was swept instantly away. The old Rivermaster's hut, which for generations had unpretentiously governed the river traffic, was hurtled from its foundations. And then the wave was gone, and Lara could see what seemed from her elevation a smear of leaden water enveloping the Mornet waterfront. She dropped her basket and the honey and hurried towards the riverbank to help.

The wave travelled beyond the sight of man, deep into the cleft that had been cut by a prehistoric earthquake through the deserts of Khalinrift, and continued remorselessly down stream. Sometimes it seemed almost thwarted by the jagged bends of the rift, but always it burst through, apparently undaunted, and thundered inevitably on.

Another day ended. The sun settled over the Plains west of
Akbar; the stars of the gods peered diffidently through the
cloak of night. Captain Jargoz's work had been interrupted
but fires still burnt on Meaak; Captain Moristal had been
less fortunate, for his commander had instructed him to work
through the night, if necessary, repairing the damage done by
the Royalists' lightning attack.

'Hurry up there,' called the captain. The light of a score of
torches illuminated him and his work. Moristal was exhausted
and frustrated equally, telling himself every time he had the
chance to think that the afternoon's events had not been his
fault, and asking himself why, that being the case, he was
expected to carry on through the night while the rest of
his army slept.

'We'll need some more wooden pegs,' his sergeant told him.

'Oh, very well,' said the captain irritably. 'See what you can
find in the town. There's surely a hardware shop somewhere
in Baoz.'

'I reckon I saw one on the Myrian Road.'

'All right then. But hurry up. I was hoping to get *some*
sleep tonight.'

The sergeant started walking out of the torch light and the
turned back. 'What's that noise?' he asked.

'I don't know and I don't care,' replied the captain. 'Just
hurry up and get those pegs.'

Thus it was that the sergeant alone amongst Moristal's
company survived the flood.

Two conscript soldiers standing on the battlements of the
Stronghold were also concerned by the noise. 'What do
you reckon?'

'Must be a storm.'

'I've never heard a storm like that before.'

'Well, what else could... Menketh alive! Look at that!'

A boil of phosphorescence appeared suddenly, bright even in
the night, where the Khalinrift ended and the river flowed into
the Plains. The sinister half whiteness spread from the familiar
river course and raced across the flat land towards them;
they braced themselves as the vanguard of the wave hit the
northernmost tower, the Tower of Asbik, and then sent silent
prayers of gratitude to the memory of the long dead builders

of the Stronghold, for the waves were parted around the tower as by the bow of a ship, and those inside were safe.

Baoz was less fortunate. The waters spread across its low streets, sweeping the wharfs clear of life and shipping, racing into the buildings, lapping like a drinking tiger. Moristal's company was caught in the swirling waves. The timbers of the half-completed siege engines were upended like mere twigs and swept away. Akbar Bridge, its western arches already brought down in Talen's retreat, was damaged further, and the wooden central section of the Bridge of Traders was smashed. Even the eastern part of Akbar Bridge was damaged, with one arch swept away and another rendered impassable. Night heightened rather than hid the extent of the disaster; night-carried screams pierced the river's rush. Horrors half seen are twice imagined, and to the watchers on the walls of the Stronghold it seemed the devastation was absolute. It was only with the slow light of dawn that any accurate assessment of the damage could be made.

Akbar had escaped virtually unscathed. True, a few cellars had been flooded, even a few ground floors, and an arch of the bridge connecting the town to the island was down, but this apart the damage to property was minimal and the damage to life was nil. The high walls, built more against the drifting sands of the Rift than against any human invader, had again stood up to the elements.

The Isle of Meaak had been less fortunate. The ravages of Captain Jargoz's engineers had already substantially weakened almost every building on the island except the Stronghold; the waters had not had to rise too far, no more than a stride, before they were high enough to tumble most of the buildings down. As the waters retreated and the day began, Meaak, sodden and dilapidated, resembled the ruts and puddles of a giant muddy road.

Relatively, Baoz looked undamaged. The bridges were both down, of course, but then one had been weakened and the other destroyed before the flood. The wharfs had been swept clear and the tethered barges smashed or washed away. But, the buildings looked intact. It was Baoz that suffered the greatest loss of life, however, for on Baoz there were more vulnerable lives to lose. Kalomn of Grav had billeted his men by the waterfront to make access to Meaak easier; he had placed most of them in groundfloor rooms. The waters had risen maybe a stride and a half above street level – it had been enough. The sleeping army was decimated, literally: one in ten men had been drowned. But more worrying by far to Kalomn was the effect on morale: when the survivors examined the ruins the following morning, they saw their own conquests washed away, whilst the Royalist positions, the Stronghold and Akbar, seemed undamaged. There is no such thing as a Holy War maybe, for all wars are unholy, but all armies like to believe there is a deity on their side. The unequally distributed damage caused by the flood caused many of the Opposition troops to wonder if maybe the Brotherhood worshipped the wrong gods after all.

Kalomn was at the edge of the water, and the water lapped the edge of the Baoz quay. As he watched the Royalist troops left the Stronghold with impunity and began the sometimes grisly task of picking over the remains of the buildings. Several of the men he had stationed there had survived, and Kalomn had to watch them surrender: neither he nor they had any choice now that the bridges were down. He turned away resignedly. Around him his officers looked to him for instructions. 'Colonel Bératon, it appears your men will not be needing the battering ram any longer. Instead, our priority must be to make Baoz defensible. We can no longer press ahead with the attack on Akbar but we can at least prevent the enemy using the crossing.' He smiled for the first time that morning. 'And the flood may have, with luck, washed away that messenger-boat they sent to Cythroné; better still there was a Royalist fleet on its way and that has been destroyed.' The smile faded. 'Anyway, we're stuck one side of the river, they're stuck the other, and consolidation seems our best policy.'

'What of our attack, general?'

The General of the East shook his head. 'The attack is over. I shall report to Wriknek at once, of course. My resignation shall be included in my report.'

Streetpoet and Od were amongst those sorting through the débris on Meaak. 'Floods, floods, storms and floods,' complained Streetpoet. 'That's been the story of my time with you. I feel like an otter.'

'It's curious,' agreed Od. 'Do you think the gods are trying to tell you something?'

'Like what?'

'Oh, I don't know. I'm not a divine. But you're being bugged by the thing you like least.' Od tried to find words for the things he thought. 'I mean, you claim looking for this Lara...'

'...Sh...' mouthed Streetpoet. The name was not unknown amongst their companions after all.

'...sorry. You claim that *our quest* is important for the future of Khalindaine, the security of the empire and so on.'

'I think it could be.'

'Well, that strikes me as the sort of thing gods tend to involve themselves in: fates of empires and so on are always high on their agenda according to legend. Perhaps the gods are taking a personal hand in all this.'

'Don't, if you'll pardon the highly appropriate pun, talk wet,' replied Streetpoet. 'I'm not the kind the gods notice. I'm one of the little people, the ordinary ones, doing my bit and doing my best, and then I'll die and be forgotten like everyone else.'

Od had a greater capacity for faith than his friend. The Brotherhood no longer convinced him but he still believed in something beyond. 'Any god worth worshipping must notice everyone, no matter how insignificant.'

'Maybe that's why I don't worship one.'

'Oi!' called a voice behind them. 'Less of the chat, more of the work!' One of Talen's promoted professionals came up, a man called Equalot, one of those who prefer to exceed than to exercise their authority. 'Stop lazing around.'

'Yes, my master,' muttered Streetpoet, not quite quietly enough.

'You being sarcastic?' The manner was that of a bullying schoolmaster; so was the gesture. Equalot took Streetpoet by the ear and slowly pulled the minstrel until they were face to face. 'You're a slovenly good-for-nothing and it's as well for you that I'm going upriver with the Vaine as soon as reinforcements arrive because I've got my eye on you fellow and I'd be drying your tongue for a shoe horn if I caught you putting one single step out of line so help me Menketh.'

'What a long sentence,' said Streetpoet politely. 'Very impressive.'

'You really ask for trouble don't you?'

'No,' said Streetpoet, as if puzzled. 'No, I can't say I ever remember doing that.'

'Just get out of my sight!' said Equalot furiously. 'Just get out of my sight!'

'All right.' Streetpoet and Od walked off, returned to the Stronghold, and sat down cross-legged in the courtyard. 'Well,' said Streetpoet. 'That was interesting.'

'I'm glad you enjoyed it. It's a good job he is going away: you could've found yourself digging latrines for the duration.'

'*Who's* going away?' asked Streetpoet.

'That bully.'

'Ah, that's what he thinks, that's what you think, but it isn't what I think.'

'No?'

'No. When Talen-vaine-Talen goes north to Mornet, we're going with him.'

'Upriver?'

'That's right.'

'It'll mean getting wet again.'

The Gros of Peltyn stood in a large chamber in Verdre, looking out of the window at the river running high over the royal lawns. In his hand was a note; in front of him was the messenger who had brought it. 'I don't understand,' admitted the Peltyn-Lord. 'Is Talen dead? Is the Vaine of Akbar?'

'Neither, your Grosarch.'

'I have an earlier communication from Talen-vaine-Talen which says he has taken over the garrison of Akbar. Now you send me a note signed by one Prothal One-Eye, of whom I confess I have never heard, telling me that Akbar is besieged and its fall is imminent.'

'It is quite simple, sir.' The messenger explained the situation as he had left it: the Stronghold still holding out, Akbar secure, but Baoz and most of Meaak in Opposition hands.

'I see. I'm not quite sure what I'm meant to do about this, however. How many days ago did you leave Akbar?'

'Three, sir. The river is extremely high, and a bore, almost a tidal wave, carried us some of the way before it ran out of power.'

'I see. But the journey upriver will take much longer.'

'Yes, your Grosarch, though the river is dropping.'

'It hardly looks it,' said the Peltyn-Lord, turning again to the window.

'Believe me, sir, it is past its height. You should be able to reach Akbar in six or seven days.'

'And then what? Discover that the Opposition has taken the whole town? Surrender myself?'

He dismissed the messenger and settled down to think. He could barely spare the men for a campaign in the east: he had enough worries about the campaign that threatened in the west. But on the other hand the prospect of an Opposition army in Akbar, controlling the Khalin and the eastern approaches to Cythroné, was terrifying. He settled behind a desk, sent for paper, pen and ink, and wrote out his orders.

Days passed. Talen's first priority was to regain contact with Akbar, and to this end he sent men to work repairing the damaged Akbar Bridge; Kalomn of Grav, still waiting for a reply from Wriknek, none the less continued to supervise the building of defence works around Baoz. It would be impossible, he realised, to defend the whole town: instead he cordoned off an area which took in the ends of the two broken bridges, in case of counterattack, and the damaged wharfs which would give him access to the river if necessary. He was a good general, defeated only by the elements, and continued to work hard even now.

Thus it was that when the Gros of Nanx rowed upriver with a fleet of hastily requisitioned barges and as many soldiers as the Gros of Peltyn could spare, he found the situation confusing. Unlike his late lamented elder brother, from whom he had inherited his title, this Gros of Nanx was far less heroic, far less impulsive, but rather more wise. His brother would have sailed straight for Meaak, risking whatever he found in the search for glory; the current Nanx-Lord preferred to moor down river and send a scouting party along the potentially safer east coast of the Khalin towards Akbar. 'Just find out who controls the town,' he told them. 'And then come back.'

They were not gone long. 'The flag of the empire still hangs over Akbar and Meaak,' their captain reported, 'and that of the Opposition over Baoz. There's been heavy flooding round here though, by the look of it, so maybe the Opposition's attack hasn't begun.'

'Perhaps.' The Gros of Nanx's cautious mind was satisfied that it would be safe to make for Akbar, and gave his orders.

The sight of the Royalist fleet coming up the river dealt another blow to the morale of Kalomn's men. Now, instead of glory and loot, if they fought at all it would be in defence of Baoz. They watched as the barges were moored on the far side of the river and the Nanx-Lord and his men disembarked.

The arrival of reinforcements coincided with the repair of the bridge between Akbar and Meaak, and Talen-vaine-Talen was able to cross to Akbar to greet the Nanx-Lord in person. It was not, if truth be known, a particularly happy meeting for the Gros. The handsome and courageous Vaine of Talen seemed awfully like the Nanx-Lord's dead elder brother, and the brothers had never been close. It was a relief to the Nanx-Lord to learn, therefore, that Talen was hoping to travel to Mornet without delay; the Nanx-Lord was more than willing to contribute a barge and its crew to the Vaine's purpose.

Talen assembled his troops in the courtyard of the Stronghold. The flagstones still bore scorch marks but the sense of siege had gone. Now it was the Opposition across the river who were besieged, and Talen could speak optimistically to his men.

'Tomorrow,' he announced, 'I shall be leaving Akbar and travelling through the Khalinrift gorges to Mornet. I have transport for only fifty men and their horses, but as all of you have shown your loyalty and courage recently there shall be no dishonour in remaining behind. I shall not select but leave it to you to volunteer. Those who wish to come must risk the power of the Khalin, and we have all seen how terrible that power can be; those who prefer to stay will stay to fight. The choice is yours.'

The comparison the Gros of Nanx had made between his late elder brother and Talen was in fact unfair. It was true that both men were gallant and impulsive but there were great differences. Until the moment of his death, leading a cock-eyed cavalry charge against overwhelming odds during the early stages of the Battle of Klau, the Nanx-Lord had never known disappointment or defeat; Talen had learnt what both felt like at the beginning of the Siege of Akbar. And Talen had a humility the Nanx-Lord could never have shared. Perhaps it was a sign of the times, but Talen, as his speech to them showed, genuinely respected his troops and their opinions: he was quite happy to let his troops make their own decisions which, after much discussion, they did. The fifty who would accompany him north, Equalot amongst them, was decided; they were ordered to be ready at dawn for the journey through the Rift.

There had been no secrecy in these arrangements nor, as far as Talen was aware, any need for secrecy. Streetpoet and Od had therefore no trouble in learning his plans: now they needed a plan of their own and the one they chose was simplicity itself.

It cost them all the money they had raised from the sale of the horses, plus a deal of Streetpoet's charm, to persuade a whore to lure Equalot and one of his comrades out of the Stronghold and into the devastated ruins, but once they were isolated it took no time at all to thump them over the head with bags full of sand, strip them of their uniforms, and leave them in the whore's charge, with instructions that neither should be released until late the following day. Then, in borrowed uniforms, Streetpoet and Od returned to the Stronghold, slept, and joined Talen's fifty by the quayside the following morning. No one noticed, because no one knew for certain exactly who had volunteered and thus the companions boarded the barge for Mornet and set off into the great gorges of the Rift.

Chapter 8

The Gros of Ra

They were lucky, and it was a bold bright day they set out on. The flood seemed to have purged the river and the level was lower now than it had been for many days; the great gorges of the Khalinrift were black and yellow, shadow and rock, and the bargemen sang as their journey began. Streetpoet and Od, in their stolen uniforms, played at being busy and keeping out of everyone's way.

The barge was wide, its width almost disguising the fact that it was also long, and had a flat bottom with only the ghost of a keel. The width and the flatness were necessary. The river was fast and dangerous and its level altered almost daily. A narrow boat would rock and maybe capsize, a boat with a deep draught would scrape on the stones. The Rivermasters who controlled the barges' motions knew the river from birth, yet even they could not always predict the depth of the rocks below nor work out the fluctuating currents.

The Rivermasters had two quite different methods for getting their boats upstream. Where possible oars were used, slicing the barge through the water with co-ordinated strokes, but where the waters frothed white at the rapids the boats were winched from the shore. The winches used for this job had been fixed in position on the banks long ago and were maintained by the Rivermasters. No one but a Rivermaster was allowed to take a boat up the Khalin through the Rift – and it was generally agreed that no one but a Rivermaster would be able to, or even want to – which meant that each boat going north had a Master aboard; when the boat reached one of the blackiron winches at the rapids there was a Rivermaster aboard to check the machinery and, if necessary, repair it. The system worked: the Rivermasters were proud of their traditions and jealously guarded their monopoly, but in return the people of Khalindaine were provided with a reliable and efficient route north. The barges were expensive to run and expensive to hire but the alternative was the long and agonising journey across the exposed deserts of Khalinrift: in the gorges there was shade at least and certainly no shortage of water.

Unlike the galleys used on the lower sections of the river Khalin, and on the coastal routes from Nerith to Comtas, the barges positioned their rowers not below the main deck but on it, high up above the waters' violence. Each barge had up to sixty oarsmen: these men were usually criminals, chosen for work on the barges because of their strength, but the traditions of the Rivermasters meant they were not treated as slaves; each was given wages, albeit low, and allowed his own home either in Akbar or Mornet, so that despite the arduous nature of the work there was never a shortage of convicts willing to risk a posting on the river. Supplementing the convicts were the apprentices, the trainee Rivermasters who had to serve five years at the oars before being considered ready for other duties. The cargo was kept in the hull of the barge beneath the oarsmen's benches. Usually this consisted of spices, wines and cloths going north or furs and ales going south, but on the Vaine of Talen's trip the entire hold was given over to horses and the horses' foodstuffs, while the men slept, like the rowers, within brightly striped tarpaulin tents rigged up on the deck. Streetpoet had once travelled north this way previously. He had not liked it then and he did not like it now. Od had never been up the Khalin before and was full of professional curiosity. On the Hasfaine, his river, the problem had been the silt that constantly altered the river-bed; here the river-bed was sound and virtually permanent, for the Rift had been cut by an earthquake rather than erosion and had not changed in many millennia, but the water level itself kept changing, exposing dangerous rocks or worse still hiding them. Od watched with a respect bordering on admiration as the Rivermaster, on a high chair, almost a throne, erected at the bows of the ship, guided his oarsmen through the gorges. He was particularly impressed by the efficient way the rapids were taken: the barge was swung to the side, moored by a ledge cut there at some ancient and long forgotten date; the oarsmen shipped their oars, disembarked and, trailing a strong hawser, made their way to the winch securely mounted on the bank at the head of the rapids; the hawser was slipped through the winch and the boat was slowly pulled through a channel that had often been artificially widened. Sometimes, at the most dangerous rapids, a single pulley, which had to be in a single direction, was not sufficient: a series of winches was necessary to negotiate the bends and changes in level there. 'It's very impressive,' Od shouted to Streetpoet over the noise of the waters. 'It's the co-operation and the planning that gets to me. I mean, someone must have actually decided that these winches were necessary and installed them and looked after them, and that's not a job for just one man. Lots of people must have got together, and pooled their knowledge, and shared their foresight, and worked out how to navigate this river. On the Hasfaine all the pilots worked independently; here they all work together. It's a fine thing to see. I wish there had been something like this on the Hasfaine. I might have stayed a pilot instead of getting messed up in religion and politics and all the rest of the silliness that's brought me here. To have a good job is a good thing.'

'I suppose so,' said Streetpoet. 'Though I'm no expert on jobs, good or not. I just make my way.'

'You've got a job you enjoy and you know it.'

'Yes,' agreed Streetpoet. 'I am now a soldier, judging from what I'm wearing.'

'That isn't really your job any more than it's mine. You're a minstrel, through and through; me, I'm a riverman, I'm realising, although I'd forgotten that fact for a while, and when this lousy war is over I'm going back to my river and back to my old job.'

'I thought you said the river would have changed too much, what with the silt and the erosion and everything.'

'That was just an excuse, really,' admitted Od. 'When we were talking before I wanted to get away from my past, my dead family and my dead faith. But being on a river again reminds me of what I did best, which was pilot boats up and down the Hasfaine. I can soon learn the ways of the Hasfaine again, I guess, if I want to; it's all a matter of wanting to enough. And now I've seen how things are organised on the Khalin I've a few ideas I wouldn't mind trying on the Hasfaine, to do with co-operation and all the pilots working together instead of against one another.'

'Well, it's up to you, I suppose,' said Streetpoet. He found his voice was getting hoarse as he tried to shout over the sound of the rapids. 'But it'd be different on the Hasfaine.' For

some reason he did not feel like analysing Streetpoet wanting
to make objections to Od's ideas. 'The Rivermasters all own
their own boats,' he said. 'You were just a pilot, not master
of a vessel. It wouldn't be in your interests to make the river
too navigable, otherwise the captains of the boats would be
able to do without you. I don't think you'd like it as much as
you imagine.'

Od looked downcast for a moment, not because of the
nature of his friend's objections but because they had been
made at all. 'Don't you want me to go back to the Hasfaine?'
he asked. 'I could be happy there.'

'It's your decision,' said Streetpoet rather petulantly.

Od realised before Streetpoet why the minstrel was being
so unenthusiastic. 'Hey! I'm not talking about going back
immediately. I'm talking about later, when the war's over
and everything's sorted out. I'm not going to walk out on you
now, you know.'

Streetpoet felt reassured, but because he had spent his
life trying to prove to himself how little he needed other
people, he changed the subject instead of showing his pleasure. 'You've not been to Northreach before, have you? It's
where I was born, and though I could never settle there, or
anywhere, I always like going back to it. It's a good place
to get to; it's a good place to leave. Everywhere I know is
rather like that.'

They sat down in the middle of the boat, between the
oarsmen, and let the boat carry them upstream.

After three days in the Rift Talen approached the Rivermaster's proud throne. 'How much longer?' he wondered.

'Another three days, I'd say. You see that big rock on
the cliff to the right?' Talen looked, but all around were big
rocks and he could not distinguish one from another. 'That's
the Gyutah-Cvav, means we're entering the Akhulatta. Say
half a day before Ghyutah-Omaron, another day to the Juy,
and then, the levels being what they are, Mornet a day later.
No problem.'

'Thank you very much.' Talen had been given much information he could make nothing of, but at least he understood
what 'another three days' meant. He returned to his place
in the stern.

The journey was becoming monotonous now. Even Od had lost much of his enthusiasm. It was always dark in the gorges of the Rift and surprisingly cold. The sun, so strong on the upper slopes, barely reached the waters even at noon. The torrents flowed by, black and heavy or white and playful, and the walls of the gorges were always much the same: unbroken, threatening, massive. Streetpoet found himself getting meditative, almost melancholy. It was an inhuman landscape he saw, that dwarfed the men and their boat and their concerns, that reduced human life to next to nothing. And yet, thought Streetpoet, who could never be downcast for long, at least we're going against the stream. Everything else in this narrow world is forced to go downwards, swept by time and the water from Northreach to the sea, but we're going the other way. Perhaps that is man's achievement, his only achievement. We cannot change much, plan much, design much outside their own worlds, a world as narrow in its own way as this, but we can at least go against the stream.

Thus the companions journeyed north.

They had given Consatiné a wing of the palace of Verdre where he could wander at will. For some reason he seemed to have taken a dislike to much of the furnishing of the palace: he kept ordering this piece or that piece to be removed, and gave instructions that all the paintings should be taken down and rested at the foot of the walls, which gave the place the temporary air of a gallery awaiting an exhibition. He was meanwhile taking little interest in the progress of the war, though the Gros of Peltyn loyally kept his emperor informed. 'Akbar has been invested, your majesty.' Only an absolute loyalty – or an absolute stubbornness – would persevere against the emperor's idiosyncratic way of seeing things.

'Infested?'

'Invested, sire. Besieged.'

'I didn't know invested meant besieged. I always thought it was to do with money.'

'It can be, your majesty, but isn't this time.'

'How very peculiar.'

Later the news came of Akbar's relief. 'So it's no longer invested,' said the emperor. 'I'm not sure how one uninvests. Is it called a withdrawal?'

'The Opposition troops have indeed withdrawn, your majesty. They are now in Baoz.'

'But it isn't their *troops* we're talking about, surely. They can't have been withdrawn because they weren't the ones invested. Akbar was invested, yes? Therefore Akbar must now be withdrawn.'

'Yes, your majesty,' said the Gros. Even his remarkable sense of duty could argue no more; he had a double reason for anxiety, therefore, when he heard the following day that Wriknek in person had marched a second force to Akbar, relieved Kalomn of Grav of his duties, and was again laying siege to the Stronghold. Not only was he uncertain how the Gros of Nanx would act – the man was cautious to a fault - but he also dreaded passing the information on to the emperor. He walked through Consatiné's bleak halls, noting how in places the paintings had been arranged on the floors in a sort of jigsaw, regardless of pattern, like flagstones, and how certain curtains had been tied into untidy bows. The emperor seemed constantly cheerful, and quite harmless, but often the Peltyn-Lord worried: even if the war were won, would Consatiné ever be able to rule Khalindaine again?

'Hello!' called Consatiné when he saw his faithful officer.

'Your majesty,' said the Gros of Peltyn. 'I have unfortunate news. Akbar has been besieged once more.'

'Re-be-sieged? Like a sort of alphabet.'

'Pardon, your majesty?' but the emperor was on a different tack by now.

'You know,' said Consatiné. 'You're ever such a helpful man. I think it's time Khalindaine had another Gyr. How would you like to be Gyr Peltyn?'

'I would be honoured, your majesty, though the state of the empire hardly encourages me to believe I have deserved this.'

'That's all right then,' said the emperor, though what was all right was less sure. 'We'll go ahead the day after tomorrow.'

Perhaps sheer audacity was the reason, or simply that there was no apparent motive why anyone *should* pretend to be one of the Vaine of Talen's troops, but no one questioned either Od or Streetpoet for the whole journey, and they arrived at Mornet's devastated docks on the day promised without either being discovered. Od had got tired of keeping his helmet on all the time, to hide his distinctively bald head, but apart from that everything had gone marvellously well. The next thing they had to do, of course, was find Lara: as this was in accordance with their orders as well as their wishes, it did not seem to present much of a problem. In fact though they found themselves attached to the Vaine's own company, which cut down on their freedom of movement, and were ordered to ride behind him up the slope to the Ranbrunsvag. Even here they were lucky, however. They were less accomplished horsemen than the Vaine's professional cavalry, but after the long river journey even the best horsemen, and horses, were a little groggy and Streetpoet and Od were again unremarked.

They rode together at the back of a column of twenty men whilst the rest of Talen's volunteers were dispatched to ask questions around the town. 'Pity about this,' muttered Streetpoet to his friend, 'but I suppose it can't be helped.'

'It looks like the flooding's been bad here too,' said Od. 'The river must have been very high, though it's calm enough now.'

'That's something else I don't like,' confided Streetpoet. 'The river.'

'You got all the way to Mornet without getting your feet wet,' Od pointed out.

'Hrrrmmmph,' said Streetpoet in reply.

Talen too was unhappy. He had met the Gros of Ra on one or two occasions: they had not been pleasant ones. The Ra-Lord's eccentricities had been getting worse since his adopted son became emperor: the man had decided he was an inventor of genius and was constantly working on some new and unnecessary device. Most recently he had invented and presented to the court something he called an 'eye-level grill' which seemed carefully designed to spit fat in your face while things cooked; in response to the war Talen was certain the Ra-Lord would be working on a secret weapon or two.

From the damaged docks their route took them through Mornet's pleasant streets and squares. They passed handsome houses decorated in the plain but effective Northreach way, and others which bore the influence of more elaborate southern fashions. There was a large market devoted to furs, which they skirted, and an even larger market, partially covered, where fruit and vegetables were sold. Then their road narrowed and rose as they climbed the volcanic plug of the Ranbrunsvag; it left the houses and circled round a wide cliff.

Streetpoet had been to the Ranbrunsvag before. Then he had been travelling with Lara instead of looking for her. It had been night and he had been younger, and had answered the Ra-Lord back and saved Consatiné from his father's bullying. At the time, when the Agaskan were rising and they had been forced to brave the Khalinrift on horseback, Khalindaine had seemed a dangerous place; now, in a civil war that tore up families and loyalties, Streetpoet found he was looking back on his previous time in Mornet almost as though it were a golden age, an age of innocence. He hummed a bar or two of a song until Od, worried, stopped him.

'What's got into you?' Od wondered.

'Sorry,' said Streetpoet. 'I was just thinking. I'm getting old.'

'You're ten years younger than me,' said Od, approximating the age gap in his favour.

'Well, there you are then,' said Streetpoet. 'And you're positively decrepit.'

'Thanks a bundle,' said Od.

They travelled through the heavily defended gate of the Ranbrunsvag and entered the outer bailey of the castle. To their left was the ancient keep, towering on heavy buttresses; ahead of them, entirely contained within the walls of the castle, was an attractive modern mansion with a drive and wide lawns leading to it. Guards in the magenta uniform of Ra bustled around the newcomers; the more senior wanted to know Talen's business, the rest wanted news of the war. The news that Akbar had been relieved was greeted with a cheer: Akbar was the key to the route south, for the only other way from Northreach to the rest of the empire – apart from overland through the Rift – was due west over the mountains to Myr, along the Nama-Ethôn, the road to Death. Talen's troops were virtually fêted, as bearers of good tidings often are, and Talen was led away from his men and ushered at once into the presence of the Gros of Ra.

The Ra-Lord was a smaller man than his reputation might suggest, with grey hair that was almost white and a neat pointed beard. He sat in the centre of a room that was obviously a study, and his desk was sprawled with yellowing vellum. 'Yes,' said the Gros, not particularly politely. 'What

can I do for you?'   'I have come by command of the Gros of
Peltyn,' said the Vaine of Talen. I am searching for a woman
named Lara.'

'Why?'

'It appears that the emperor, your adopted son, has asked
for her.'

'Who are you anyway?'

'Talen-vaine-Talen, your Grosarch. Of the House of Vois.'

'Never heard of you. Have we met?'

'Yes, your Grosarch.'

'Really? Don't recall, must say. Still, you look like a soldier.
I've something to show you that might interest you.'

Menketh! thought Talen: here we go! But there seemed no
way of getting away from the old fool, and Talen prepared
to follow him to whatever workshop in which the Ra-Lord
and his assistants prepared their inventions. The Ra-Lord,
however, was not going anywhere. Instead he took a book
from the shelves surrounding them and searched through for a
page. 'Peculiar old book, this,' said the Ra-Lord. 'Came from
Ehapot, but it's not Ehapot work... Can't read a word of it
of course, but there are some funny pictures... What do you
make of this?'

The Ra-Lord showed Talen a picture, beautifully painted
but in an unfamiliar style, of a man on horseback. The man
seemed to be pointing a stick, looking along it almost as though
he were aiming it at something, and from the far point of the
stick the artist showed what looked like a blast of smoke. 'What
do you think?'

What am I meant to think? wondered Talen. 'Very nice,'
he said.

But the Ra-Lord had not finished yet. A few pages on was
a picture of a man on foot, pointing a similar stick at another
man; the second man was apparently wounded in some way,
but was the pointing-stick a weapon or a way of curing him?
It was all very curious and had Talen had more time he might
even have been interested, but there was a war to be fought
and pointing-sticks were irrelevant.

The Ra-Lord still would not let Talen get away though.
'Follow me,' he said.

There was no arguing with the Ra-Lord as many before
Talen had learnt. It was better by and large to let the old

man have his way for he never detained anyone long; his mercurial mind soon found something else to occupy it. So Talen followed the Ra-Lord through a long and handsome hall, down a flight of broad marble stairs, and out of the modern building. Across the courtyard he could see his men. Most were looking cheerful in the company of the Ra-Lord's guards, though two seemed to be walking off towards a maid who was hanging out washing. Talen wondered vaguely where they were going, or where he was.

That question was soon answered. Set at the foot of the keep's high walls was the workshop Talen had anticipated and in there were forges, anvils, vices and benches, as well as a number of muscular men in long aprons. The Ra-Lord paid the workmen no attention, however, and hurried through the workshop to a rough wooden table at the far end. 'Just look at this!' he enthused.

Talen looked. Rather as he had expected, it was a pointing-stick. 'I had it made from the drawings. Have a look at it.'

Talen picked it up. It was well made in wood bound with silver, and Talen had to admit that when he raised it to his shoulder in imitation of the men in the pictures, it nestled there comfortably enough. But he still had no notion what it was for. Neither, apparently, had the Ra-Lord, because though he patted the pointing-stick with paternal pride, he clearly had no more idea than Talen what to do with it.

'I'm afraid it doesn't work,' admitted the Ra-Lord. 'We've pointed it at all sorts of people but nothing seems to happen. If they're poorly they stay poorly and if they're well they stay well. But I'm sure we'll get it right in time.'

'I'm sure,' said Talen, laying it down on the bench. There was something intriguing about it, with its purposeful stock, the moulded bulge where it fitted the shoulder, and the delicate bit the forefinger gripped round, but Talen had no time to worry. As he put it down the solid pointing-stick banged on the table. They made their way back to the open air.

There was something of a commotion. Talen saw one of his soldiers embracing a woman. He's moved fast, thought Talen: we've only just arrived. And she's a very pretty lady too, he noted admiringly. It did not seem particularly good for discipline though, to have his soldiers accosting women left, right and centre, and so he moved to break the couple apart.

The Ra-Lord moved even faster: there was little the Ra-Lord enjoyed more than shouting at people. 'What is the meaning of this outrage!' he spluttered.

The soldier moved away from the girl. He was a young man with an attractive, slightly insolent face. Talen did not remember having seen him before. 'Oh dear,' the soldier said. 'We may have some explaining to do. Sorry Lara.'

'*Lara!*' Talen-vaine-Talen was astounded. '*The* Lara?'

'Well,' said the soldier. 'She's a Lara, certainly.'

Talen turned to the woman. 'Are you the Lara who knew the Emperor Consatiné? The one the emperor loves?'

'I knew him, yes sir,' she said, composedly.

The Ra-Lord made himself heard again. 'Consatiné can't love her! He's never met her. She's a serving maid. Look!' he said, as though this made it conclusive: 'She's carrying the washing!'

'Apparently he has met her and does love her, your Grosarch; he intends to marry her, though I would prefer you to say nothing of this until we have returned her to Cythroné.'

The young soldier now looked surprised. 'Is that what you want her for?'

'You're not meant to know. Who are you anyway? You've done well to find Lara here, and I'm sure we're all grateful, but your face is beginning to worry me.'

'I know. It sometimes worries me too,' the soldier said, playing for time. 'Perhaps I should change my soap, do you think?'

'Well, I'd like to know what you're doing here too,' said Lara. For a serving girl, Talen thought, she did not seem terribly humble; on the other hand, his mind told him, he had never met a serving girl who was loved by an emperor before. 'I didn't even know you were still in the army. I thought you left, when I did, after the Battle of Klau.'

'When *you* did?' interrupted Talen-vaine-Talen. 'How can you have been in the army? You're a woman!'

'I am indeed, sir,' she replied, not that any of them had any doubt. 'But with my hair cut short and the help of my friends, including Streetpoet here, I managed.'

'I'm Streetpoet, by the way,' said the soldier by way of introduction, but the two noblemen were busily ignoring him.

'Deplorable hussy!' said the Ra-Lord.

'How dare you speak of this woman in that way!' said Talen-vaine-Talen, surprised at his own vehemence, and consoling himself with the thought that this Lara was obviously not a hussy, as anyone with eyes – or his eyes at any rate – could see.

'Thank you for your defence of my reputation, sir,' said Lara, modestly. 'But I assure you it is not necessary. My reputation means nothing to me as long as my honour remains intact.'

'Which of course it is?' asked Talen eagerly. What a remarkable young woman, he thought, and understood how the emperor could love her.

'Yes sir.' She smiled at him prettily, and he saw her eyes were grey.

'Have you two finished? asked the Gros of Ra. To his surprise, Streetpoet found himself agreeing with the Ra-Lord: Lara and Talen seemed to be spending too long looking in one another's eyes and not enough time working out what to do next for the minstrel's taste. 'There is still some explaining to be done,' the Ra-Lord continued. He sounded fierce and Talen was reminded that he had contradicted the old man rudely.

'Oh yes,' said Talen, trying to make amends. 'Soldier, explain who you are.'

'I'm an old friend of Lara's, and my name is Streetpoet. I knew both Lara and Consatiné, before he became emperor. Lara and I, with Consatiné and Ormaas and Khayrik...'

'Who?'

'Khayrik,' said Lara. 'He's a wonderful old soldier and the wisest man I've known. Where is he now?'

Streetpoet had not realised she would not know. 'I'm afraid he's dead,' he said, as gently as he could, but such news always sounds harsh and Lara looked shocked and hurt. Talen wanted to put his arms around her and comfort her yet did not want to intrude on her brave grief.

'Continue,' said the Ra-Lord. 'You were somewhere, we don't know where, with this miscellaneous list of people.'

'I was here,' said Streetpoet. 'In this very castle.'

The Ra-Lord looked as if he was going to contradict, and then corrected himself. 'Menketh alive! At the time of the Ingsvaal? That Khayrik man had no legs, and you all accompanied my wife to safety across Khalinrift?'

'That's right,' said Streetpoet. 'Although as things turned out we'd have been safer here. But that's by the way now. We travelled through the Rift but met an army of Agaskan that was moving south and were separated. Consatiné and the Lady Ra made their way to the castle of the Vaine of Akbar.'

'Yes,' said the Ra-Lord impatiently. 'He's some kind of relation of my wife, hideous man.' Talen knew enough of Leutah-vaine-Akbar to agree wholeheartedly with this judgement. 'But I've heard all that.'

'That explains where two of our party got to, but we others had different fates. Ormaas was arrested by the order of the Gros of Weir and the rest of us met again in Cythroné. The Gros of Weir and his brother, the Gyr Orland as he was then, thought that Ormaas was the bastard son of the Empress Elsban, you see, and they had him killed.'

Again Talen saw misery cross Lara's lovely features.

'But they'd got it wrong,' continued Streetpoet, 'because Ormaas was nothing to do with it, and when the Gyr Orland tried to perform the Rite of Endyear he died. He wasn't the true heir, Consatiné was. Then we fought the Agaskan at the Battle of Klau, and Consatiné showed that he was the true heir and carried the atavar of Akhran the Golden, and we all thought that everything was finished and went our own ways. Ormaas was dead, Khayrik went to live with a widow he knew on the Rhalman Road, Lara came back to her family in Northreach, and I carried on wandering as I've always done. But everything wasn't finished at all. There were all those people, the Hedchites they were called at first, and then the Brotherhood, who believed Ormaas *had* been the rightful heir, and they were clamouring for acknowledgement. And Consatiné, because he was in love with Lara here and because Ormaas had been her cousin, was daft enough to agree that Ormaas had been the true emperor, and then dafter still because he said Ormaas's ghost had led the troops at the Battle of Klau, which was hard to contradict as the atavar looks like Akhran rather than either Ormaas or Consatiné. This really confused things, as you know. The Hedchites got together and formed the Brotherhood, and the Gros of Weir was forced to include them in the government. And their power grew every year because Consatiné, Menketh alone knows why, refused to perform the Rite of Endyear himself and therefore refused to confirm he was the rightful emperor. And that's about that,' the minstrel concluded.

'You still haven't explained what brings you back to Mornet,' said the Ra-Lord.

'I was looking for Lara. Lara and I must be the only ones, apart from Consatiné, and you now, who know the whole story. I was getting tired of the Brotherhood and their silly ways and wanted to see if I could shake some sense into Consatiné. Then the war started and that only made things more urgent. And I'd heard the Vaine of Talen was looking for Lara too, so I joined you.'

'But how?' asked Talen. 'And how did you know about my mission?'

'There are ways and means,' said Streetpoet, elaborating no further.

'It's all very odd,' said the Ra-Lord.

'Od!' cried Streetpoet. 'I'd almost forgotten him: you haven't met him yet! He's been travelling with me from Ordagyn.'

'Where the wine comes from?' asked Talen. He was feeling somewhat bewildered.

'That's right. Od, come over here.'

Obediently another of Talen's soldiers came over. 'Hello,' he said. 'I overheard a lot of what was said so there's no need for explanations and introductions. It seems we're all after the same thing anyway, which is to get Lara married to the emperor.' Lara looked up, as if to question this, but Od did not notice. 'I'm very pleased to meet you all,' he said, taking off his helmet with relief and exposing a shiny bald head.

The investiture of the new Gyr Peltyn was performed with minimal ceremony, which was as well because Consatiné's speech, though fascinating and occasionally very funny, was also quite incomprehensible. Even the feast afterwards, to which Consatiné, to general relief, had decided not to go, was rather a quiet affair for news had just come through that, after a gallant struggle, the Stronghold on the Isle of Meaak had despite everything fallen to the Opposition.

The Gros of Ra surprised everyone by offering his friendship and hospitality to the newly formed group. He even introduced them all to his wife which was less of a shock for them than for her: normally he barely acknowledged her existence; she was also surprised when she was introduced as an equal to the girl who had recently been her maid, though she said nothing that could spoil her husband's rare good humour. The fact was that, though he would admit this to no one, the Ra-Lord's imagination had been attracted by the intrigues in Streetpoet's tale; after years of self-imposed seclusion in Mornet, the Ra-Lord suddenly had a hankering to be involved in Khalindaine's events. So he wished the companions well and gave them all the help he could.

The Rivermaster of Mornet had been drowned in the flood and many barges destroyed. Although work was being done to repair the damage, there was little co-ordination, and none of the Mornet barges was in a fit condition to make the journey to Akbar, which from the companions' point of view seemed a shame, though not an insurmountable objection to travelling back the way they had come: they still had the boat in which Talen-vaine-Talen had travelled upriver, though Talen was aware that another boat, or better still two, crammed with the Gros of Ra's magenta-dressed soldiers, would make him feel a lot safer. He did not want to lose Lara now he had found her and he thought this wish was merely an expression of his sense of duty.

Plans were still being made two days later, when it was announced that another barge had just been seen coming up the Khalin. 'That's useful,' said Talen. He was wrong.

The barge brought the news of how the Stronghold had fallen to the enemy; Akbar was still holding out but the Opposition had put a boom across the river, making it virtually impossible for boats to get either up or down. 'What do we do?' asked Streetpoet.

'We'll just have to make a dash for it,' said Talen with bravado, though he was worried about the fate of the men he had left behind in Akbar. 'We've two boats now. This boom of theirs can't be too strong, surely.'

'It seems awfully risky,' said Od.

'What choice do we have? We can hardly stay penned in up here for the rest of the war.'

'I suppose not.' There was a silence that contained little hope and then Od spoke again. 'Isn't there any other way out of Mornet?' he asked.

'None any good to you,' said the Ra-Lord. 'Go north, further into Northreach, safe enough, though there are still a few stray Agaskan around, but that won't get you to Cythroné. And other two routes hopeless.'

'Why?' asked Od.

'Because they lead straight to Brotherhood territory. You could go across the Rift, maybe, and get to Akbar that way, but you'd end up on the wrong side of the Khalin and walk straight into the Opposition armies. Or you could go along the Nama-Ethôn, through the mountains to Myr, but that would be no use either. You'd still be in middle of Brotherhood lands.'

'I'm not sure that matters,' said Od, speaking slowly for he was thinking as he spoke. 'There's a chance we might get away with that.'

'With what?' asked Talen.

'With being in Brotherhood territory. Streetpoet and I have already been through the Plains of Myr once since the war began, and it wasn't so terribly difficult.'

'It's true,' said Streetpoet. 'They even asked us to join one of their clubs, so we did. Od and I are both members of the Brothers Militant.'

He paused for effect. There was none. News of the Brothers Militant had not yet reached Mornet. 'So?' asked Talen. 'What about me, and Lara, and all my soldiers?'

'We'd have to leave your troops behind, of course,' admitted Streetpoet. 'But then fifty men would hardly be much use against the massed armies of the Opposition anyhow.'

'Perhaps we could steal a boat from Myr,' said Od.

'No boats!' said Streetpoet firmly. 'But I'm sure we could find a way of getting from Myr to Cythroné.'

'It sounds dafter than risking Akbar,' said the Ra-Lord.

'Not really.' Od had convinced himself by now; all he had to do was convince the others. 'If we travel down to Akbar, either by barge or through the Rift, they'll know where we're from and that we're enemies.'

'Couldn't we pretend to be Northreachers deserting for the Opposition cause?' asked Talen. It had worked before, after all.

'No,' said Od. 'That's the whole point. No one would desert that way, surely. You wouldn't go across the Rift if there was an easier way through the mountains to get to Opposition territory, which there is now the Agaskan on the Nama-Ethôn have been subdued, and you certainly wouldn't come sailing down the Khalin on a barge borrowed from the Gros of Nanx!'

'He has a point,' conceded the Gros of Ra. 'If subterfuge is needed the Nama-Ethôn is the route to take.'

'Exactly,' said Od. 'And subterfuge is certainly needed here.'

Outside the Stronghold, which was Wriknek's new head-quarters, a rabble of beggars had appeared and refused every attempt at removal. Some of the beggars were recently maim-ed, victims of the war one way or another: the raped or the homeless or the injured. Others were veterans who had spent years or lifetimes on the streets. Amongst them the syphilis victims were perhaps the most disgusting. Primary syphilis affects a small part of the body. It can be ignored, and often is. Secondary syphilis works on the skin, causing rashes and sores. Tertiary syphilis affects the bones, the muscles and the brain, and the disfigurement is often horrific. In a sense, Wriknek had been lucky. His disintegration was largely internal: the sores he had were minor and hidden; his muscles sometimes ached but were not yet wasted or eaten by the disease; his bones were scarred but not yet distorted. But this was a bad day. The energy the disease sometimes gave him seemed drained that morning; the aches and pains seemed intensified. He looked down at the crowd of beggars outside the Stronghold's gate as they waited for the army's refuse and felt hatred. These people were impurities in his system and he wanted them purged, driven out. His Brothers Militant was still not as well organised as he would have liked, but this surely was a job for them. He called for their Undermaster, who had travelled with him, and gave his instructions. The beggars were to be dispersed with force, and Wriknek gave specific instructions about the syphilitics: every one of them was to be killed; each body was to be burned. The Undermaster, happy in his task, performed it with a will.

It was decided, or so Talen thought. Streetpoet and Od would be going because their credentials, he was assured, could get them through the Opposition territory; he would go himself because he had the credentials to get through the Royalist lines; and Lara would go, of course. They would be accompanied part of the way by the Gros of Ra's men – who with any luck would scare off Rhav bandits or any remaining Agaskan – they would wear the usual Northreach outfit of coarse trousers, high boots and furs (worn by both men and childless women) and they would leave at first light. But with first light came a problem.

At first the companions were too polite, or too taken aback, to say anything but then Streetpoet spoke up. 'Excuse me, your Grosarch, but why are you dressed like that?'

'Like what? Oh, rags and tatters you mean? My disguise.'

'Disguise for what, if you'll pardon the question.'

'Question pardoned, say no more. Disguise for going through Plains of Myr. Can hardly go whole journey dressed as Gros of Ra, agreed?'

'But why are you going through the Plains of Ra?' This time it was Lara who asked the question.

'Take you to Consatiné, naturally. Why are any of us going, come to that?'

'But, your Grosarch...' It was Talen's turn to speak. 'We naturally assumed... Never thought...' He found he was adopting a sort of parody of the Ra-Lord's idiosyncratic way of speaking, and shut up before he caused offence.

'We naturally assumed,' said Streetpoet for him, 'that someone as eminent as yourself would be staying here to guard Mornet.'

'Guard Mornet! Guard against what! No danger here, no excitement. Missed out on Ingsvaal by staying here to defend the place – silly Agaskan blighters just walked straight past! I'm not doing the same trick this time round. I'm coming with you.'

They tried to talk the Ra-Lord out of his notion and failed. He was still in his remarkable good temper but he was entirely stubborn. And anyway, there was no real reason why he could not come. His age made him less conspicuous than Streetpoet or Talen, for instance, who might find they had trouble explaining why they were not in the army; his sheer personality made him a force to be reckoned with. With as good a grace as they could muster, they agreed he could come along.

Chapter 9

The Nama-Ethôn

The Nama-Ethôn, the Road to Death, had once been well named, for in the days before the Ingsvaal, which had led to the virtual destruction of the Agaskan nation, the passage westwards through the mountains had been more than perilous, it had been fatal, though the existence of the route was well known. But in the reign of Consatiné the route was being reopened and today the pass is familiar and virtually safe, though there is always the risk of bandits. From Mornet one travels a day's journey north, to Levafoln, and then west, through mountains which have no name in human tongues; in time one reaches, with luck, the Folhn river; the Folhn feeds the mightier Edo on which Myr is built, and from there the journey is a pleasant, though long, riverside stroll through pastureland and simple villages, crossing and recrossing the river on the characteristic humpbacked bridges of the region, until eventually one comes to Myr. The whole journey can be done in perhaps fifteen days. But that is today, and we are not talking of today. We are talking of the time barely five years after the Ingsvaal, when the Nama-Ethôn had not yet shaken off the implications of its name.

The companions travelled north. They passed the magnificent, terrifying, Mornet Falls and followed the Khalin as far as Levafoln. Streetpoet and Lara talked a lot at this time which Talen resented but forgave, for he knew them to be old friends and anyway his was a forgiving nature.

'You've changed,' said Lara.

'Do you think so?' asked Streetpoet.

'Yes, I do. You used to be afraid of nothing and would risk your life for a dare. But you seem more sober now, more sombre.'

'I'm sorry,' said Streetpoet, recognising the truth in what Lara said. 'It must be age catching up on me.'

'Why?' Lara asked. 'You're still young.'

'It must be Od's influence then. Like I told some woman, somewhere, Od is my conscience.'

'No,' said Lara. 'You're wrong. Before you didn't need a conscience, and now you do. Whatever has changed in your life isn't Od's doing, it's yours.'

Streetpoet thought for a moment before replying. 'That's half true,' he said, 'and half untrue. I hadn't known I needed a conscience before I met Od; having met him I know I do.'

'Then you really are getting old,' said Lara.

They reached Levafoln, a small walled town with nothing to recommend it except its fine and ancient carved gates and the fact that it was there, and stopped for the night. The Gros of Ra surprised them all by accepting the meanest rooms on offer, because he was wearing the tattiest clothes; Streetpoet, perhaps to prove to himself and to Lara that he had not reneged on his past entirely, earnt himself the best. 'I'll sing for my supper as I've always done,' he said.

He sang them a drinking song, borrowing a mandola to perform. One verse alone will convey the tone of the song.

> I can keep it up all night:
> Can you?
> Keep it for your delight
> The night through
> Keep it up without a fight
> Just for you.

And so on. It seemed to satisfy the tastes of the simple folk of Levafoln, however, if not Streetpoet's companions. The Gros of Ra was exhausted anyway by the day's unaccustomed travel, and went straight to his uncomfortable and even more unaccustomed bed; Lara and Od were disgusted by Streetpoet's performance, and soon followed the Ra-Lord upstairs. Only Talen amongst the travellers stayed for the whole song, for the troops were sent to sleep elsewhere, and he stayed only from politeness; he was so tired by the end of the evening that he could have described nothing of what had occurred anyway, which was as well because Streetpoet, in a rush of youthful abandon which in the morning was to shame him, managed to persuade not one but two barmaids to share his bed with him.

The following day their journey proper began. From Levafoln they travelled west, into the mountains. Streetpoet, Lara and the Ra-Lord were all natives of Northreach, yet none of them had ever journeyed that way before. It was a strange, dangerous, compelling route that opened before their eyes. For a few thousand strides they were able to follow a river, a tributary of the Khalin, but then their path took an unexpected lurch upwards through a sweet smelling coniferous wood, until they reached the tree line and were isolated among the peaks. They travelled with a hundred cavalrymen, and a hundred was not enough; in that sudden shift from valley to mountain, a thousand would not compensate the loss of human perspective. They crossed strange fissures and ominous gorges, and then their path dropped. As none amongst them had travelled that way before, no one knew what to expect, but the cavalrymen at least knew they would be setting back for Mornet soon, and for that they were grateful. Vast vistas opened ahead and then were closed again as they wound their rough way round the mountains; tempting inaccessible valleys were displayed for a moment before being hidden behind the next bend. There was a danger of Agaskan on these mountains, and of Rhav tribesmen; the fear the companions were aware of most was vertigo.

Four days passed. The Nama-Ethôn became almost familiar and seemed less hostile as it did so. They saw no Agaskan or bandits; the only living creatures they saw at all were the eagles that sometimes circled, curious, overhead, the swift mountain goats that leapt recklessly from ledge to invisible ledge, and once, in the distance, a great black bear that ambled and shambled alone. They got used to the heights, fond of the clear cool air, and when night came their sleep was unbroken and refreshing. But then came the time that the escort must return to Mornet and the companions were left alone. They had their first lonely night on the mountainside and felt deserted and strangely desolate. They chose a rough gully perched high on the side of a mountain, where a few stunted trees grew in the shelter, and arranged to take turns to keep watch. Suddenly, now that their escort had gone, the Northreach night seemed to have a different character. Was that the wind that howled or wolves? Were those eyes really there or was it a trick of

the light? Lara was given the first watch and as she sat in
the darkness she remembered, without choosing or wanting
to, her first experience of a night on the bare mountains, and
how a group of Agaskan degenerates had almost ambushed
her and her companions on the Agilla Pass six years or more
before. Around her were sleeping figures. Streetpoet dreamt
of lions, of which he had heard from sailors who had voyaged
to Ehapot; he had never seen one though and his lions had
the shape and colouring of giant tabby cats. Od dreamt of the
Agaskan though he had never seen one either. Only Talen and
the Ra-Lord seemed to sleep soundly: perhaps noble blood
is worth something after all, Lara mused, as she counted the
time by the stars and willed her watch to be done. It felt
lonely to be the only one awake on such a night, and she
missed the comforting jingle of the cavalry horses' bridles and
the comforting sound of the guarding cavalrymen's talk.

The moon was a narrow crescent. It gave little light and
no friendship. A twig snapped distantly on the edge of her
perception. It was getting colder, for although it was summer
they were high in the mountains and Lara drew her fur tighter
round her. She wished they had a fire but they had debated this
and decided it might attract the wrong sort of attention. She
heard another sound, nearer this time, as two rocks clinked
together, and her hand tightened around the grip of the small
bow she carried.

And then it pounced. A black shape, red eyed, leaping
from above them, clearing Lara's head, landing on Streetpoet.
His dream-lions fled at this new attack. He raised his arms
to protect his face and saw between them a snapping snout
and yellow fangs. Everyone was awake now. The dark shape
savaged at Streetpoet's prone body, snarling and pawing while
the minstrel tried to fend it off. Lara dared not fire her bow in
case she hit Streetpoet but she was on her feet and approaching
the struggle. She saw – with the clarity that comes with urgency
and the sense that time stands still – that the creature was an
ugly old wolf with a ragged pelt, that Streetpoet was bleeding
but fending it off, and that its ferocity seemed to be lessening.
Then Talen had rushed the wolf with his sword and struck it
a blow to the heart.

The wolf howled and fell away leaving Streetpoet to cope
with his wounds. His face had been mauled and his hands

were over his eyes, which meant he did not see what the others saw. For the wolf, lying on its back, writhing, was somehow changing form. Its legs and arms grew longer, its back seemed to shorten, its muzzle shrank back into its face, and suddenly instead of a wolf it was a withered and incredibly ancient old man with a matted and miserable beard, who clutched at his wounded heart and then cracked and crumbled to dust.

For a time no one spoke and then Streetpoet sat up. There was blood across his forehead and down his cheek, and a flap of skin hung loose beneath his eye. 'Has it gone?' he asked.

'Yes,' said Od. 'It's gone. Whatever it was.'

'It was a wolf,' said Streetpoet. 'I saw it.'

'It was a wolf,' his friend replied. 'And then it wasn't any more.'

'What are you talking about?'

They told him, and though their telling was confused by their shock he understood enough. He turned to the pile of dust next to him, which was still undisturbed, and saw white hairs tangled there and a handful of broken yellow fangs. 'But what could it have been?' he asked. He found he did not want to touch the dust and shivered and edged away from it slightly.

'Va'samroth,' said Lara in a low voice.

Talen and Od could make nothing of this but for Streetpoet and the Ra-Lord the word seemed to have meaning. 'Do you think so?' asked the minstrel. 'But surely that all happened sixty years or more ago, if it ever happened at all.'

'Oh, it happened all right,' said the Ra-Lord. 'Time of my father. He told me the tale.'

'Can someone explain what you're talking about, please?' pleaded Talen.

'Not heard of Va'samroth?' asked the Ra-Lord, puzzled. 'Surely everyone's heard?'

'I haven't heard of it either,' said Od.

The Ra-Lord shook his head with pity for these southerners and their deplorable ignorance of Northreach legend, but told his tale patiently enough. 'Va'samroth was a shaman from Toothaas. Don't know how much you've heard about our religion here, because though it's the Old Religion, the one on which the southern religion's based, from what I've seen of

Cythroné at any rate, there's not much comparison to be made between them, what with the Rite of Endyear down there and the hoarstones up here and so on. Biggest difference of all is the shaman. Officially a shaman is a shape-changer, though not many of them do that; mostly they just hide away and sell potions which don't work, and pretend they understand what the hoarstones are saying, and come out about twice a year for the Initiation of Youth and the Burial of the Dead. They're all known as Va'-something, and that should interest you, Talen-vaine-Talen, because your title of Vaine comes from the same word, Vant, which means 'honoured' in Old Northreach.

'Anyhow, this one shaman, Va'samroth, was known as a particularly powerful magician. Don't ask if all the stories about him are true – how he once flew across the Mornet Falls in a buzzard's beak, and how he made friends by turning lead to gold, and made gold by turning enemies to lead – but one story is certainly fact, because my father told me, and the House of Ra has no liars in it. Happened like this. One day Va'samroth was looking for herbs in the valley, when he met a woman from the town who was walking with her children. Don't know how old Va'samroth was then, but he wouldn't have been young: no such thing as a young shaman anyway, as it takes so long to learn the tricks. Anyhow, he takes a bit of a shine to this woman, and asks her for a favour or two, which we won't go into in mixed company, and she says no. Now, she lived in a farm outside Toothaas, along the valley, and because he's annoyed she's turned him down, Va'samroth takes a stone no bigger than my fist and throws it at the house. Poof! No house. And then he picks up the youngest of her children and threatens to throw that in the air too, which will be the end of the child, unless she changes her mind. Which she does, and having nowhere else to live she goes to live with him, as his mistress. And don't ask me about her husband because I don't know. She might not have had one, though some say he was in her house when Va'samroth threw his stone.

'Well, life with him was no fun, all humping and thumping as they say round here.' He avoided Lara's eye, which was unnecessary: she had heard far worse expressions. 'The only work she didn't have to do her children did, and all of them were set to work day and night, while he sat in his study messing with his potions and reading his books.

'A few years must've gone by like this, and then suddenly, one night, Va'samroth disappeared. Don't mean magic, just mean went, vanished, was never seen again. Thought he might have been murdered, so my father was sent for, told what had happened, asked if he'd judge the case. He was only young at the time, only Vaine of Mornet, his father still being alive, and I wasn't even born. And he asked the woman what had happened, so she told him.

'It seems old Va'samroth was in the habit, now and then, of turning into a wolf at night, going into the mountains, savaging a few sheep, and coming back. Not much fun in my opinion, but there you are, everyone to their own. Anyway, the woman discovered that to change back to a man he needed to drink a potion of some kind, which he always left in a bowl outside his house. That was sensible, if you think about it, because as a wolf he'd not be able to open a bottle, would he? And he also locked the woman and her children up, to stop them meddling with things. But the woman had made a spare key without the shaman knowing, and one night when he was out with his sheep she stole out to the yard and poured his potion away. Then she locked up the house again, and warned the neighbours there was a wolf about, so when Va'samroth came back he wouldn't be able to get his drink. And that's what happened. Wolf came back night after night and was driven away, and in the end it stopped coming back and went off to the mountains.

'And that was that, really. Not much of a story. Silly domestic dispute. Only proves that though a man can beat his woman she can get her revenge other ways, and every man worth his boots will know that already.'

'But what happened to the woman? asked Talen-vaine-Talen, always concerned by matters of gallantry.

'Oh, she was burnt as a witch, as a precaution, in case she ever decided to turn anyone else into a wolf. And every so often the people of Toothaas would see the wolf hanging round, and drive him off again. He must have eventually wandered up here.'

There was a pause. They looked at the pile of dust and hair with pity and disgust, and then Lara spoke for them all when

she suggested they move on, despite the night, because she
was not happy about sleeping next to Va'samroth, whatever
form he was in.

It was only when they moved that they discovered the
severity of the wounds to Streetpoet's face. His eyes were
undamaged, but the skin that hung loose beneath his left eye
was certain to scar badly, and there was another mark across
his forehead that looked equally ugly. They found a place
where a stream ran brightly down the dark mountainside and
bathed his wounds, but they could do nothing else for him.

The night was almost over and the sky was lighter now
to the east. They decided to rest there. Lara had not slept at
all and the others had slept but little; in addition, Streetpoet
had lost quite a lot of blood from his forehead. Head wounds
always bleed profusely. Yet despite this lack of sleep only the
Ra-Lord settled down straightaway while his companions took
turns to keep watch.

They rested until almost noon and then set off again. The
previous night's events, as so often happens when the sun
shines and birds sing, seemed distant and dreamlike, but
Streetpoet's face still bore the scars and he would carry them
for life, disfiguring his handsome face and drawing his left
eye down as the cuts healed. The travellers walked in virtual
silence. Their path had dropped again into a wide wooded
valley and they found a river, but it was flowing eastwards,
back the way they had come, which meant they had not yet
reached the watershed. The trees here were deciduous, elms
and oaks mostly, and the undergrowth was thicker. The path
was not hard to follow, however, for someone in ancient times
had paved this section with giant flags of stone. Or perhaps the
engineers had not been human at all, but Agaskan, for once
this had all been Agaskan territory.

Streetpoet's face hurt him but it was not the pain he minded.
He had examined his face that morning in a pool at the river's
edge and had recognised that these were not scars that would
fade. Almost all his life, from the time he had run away from
his fur trading bully of a father, Streetpoet had lived on his wits
and his looks. Now his looks were gone and he even suspected
his wits might be failing: certainly Lara had hit home when
she had said he seemed more sombre, less reckless, than he

had been when she had known him before, and somehow his wild night with the Levafoln barmaids had improved neither his self-image nor his self-esteem. He looked around him. Two courting doves chased across a glade. A molehill by the path indicated the activity beneath. The trees rustled and budded. The river chattered away to itself. Everything seemed the same as ever, seemed safe and normal and a long way from the war, yet here the night before a creature from a nightmare had scarred his face before crumbling to dust. Is it the world that's changing, he wondered, or is it me?

A wandering minstrel leads a bastard existence, part bard and part bawdy entertainer, for his trade is as ancient, as honourable, and as base, as man. Streetpoet's living depended on his memory for drinking songs and his ability to conjure rude rhymes, yet he had also learnt, from the masters he had met and studied with at the Grove of the Red Rock – a secret place known only to minstrels – the ancient verses that told the history of Khalindaine. Perhaps it was the antique track they travelled, or the melancholy he felt, but Streetpoet's mind turned to that history and to the songs that retained it.

There were many versions yet the theme was always much the same. In the beginning there was Hrakar, the father of gods, and were one to travel high enough in the sky one would see him, for Khalindaine lies on his skull. This explains why the world seems round, with its horizons always shifting – we see this most at sea – yet we never fall off because Hrakar is the father of all and everything is attracted to him, and this is also why an apple drops or a bird when hit by a stone. After Hrakar came his sons, Menketh and Araketh. Menketh wanted all things free, Araketh wanted all things bound. They argued and fought for many years, and then Hrakar, tired of his sons' bickering, told them to make an experiment to prove which one was right. So Menketh made man, and Araketh made the Agaskan, each in his own image. Man was free and able to do certain things because of this; the Agaska was bound, yet the Agaskan as a nation could all work together in harmony and without trouble. The Agaskan had no poets and no civil wars. And these creations were placed on Hrakar's skull, in a land that was surrounded by water, and told to do what they could.

In the beginning the Agaskan did much better. They controlled most of the land, and the men were contained in one corner, where they kept their freedom yet could neither agree nor fight back. But then came Tlot – or Hlot, as some tellings have it – who was a leader and a hero. He galvanised the men and led them north, driving the Agaskan from the plains and forcing them into the mountains. But even Tlot could not do the impossible: he challenged death, and was beaten, and taken to Rathkerid, the land of the dead.

Khalindaine is well named, for the river that runs through its heart has dominated and shaped its destiny. Tlot died in the north, in the region that is now called Northreach, and left a line of descendants who still feared and faced the Agaskan; in the south, people had an easier life, and though they never forgot the Agaskan nor neglected to patrol the Khalinwatch, the line of fortresses at the edge of the Thatter where many Agaskan still flourished, their lives became dominated less by battle than the change of the seasons. They still had wars, of course, for they were men, but they also had periods of long peace and times when beautiful buildings were made and beautiful songs composed.

Then suddenly there came Akhran, leading his hordes from Northreach, following the Khalin southwards in what has been known since those times as the Riverrun, and establishing in Cythroné, on the great river's mouth, his capital and his dynasty. Akhran the Golden, the founder of Khalindaine's empire, yet at the same time barely human himself: a man whose face was almost Agaskan in appearance, with narrow cheeks beneath high bones and sharply pointed teeth; a man who could, with an Agaska's ritual delight, tear another man apart; a man who would not die but who recurs to this day in his descendants. Streetpoet was a bard, a poet, despite his rough life and his taste for low dives. He could, at times at least, understand how another man thinks and why. He knew better than any why Consatiné rejected his destiny, why that mild, mellow, intelligent young man loathed to carry within him the avatar of hideous Akhran, and why therefore the emperor refused to perform the Rite of Endyear, which summoned Akhran and gave strength to the empire. But, because Streetpoet was a bard and a poet, he also knew that Consatiné must accept destiny, be emperor, do what history demanded of him. Because the alternatives, the civil war in which brother fought brother and Khalindaine tore itself to pieces, would never work. And therefore Streetpoet saw, without realising it, the great truth of man's existence: that life is a compromise between the freedom Menketh wills and the rules his brother imposes; that sometimes duty must come before individuality, though individuality must never be lost. Araketh would bind us, hold us down, regiment and organise and dictate to us, rooting out our individuality and our impurities; Menketh would allow no rules and split everything asunder, until with the final split of the smallest thing, Khalindaine would be finally destroyed.

Streetpoet shook his head. There were many things he did not understand, and a few things he did. It must be the atmosphere beneath these trees that makes me philosophical, he decided, as he walked on.

They came to a form in the road. This was unexpected.

'Which way do we go?' asked Lara.

'I don't know,' said the Ra-Lord.

'No one else is going to,' said Streetpoet.

'Oh, all right: this way.' The Ra-Lord's choice was arbitrary, and as it happened wrong, but at least someone had taken a decision. The Gross of Ra had never been afraid of authority, which is perhaps why he pretended to treat his adopted son with contempt.

They climbed a long hill through the woods and reached the top. Looking out they saw another deep valley, and within that valley was something that stopped them in their tracks. For it was a town of sorts: a gigantic town, as big as Mornet at least, made of pyramids of stone, and apparently quite deserted.

'Where in Khalindaine are we?' asked Talen, awed.

'Menketh knows,' said the Gros of Ra. 'The wrong place, certainly.'

The pyramids were all square at the base, all identical, and all equally spaced, so far as the rather uneven valley floor would allow. Between them ran regular roads; the one they were on descended the valley to join these.

'It must have been an Agaskan city,' said Streetpoet, and Od shivered. 'If the Agaskan lived in cities, that is.'

'This wasn't built by humans,' said Od. 'But where have they all gone?'

'I think I can answer that,' said Streetpoet. 'As can Lara. We saw them marching south, millions of them, in the Ingsvaal. They'd have been enough to fill a city this size, and more.'

'Where are they now?'

'I don't know. Dead? In the Thatter? A lot of them died trying to cross the Khalin. They're not here, at any rate. Look at the plants growing all over everything.'

'Perhaps the Agaskan like plants,' worried Od. But what Streetpoet said seemed true. The pyramids were terraced and the terraces dotted with round windows, but these were already as overgrown as the paths they had travelled along. 'Well,' said Od who, having never met an Agaska, was perhaps most fearful of them all. 'I think we now know who built this road, and the one we left, and now we know that can we get out of here please. There may be one or two Agaskan left around still, and it's a big city. They'd have no trouble finding somewhere to hide.'

It certainly was a big city: each pyramid could hold maybe a thousand, maybe more, and there were hundreds of them in the valley. Even Talen, who was not used to fear, felt intimidated. 'Yes, let's go,' he said. 'This obviously isn't the right route and we're wasting time.'

No-one disagreed. They regarded the dreadful splendour in silence and turned to go.

'I wonder what the Agaskan called this place,' said Lara. 'It must have had a name.' She took a last look over her shoulder, but the others were not interested enough to speculate nor answer her question, so she turned and followed them and therefore did not see the crouched figure of an Agaska that had scuttled for cover when she turned, nor the slightly larger figure behind it.

Even though they did not know they had been seen, the companions returned to the fork in the road rather more rapidly than they had left it, and set off in the other direction. At once their path began to climb again, quite steeply, though still they were surrounded by the woods.

'How many people have been this way before? asked Talen of the Ra-Lord.

'I don't know. Enough to have found that place.'

'That's what I'd have thought. Then why has no one heard of it before. You hadn't, obviously, from the expression on your face, and neither had Lara, yet you've both been in Northreach all this time.'

'Are *you* going to tell anyone about it?' asked the Ra-Lord. 'I'm not. There's plenty think I'm in my dotage without me encouraging them in their views.'

Talen half followed the older man's thoughts. After all, who would believe they had actually seen an Agaskan city. But he was not convinced entirely. 'On the other hand,' he said, 'I've heard plenty of traveller's tales. They're usually incredible. Why hasn't anyone told this one?'

'Which one?' asked the Ra-Lord, and Talen gave up.

Instead he went to talk with Lara, which was his special pleasure. 'What a strange place this is,' he remarked.

'I know,' she said. 'Nowhere has a name.'

'That's right. And that makes it all a sort of Nowhere. I'm not sure I don't like it though, for all that.'

'There's a lot of beauty here,' said Lara.

'There is indeed,' said Talen, and she knew he was looking at her.

'Look at the squirrels!' she said, attempting to change the mood, and failing.

'Wonderful,' he agreed. 'I love you.'

She had expected this declaration. She was older than he and had spent the last years in a busy castle's domestic quarters. She had recognised the way Talen looked at her. What she had not expected was her reply. 'I love you too,' she said, and as she said it she knew she meant it.

Behind them walked Od, thinking his own thoughts. Perhaps there was enchantment in that valley, or maybe it was just the contrast with the bleak mountains they had been through and the hideous night they had suffered. But the same warm air which had made Streetpoet first melancholy and then philosophical, and had turned Lara and Talen into lovers, was making Od feel nostalgic. They had left the river behind now but there was still a river in his mind, his glorious beautiful Hasfaine, where the banks seemed so domesticated and calm, and yet where a night of flooding or a season of drought could find new sandbanks, new outlets, new routes to navigate. A man does not need a religion, Od decided, nor even someone to love. What a man needs, he felt, was a trade and a river on which to ply it, and he knew he would be returning to the Hasfaine soon. The thought delighted him.

Meanwhile, the Agaskan who did not like the woods and preferred to hunt on the peaks watched them from a distance and plotted what best to do. These were not the true, terrifying Agaskan of the legends; the warriors were dead or dispersed to the Thatter in the centre of Khalindaine, where they planned their next attack on the people who had driven them from the valleys. Instead, this bunch was barely Agaskan at all, in the sense that Araketh had planned it, for they were minor mutants who had failed to respond in the programmed way to the call of the Ingsvaal, the call to war, which was why they had remained in the city when the others had left. They were Agaskan enough, however, to have retained their sense of duty. They looked after the city as best they could and guarded its precincts. It was not surprising that neither Talen nor the Gros of Ra had heard tell of the Agaskan city before; none who had ventured that way before had survived.

The path the companions took seemed suddenly steeper. It had been a long day's walk, the evening was drawing in, and they wondered where they should stop for the night. The valley was beautiful but too close to the city; the peaks ahead were bleak but more easily defended.

They continued on their way. In these northern climes the evening was slow, a gradual change, as much of mood as light, that spread from the east. The insects seemed to feel it first. The sound of crickets and bees was replaced by the threatening buzz of mosquitoes, and clouds of gnats could be seen, circling like dust around the branches of trees. Then the birds noticed the night. The sound of the doves and blackbirds faded, and instead came the melancholy call of the owls. The gaps between the trees grew darker; the distance they could see decreased. Yet even in night the valley's enchantment continued. The Agaskan stayed clear, unnoticed, and the companions thought their private thoughts.

The Gros of Ra thought about his pointing-stick. Was it magic or science? he wondered. He did not have much skill with magic, and less understanding, but he could not figure how else the pointing-stick might work. Behind him were Lara and Talen. They walked hand in hand and exchanged their lives.

Following the lovers were Streetpoet and Od. They walked together but did not talk. Silence was pleasant enough. Streetpoet thought about a poem, a new one to rival the work of the great bards, which might earn him immortality or better still a state pension. He might be needing a state pension now his face was damaged. It would be a poem about the Ingsvaal, yet also about Menketh and Araketh, and the way matter responds to freedom and rules. It would be a good poem.

Od was still thinking of rivers. He loved the sound of water, especially the noise it makes when it meets an obstruction. He liked too the way it behaves when its way is blocked: it is stubborn, but not too much so; it gurgles but divides to pass round, and then reunites as though it had never been split. He was so busy thinking of water that for a moment it did not register that he was also hearing it, and sure enough ahead was a stream. For a moment the implications of what he saw were lost on him, and then he suddenly danced with excitement; Streetpoet, who felt he had known Od a lifetime by now, was not disconcerted by his bald friend's strange behavior in the half-light. 'What's up?' he asked.

'Look,' said Od. 'Look.'

Streetpoet looked. 'Water,' he pronounced.

'Yes,' said Od. 'But look at the way it's running. It's going the same way we are. We've crossed the watershed. It should be downhill all the way from now on until we get to Myr!'

They were not yet even at the Folhn, much less at the Edo that flows through Myr, but this stream was going their way at last, and as Od said, it should have been downhill all the way from now on.

Od should also have known better. He had seen enough of life to know it is a little rascal, quite incapable of doing the right thing at the right time. They had barely followed the river for a thousand strides before the Agaskan attacked.

Suddenly all was chaos. The attack was clumsily planned and clumsily executed, but still it caught them by surprise. They were forced together in a rough circle, back to back with their swords drawn, while the Agaskan tried to break through. A better ambush could have separated and killed them in an instant; it was as well for the travellers, and for our traveller's tale, that these were not the crême of the Agaskan hordes.

Talen's youth and bravery made an instant impression. He had killed one Agaska while his companions were drawing their swords, and this at least gave them all time to think. For himself, he barely thought at all. All his life he seemed to have been swinging a sword, but never before in defence of the woman he loved. He tore into the enemy with a will.

Lara too was fighting. She would not let her hero die if she could help it, and if he died he would not die alone. She fought well: in Northreach they teach their womenfolk such things, which is sensible; why limit half a population simply because of some quirk of biology? Beside her was Streetpoet. They had fought side by side before against the Agaskan, in the famous Battle of Klau, and understood one another's reactions well. Next to Streetpoet was the Gros of Ra, always ferocious, waving his sword with the abandon and certainty of a man who knows he shall not die here. And finally, completing the circle, was Od of the bald head, the cool head, fighting sensibly, keeping their loose formation together, trying to assess where their best chances lay.

Unfortunately for Od, this did not need much working out. They were outnumbered, and unless they could drive their enemy off, all was lost.

And then he noticed, by his side, another arm, unmistakably human, undeniably unknown to him, with muscles and tattoos that rippled in the dusk. And now the fight had a different complexion, for it was not one arm but fifty that had joined them, and now the Agaskan were in retreat.

None of the companions quite knew what had happened, nor who their saviours were; Talen, for one, felt vaguely cheated that the fight had ended so abruptly. Nor was their curiosity satisfied immediately: with a harsh 'Follow me!' they were led from the path.

Darkness had now almost closed and none of them knew where they were anyway, so they were surprised and even a little offended when they were told they would have to be blindfolded. Still, they reasoned, better blindfolded than dead.

Their path was impossible to follow; it occurred to Od early on that he doubted he could have sorted out all the twists and turns at noon with the blindfold off. The only things they knew for certain was that the trees all wanted to grab at their hair and that the path led always upwards. At last they reached somewhere else. Through their blindfolds, dimly, was the outline of a good fire and around them was the sound of voices.

The companions were arranged in a line and their blindfolds removed. They found themselves facing a large and rather fierce-looking man with a full beard and a goose leg in his hand. The grease from the goose, bright in the firelight, dribbled down his muscular arm and matted the many black hairs there. There could be no doubt that this man was a bandit, and no doubt that he was a chief.

'Who be you lot then?' asked this bandit chief to the companions. He had a strange way of speaking for that region, a little like Od's although broader. There was no mistaking the distinctive southern twang.

There was a pause. 'Travellers,' said Talen, speaking for them all.

'And where be you travelling?'

There was no point in lying. 'To Myr.'

'And what be you going to do there, pray?'

Menketh knew what the right answer might be! Each of the companions racked his or her brain for something sensible to say, and came up with a nothing which was as incriminating as anything they could have contrived. 'I see,' said the bandit chief. 'You's not be telling me then. Which means it's as well that I knows.'

Do you? they all wondered, after they had sorted out the grammar of that sentence, and then they felt themselves caught between disbelief and alarm.

'Yes, you're spies for the Brotherhood, or spies for the Royalists, one or the other. And how do us know? Because only a sneaking spy would bother going between Mornet and Myr the route you've taken, that's why.'

'Well, that's not true,' said Streetpoet. He was very grateful to have been saved, and all that, but he was getting fed up with being accused of being a spy. 'Akbar is besieged by the Opposition. There was no other way to get out of Northreach.'

'Aye, well, if you'd not been travelling these past few days you'd maybe have heard that Wriknek and most of his lot have left Akbar now and are marching towards Cythroné, and that the Gyr Peltyn is on his way to meet them.'

'The *Gros* of Peltyn, surely,' corrected Talen, out of habit. His nurse had always been very insistent that titles should be allocated correctly.

'I said Gyr and I meant Gyr. He's been promoted.'

'Elevated,' said Talen, correcting again and then wishing he had not. 'You seem very well informed,' he added, hoping to rectify his bad manners by displaying his good.

'Got to be in this game, son. No choice. Us can't go frigging all over Khalindaine in the hope that the war'll go away, oh no sir. Got to make a living. That's why us come up here, but that been a mistake. No one on this route but lousy useless bastards like you.'

This judgement seemed a little unfair, yet none of the companions complained. And anyway, the bandit chief was still speaking. 'Now, me and my lads, we be in business, and our business be to relieve them what's got money of their surplus. What with the war and all us've come north, because business was looking very bad in our part of the world, what with armies all over the place an' the rest, but I reckon us've overstepped ourselves here; I reckon this be too far north and there be too many of them pesky Rhav about offering us competition, to say nothing of those green-skinned Agaskan. Which is a good thing for you. Because if I was staying round here I'd have your throats cut like that, so'd you'd not give me away. But as it is I'm leaving, and all of the boys going too, and I don't need to bother now, do I. So I'll tell you what us'll do to you, and you'll listen careful if you've got the sense – not that folks can have much sense, thinking on, because otherwise they'd never have left their mothers' wombs. We're going to truss you up, and take you somewhere, and dump you, and you can reckon yourselves lucky.'

'Thank you,' said Talen, but the bandit's mind had moved on to the next matter.

'Food!' he cried. 'Where's the grub?'

A fat man in a stained apron pushed forward. 'Here you are, Frahko,' he said holding a leg of lamb, and then taking a bite. The bandit chief grabbed it out of the fat man's mouth.

'Mine, brother,' he said. The fat man turned and Frahko aimed a kick at him, which the waddling bottom absorbed fairly effortlessly. 'You'll want feeding too, I reckon,' added the bandit chief, looking at the companions.

'You come with me,' said the fat man, while Frahko bit into the lamb and thick trickles of grease ran off his chin to mingle with the hairs on his chest.

The friends followed the fat bottom across a large grassy clearing surrounded by caves. It was easy to see why the bandits had thought this a suitable place for a hideout; it was a shame, from their point of view, that there were so few victims about.

A good fire in the mouth of a cave played on what was left of a roast sheep while a couple of lads pulled a clay pot from the flames, handling it carefully as though it were precious and then smashing it. Inside was a loaf of heavy black bread. The fat man broke the bread in his unsavoury fingers, tugged lumps of meat from the roasting carcass, and handed them out. 'What's your name then?' he asked Lara.

'I'm Lara,' she replied, and seeking to deflect his attentions – she knew the look in his eyes well – she introduced her companions as well, though she omitted Talen's title and the Gros of Ra entirely.

The fat man was unimpressed. 'I'm Lhink,' he told her. 'Frakho's my brother. Frahko's the boss.' He obviously sought to impress her with this connection.

'Really,' said Lara. She was about to remark the brothers looked nothing like one another, then reflected that Lhink might not want to hear this. 'I can see the likeness.'

'That's what I say. My brothers don't see it.'

'You've another brother apart from Frahko?'

'Yeah. Hruhnk. Him and Frahko, though, they reckon I'm the simpleton in the family. Frahko's got the brains, Hruhnk has got the muscles, and it's yours truly, Lhink, do the cooking.'

Lara tried to picture this Hruhnk – Frahko seemed to have muscles for two – and failed. 'Still, somebody's got to do the cooking, I suppose,' said Lara comfortingly.

'That's what I always say,' said the cook.

Frahko arrived and gave his brother a playful cuff round the ear: the cook landed about five strides away. 'Ignore him, love,' said the bandit chief. 'He be stupid but harmless. And now I guess it's time for bed.' Big Frahko looked hard at his sprawled brother. 'And no funny business.'

'Who? Me? asked Lhink.

The following morning they were pulled from their beds rather than woken. Big Frahko was not in sight but his deputy, who was almost as big, had obviously been given instructions: 'Right! Deal with them, lads.'

Od felt a sharp blow on the back of his head, and then nothing. Streetpoet felt a similar blow, resisted for a second, and passed out. The Ra-Lord's thick skull required a second tap. Talen stepped forward, involuntarily, as Lara dropped to the floor, and then was felled himself. The last thing he remembered was seeing the faces of two children, a boy and a girl, and thinking how strangely familiar those faces were. And then the world turned grey and cellular to his eyes, and he too dropped to the floor.

The Gros of Ra was the only one who could say anything at all about the journey, and even his recollection was hazy, though he probably would not have been able to say much more had he been wide awake. They were each strapped to the back of a mule, face down, and led downhill a long way. All the Ra-Lord could see was his arms, tied to the mule, and beneath was the dusty ochre road, cracked now as summer approached. Then they were unstrapped, and carried, each slung between two bandits, down to the banks of a river. The Ra-Lord smelt this rather than saw it, for he did not dare open his eyes in case they slugged him again. The scent was slight yet pervasive, clean, unwooded. It reminded him of ducks. He was dumped onto something that resisted and rocked, and knew he was on a boat. Then another body was dropped on top of him, and another on top of that, until he found himself virtually crushed to the planks. He had just decided he might have been more comfortable if they had slugged him again when he felt the boat move beneath them. They were being pushed away from the banks, and the next stage of their journey was under way.

Chapter 10

Charisma

If there is something undignified about floating downstream at the bottom of a boat while being crushed by your four companions, then the Ra-Lord did not seem aware of it. On the contrary, he seemed to be keeping his composure remarkably well, assessing the situation and admiring the view. From where he lay he could see: one hand, masculine possibly Od's; one hank of hair, long and feminine, surely Lara's; one knee, unidentified; one gunwale, brown, varnish blistering to reveal lighter colour beneath; and one patch of sky, duck-egg blue occasionally cracked by the silhouette of dark branches. He was not comfortable, nor was he uncomfortable; he would be glad when the others woke, but was not desperate for that moment.

The unidentified knee stirred first, pushing itself into the Ra-Lord's chin 'Careful,' cautioned the Ra-Lord. The knee was still then stirred again.

'Oooooooo,' said Streetpoet. The knee in the Ra-Lord's face suddenly moved away, rather to that nobleman's relief, and Streetpoet tried to extricate himself from under Lara. Lara was no weight, yet Streetpoet seemed to be having difficulties. The boat rocked and water splashed the Ra-Lord's upturned face. 'Careful!' the Ra-Lord said again.

At last Streetpoet had struggled free, though the dislodged Lara now hung, unnoticed, perilously close to falling overboard. 'Where are we?' he asked as he rubbed his eyes.

'In a boat,' called the Gros of Ra.

'*In a boat!*'

'Don't believe it! Look for self.'

'Oh, I believe it all right. We're in a boat, Naturally we're in a boat. Where else could we be but in a boat?'

'Don't sound very well,' observed the Ra-Lord.

'Me? Oh, I'm fine. I'm in a boat, that's all, another Menketh-blasted Hrakar-hating sodding lousy boat.'

'Give hand, help out. Everyone on top of me,' said the Ra-Lord, his normally abbreviated sentences made even shorter by the difficulty of breathing.

'Oh. Yes. Of course.' Streetpoet was still trying to work out which of the ironic fates was responsible for putting him on yet another river, and his responses were slowed down anyway by the after effects of the blow to his head. 'Right.' But the minstrel did nothing.

'Good chap, give hand. Help out.' cajoled the Ra-Lord.

Streetpoet shook himself together, almost literally, and the boat rocked: he was just in time to stop Lara falling overboard, and as it was one of her legs fell into the water.

These sudden transferences of weight above him were not doing the Ra-Lord any good. 'Say! Steady on.'

'Sorry,' said Streetpoet. From the top of a heap of bodies Lara hung over the side, with Streetpoet clinging to her; it was not surprising that the boat had developed a list. 'Lara's falling out.'

'Pull back in then,' advised the Ra-Lord.

'Why didn't I think of that?' He had Lara by the waist and tried pulling, but every movement he made was magnified by a rocking of the boat, and accompanied by a grunt from the Ra-Lord. It was not a big boat. Five people might have been able to sit upright in it without too much discomfort; five people sprawled haphazardly in it was at least four too many. Meanwhile, the boat, which had been going gently down the stream, was now turning, dragged by Lara's dangling leg, and Lara was beginning to stir.

'Give her a push and let her swim!' came a youthful cry. Streetpoet looked up. Lolling on a bridge, watching them, were two fat boys. Each munched an apple.

'Haven't you anything better to do?' he called back.

'No,' said the fat boys, contentedly.

Streetpoet tried to ignore them but it was hard. He pulled Lara as best he could and spoke to her gently as she came round. 'It's all right. There, there. It's all right.'

After a short time of this, while Lara tried to rearrange the jumble in her head and Streetpoet tried to help with reassurances and answers to her questions, one of the boys on the bridge had obviously had enough. Watching a boat piled high with bodies is an unusual spectator sport, but a potentially exciting one, and the fat boys wanted some action. The apple core hit Streetpoet behind the ear.

'Ugh, my head,' said Lara.

'What about mine?' wondered Streetpoet. 'I'll murder the little swine. I'll tear him limb from limb, I'll...'

Odd had started to move now, beneath them. The bandits' clumsy anaesthetic left unfortunate side-effects, and Od seemed completely unaware of all that had happened since the previous winter. 'What do I do?' he asked. 'They'll kill me if they find out where I am...they'll tear me limb from limb...'

'What's he talking about?' asked Lara.

'I'm not sure,' said Streetpoet. 'Probably, being bald, he took a worse knock than the rest of us. No hair to absorb the blow.'

Another apple core was tossed at them, with the injunction to get on with it. 'Who are those lads?' asked Lara.

'Future victims of an axe murderer,' said Streetpoet with optimistic relish.

Now that three of them were awake, and Od on his way, it was possible, with a certain degree of co-ordination, for them all to ease into more comfortable positions. Meanwhile, however, Lara's foot was no longer in the water and the boat was free to go downstream unhindered again: it hesitated, broadside to the flow, seemed to sniff and fidget, and then chased beneath the humpback bridge. The fat boys threw stones at them, which missed, then chased along the towpath behind them.

It was a quiet stretch of river used a lot by barges. These Folhn barges were not the dramatic wide barges of the Khalin though, but were long, sheer-sided, narrow and graceless, pulled by horses. The barges went from level to level through simple locks that had a cumbersome single gate at each end and sluices which needed to be raised by hand. The locks reduced the drift of water seaward, and thus slowed down the companions. Even two fat boys had no problem at all keeping up.

Talen was still out cold, watched over by Lara. Od was uncertain where he was, and Streetpoet splashed water at his friend to let him know. The Gros of Ra sat at the back of the boat, impervious both to the incongruity of the situation or the jibes of the panting fat boys.

Soon they reached a lock. The upper gate was closed and they ran straight into it but the lower gate was open to admit a barge. Od's professional curiosity got the better of his grogginess and he started to take an interest in his surroundings. The fat boys decided, prudently, that their entertainment's access to dry land made their position perilous and stayed clear of the lock.

The Ra-Lord was the first to climb from the boat onto the rickety walkway at the top of the gate. He looked down as the barge was manoeuvred into the lock, the bargees pushing with poles against the stone walls while their horse, untethered, chewed grass on the bank. 'Give us a hand,' called one of the bargees.

'What do you want me to do?' asked the disguised Gros of Ra.

'Just open us the sluice.'

There was a fall of about two strides between the two levels of water. The Ra-Lord had heard of locks but did not yet understand them. Without waiting for the bargees to close the lower gate he raised the sluice. 'Oi!' cried the bargees. 'Hold on!' But the Ra-Lord, trying to be helpful, could not hear over the rush of water, and when he next looked the barge had been washed out of the lock, through the lower gate, and was floating slowly downstream. 'That can't be right,' he thought.

Od had joined him on the walkway. 'You should've let them close the lower gate first,' he explained, 'Then when you open the sluice the lock fills up, their boat rises, and they can open the upper gate and let themselves out; we'd go in, open the sluice on the lower gate, the lock would empty, and then we could get out. We'd better get this sluice closed before the water level on our side gets too low; at the moment we're just draining the river.'

The barge by this time had backed delicately into the bank, and the bargees were hurrying about, rounding up their horse and tethering it to the barge so they could move upstream again; Od and the Ra-Lord tried to lower the sluice and found it jammed. 'It isn't designed to be closed while there's water flooding through,' said Od. 'Normally it's only closed when the level is the same both side of the gate, and there's no pressure on it. We'll have to see if we can close the lower gate."

He ran down to explain what he wanted to the bargees. They were getting fed up by now, but what Od said made sense; they wondered if they could get their barge into the lock before the lower gate was closed, but decided they could not push against the flood and instead moored their barge outside the lock and went to help with the gate.

It was hard work getting it closed, even after Streetpoet and Lara had joined them, for like the sluice it was not designed to be moved except when the waters were calm; at that moment the upper sluice was pouring water like the Mornet Falls. But they managed it at last. The Ra-Lord watched with fascination how the lock filled up; in time the water reached the level of the sluice, reducing the sound of the rushing water to almost nothing, and eventually it reached the level of the water on the upper side. Now that the pressure was equal on both sides of the sluice, closing the sluice gate was easy, as was opening the upper lock gate. With Talen still aboard, their little boat was floated in, the gate refastened, and the lower sluice opened to let the water out.

The bargees were still fretting over the waste of time, but it was a pleasant day and they were essentially pleasant people: after a few minutes of annoyance at these bloody amateurs who shouldn't be allowed on the river they settled back, waited for the lock to fill and re-empty, and let the companions tell them an edited version of their story, from the fight with the Agaskan to waking up on the barge.

The Ra-Lord was uncharacteristically contrite but also secretly rather pleased by all he had learnt. Locks were fun, he had decided, and he set about trying to devise new applications for the principle. He had been trying to design some sort of perpetual motion machine for a while now, and wondered whether this exchange of waters might not be the solution, though he could not see quite how water-power could open the gates at the right time, nor how he could arrange his levels without pumping the water back uphill. Never mind, this was exactly the sort of problem he loved best, intriguing, impractical, insoluble.

His revere was disturbed by the return of the fat boys, reinforced now by friends: the village was nearby but hidden from the river. *'Simpleton, simpleton. Doesn't know how locks are done!'* they chanted, which was a familiar chant among the river-children. They had picked the wrong man to annoy.

For days now the Ra-Lord, pleased by the novelty of his situation and the curious job in hand, had maintained without effort his good humour. But these children pierced him doubly: they derided him, and they derided his mechanical competence. He, the Ra-Lord, the inventor of the eye-level grill, the (admittedly impractical, but rather ingenious) machine for pressing pats of butter, and the heating system for the royal palace at Verdre. He drew himself up to his full height, which was not great but was enough to impose, and in a clear commanding voice said, 'Come here!'

Generally speaking, under these circumstances this is an impotent demand. The child sensibly prefers to stay away; the adult can bluster all his likes. But such was the authority in the Gros of Ra's tone that meekly, contritely, the children came forward. 'Stand in line,' the Gros ordered, and the children did so.

'Right, you disgusting, ill-mannered, ill-bred children, perhaps you'd like to apologise for your appalling behaviour?' The Ra-Lord wheeled suddenly on one of the fat boys. 'You!'

The fat boy blanched and his lip trembled. 'S-s-s-sorry, sir.'

'Louder!'

'Sorry, sir.'

'I should think so too. And maybe you could add an explanation for your unwarranted impudence? Yes?'

Plump tears pumped down the fat boy's face. 'It wasn't me, sir.'

The Ra-Lord's voice grew even deeper, even more menacing. What do you mean, 'It wasn't me'? of course it was! I saw you!'

'He made me do it,' said the fat boy, turning to his erstwhile friend.

'Did he now. Then maybe an apology from him might be even more relevant.'

'It's not fair,' burbled the other fat boy.

And so it went on. Each child in turn was admonished and reduced to tears, and then the whole pack of them dismissed with contempt. As the children left the Ra-lord was aware of applause behind him. He turned to look: there, sitting on the bank, were Lara, Od, Streetpoet and the two bargees, and each was clapping in admiration.

'I've been wanting to get 'old of them 'uns for years,' said one of the bargees. 'Rude little buggers they are an' all, begging your pardon.'

'Aye,' said the other. 'But you've told 'em right proper. They'll not be up to their tricks for a while, I shouldn't wonder.'

'Aye,' agreed the first. 'You told 'em right proper. Right proper you did.'

Od took advantage of the bargees' delight to question them about the journey ahead. 'Simple as you like,' they told him. 'Just stay on the Folhn till it meets the Edo and then you're next to there. You can't miss Myr! It's a big sod of a place, begging pardon. That's all there is to it. Though I'd not want to stay there long, myself. Place is full of weird religions, all trying to go one further than the Brotherhood. Thee'll never have seen such a load of halfwits.'

'It's a shame we've only got this little boat,' said Lara, bringing the subject back to the more urgent question of getting to Myr. Once they had got there there would be the time to worry about what to do next, she thought. 'There's not really room for all of us.'

'Shame we're not going that way ourselves,' admitted one of the bargees, 'but we've an order to deliver to the mines at Kelgramm and we'd best be on our way pretty soon.'

'Wait on,' said the other. 'What about Yrgé. He'll be about due here on his way back to Myr. He'd give this lot a ride if we told 'im about them kids.'

'Aye, he *hates* them kids more'n any of us. One of 'em fired a catapult at 'is 'orse. Poor bloody animal near ruptured itself tryin' to gallop off with a barge tied on.'

'Right. That's settled them. We'll tell Yrgé 'bout you, an' 'e'll take you to Myr.'

'That's ever so good of you,' said Lara.

'No problem. Anyone who can put them kids in their place is all right by us.'

And so it was arranged. Yrgé's barge, loaded with mineral ore but infinitely roomy compared to the little boat, picked them up. Yrgé was an ageing man, good humoured and generous except when it came to 'them' kids. 'They're a blight on the river, them buggers,' he said, jabbing with the stem of a pipe – all Myrians seemed to smoke pipes, yet elsewhere in Khalindaine it was almost unknown. 'If half of what them two says is true, I just wish I'd heard thee. I'd love to give 'em a piece of my mind myself, but they just run off 'fore I've chance.'

Yrgé, and his companion Hyat, had comfortable quarters at the stern, and another, smaller room in the bows, which was given over to Lara. The others were to sleep in the open, but none of them minded. Talen was carried carefully from the boat to the barge and given temporary accommodation in Hyat's bunk, where Lara tended him; the others sat on the roof of the sleeping quarters, ducking when the bridges came, or walked along the towpath. Even Streetpoet's notorious dislike of water could find little to complain about here. The sun was shining, the water was glimmering, and the speed of the barge seemed exactly suited, exactly appropriate. From the banks came the sweetly sour smell of freshly cut grass and the soft aroma of gentle spring flowers.

It was an idyll that lasted for days, an arcadian delight. They rested their weary limbs, recovered from their concussions, and relaxed and basked in the sun. There seemed no shortage of food aboard: the war had made little impact this far north, and it was a prosperous land of both good mineral deposits and fertile soil. Even ale, the strong dark Myrian kind, was available, though Yrgé made it clear that this was an illicit treat. 'None of them Brothers Militant round here, Menketh-be-thanked,' he said, and the others heartily agreed. Indeed, it became almost a holiday.

Streetpoet was the only one with worries and he kept these to himself. His biggest worry was their shortage of cash: they had none, since the bandits had reasonably extracted all they could from their pockets after knocking them out, and no way of getting any. To be short of money is a fairly standard condition: even the Gros of Weir, reputedly the richest man in Khalindaine, did not always have quite enough money to fund his next venture or make his next investment, and so it worked down the social scale; there is always something we want that is just out of reach. But to have no money at all is a different thing entirely. The Gros of Ra was a rich man, Talen-vaine-Talen was doubtless worth quite a few talents, even Lara and Od, prudent types, were unlikely to be without savings. Only Streetpoet amongst them knew what absolute poverty is like, how impotent it can make a man, how awful it can be. The others, comfortable for the moment on the barge, did not seem to have given this a thought; Streetpoet's experience made him worry. Before his face had been scarred he would have got by: he had lived that way for years, and provided for Od too when necessary, but now he was not sure, and because his confidence was sapped, his ability was sapped, for a confidence trick is rightly named. He looked around at his companions. Lara and Talen were walking along the bank ahead, skimming stones across the river. Od was teaching the Ra-Lord to fish. It is probably better to starve with friends then to starve alone, just as it is doubtless better to lose a finger than a whole hand; it is better still to survive intact. Streetpoet doubted if the Gros of Ra had given money a thought: certainly the Ra-Lord's credit would be good in most of Khalindaine; he doubted if it would be quite so good in republican-held Myr, however. The sun went behind a cloud as the minstrel thought, and then suddenly came out again; Streetpoet, warm again, suddenly remembered something the bargees had told them, and had an idea that could turn his disfigurement to their advantage and utilise the Gros of Ra's remarkable aura of authority. The only question was, would he be able to convince the others.

That evening, as they sat round a small fire by the side of the river, with the horse chomping contentedly in the background, Streetpoet explained his idea. His companions listened with amusement that bordered on amazement, but heard him out before voicing their objections: then came the objections.

'It's impractical.'

'Why?' answered Streetpoet. 'It seems perfectly possible to me.'

'Then it's outrageous.'

'All the better. Who'd believe they were being fooled.'

'It's daft.'

'Exactly, but it's inspired daftness.'

'Surely there's a better way.'

This was exactly the objection Streetpoet was looking forward to most. 'Then find it,' he invited.

And that, of course, was the problem. In the end they all agreed, though with differing degrees of enthusiasm. The

Gros of Ra was rather flattered that he would be playing the leading role; Od had faith in his friend. But Lara and Talen were less sanguine, though they accepted they could think of nothing better.

Finally, they had to convince Yrgé. This was easier than anticipated: he was perfectly agreeable, though equally sceptical. 'Can't see the point, mysen,' he told them. 'There's enough daft buggers about wi'out you lot joining them.' But apart from that he had no objections. 'No skin off my nose, any road. I'll just say you was paying passengers, which you are in a manner of speaking, since you gave those kids a good lesson, and I di'n't know you was bonkers till too late.'

It was decided then, and they planned ahead.

The innocent folk of Myr were getting used to strange sights. Every religious fanatic in Khalindaine seemed to have thrown her, or more often his, lot behind the Brotherhood, and then tried to outdo them for extremism. There were religions springing up all over the place: the Church of the Second Coming of Ormaas, the Free Church of the New Martyrs, the Advent Day Seventists, the Church of Menketh the Fishmonger. Even more surprising was that each new religion actually seemed to find adherents. For some the ban on alcohol was not enough, so they banned all liquids except water from amongst their number. For some the regulations on dress were too lax, and they made all their co-religionists wear only black, or only white, or only grey. Some thought women should have a larger say in their religion; others thought women should have a smaller say. Some argued for free sex, and others for no sex. Several wanted impurities within the race eliminated, and turned their attentions on the nomadic innocuous Kapatans or the rarely seen and private Rhav. Even so, the arrival of a new religion, especially one as weird as this one seemed to be, was bound to provoke a stir.

It began at the waterfront: The markets of Myr are held along the riverside. Suddenly the morning's fair was interrupted by a man dressed only in a loin cloth, sitting astride the short bowsprit of a barge, banging out a rhythm on the bottom of a bucket. 'People of Myr! People of Myr! Listen to the Word of the Truth!' More bangs, and then it was repeated. 'People of Myr! People of Myr! Listen to the Word of the Truth!' Behind the drummer were three others, two men and a woman, who encouraged him at appropriate intervals with cries of 'Ormaas be Praised!' and 'Listen to the Word!'

When the attention of sufficient had been drawn, the drummer changed his beat, playing a low, ominous roll on the base of his bucket. 'The time has come for the Truth to be known,' he told his audience. 'You must listen for the Word of the Truth!' and as he spoke this last word from the centre of a barge, lifting the tarpaulin in which he had been hidden as though it were a cloak, rose a most amazing old man. He was not tall. He certainly was not well dressed, being solely clad in what can only be described as a sort of sock over his private parts. Yet he had enormous power and authority.

'People of Myr,' he said, somehow fixing each of them with his glare. 'Know this. THIS IS THE LAST YEAR OF THIS WORLD!!!!! Soon we shall all be born again. For some of us this will be a terrible experience. Our sins will catch us up. Our deceptions will catch us out. There will be the stench of sulphur and the pains of fires. There will be the rack and the turnscrew. Flesh will wither on the bone. Bones will bend and distort. Your skulls will be opened with blunted knives; your brains shall be thrown to the wolves; and this will last for ever. There is no apologising on the other side. There is no forgiveness.

'But for others it shall be different. Not for them the agonies of an eternity of torture. Not for them the pains of infinite death. For the BORN AGAIN TRUTHKNOWERS the end of the world shall hold no terrors. For them there will be safety and comfort.'

Again the weirdly wonderful old man fixed them with his stare. 'For I am the PROPHET WITH NO NAME, I am the first of the BORN AGAIN TRUTHKNOWERS, I am the future for those who would follow, and the destruction of those who turn away!'

There was a great banging on the bucket again, and the old man slipped back to the floor beneath his cowl.

It was the turn of the three disciples now. In an apparent frenzy of belief they walked among the crowd, begging money, asking people to throw off the world and rejoice that salvation was at hand, saying anything they thought their audience might want to hear, in short. By the time they had finished they had collected a large tribute, some of which they offered to Yrgé, who declined, saying they were all daft anyway; and most of the rest they spent immediately on printing notices of a forthcoming meeting. Then as it was growing late, they found somewhere to spend the night, and slept.

The following day was spent handing out the crudely printed but effective notices which announced the general meeting, to be held in the main square. Streetpoet's charm, Od's conviction and, it has to be said, Lara's legs, made quite an impact. By the third day of their stay in Myr, they had raised a considerable following, and a considerable amount of money.

The meeting, held that day, was quite a success. The PROPHET WITH NO NAME certainly had a way of dealing with hecklers: his stares virtually turned them to stone. And the chief rabble-rouser, the bucket-beater, showed a surprising virtuosity as a musician when lent a mandola. One or two in the crowd said he reminded them of this or that minstrel seen in this or that inn in the past, but the scars were unfamiliar. And anyway, why should a minstrel be barred from joining the BORN AGAIN TRUTHKNOWERS? The truth, if the PROPHET WITH NO NAME was to believed, was open to all who were prepared to put a few rubecks in the coffers or follow the prophet on his great pilgrimage south.

This pilgrimage, indeed, was the main subject of the prophet's address. His idea was to raise a sort of crusade of what he called 'normal, everyday BORN AGAIN TRUTH-KNOWERS' (which rather begged the question of what an abnormal TRUTHKNOWER might be like) which would join the Opposition Army of the West, which had now been joined by the Army of the East and was marching towards Cythroné, though its way was known to be blocked by a Royalist army under the command of the Gyr Peltyn. Having joined the Opposition armies (and of course passed on the Word of the Truth) the PROPHET WITH NO NAME then planned, he said, to cross the lines by miraculous means and convert the Royalists too. 'For even the misty-eyed and most misguided men who serve the régime of the upstart Consatiné have not yet forfeited the right to be told the Word of the Truth... WHO SHALL FOLLOW ME?????'

The numbers who volunteered were not large in terms of an army, perhaps, but they still surprised at least one of the disciples. 'Four thousand three hundred and twelve,' Talen-vaine-Talen counted with mounting disbelief, as he walked round the crowd that had remained. 'Four thousand three hundred and thirteen.'

That night the PROPHET WITH NO NAME held a meeting with his original followers in a rather expensive private room hired for the day with some of the money raised. 'I feel filthy,' he said to his chief disciple, and Streetpoet smiled apologetically.

'Never mind. I think we can make the transformation now from dusty hermit to full-blown leader of a new sect. You can have a wash and comb your hair now, if you like, and I'll go out and see if I can get you a new costume tomorrow. Something splendid and startling, to set you apart from the crowd.'

'What about for the rest of you?'

'I want something a bit less scanty,' complained Lara. 'I'm tired of being mauled.'

Talen, who was tired of her being mauled too, agreed wholeheartedly. Streetpoet had no objection. 'Look, with the money we've raised we could buy out a tailor's shop lock, stock and barrel. We could buy out thirty tailors' shops.' He laughed. 'Isn't everything going splendidly!'

'Maybe,' said Od. 'But what about this miraculous way of crossing the enemy lines?'

'Yes,' said Streetpoet. 'I meant to ask about that myself.'

'Oh, I don't know,' said the Ra-Lord. 'Just seemed a good thing to say at the time: get quite inspired, standing there in front of all those people. Quite excited too.'

'Well, we'd better think of something quick. You told them we'd be setting off south in three days' time.'

Streetpoet was glad he had heard that 'we' from Od. He had begun to feel strangely isolated, as though he and the Ra-Lord were dragging the others along, rather than all pulling together, and said as much to them.

'We've worked hard enough, I think,' said Talen-vaine-Talen rather primly.

'Sorry, no. I wasn't criticising that at all. You've done everything you could have done and more. But you don't seem to be making suggestions any more, just doing what you're told, as though it's my conspiracy and the Ra-Lord's conspiracy and you are just conscripts or paid extras.'

Od ran his hand through where his hair should have been. 'I think it's the money that bothers me.' he said. 'We're virtually robbing those people. Now we're even breaking up their lives and their families. When it was just us, escaping Cythroné, getting to Akbar, going up the Khalin, even travelling to Myr – no, especially that bit – everything seemed good. We were doing what we had to do and only harming those who got in our way. But somehow all this BORN AGAIN lark seems gratuitous, extravagant, unfair.'

'But is *is* working,' pointed out Streetpoet. 'We are going in the direction we want. We've even got an excuse to try to cross to the Royalist lines now. Surely that justifies inconveniencing a few Myrians who, in an age of civil war, already believe that the end of the world is at hand. We're not even convincing them, remember; we're confirming what they already suspect. Their lives had been inconvenienced, disrupted, torn apart before we even got here. They've sent sons and brothers and husbands to the war. They've seen the value of what they own drop. They've seen the market for what they produce fluctuating depending on what the armies are short of or the generals fancy, and their pride in their workmanship goes. They already *know* it's the end of the world, and sometimes I almost believe it myself. At least this way we're trying to end the war. If we can get to Consatiné, if we can persuade him to perform the Rite of Endyear, then everyone will know he is the rightful emperor of true heir or whatever it is he isn't, and lay down their weapons and go back to their fields and their workshops and their forges. Isn't it worth inconveniencing a few people for that?'

'And Lara will marry Consatiné,' said Talen.

'That's right. That way everything's nicely...' Streetpoet faltered mid–sentence. Suddenly he understood why Talen and Lara could no longer put their hearts into the mission.

'Exactly,' said Lara, putting her hand over Streetpoet's. 'We've talked it over, Talen and I, and we've decided we must do our duty: if his duty means taking me to Consatiné, then that's what he must do; if my duty means I must marry him, then I must do that too. But don't expect us to enjoy it.' She gave Streetpoet's hand a squeeze, withdrew it, and returned it to her lover.

The Gros of Ra broke the silence. 'Consatiné doesn't deserve you,' he said. 'Even though he is – almost – my son.'

'That's not fair,' said Lara.

'Why not? It's true.'

'No it isn't. He was a nice enough young man when I knew him last. I didn't love him then and I don't love him now, but then I had just realised how much my cousin had meant to me and now I know Talen. That's not his fault...'

'Not what I'm talking about,' said the Gros of Ra. 'And if there's a fault here it's probably mine. I brought him up, I didn't trust him to behave like a member of the House of Ra because I knew he wasn't, and I didn't give him enough responsibility.' The old man chuckled; even blaming himself for Consatiné's weakness, and therefore the weakness of the empire, did not seem to disturb him. 'Must admit, never thought I was meant to be grooming future emperor. Might have taken more care. But that's the way it is: Consatiné won't accept the responsibility of being emperor, and because of that he's messed the whole thing up. He won't do his duty, and when I hear you two lovebirds talking so bravely about how you're going to do yours, it breaks my heart.' And he surprised them by embracing them both.

'Perhaps I wouldn't feel so brave if I knew I'd got the avatar of Akhran the Golden inside me,' admitted Lara.

'Akhran the golden never killed anyone,' said the Ra-Lord and sometime PROPHET WITH NO NAME, and then he guffawed as he realised his mistake. 'Well, no one whose body he was wearing at the time, at any rate.'

'Never seemed to do anyone any good either,' mused Od. 'Look at Elsban, old before her time, and that bloke that succeeded her, Ravenspur's son. He didn't even make it through *one* Rite of Endyear.'

'That's because he wasn't the true heir!' said Streetpoet, in comic exasperation. 'Don't you ever listen to a word I say?'

'Menketh alive, no,' replied Od. 'How do you think I've kept my sanity so long.'

The pilgrimage began as promised. Not quite as many turned up as expected – it is curious how much initial enthusiasm can fade after a night's sleep and a chat with someone unconvinced – but even so there were nearly three and a half thousand people gathered behind the now splendidly dressed PROPHET WITH NO NAME, and there was great confidence that others would join them on their way. As Streetpoet had said, it was less a matter of converting people than confirming what they already believed, and for people who had already seen their livelihoods or their menfolk taken away by the war, there was not so much to lose.

The disciples seemed more vigorous and enthusiastic than ever that day, marshalling the rabble for the long walk south. One of them, a good-looking chap they realised, now they saw him properly dressed instead of the rags he had worn before, showed exceptional ability in lining people up and making them look almost military. The BORN AGAIN TRUTHKNOWERS were on their way.

Of the march, the less said the better. The rabble got out of hand and rowdy, or disgruntled and depressed; the PROPHET WITH NO NAME never let this disturb him, however, and with that awe-inspiring power he had, that reduced everyone even in a crowd of thousands to a rather ill-behaved schoolboy, order was retained, just. At Frath they encountered some resistance from the Opposition garrison, but the PROPHET WITH NO NAME was eventually able to assure the local commander that, though noisy, they were harmless and essentially on the same side: the commander was not exactly convinced but he felt so small in the company of this peculiar prophet that he let them by anyway. In Ghell, where the Opposition armies had already stripped the land bare, as flying grasshoppers did in the Comatas province, provisions for the BORN AGAIN TRUTHKNOWERS were hard to find, so the PROPHET WITH NO NAME climbed (illegally, but who was going to stop him?) the watch-tower at the south of the now largely abandoned camp, declared it his PRAYER-TOWER, and said that the gods would strike him dead if food was not found for his followers. The word got around; the food was found.

Actually, even the Ra-Lord almost lost confidence at this point, and none of them quite knew what sort of omen it was that when, on the last day of their stay in Ghell, a summer storm brewed up, and lightning struck the tower.

And finally they reached the rear detachments of the Armies of the East, who were operating a picket from Akbar to Morn along the Rhalman Road, and saw in the distance the low but well-defined hills of the Itor Range, where Wriknek had made his camp. They were seven thousand strong – which somedays felt like seven thousand weak – and still marching, still full of enthusiasm. Meanwhile, the Day of Endyear, which in the Khalindaine calendar is the longest day of the year, was approaching; if the companions were to reach Cythroné in time to persuade Consatiné to perform the Rite they would have to hurry.

This time it was Od who had the bright idea.

Chapter 11

Crossing the Lines

Wriknek sat in a tent in the Itor hills, engaged in his usual occupation of writing and signing orders. He no longer doubted his ability as a soldier: his remarkable triumph at Akbar, and the degeneration of his brain, had persuaded him that he was indeed a great general, capable of commanding his troops alone.

Yet perhaps this belief was not only megalomania; perhaps he did have a genuine ability. Certainly he had been fortunate at Akbar. The cautious Gros of Nanx, fearing that his forces would be split, had given up the Stronghold without a fight, on condition that its Royalist garrison was allowed to retreat to Akbar. This saved there being a fight, and a long-drawn costly siege which the Royalists might eventually have lost, but gave the Opposition two distinct advantages, though the inexperienced Nanx-Lord did not realise it at the time: first, the Opposition did not have to waste time trying to wear down the Stronghold in what would inevitably been a battle of attrition; secondly, Wriknek found himself in possession of an almost invulnerable castle that not only dominated the bridge across the Khalin, but also all river traffic. The Royalists in the east were quite contained; the battle for Akbar was a stalemate but the Opposition now controlled the river. Only a very strong Royalist naval force would be able to break through the Opposition blockade and that was something the Gyr Peltyn did not have, which meant he had lost contact entirely with his allies in Northreach.

Wriknek had been lucky but all successful generals are lucky. The trick is to take advantage of that luck, and Wriknek had capitalised on his control of the river by immediately redirecting the bulk of his troops and the focus of his attack to the west. The east could now take care of itself: it would be in the west that the war would be won. Moreover, he had recognised that the initiative was now entirely his. He had complete freedom of manoeuvre in the entire area north of the Khalin and west of the Rift, and marched at once towards Cythroné: if he could capture Cythroné he would surely have won the war, for though Northreach and Comtas were both Royalist bastions, they were isolated in the east and could be ignored until he had consolidated his position in the west, when he could capture them at his leisure.

Only a hundred thousand strides to the south another general, with greater experience but less luck, was also reviewing the situation and coming, more reluctantly, to the same conclusions. The Gyr Peltyn had few advantages. The loss of the Stronghold had been a severe and unnecessary blow, cutting his communications with Mornet. For all he knew the Gros of Ra might have died, or gone missing, or be marching through the Plains of Myr disguised as a visionary prophet who foretold the end of the world. Equally, Cythroné was a major problem. The city was physically very difficult to defend: not only were the walls in a poor state of repair – he had done his best to rectify this, but it was almost impossible to repair the ravages of generations of neglect – but the sheer size of the population made evacuation to within those walls virtually out of the question. His best option, practically, was to let the Opposition take northern Cythroné while he retreated across the river into southern Khalindaine, pulling down the bridges behind him and virtually partitioning the land, but this he was reluctant to entertain. Not only would it mean that the war could drag on for years, but also that almost all the important buildings of government, including the royal palace and the Keep Akhranta, would fall into Opposition hands. The blow to morale would be immense.

He went through his other choices, and they boiled down to two. Either he could allow the Opposition to march all the way to Cythroné, risking the city's dubious defences and the threat of republican insurrection in the city – for if anything Consatiné's credit had fallen still further since the war had begun – or alternatively he could march out and engage the enemy in the field. Of the two the latter held more appeal for him. His army was smaller than Wriknek's but it was also more experienced. A good half of the Opposition troops had never seen active service before: at least most of his troops had and were familiar with their officers. His chances in the field would surely be at least even which seemed better than his chances in a siege. And anyway, he was tired of inactivity. He called his aides to him, and made his preparations. The Royalists were marching north.

The BORN AGAIN TRUTHKNOWERS marched towards the hills, singing

> Brother, sister, son and daughter,
> All will face the final slaughter
> Rocks and stones and bricks and mortar,
> – All will be destroyed!
> We alone, the strong can bear it,
> We who've heard the truth and share it,
> We can face great death and dare it
> – Dying overjoyed!
>
> Great the words the prophet uses,
> Death to he who truth refuses,
> They shall be the final losers
> – When we are destroyed!
> We have strength to face disaster
> Following our one true master,
> We face death with scornful laughter
> – Death no one can avoid.

The words were Streetpoet's. He was quite pleased with them. The last line in particular seemed universally appropriate. And it seemed to him that perhaps the next year would see the end of the world, and that they really were dancing on the edge of a precipice. It did not seem to matter much.

In fact, this sense of doom and gloom was working its way through all the companions. Streetpoet's melancholy was no greater than that of Talen or Lara, who for all their courage still approached their parting as though it were an execution, and contrived to steal every moment they could together. Even the Gros of Ra, though buoyed up to a degree by a natural self-confidence and self-centredness, seemed to be suffering from the effects of his prolonged performance as the PROPHET WITH NO NAME, and sometimes spoke in private in the same apocalyptic tones he used in public. And Od, of course, had always been sober and inclined towards melancholy, which was one of the reasons he had been attracted to the Brotherhood all that time ago.

Yet actually, though Od retained his serious demeanour, he was in fact full of a quite unwholesome degree of glee. For Od had his idea.

The evening before they reached Wriknek's camp the friends held a council. It was a sombre affair to begin with. The idea of the BORN AGAIN TRUTHKNOWERS had taken on a life of its own, dominating their thoughts until they found it almost impossible to see further than the next day's meals or the next day's speeches. But now the next day was a special day, the day they were to arrive at the Opposition lines. What was to happen after that, and how they were to cross to the Royalists, was beyond them. The PROPHET WHO HAD NO NAME had spoken of crossing the lines by miraculous means: now they were almost there; the miracle had failed to happen.

It was then that Od explained his plan. The others thought about it and laughed in disbelief; then they thought about it again, and this time they laughed from pleasure. The miracle had happened after all.

The following day was windy and grey, a day of crows and curlews, a day without promise. As the BORN AGAIN TRUTHKNOWERS marched into the low hills west of Marq and north of Cythroné where Wriknek had established his headquarters, they were halted by a picket of Opposition troops. With the troops were a number of men of the Brothers Militant in their distinctive tabards. But despite the weather, despite the obstacle, the companions had confidence in Od's idea, and were determined they would not be thwarted.

'Right,' said the Undermaster of the Brothers Militant. He addressed Streetpoet who, at the head of the column, was leading the customary communal singing; the PROPHET WITH NO NAME was resting in a horse-drawn cart further down the line. 'You lot have travelled far enough.'

'What's the problem,' said Streetpoet. He looked back on the column behind him: the rabble was looking better than usual because the road led through a defile and the valley confined them; Streetpoet felt almost proud of them. 'We are loyal to the Opposition cause.' he said. 'Now we wish to spread our word amongst your troops.'

'Yes, we know about your words. Doom, death and destruction, they mostly seem to be,' said the Undermaster succinctly. 'We've been hearing reports about you for days, with your noise and your prophecy, and though you've spoken no treason, the commander in his wisdom doesn't think a deal of you coming near his army and messing things up.'

'How can the word of a prophet mess things up?' asked Streetpoet. 'It is known that many prophets are in Wriknek's army, encouraging the troops to resist the temptations of the flesh and to fight for the spirit and the truth. Wriknek himself has, it is said, encouraged this.' Streetpoet was drawing the Undermaster away from the crowds as best he could. The BORN AGAIN TRUTHKNOWERS looked patiently at the troops, certain both of their loyalty to the Opposition and the infallibility of their leader, while the troops looked as patiently back.

'We're not denying that. But this talk your bloke has, about the end of the world, it's no good for soldiers. Their morale is high, they're undefeated' – which was true if the flooding of Baoz was discounted – 'and Cythroné is virtually in sight. You seem a sensible enough man. How is telling them that they're all going to die anyway going to help them fight the Royalists?'

'Because the PROPHET WITH NO NAME is also going to announce that there will be a special life-beyond-death for any man who kills those who would deny the truth. It's all been worked out, believe me. Is there anywhere private we can go.'

'Why?'

'Because I'm a member of the Brothers Militant and I have the scar to prove it.'

'You've a lot of scars, mate.'

Streetpoet ignored the interruption. 'So is another of the disciples of the prophet, Od the Hedchenlightened of the Ilynés Chapter.'

'Never heard of him.'

'It doesn't matter. The point is, would two of your own most staunch company be engaged in this if we thought it could do the cause of the Opposition any harm? Come off it! Let us through; let us prove what we can do.'

'Look, it's not on.' The Undermaster was a strange but not uncommon type. In the service of his beliefs, the Brotherhood, the Opposition, and Wriknek in person, he would zealously perform any cruelty, as he had proved to the vagrants of Akbar. Yet though unimaginative, an obeyer rather than giver of orders, in private – and as long as his prejudices were avoided – he was not an unreasonable man. This bloke standing in front of him, for instance, was obviously loyal to the cause, claimed to be a member of his own organisation, and talked a certain amount of sense; orders are orders, and the Undermaster knew his duty, but that didn't mean the bloke wasn't owed an explanation. 'It's this way,' he said. 'Like I say, we've heard a lot about your prophet, and we don't dislike what we've heard. He's never questioned Wriknek or the Brotherhood, never suggested he's right and we're wrong or anything, just said he knows something extra. He's stirred up a lot of feeling, and it's the sort of feeling we don't mind. But just look at the rabble he's brought with him! First, how do you expect us to feed them all. We've mouths enough of our own, thank you. And secondly, look *who* you've brought. Our soldiers' mothers and fathers, wives and kids. A fighting soldier can do without that sort of distraction. You'll have heard the rumour that the Royalists are marching out to meet us. Well, it's true. There's a Royalist army forty thousand strides off and heading our way: our troops are going to be going into battle in only a few days. Now if we were besieging somewhere it might be different. A bit of nookie with the wife might be good for morale then, when there's plenty of hanging around and not much to do, though by and large it's best to keep women out of army camps. But when a soldier's going into battle, then it's a different thing. He's enough to worry about looking after his own skin, keeping in formation and listening for commands. He doesn't want to be thinking about what happens if his line breaks, will his camp be overrun, will his mum and dad be killed? You might think thoughts like that would do him good, make him determined, but in a battle he's no time for them. They just take his mind off his job. I used to be in the army, the Royalist army you'd call it now. Fifteen years a sergeant before I saw the light. Believe me, I've seen a thing or two. I know.'

It was common sense, but Streetpoet was not to be denied so easily. 'So the objection isn't to the prophet, it's to his followers. Right?'

'I suppose so.'

'Then why doesn't the prophet come to the camp, in person, with maybe fifty or so followers, all men if you think best, though some of the women we've with us are so ugly they won't cause much trouble in your ranks, and let the PROPHET WITH NO NAME do his bit.'

'And what are the rest of them going to do? Go home? No, the only way this can be sorted out in a satisfactory manner is for all of you to go together.'

'You don't know the prophet. He can get them to go if he asks them, while he stays here, and there won't be only trouble, believe me.'

The Undermaster adopted his it's–more–than–my–job–is –worth look. 'I don't know.'

'Look, I don't want to cause you any trouble: it's the last thing I want to do. But I really believe that the PROPHET WITH NO NAME can inspire your men; he's even talking of crossing the lines and putting the fear of Menketh up the Royalists, because he's nothing if not brave. Why don't you let him speak to this lot, tell them to retire back to, say, Morn, where there's plenty for them to eat now the summer's coming, and then let him join the army?'

'I've got my orders,' said the Undermaster, but he was wavering.

'Look, what've you got to lose? If the prophet can't persuade them to leave without him, he'll leave with them. It's as simple as that. Either way, there's no problem, but if you could just see how he can command a crowd you'd see why I want him to speak to our soldiers.'

'I'm not sure,' said the Undermaster, wavering further.

'He's got to speak to them anyway, to get them to turn round after going so far. Why not let him ask? It's not your problem, whatever happens.'

'Oh, all right then, go on.'

Streetpoet returned to the Gros of Ra, who was sleeping despite the noise of the crowd and enjoying the moment's peace. He woke up to find he was still the PROPHET WITH NO NAME, which was a blow. Streetpoet explained the problem and the possible solution to him, and went off to look for his fellow disciples; the PROPHET WITH NO NAME thought about what he was going to say.

The crowd, meanwhile, as often happens with crowds that have nothing to do, was growing restive. They need something to do, thought Streetpoet, and as he passed amongst them in search of Od, Talen and Lara, he urged them into song.

> Men, who know destruction faces them
> Either stand or scuttle away.
> We who know the prophet tells the truth
> Can stand staunch and face that day.

When one group were singing confidently, he moved to another, and started them on the next verse.

> We are mighty in our sense of truth.
> We are mighty and we're strong.
> We fear neither death nor mortal man.
> We are right, the rest are wrong.

In time he found his companions, while the crowd, having finished one song, moved without bidding to the next. The words of the songs were predictable, really rather monotonous, but the tunes, most of which Streetpoet had unashamedly stolen, were all good rousing ones, exactly what a crowd needed. While they sang Streetpoet described the situation to his friends, drawing them to one side and speaking quietly, though the sound of all those voices would have drowned a thunderclap.

'Do you think the Ra-Lord can do it?' worried Talen. 'It can't be many days to Endyear: if we don't get the chance to cross the lines soon it'll be too late anyway.'

'Of course he can,' said Streetpoet. 'He's got them eating out of his hands.'

'And will Wriknek accept it if they do go,' asked Od. 'He's a lunatic but he isn't a fool. He isn't going to want all these people behind his lines and getting in the way. He doesn't want them here at all by the sound of it, and I don't blame him. At least if the Ra-Lord stays with them there's a chance they'll keep together in one place; without him they'll just go anywhere they fancy. We've had enough trouble ourselves, even with the Ra-Lord with us. There's only him and your songs that have stopped half of them wandering off as things are. Why shouldn't Wriknek see it that way too?'

'It's true,' said Talen. 'There are so many of them. I can't actually remember why we brought them anyway.'

'A miscalculation,' admitted Streetpoet. 'I thought it would be easier to get into Wriknek's camp if we could prove how popular we are. And anyway, they wanted to come.'

'Exactly,' said Lara. 'So they won't want to just turn and meekly go away now, will they.'

Once more Streetpoet found himself feeling isolated. The plan had been his, and now the responsibility was his, and he neither liked the fact nor saw any way to avoid it. What Od had said was true. Only the Ra-Lord and the songs had kept the BORN AGAIN TRUTHKNOWERS together. Only the Ra-Lord and the songs...

He did not like the prospect at all, but there was no other way. He turned to his friends. 'I'm going to have to stay with the BORN AGAIN TRUTHKNOWERS,' he said, 'and lead them off singing. When they've gone there's no reason for Wriknek to refuse you access to their camp. Od's idea is too good to throw away. What have you got to lose?'

'You,' said Od, seriously.

'I'll be all right,' said Streetpoet, but for the first time since they had met, Od was not sure. His friend seemed downcast, tired, almost broken.

They were distracted at that moment because the singing was faltering, failing. The Ra-Lord, the PROPHET WITH NO NAME, had climbed up a slope at the side of the defile and signalled for silence.

'Followers, friends, BORN AGAIN TRUTHKNOWERS! Today is our greatest day yet, though there will be greater days. I have a task for you, a mission you will not like. I ask you to perform it.' His voice carried clearly over the crowd, who listened carefully. This was an uncharacteristic way for the prophet to begin a speech: normally he more or less beat them into submission by threatening them with the future; today he seemed almost friendly, almost – though they could not believe it of him – pleading. 'There are too many of us here. Wriknek fears that we may consume the provisions of our armies, and therefore asks you to turn back, return to Morn, where I shall rejoin you later.' There were murmurs of discontent among the crowd. Had they travelled all this way for nothing? Was there something the PROPHET WITH NO NAME could not do? 'Wriknek asks you. I ask you.' The murmurs grew louder, more mutinous. They had not followed the prophet so far because he had asked them to, but because he had told them to.

'We're not going!' shouted a voice.

'We're staying here!' added another.

The clamour became general. Until this point the Ra-Lord had been concerned only with getting on to the next stage of their mission, and had expected the crowd to do what was needed. But now he was being opposed, and the Ra-Lord was *never* opposed.

'Cretins!' he bellowed. 'Morons!' His eyes glared across the crowded valley, and as if it too were at his whim, the sun suddenly came through the clouds. 'How dare you question my will.' The Ra-Lord's determination combined with the PROPHET WITH NO NAME's rhetoric. 'I command thee get hence. Shall you burn forever in vats of acid? Shall your teeth be made of fiery coals? To oppose me! To stand against me! You wretches! You monstrosities whom I have brought here and I can destroy? Without me you are nothing, condemned to die at the great world's end! With me you are saved for an eternity and more.' He slowed down his speech now, clearly enunciating every word to give it weight; his pointing finger seemed to alight on each of his followers in turn, withering their mutiny, commanding their destiny. 'Not one of you dare question me. Not one. For I am the PROPHET WITH NO NAME! Get hence! Be gone!'

And with that he turned his back on them and crossed his arms, and even his back seemed to quiver with potency and threat.

There was a long silence, and then a voice struck up a song.

> The prophet tells us and we learn,
> We must hear or we shall burn,
> The prophet orders we return.
> – Praise him and obey!

It was a new song, though another familiar tune. The companions looked for the singer. They had not seen Streetpoet go, but they recognised the voice at once. The singer repeated the verse and many round him joined in. People started to turn, to move down the valley away from Wriknek's camp, to go back towards Morn. Again and again that single verse was repeated, mournful yet accepting, and the crowd filed away.

Streetpoet tried to force his way through the claustrophobic crush of bodies to its head. He felt he had never been amongst so many people, never been so alone. His mouth kept singing the words but his mind flashed and spun. He remembered the careless youth who had saved and seduced Amila, the easy-going bloke who had charmed landladies throughout the land, the happy-go-lucky young man who with neither plans nor misgivings had joined the Brothers Militant out of sheer bravado. Where was that man now? Where had he gone? Instead there was this walking cadaver, scarred on the outside, hollow within, a slave to his destiny, captured by responsibility. He had been Streetpoet so long he had almost forgotten his given name; now Streetpoet was a mockery, a reminder of things long gone. He was Streetpoet no longer, he was nobody, a face in a crowd going along with the crowd, without freedom and without friends.

His thoughts were broken by a tap on his shoulder. 'Do you think I'd let you go off alone?' said Od, and despite the crowd, despite the crush, despite the risk, the two men turned and embraced.

The sun had gone in again. Talen and Lara joined the Ra-Lord on the slope. He still stood, back to the receding crowd, full of force and passion. 'They've nearly gone,' said Lara. 'You can relax now.'

For a moment the Ra-Lord stayed rigid, and then he turned to them. His face, which had been so red with pent fury before, was suddenly ashen. 'Thank Menketh it's done,' he said. 'It was awful. Never been afraid before; terrified then.'

'But you had them in the palm of your hand,' said Talen, misquoting Streetpoet's phrase. 'Not to start with maybe, but later. There was never any problem.'

'Wasn't that.' The Ra-Lord put his hands to his face. 'At the end, when I said "For I am the PROPHET WITH NO NAME", that was when it was bad. Because I *was* the

PROPHET WITH NO NAME, don't you see. I wasn't the Ra-Lord any more, I was somebody else. I had become the prophet and stopped being me. Awful,' he said again.

'Never mind,' said Talen, dismissing this crisis of identity. 'You'll have to go back to being the Ra-Lord now. We need his technical skills if we're to carry out Od's plan.'

The Ra-Lord looked up, and looked better. 'That's right,' he said. 'Od's plan. You know, I'd nearly forgotten. Of course, Work to do. Plans to draw up. Men to organise. Od's plan: where is Od, anyway.'

'He went with Streetpoet, to lead the crowd back to Morn.'

'Pity. Still, just have to get on without them both.' The Ra-Lord was himself again, though a little older, a little wiser, and just a little – just a fraction – less secure.

The Undermaster escorted them to Wriknek's tent in person. 'He'll be busy,' he warned. 'Always is. I'll just have a brief word, to introduce you, and that'll be about the lot.'

They went through the flap, into the unhealthy mean light of the tent. The Commander was looking old and shrivelled, a hungry spider in a web of weapons and ink. 'Yes,' he said. 'What is it.'

His voice was strange. Lara got the impression of someone holding and releasing his nose as he spoke, or as if something was working loose inside.

'This is the PROPHET WITH NO NAME. Commander.'

Momentarily, Wriknek looked angered. 'I told you to lead that rabble away.' But is was as if the emotion exhausted him, for having half risen from his chair he slumped back.

The Undermaster took advantage of this. 'The rabble have gone, sir. He sent them away.'

'Sent them away?' Wriknek looked up at the Ra-Lord with new respect. 'And they obeyed him just like that?'

'Yes, Commander.'

'In good order? They're not spreading all over the fields or anything like that?'

'No, Commander. They went off singing?'

'Singing!'

'Yes, Commander.'

'Well, well, well. And what does this PROPHET WITH NO NAME want?'

The Ra-Lord started to speak. 'Want to address your troops, then want to speak to Royalist troops. Got a plan. Need plenty of wood, few lengths of canvas, long rope, some of your...'

'Yes, yes,' said Wriknek, addressing the Underofficer rather than the Ra-Lord. 'Let him have anything he wants. Dismissed.'

Perhaps the Ra-Lord had lost that tiny amount of self-assurance just in time. For the first time in his life he let himself be silenced. The Undermaster led them away.

Wriknek picked up his quill and began to write, but his finger joints seemed to be getting thicker daily. The quill dropped out of his grasp.

Outside seemed bright and clean after the tent, though there was no more sign of the Ra-Lord's miraculous sun. The Undermaster shook his head and looked worried. 'Commander's working too hard,' he said. 'He looks ill.'

He looks terrible, thought Lara, all eaten up from inside. 'Has he always talked like that?' she asked.

'Only for the past day or so,' answered the Underofficer. 'He really works much too hard.' Saying this was like a charm; to speak otherwise would be a curse. 'Anyway, you'd better give me a list of the things you want. You'll want a tent or two, I guess.'

'Please.'

'I'll see what I can do. I warn you though, you'll be a fair way from the front, and from most of the troops. This woman you've got with you is far too pretty to let them see. I don't know what I was thinking of letting her in.'

He did, however. He had seen her with the prophet, thought about refusing her permission to enter the camp, remembered how the prophet had dealt with the crowd, and decided to keep his mouth shut.

'It's all right,' said the Ra-Lord. 'Married them myself. Give them a tent they can share. Haven't got long together, poor things.'

'Eh?' asked the Undermaster. 'Why not?'

'End of the world,' said the prophet succinctly.

That evening the three of them gathered in the Gros of Ra's tent. 'Sorry to keep you two lovers up,' said the Ra-Lord. 'Lists need to be made.'

He placed a few rough sketches on the bench in front of him. 'Wanted to use lock ideas, water pressure, that sort of thing, but couldn't. Settled on this instead.'

The advantage of their secluded position was that they could talk relatively easily, but what they were discussing now was hardly secret anyway. They were going to build it with the help of the Opposition engineers. After all, as Lara reminded them, Wriknek had said they could have anything they wanted.

'Wood, lots of wood. Planks. Must be wood round here: saw engineers making artillery weapons. And lengths of canvas, sown into loops. Need one each for eyes and mouth of machine. And several lengths of blackiron.'

'What about the platform? Where are we going to stand?' asked Talen.

'In crown of head, here. Make sure you understand. Work must begin tomorrow, and tomorrow I'm addressing the soldiers.'

The puzzled over the plans until it was late and Lara and Talen went to bed. The Ra-Lord stayed up a while longer, putting the finishing touches on his ideas.

An advantage of totalitarianism – the only advantage, many would say – is that once an order is given, it stays given. The PROPHET WITH NO NAME had been told he could have everything he required, and therefore that is what he got. He spent the morning arranging his workmen, co-opted from Captain Jargoz's company, and in the afternoon gave his usual speech while Talen supervised the construction.

They started off with a great square platform of wood, as solid as could be made under the circumstances, which they put together on four short pillars: the pillars were there because eventually wheels would be put on, and no one fancied lifting the platform to do that job. At what was eventually to be the front no axle was needed, so none was fitted, but at the back a length of circular blackiron, polished smooth and coated with grease, was pushed in at one side of the platform, threaded through a pair of wooden cogs, one bigger than the other, that were buried half way into the platform, and out the other side. Now the wheels could be fitted, the back ones at each end of the axle, those at the front pinned on separate short lengths.

From time to time the workers heard cheers as the PROPHET WITH NO NAME made a particularly pertinent or popular remark. They secured the wheels with giant wedges, all cut from a section of the same huge oak, and then knocked away the pillars it had stood on. The platform was now a chassis ready for the superstructure.

This was all that had been completed by the end of the first day; meanwhile, news had reached Wriknek that the Royalist army, a mass of colour, was approaching. 'Let them come,' he said. 'We'll stay where we are, where we're safe.'

'I wonder where Od and Streetpoet are,' Lara asked as she lay in bed.

'I don't know. If they're still with the BORN AGAIN TRUTHKNOWERS they'll be in Morn by now,' her lover replied. 'I'm glad I'm not with them though.'

'Why?'

'Because then I wouldn't be here,' he said, and gave her a long, adoring kiss.

The friends had indeed reached Morn, in the company of the BORN AGAIN TRUTHKNOWERS. Already that company was diminishing: as Od remarked, you can't keep singing forever. Some of the Truthknowers were wandering around the town, causing something of a nuisance but – because they were still so numerous – as yet unhindered; others had set off for their homes. The most tenacious, perhaps simply because they were the ones with the furthest to go, were the Myrians. They hung around Od and Streetpoet all the time and gave them hardly a moment's peace. The first night had been impossible: they had been pestered constantly to tell and retell the story of how they had met the prophet, and as the night wore on their fabrications grew more and more careless. But on the second night the disciples managed to slip off unnoticed; having got away, they intended to stay away.

They travelled under cover of darkness, navigating by the stars and heading south.

The camp was full of rumours when Lara and Talen got up. 'The Royalists are in Belariath', 'The Royalists have turned back', 'The Royalists have headed straight for Morn and we're behind them', 'The Royalists have headed straight for

Morn and they're behind us.' Trying to ignore each conflicting report, for they had work to do, they joined the Gros of Ra at the construction site.

'I just hope to Menketh that Wriknek decides to stay on the hillside,' said Talen. 'If he advances onto the plain we've had it.'

'You've seen him,' said the Ra-Lord. 'Cautious type. Lawyer type. He'll stay here.'

The Ra-Lord's confidence was justified. Apart from occasional scouting parties of cavalry, the rest of the Opposition troops spent the day digging in.

The Ra-Lord's task for the day was to erect a scaffolding skeleton for his superstructure, a framework which would support both the various simple mechanisms and the outer shell. The first thing they did was put up four strong posts in a square pattern on the chassis; these were firmly held in place by nails, struts and angle irons. 'It looks a fairly smooth slope,' said the Ra-Lord. 'And of course we'll be lowered down which will limit the vibrations, but we still don't want these to give way, no sir.' Four more poles joined the posts at the top, like an empty box four strides by four, and again struts and angle irons were used to keep the structure rigid.

Next came a vertical piece of blackiron, which was pushed between a hole in the chassis and a similar one in the horizontal post directly above. Another large cog was fastened to it, horizontally, so that its teeth meshed with the larger vertical cog on the rear axle. The wedges were removed and the whole massive construction was pushed back and forth: the movement of the axle was translated by the cogs into a vertical movement by the blackiron pole.

Around the base of the box the beginnings of the outer shell were fixed. The back was kept open, but at the front was a piece of wood nailed at an angle which jutted forwards. This the Ra-Lord referred to, in all seriousness, as the chin.

The day was growing late but the Ra-Lord allowed no slacking. There was much to be done and little time in which to do it. Another large cog had to be fitted at the top of the blackiron pole, and a pair of smaller ones – one with great teeth like paddles – were put in place on a horizontal axle behind the chin. Even then the Ra-Lord was not satisfied, and ordered that two long belts of canvas be made, with holes, like buttonholes, sewn at specified distances along their length.

Few of those who had been working on the prophet's construction had trouble sleeping that night.

The flight of Od and Streetpoet had been precipitate and unplanned. Wiser heads would probably have advised caution, and it was of little comfort to the friends to conject that wiser heads would probably not have got into such a situation in the first place. There they were, lost somewhere between Morn and the Khalin, with a picket line of Opposition troops somewhere ahead and fifty thousand strides at least to travel until they reached the river. The only consolation was that evangelism had proved lucrative: they both had money in their pockets; what they needed now was somewhere to spend it.

'What we need,' said Od, 'is to bump into some family of actors you've rescued from certain death that can put us up for a while. Find me one of those and I'll not even moan if you sleep with the daughter.'

Streetpoet looked at Od in amazement. 'Fine conscience you're turning out to be.'

'I'd been made redundant already,' replied Od. 'You've found a conscience all of your own.'

'You realise that if we carry on exchanging attitudes at this rate I'll soon be telling *you* off for sleeping with women?' said Streetpoet, only half joking.

'None would have me,' said Od.

'Don't be unfair to yourself. Look at you. A season in the open air, plenty of travel, a varied active life, you're a changed man. Look at the muscles you're getting. When I first met you that was all flab. Nowadays no woman in her right mind would turn you down.'

'I could still do with some hair on my head,' decided Od, thinking about what Streetpoet had said and deciding, rather proudly, it was true.

'I don't know. That shiny head of yours is really quite distinctive. Women always go for gallants in their helmets; you've got a sort of helmet all the time. If you'd let me teach you a few opening lines, ways of breaking the ice, you could become the demon-lover of the Hasfaine.'

Od laughed. 'I don't think so somehow.'

'Pity,' said Streetpoet. 'It seems a shame to waste them. I'll not be needing my gambits any more.'

'What do you mean?'

'I don't know. Partly it's this' – he indicated the scars that disfigured one side of his face and drew his eye down – 'and partly it's a change in me. I don't know why, but I have changed.'

'And I've noticed. I don't think it's for the worse, myself, scars or no scars. You're getting wiser as you get older, that's all. It happens to everyone, only some of us don't have so far to go.'

Streetpoet thought about this. 'Is that an insult?' he wondered aloud.

Od shook his head. 'Not at all. A wiser man wouldn't have saved my life that time in Ordagyn; a more foolish man wouldn't have led the BORN AGAIN TRUTHKNOWERS away from Wriknek's army. Your experiences have changed you, that's all. Experiences do that to us all.'

'What about you then. You've been through exactly the same things, and you haven't changed. You're sensible, loyal, brave...'

'Hold it! You'll spoil me. And anyway, experience has changed me, only with me it all happened at once.'

'When?'

'The night you saved me, of course. Before that I was a normal, bigoted, mean-mouthed member of the Brotherhood, and you stood for everything I detested. And then you saved my life. I might have stayed much the same all the time I've known you; I'm a different man from the one I was *before* I knew you.'

Streetpoet mused. 'Life really is peculiar, isn't it.'

'It certainly is,' agreed Od. 'And you've taught me that it's the peculiarities that make it so much fun.'

'Fun! Being chased out of Ordagyn, lost in a blizzard, shipwrecked and captured, nearly killed in a siege, attacked by Agaskan, saved by bandits, playing at being prophets and then getting lost and having nothing to eat? You call that fun?'

'Yes I do,' said Od firmly.

Streetpoet smiled, wrinkling his nose, recapturing all the old charm of his once-charming face. 'And so do I.'

They continued to head south.

It was the third day of building and the construction was beginning to take shape. The cogwheel with the paddles behind the chin was linked up to a ratchet arm that moved a heavy wedge of wood. When the paddles hit the ratchet they pushed the wedge up; when they moved further and disengaged the weight of the wedge made it drop on its pivot. They tested it, and then satisfied, fixed another wedge above the mobile first. The lower one snapped into the upper one like a mouth, which was exactly what was required. Meanwhile, the shell was being built up: the slats of wood reached smoothly up the sides of the box, but at the front various structures were being added, the most significant and precarious being a large protusion above the mouth. Whilst this was being fitted there was a sudden sound, part anxiety, part anticipation, from the troops on the other side of the hill. These soldiers overlooked the plain. Talen asked, and received, permission to go and look: he was not surprised to see, assembling on the plain beneath, the vanguard of the Royalist army.

He watched awhile, noting with approval the professional formations of the Royalists, and then reported back to the Ra-Lord; returning, he was astounded to see that, now the protrusion above the mouth had been boxed in, the thing really was beginning to look like a head. A crude head, huge and comic to be sure, with flat cheeks and a wide mouth, but a head none the less.

The Ra-Lord nodded his own when Talen brought the news. 'Will there be fighting today?' he asked.

'Not unless Wriknek wants to risk an early attack before the Royalists get their disposition sorted out. And I don't think he'll do that as it would mean exposing his troops to the Royalist reinforcements that keep arriving.'

'What about tomorrow?'

'Perhaps, but again it isn't likely. There's no reason why Wriknek should give up his defensive position, and the Gros of – the Gyr – Peltyn isn't the sort of man who will rush in until he's weighed everything up. I should think tomorrow will be a quiet day. There may be some cavalry skirmishing but beyond that I'd be surprised if anything happens.'

The Ra-Lord accepted this professional judgement. 'Then we'd better get this monster finished,' he said.

One of the lengths of canvas was tied in a loop from the small wheel on the axle to the cog behind the chin. The buttonholes fitted the cogs' teeth exactly. Again the contraption was moved, though this time forwards only – the ratchet only worked that way – and again everything worked.

As soon as the testing was complete the eye mechanism was installed: a securely fastened platform behind the nose supported two meshed cogwheels, one below each eye. Above each cogwheel, rotating with them, was a white barrel with six eyes painted at regular intervals round its waist, while from the top of one of the barrels a further cog was linked by the second canvas belt to the cog at the top of the blackiron pole. This linkage was severely geared: the mouth could chatter like anything but the Ra-Lord wanted the eyes to move in a more stately fashion. The whole thing was completed and tested in torchlight; the following day would be the important one.

They got up at dawn. Captain Jargoz had at first been annoyed that the Ra-Lord had borrowed so many of his men, but as the contraption took shape he grew quite fond of it, intrigued by its ingenious though simple mechanism. He had suggested practical improvements from time to time, and that morning he was at the head even before the Ra-Lord and supervising the building of a platform above the machinery. The face was virtually complete already. The eyes, somewhat protuberant – they had been barrels once, after all – were partially boxed in so that only the area in which the many eyeballs moved showed, and the forehead, which was angled back and gave the grotesque face an appearance of stupidity and surprise, had also been planked over. Only the side panelling needed completing, and that was a fairly simple job, and then the whole thing would be ready.

The Opposition troops had, of course, known of the construction of the prophet's giant head, and had followed its rapid progress with some interest; the Royalists were quite unprepared when, with incredible slowness, they saw a large wooden contraption appear over the crest of the nearest hill. At first they assumed it was some kind of weapon of war, but as more and more appeared, thanks to the strenuous efforts of a whole company of men at its rear, they were not so sure. Certainly, it was like nothing any of them had ever seen before: a giant wooden head, six strides or so high, with a mouth that jabbered and twitched, and strange lunatic eyes that continually crossed and then crossed again. It browed the hill and started to descend. The prophet was about to make more conversions.

The Gyr Peltyn was sent for but he had already seen it. 'Tyroq,' he said to one of his aides. 'Your eyes are good. Are those people on top of it?'

'They appear to be, sir.' Tyroq screwed up his eyes further. 'One of them seems to be a woman.'

Behind the head a crowd of soldiers, stripped to the waist and taking the strain, paid out the long rope attached to its back and let it move down the hillside. On top, with the rope ladder they had ascended by curled at their feet and with expressions of frightened delight on their faces, were the Ra-Lord, Talen and Lara.

Then suddenly their expressions changed. With an unexpected jerk the head shot forward, throwing the companions together. It was picking up speed down the hillside; Talen looked behind. A line of half-naked soldiers, lying comically on their backs, showed him what had happened. The rope had parted and they were out of control.

As the head speeded up a series of alarming things began to happen. It had been making odd noises all along, creaking and groaning and clicking, but now the noises were coupled with a sort of juddering thud, irregular and wild, that sent shivers – literally and metaphorically – through the passengers. Boards that had seemed firm started working loose. Nails popped and twanged. And still it was accelerating, still racing towards the enemy lines.

This sudden acceleration was matched by an equally rapid movement on the part of the nearest soldiers, who hurled themselves out of its path. The head careered down and ever down, shedding planks as it went. It reached where the front lines had been. The slope flattened into the plain here, but the head did not want to stop. Suddenly there was a boom and a twang. A great wooden cogwheel flew through the contraption's back and bounced harum-scarum, scattering a squadron of cavalry. A long band of canvas seemed to unfurl itself like a flag before getting caught up in one of the wheels. The mouth gaped open. The eyes still spun. And the head fell apart, shaking pieces of wood loose all over the place: it rocked, it juddered, and it came to a halt.

Only it was no longer a head. It was a frame, a box, and huddled together on top were three figures, suddenly very exposed and a long way up. All of them had their eyes closed.

Streetpoet and Od reached the picket line. The Opposition was using a time-honoured line of defence, the Khalinwatch, a series of watch-towers along the river. The Khalin by this time was a statelier and slower river than the headlong adolescent who plunged down the Mornet Falls or the ambitious newly wed who, after linking with the Heront, made her way through the Rift; now she was noble, mature and dignified.

She was also, as is her privilege, sometimes capricious, and though the Khalinwatch had been built on the banks of the meandering river, sometimes the river had preferred a new course to the old and deserted the towers. Where Streetpoet and Od emerged from the undergrowth, for instance, five score thousand strides above Cythroné, the watch-tower was one of those that had been abandoned. It stood at the head of a sandy bank that showed the river's old course, but between the tower and the river was a flat, scrubby embankment which had once been the river-bed. The embankment offered no cover at all.

'What next?' asked Od.

'Brothers Militant.'

'All right.'

They walked openly across to the tower. It was sheer sided, about the height of a windmill, and access was gained via a flight of steps that led to a high door. Like many of the Khalinwatch towers, it was not in perfect repair; advances in miliary technology had rendered it defensively almost obsolete, but it still served as a viewing platform. They climbed the steps. Overhanging them was a threatening series of spouts, down which boiling water, pitch or oil could be poured onto attackers.

The door opened and a guard, with a flagon of ale in one hand and his sword hanging casually in the other, stepped out and looked at them. 'What do you want?'

'What is in the flagon?' asked Streetpoet.

'What's that to you?' replied the guard, belligerently.

'Perhaps you will have heard of us: we are from the Brothers Militant.'

'Oh bugger.' The guard's face went slack; he did not need to be told what this would mean. Men had received sixty lashes for drinking in their own time, and he was meant to be on duty.

'However,' continued the scarfaced Brother Militant. 'We are not here on an inspection. Our mission is a delicate and complicated one. If you are lucky, and co-operative, perhaps by the time we make our report to the commander we shall have forgotten this incident.'

'Oh... yes... er...' The guard thought he had never seen such sinister people as the scarfaced man and his bald companion. Their clothes were once expensive though now dusty, their faces were weatherbeaten and hungry looking, and they had a look of calm, dangerous experience about them that made his blood run cold. 'Er... come in.'

'Thank you.'

The guard scurried ahead of them, calling out. 'Lads! Lads! We've got visitors.'

'What? Them blokes we saw?' called back a voice from inside.

'They're not blokes. They're Brothers Militant.'

'Oh bugger,' said the second voice, a belated echo.

They entered the bleak round chamber in the centre of the tower. Five guards were sitting at a table playing cards. They caught sight of a sixth man disappearing up the spiral stairs to the roof, and then saw a seventh hiding clumsily beneath the table.

'Irregular,' said Streetpoet. He turned to his bald companion. 'Despite the urgency of our mission, I should be interested to hear what these men have to say for themselves.' He nodded towards the figure under the table and Od, with the willing, obsequious assistance of the first guard they had met, dragged the man out.

'Well, well,' said Od. 'And who are you?'

One of the guards answered first. 'His name is Krunf, Captain of the the Guard of the Vaine of Akbar.'

'Really?' The bald man smiled, rather dangerously it seemed to the guards. 'And what's he doing here?'

'Um... He's our prisoner.'

'That's right,' agreed the others, with obvious relief.

'And who was that we saw disappearing up to the roof?'

'Who?' asked one of the guards innocently, till his neighbours kicked him to shut up.

'That was the Vaine of Akbar himself.'

'Another prisoner?' asked the bald man.

'That's right.'

'And how long have they been captive here?'

'Since winter…since the day before yesterday.'

Very irregular. However, your capture of two such important prisoners will in some way mitigate against your dereliction of other aspects of your duty. I suggest you send for troops to escort them to prison immediately. How did they arrive here?'

'By boat, sir.'

'By boat? How curious. And where is the boat now?'

'By the river, sir.'

'Lead us to it.' They left the tower, scrambled down the sandy bank, and crossed the flats. Pulled up at the head of the flats was a small dinghy. 'They arrived the day before yesterday, you say?'

'Yes sir.'

The boat looked as if it been there since the Khalinwatch was built. A layer of mud and rainwater in its hull was sprouting weeds, and the paintwork had faded to nothing. 'The oars?' asked the bald man.

'In the tower, sir.'

'Then fetch them!'

'Yes sir.'

When the guard had gone Streetpoet looked distastefully at the boat. 'It looks the worst yet.'

'Have we any choice?'

'I suppose not.'

With the eager help of the guards they checked that the hull was still watertight, cleaned the boat out, and set it on the water. Streetpoet was by now almost adept at getting aboard. 'Remember to report your prisoners,' he called.

'Yes sir.'

Od rowed downstream a little way. 'We never told them where we were going,' he said.

'They didn't care,' said Streetpoet, 'so long as it was away.'

Talen-vaine-Talen did his best, but the Gyr Peltyn still could not follow all the details. After a while the Gyr got fed up with asking 'Why?' all the time, and just accepted that these things had happened.

'Are you fit to fight?' he asked the Vaine of Talen.

'Sir?'

'I'll want you to rejoin my staff. I'm sure we can find a uniform for you and a mount. And we'd better get this Lara and the Ra-Lord off to Verdre as quickly as possible, to see if they can knock some sense into the emperor.' The phrase was doubtless disrespectful but the Gyr Peltyn did not care: he was entirely fed up with his emperor, his charge. 'Personally I doubt he'll even recognise you, but it's worth a try. I think, Talen, your time would have been better spent defending Akbar, but we were neither of us to know that.'

'Sir'.

There is no need to describe the parting of Lara and Talen: it was a clichéd scene and they spoke in clichés, and believed every word they said. Then transport was found for her and the Ra-Lord, and an escort of two – even that was more than the Gry Peltyn could spare – was provided, and they were off on the day's journey back to Cythroné.

They left just in time. From the hilltop it had been difficult to make out the fate of the PROPHET WITH NO NAME and his disciples; the whole thing had seemed rather bizarre. The disintegrating head had apparently stopped safely with its occupants still inside. There had been a long period of inactivity; the prophet was led down – and treated, the Opposition was pleased to note, with great courtesy, and then the whole affair seemed to be over. No conversions, no desertions, no thunderclaps or divine signs at all. But certain of the Opposition troops, inflamed with zeal by the prophet's words, and uncertain about his fate, suddenly broke rank and started running down the hill. The Battle of the Itor Range had begun.

Chapter 12

Responsibilities

At once horns began to blow on all sides. As usual, Wriknek was in his tent, away from the sun: daylight was beginning to hurt his eyes. He blinked aggressively as the silhouetted messenger lifted the tentflap: 'Yes?'

'The fighting has begun, Commander.'

Wriknek remained calm. 'Thank you,' he replied with chilling courtesy. He walked stiffly to the tent flap; aides helped him onto a horse and led him to a brow overlooking the plain from where he could study the situation. Two things struck him at once: the great wooden frame of the prophet's head had opened a gap in the enemy ranks; the unplanned attack by certain of his troops had made that gap wider. Once more Wriknek took advantage of his luck. 'Send in the cavalry,' he said, pointing. 'There!'

He watched as the cavalry prepared. Meanwhile, the Royalists, recovering from the initial assault, were beginning to rally. Wriknek ordered his archers forward; so did the Gyr Peltyn. Despite its messy beginning this was beginning to look like a textbook battle.

But Wriknek had two special factors in his favour. The first was that he, not his enemy, had chosen the terrain. His scouts had told him of every gully and ditch on the plain below; he had instructed that each tree that obstructed his view should be chopped down and, with his usual almost pedantic thoroughness, had learnt even where cavalry could charge safely and where molehills could do damage.

The second was that he could see what was going on. He could react at once to changing events, and rectify them in the speed it takes a horseman to carry a message; the Gyr had to receive a report and assimilate it before he could respond.

Wriknek looked round. His cavalry were ready, lined up in orange and black along the ridge, preparing to charge. The autocrat watched as their commander lifted his sword; the subcommanders raised theirs. The kettle drums of the heavy armoured regiments began to play; the bugles of the lancers answered.

Slowly, but with ever-increasing momentum, the charge began.

Down the hill, following the deep ruts made by the prophet's head, your weight back in the saddle, your hands gripped hard to the reins. A missed footing, a grimace. Then spurring on and hanging on as you rushed headlong at the enemy lines. The first blow, a shockwave. A pause for breath, to see where your companions are, and then the fighting begins. Parry, counter, thrust. The slash that misses wildly. Balancing, trying again. The slash that severs flesh.

For Wriknek on his hill perhaps there was a pattern, but not for those fighting. Sheer chaos now: cutting-twisting-rending blows that flash the air with silver, stain the earth with red; the taut, too-taut tension of the bowstring; the horse, its nostrils flaring, rearing above the broken lance; the sudden swift swish of the arrow.

The Gyr Peltyn ordered a counter-charge. The cavalry went in. The noble cavalry first, in their ancient heraldry, a pageant of the colour, the tumble, the blood-and-the-guts that is history. Behind them the regulars, dour and disenchanted, and the irregular musters who'd rather be far from the field. Arrows strike, piercing the history, the disenchantment, the fear. Horses whine, whinny and neigh. Then contact, the ranks break, you are alone and the battle rages over you, around you, beneath you. The world is nothing but war. Faces distort with fury and pain. Muscles tear and are torn. Sweat runs into your eyes. A man with an arrow through his throat is carried by, bolt upright, on a horse that is wild with fear.

The ranks wheel and thread, collide and break. Wriknek watched the battle with surprise. He had never seen a battle before. The careful plans he had made at his desk seemed irrelevant to the carnage he witnessed. Yet the carnage neither disgusted him nor caused him despair. Instead it filled him with emotion, exaltation. He was winning! He was pushing them back! He was going to triumph at last!

Heavy armour, heavy helms. Tiredness. The wide anguish of despair. Not to live but to get away: what is life but a battlefield anyway. Turning, running, fleeing, the enemy at your rear, the special sound of the cavalryman who's going to kill you.

The panic spread. Talen watched as the Royalist left flank wavered. The centre was already weak where the prophet's head still stood. A single company seemed to hold, their standard high, and then the standard was trampled and the men had turned. He rode over, to try to stem the tide, waving his sword and shouting Menketh-knew-what at the men.

Stumbling, felled, your breath tastes of steel. The flash and the pain and the end.

The Royalists were being steadily forced back. Wriknek urged his horse forward down the hillside. His companions, his Brothers Militant, their black standard limp in the windless afternoon, followed. Riding downhill is not always easy, and Wriknek was never a good horseman, but he did not seem to notice. His eyes were fixed on the killing fields ahead.

Talen rode back to his general. The left flank had collapsed towards the hollow centre, and a wheeling claw of Opposition troops threatened to cut off their retreat. 'You've got to withdraw!' he shouted to the Gyr Peltyn, but the older man made no response.

As the left flank gave way the front line shifted, angled itself on the plain. Had Wriknek been in a position to see, he would have noticed the right flank of the Royalist army was exposed now and sent in his reserves. But he was still riding slowly down the hill, silent, in awe. Had he seen, the Royalist defeat might have been a rout.

Suddenly the Gyr Peltyn seemed to register Talen's words. He pulled back his reins with unnecessary force and turned his horse round; he retreated two hundred strides and turned again. 'Take a message, Talen, to the Vaine of Honiman on the right flank. Order his men to pull back.'

Talen nodded and left at once. He was always happier with something to do, even if it was bearing bad news.

The drums still beat remorselessly, driving the Opposition forwards. Talen delivered his message. From the Royalist ranks came a different beat, harsh and urgent, against the regular rhythm of the Opposition. The right flank fell back and the retreat had begun.

The prophet's head was abandoned now. The tide of war had passed over it, leaving it strewn with bodies. It was there that the fighting had been thickest. It had been a focus and a fulcrum for the wheeling armies. Now, as the shadows lengthened and evening drew on, it became a memorial, a landmark, a scaffold.

Streetpoet and Od let the current carry them, rowing only to steer. On both sides of the wide river there were villages, and as night started to approach they settled for one on the southern, Royalist bank. They moored at a wooden jetty of haphazard poles and irregular planks, and went in search of a tavern. Their money jingled in their pockets.

They ate and, exhausted, retired to their room. A tin tub had been filled with hot water.

'A drink and then a good bath,' said Streetpoet. 'Ah, life!'

'Food in the stomach,' added Od. 'And sleep.'

A boy in a soiled apron kept coming up stairs with more water. Streetpoet bathed first, then Od. 'How far are we from Cythroné?' Streetpoet asked the boy.

'A day's journey downstream in a barge, sir. And two days by horse.'

And how many by rowing boat? he wondered.

Relaxed, at ease, they slept.

The pursuit lasted until nightfall, and then the Opposition, as tired as their enemies, called it off and regrouped. The Gyr Peltyn left command of the retreat to the able Vaine of Honiman, and set off, travelling by night, for Verdre. Talen, and a company of horse, accompanied him. They barely spoke; there seemed to be nothing to say. Only once, when the horses travelled slowly, fording a river, did the Gyr Peltyn communicate his thoughts.

'I should resign, I suppose,' he said. 'But if I do, who will defend the empire then?'

Talen looked for an answer, realised there was none, and left his general to his own harsh, bitter thoughts. Talen's thoughts were quite bitter enough.

The Gros of Ra was not going to be stopped by anyone, and few were going to try. He strode through the great halls of Verdre as though he owned them, burst into his sleeping son's chamber, and shook the emperor awake.

'Get up!' he commanded. 'We've two days until Endyear. You've got to pull yourself together.'

'Have you ever looked at flowers really closely,' asked Consatiné sweetly.

'Stop babbling,' said the Ra-Lord harshly. 'I've brought a friend.'

'How nice. Anyone I know?'

'It's Lara, you Menketh-blasted fool.'

'Lara!' The change that came over the emperor's face was absolute. The tranquil blank look of the moment before was replaced by real comprehension, real love. For the first time he recognised the girl at the foot of the bed. 'Lara!' he cried again, and embraced her passionately. 'Lara!'

'She's come here to be your wife,' said the Ra-Lord, sending Consatiné into further raptures of tears and endearments. 'But only if you'll perform the Rite of Endyear.'

At once Consatiné let her go. Lara looked modestly down at the expensive rugs on the floor while the Ra-Lord continued. 'You must perform the Rite of Endyear. Khalindaine is crumbling round your ears. Lara says she will marry you if you do it; she is a very remarkable girl. Will you?'

'I want to marry Lara!' he declared.

'Therefore...' encouraged the Ra-Lord. For the first time in his life he was begging, rather than ordering, his son.

Consatiné stood in the middle of the darkened room. His nightgown almost glowed in the partial light of a midsummer night. 'I can't do it,' he admitted.

'Why not?' asked Lara, concerned for him. She took his hand and sat him on the high bed beside her. 'Why can't you do it?'

'I can't! I can't even talk about it!' Consatiné turned to Lara, buried his face in her breast. 'No one knows what it's like! No one!'

The Ra-Lord made a move towards him; Lara stopped him with a look, and stroked the emperor's curls. 'It's all right,' she said. 'Shhh now. It's all right.'

Consatiné sobbed a little more and then raised himself. 'All my life I thought I was going, in time, to be the Gros of Ra. I saw how my father treated people and thought I was going to be different. I thought I would be a gentler Ra-Lord, more loving, more careful.' There was no venom in his voice as he spoke, just a calm statement of facts. 'I wasn't going to make my wife cry as he did. I wasn't going to bully my children into being something they weren't. I wanted to be good, and noble, and loved.'

Again Consatiné paused. He sat in silence for a while, then shook his head and continued. 'And then the avatar found me, took hold of me, made me into something else.' The desperate tears began to flow again as Consatiné's face crumpled with the memory. 'At the Battle of Klau, when the avatar filled me and used my body...used my body, as though I were a whore...it was dreadful, appalling. I was the very thing I hated most. I had become a monster, a man without sympathy or love, a killer who kills without feeling. Akhran was the real me and I was a shadow, a shade in my own corpse. And afterwards, after the confusion, I said it was the ghost of Ormaas that had done it, when really it was the ghost of Consatiné.' He buried his head again into Lara's shoulder. 'I wanted to disown the avatar, pretend it had not happened. I wanted to go back to Northreach and be the Vaine of Mornet again, and marry you Lara, and tell my father I forgave him for, however hard or harsh he had sometimes been, he had never been anything – anything at all – as hard or as awful as I.

'But I couldn't. The Gros of Weir had me crowned, made me emperor. I couldn't return. I couldn't even return to being Consatiné any more. I was a ghost inside my own body, vying with Akbar, and he was always, always, always so much stronger.

'So I refused to perform the Rite of Endyear. I had to. I did not dare invite Akhran into me again. I did not dare. I didn't care that people thought I wasn't the rightful emperor: they could think what they liked. I didn't care if the Brotherhood ruled the empire – Menketh knows I wanted no part of it. All I wanted was to be me.

'Yet even then Akhran couldn't leave me alone, and when Kamrot tormented me, Akhran killed him.'

'So that's what happened,' said the Ra-Lord quietly.

His son nodded. 'Ever since then I've been living two lives, playing the fool, doing anything, anything, to avoid being emperor still, while inside I burn with guilt and despair. The madness people saw was fake; inside was a deeper madness, quite real. The only thing that kept me from throwing myself from the window, from the world, was the thought of Lara. Lara, Streetpoet, Khayrik, Ormaas. They were the only friends

I have had, the only ones I've known. And Lara, Lara I loved! Lara I love!'

'Shhh,' said Lara, holding him. 'Shhh. I'm here now. Shhh.'

'You'll perform the Rite of Endyear if she marries you and supports you?' asked the Ra-Lord.

Again there was a long pause. 'I can't,' the emperor said, in quiet despair.

'But you must,' his father insisted. 'Empire needs to see you are emperor. People need to know. Then they'll stop fighting.'

Consatiné remained silent.

'Look,' continued the Ra-Lord. 'Lara doesn't love you. She loves the Vaine of Talen and he loves her. But for the empire she'll marry you. She'll love you as best she can. She'll be your wife. She'll do her duty to the empire; so should you.'

'Is this true?' asked Consatiné.

Lara nodded. 'But it makes no difference,' she said. 'I shall be your wife in all things. I shall never betray you or let you down.'

'And this Vaine of Talen?' asked Consatiné. 'What does he say?'

'He knows his duty too,' said the Ra-Lord. 'They are both very brave.'

Consatiné buried his face in his hands. Fear and shame and self-loathing ran through him. And then he looked up. 'I shall do it,' he said in the quietest of voices. 'I shall perform the Rite of Endyear.'

By the time the Gyre Peltyn and Talen arrive at Verdre, early the next day, the word was out: Consatiné was to perform the Rite of Endyear. Few were impressed. News of the defeat of the Royalist armies had reached them. 'He might as well stick the knife into himself as wait for Wriknek to do it,' they said.

The Gyr Peltyn, with Talen by his side, went immediately to see the emperor. Both had reservations: Talen's only thoughts were for Lara; the Gyr doubted if, after all this time, Consatiné would really go ahead. Outside Consatiné's chamber their way was blocked by the Ra-Lord. 'Lara's with him now,' he told them.

'Are they...?' Talen could ask no more for dread of the answer.

'Consatiné asleep on Lara's knee,' replied the Gros of Ra, reassuring his young friend. 'Lara stroking his hair.'

The Opposition armies were drawing nearer all the time. By noon skirmishing was reported in the very outskirts of Cythroné, and few doubted that soon the capital must fall. The population braced themselves for the end as best they could. They could not win, so they hid their valuables and prepared to lose.

As the Eve of Endyear came and went, marked by none of the traditional feasting, the first of the Opposition troops entered Cythroné. They encountered little defence. The people of Cythroné had no faith left in their emperor: Wriknek, by right of victory, had a least earnt their respect.

Yet despite their conspicuous success there was consternation among the Opposition commanders. Wriknek's health, which had been causing them increasing concern for many days, seemed at last to have collapsed entirely. He was transported in a closed wagon; he was virtually blind now and totally incoherent, and had nominated no successor should he die. Already the Opposition leadership was splitting into factions and preparing, in secret, for the future: the end of Consatiné would not necessarily mean the end of the war. But for the time being their first objective was to capture the capital and the emperor: if there was to be another war, it would be as well to finish this one first.

As night fell on that last day before Endyear the vanguard of the Opposition army had almost reached Fragma Square, but the defence was more stubborn now as they ran into the veteran royal guards. The Opposition pulled back slightly and rested. Tomorrow, the day of the Rite, would be time enough to secure their victory.

Dawn found the city almost quiet. There was looting in the north, blamed on the Opposition soldiers but often the work of the Cythroné mob, and there was some desultory fighting in Fragma Square, but the royal guards had retreated towards the palace of Verdre, and all the Opposition had to do was march straight in.

As the sun rose so did the Cythrons. The streets filled as the citizens came out to greet their conquerors. Sometimes the crowds were enthusiastic, cheering because they had always believed in the Brotherhood's cause or because they wanted to curry favour; sometimes the crowds were silent, hostile and tense. As Streetpoet and Od made their way down the river, to moor by one of the great galleons in the port, they heard the crowds and the sound of city bells.

'It sounds as though Consatiné is going to perform the Rite of Endyear,' said Streetpoet. 'This is how Cythroné used to be, in the days of the Empress Elsban.'

Od shook his head. 'Look at the troops. They're Opposition soldiers. This is a victory celebration.'

They climbed from their boat and onto the crowded quay. The enterprising citizens of Cythroné had already begun to make defeat pay, offering rooms and goods to the battle-weary soldiers. They passed a large bonfire. The troops were good-humouredly burning the portraits of the emperors seized from the government buildings, with the willing help of many civilians.

'Have you heard?' one of the civilians was saying. 'About Consatiné performing the Rite of Endyear?'

A large soldier laughed. 'Is he now? Well, I reckon if he kills himself it'll save me the trouble of doing it for him.'

'Do you think it's true?' Od asked quietly.

'I don't know. We'll stay here, by the river, and find out. We can see it all from here.'

True or not, the rumour was certainly spreading. Someone by the quay had opened a book on Consatiné's survival, but despite ridiculous odds he was getting few takers. The general feeling seemed to be that the emperor had nothing to lose; as the soldier had said, if he stuck a knife in himself it would just save someone else the trouble.

The quay was getting crowded. Sideshows were set up: baked apples, sweetmeats, glasses of water with lime. Troupes of performers, risking the Brotherhood's wrath and trusting to the good mood of the soldiers, set up their wagons. Pedlars hawked flints and patent medicines. More and more it resembled a typical Endyear.

Streetpoet and Od established themselves at a good spot on the south bank. Directly opposite them was the long, menacing stonework of the House of the Condemned. There were many figures on the roof of that notorious jail. At first Streetpoet wondered if they were released prisoners, pardoned as he once had been, to mark Endyear, but then he dismissed the thought. Those weren't prisoners: even at this distance he could see they were soldiers, and in the middle of them, carried into a position from where he could overlook the river, was a withered figure slumped in an open sedan chair.

He was interrupted by a voice just behind him. 'Od!' said the voice, a woman's, and it was full of surprise and delight.

Streetpoet turned round, to see Od being embraced by a heavily pregnant girl. 'O Od,' the girl was saying. 'I've been looking for you for ages.'

'For about eight months,' agreed Streetpoet, laughing.

And then the laughter died as he recognised the girl. 'Oh. Hello, Amila.'

'Streetpoet?' They stood facing one another, embarrassed. 'It is you?'

'It is.' He turned round slightly, to show her the unscarred side of his face in profile. 'You see.'

'O Streetpoet,' she said, flinging herself at him suddenly and sobbing painful sobs.

For a while Streetpoet let her rest in his arms, and then he began to stroke her hair. Od, courteously, looked away, looked up river.

After a while Amila's crying had stopped. 'I'm sorry,' she said. 'I must be going now. I didn't mean to cry.'

'Going?' asked Streetpoet.

'I'm working. A new company. I left my parents when I discovered.' Her voice tailed off but she tapped her swollen womb. 'I came to look for you.'

'Well. Now you've found me. Aren't you going to stay?'

'I don't think I'd better. No, no I must go.'

'But the baby?' Streetpoet too tailed off midsentence, but Amila understood his question.

'Oh, yes,' said Amila. 'Yes it's yours.'

Streetpoet, slightly hesitantly, embraced her again. 'I've always wanted a son,' he said, and as he said it he meant it, though Menketh only knows he had never had the thought before.

'It might be a girl,' warned Amila.

'Oh no. No, it's a boy. I can feel it in my heart.'

Amila smiled, the first real smile she had managed for months. 'A boy just like you,' she said happily.

Od was laughing. 'I hope not,' he said.

Quite suddenly there was a change in the mood of the crowd. Even Wriknek, in his sedan chair on the roof of the House of the Condemned, was aware of it, and he raised his head slightly. 'Yes, Commander,' said his aides, 'the Royal Barge is coming down from Verdre.'

Alone in the canopied throne of the Royal Barge, Consatiné sat rigid and afraid. Around him, also seated, were his father, Lara, and Talen, but they could all have been ten thousand strides away for the difference they made for him now. The barge passed beneath a bridge. Above, Consatiné could see the crowd looking down on him. The faces he saw were neither hostile nor friendly, but watched with curiosity and even pity. Consatiné straightened his back slightly in his throne and raised his chin. Despite his fear, he was still emperor, descendant of a line of emperors. Whatever was going to happen – and he neither knew nor cared – he had found his dignity and was determined never to lose it again.

The barge moved slowly, ponderously, downstream. If there was noise from the crowd Consatiné did not hear it. There was a jerk as the barge moored at the foot of the great Keep Akhranta. Someone made to help him from his throne, but Consatiné, gently, pushed the hand aside and stood without assistance. He walked down the gangplank, hastily placed between the barge and the wharf, and walked into the keep.

In other years the Rite has been celebrated with greater pomp. All the state barges of Cythroné accompany the emperor; the city is strewn with flags; magic is prepared whereby the emperor can pass through the heavy gates of the keep in a blaze of fire. But not this year. This year there was no ceremony. Just a small figure, dwarfed by the giant portals, who opened the gates himself and then stepped through.

There was a long wait. Wriknek's head slumped again. His aides, however, continued to commentate. 'He's inside the Keep now'; 'He'll be climbing the stairs'; 'There he is! On the roof! With the knife in his hand!'

Consatiné stood, exposed, silhouetted, on the roof of the high keep. He raised both arms above his head. In his right hand he held a curved knife. There was a pause a heartbeat long and then the emperor seemed to crumple, fold in on himself, as the knife plunged into his breast. Bright blood seemed to well through his fingers, and then the emperor fell, out of sight of the crowd.

There was another pause. 'That's that then,' said a man near Streetpoet. 'When does the eating start?'

'Wait!'

As quickly as it had been lost, attention returned to the keep. Slowly, painfully, Consatiné was returning to view. His face was drawn, but not only by pain; this was the face of Akhran. In movements agonising in their deliberateness the avatar, his teeth exposed in a savage snarl, took the hilt of the knife in both hands and pulled it from his chest. His arms were raised again, but this time the gesture spoke only of triumph. 'Akhran!' he cried, bellowing, echoing. 'Akhran! Akhran! Akhran!'

For a moment more he remained there, reassuring and terrifying at once, and then he returned to the bowels of the keep.

'Now what,' asked one of the senior Brothers on the roof of the House of the Condemned. He turned to his Commander for support. 'Commander?'

Wriknek sat there still. His mouth was open. He seemed asleep. One of the aides approached him, reached out towards him, touched him. That one touch was enough. Wriknek fell untidily off the chair and landed head first on the stone. The bones of his skull were brittle. His maggot-ridden mind spilt out.

The war was over.

The emperor, his face white but his features restored, returned to the Royal Barge. He staggered on the gangplank and seemed about to fall, but shook his head impatiently and continued. He heard the voices, saw the faces, about him, but what he heard and saw made little sense. His father, smiling as he had never done, looking at Consatiné with a look that spoke of pride; Lara, looking at him almost with love; the brave Talen-vaine-Talen with tears in his eyes. The barge got under way.

There were cheers now, cheers from each side. Consatiné smiled, too tired to make any other acknowledgement. Though the wound on his chest had healed, knitted by Menketh only knew what power, it ached and throbbed without mercy. His shoulder too ached, numbing his arm where he had fallen, conspiring with his exhaustion. He rolled forward on the throne then rolled back, head lolling towards the crimson canopy above, but the eyes that finally focused there were bright with intelligence, and beneath the exhaustion and the pain that crossed his face there was, unmistakably, satisfaction.

'Come on!' said Streetpoet as the barge approached. Od realised at once what the minstrel had in mind, and the two of them bundled Amila across the boards of a moored galleon and into the little rowing boat, waiting where they had left it, on the other side.

Od rowed, Streetpoet sitting in the stern with an arm round Amila. The barge was catching them fast: the barge had fifty oarsmen and Od was rowing alone. But Od did not hurry his strokes: he let the rhythm build naturally.

Inspired by this example, other craft had now put out, to fête their emperor. The river became almost crowded, with Od only slightly ahead of other boats that had chosen other routes. Streetpoet stood up uneasily, to shout, and Od had to rest his oars. 'Consatiné! Lara! Ra-Lord!' shouted Streetpoet. 'Talen! It's me! It's Streetpoet and Od!'

Streetpoet sat down again with a bump, but he had been heard. Talen was waving to them, and then so were Lara and the Ra-Lord. Even Consatiné managed to lift an arm in acknowledgement. The oarsmen on the barge were ordered to rest.

Skilfully, Od brought the little rowing boat to the stern of the barge. They were being jostled now by the other craft that had put out to meet their emperor, but nobody noticed or cared. First Amila was helped up, and then Streetpoet, and then Od. By the time Od arrived Streetpoet was already explaining Amila and her condition. 'My fiancée,' he said. 'If she'll have me with these scars.'

Amila was glowing, jubilant. 'Of course I will.'

'Congratulations,' beamed the Ra-Lord.

'Oh yes,' agreed Lara. 'Congratulations.'

Consatiné stood and stepped forward unsteadily. 'Hello, old friend,' he said to Streetpoet. 'It's been a long time.'

'More than five years,' agreed Streetpoet.

'I have a lot to thank you for,' said the emperor. 'And now you too are getting married? Then it must be a double wedding.'

Suddenly, faces fell. It was as if, in the euphoria, they had forgotten the condition Consatiné had attached to performing the Rite of Endyear. Now they were reminded.

Consatiné, selfishly it seemed to the Ra-Lord, was still smiling, and the pride the Ra-Lord had felt disappeared.

'Why so sad?' asked the emperor. 'It's a wedding we're talking about. No. Better than that. Two weddings.' Those around him tried to smile, to share his enthusiasm, but it was a feeble effort. Undeterred, Consatiné continued. 'It isn't every day such close friends wed. Streetpoet and Amila, Lara and Talen.'

There was a pause, a look of surprise and then of joy. 'Me?' asked Talen, stupefied.

'Of course,' said Consatiné. He sat down on the throne again. This was not as easy to do as he wanted to make it look. 'That's what you both want, isn't it?'

Lara looked at Talen; Talen looked at Consatiné. 'Yes,' they decided together.

Consatiné hoped the strain in his eyes would be put down to the strain of the Rite. 'Good. Then that's settled.'

It was the Ra-Lord who was next to speak. 'Consatiné,' he said, feeling for words. 'My boy. My son.' There were tears in the Ra-Lord's eyes.

Consatiné stood. He held out a formal hand to his father, but the Ra-Lord did not take it. They looked one another in the eye.

'I'm so proud,' muttered the Ra-Lord.

'And I,' his son replied.

They embraced. So did Lara and Talen. So did Streetpoet and Amila. Od looked on. He felt uncomfortable and forgotten. But the boat rocked beneath his feet, dispersing any bitterness, and he looked round to see the boats all around them, full of faces who watched and smiled. The oarsmen of the barge were watching too, letting their oars dangle untidily in the heavy waters of Khalin.

'What are you lot looking at?' he asked the oarsmen. 'Let's get this boat under way. Stroke, two three four, stroke two three four.'

Slowly the barge pulled up-river, Od in command.